Also by Diana Palmer

Wyoming Men

Wyoming Tough
Wyoming Fierce
Wyoming Bold
Wyoming Strong
Wyoming Rugged
Wyoming Brave
Wyoming Winter
Wyoming Legend
Wyoming Heart
Wyoming True
Wyoming Homecoming

For a complete list of books by Diana Palmer,
visit www.dianapalmer.com.

DIANA PALMER

WYOMING PROUD

CANARY STREET PRESS

CANARY
STREET
PRESS™

PLEASE RECYCLE
THIS PRODUCT IS RECYCLABLE

Recycling programs
for this product may
not exist in your area.

ISBN-13: 978-1-335 -09139-0

Wyoming Proud

First published in 2023. This edition published in 2023.

For questions and comments about the quality of this book, please contact us
at CustomerService@Harlequin.com.

Canary Street Press
22 Adelaide St. West, 41st Floor
Toronto, Ontario M5H 4E3, Canada
CanaryStPress.com

Printed in U.S.A.

To Dr. Max E. White (1946–2023)

My anthropology professor at Piedmont University in Georgia

He made archaeology as adventurous as Indiana Jones.
All he lacked was the fedora hat. RIP, dear professor.

CHAPTER ONE

Ty Mosby was bored out of his mind. He could have been home with his sister, Annie, watching that dragon drama on cable. Even that would be better than this stupid office party with two women drooling over him. One was recently divorced. The other was married. Women!

He turned around and almost fell over Erianne Mitchell. Well, her name was Erianne. Nobody called her that. She was just Erin to Ty and his sister, Annie. He glowered at her.

"It's not my fault that you're gorgeous," she teased. "Mary over there has forgotten her ex-husband in her fever to get you into a dark room. And Henrietta—" she nodded toward a gangly woman with wild dark hair who was sighing into her drink as she studied him over it "—hasn't given her husband a thought all night. Just as well," she added under her breath, "because he's running around with the Tarver woman."

"What are you, the town crier?" he chided.

"It's a nasty job, but somebody has to do it," she replied with sparkling gray eyes. She laughed and half turned away, her dark hair in an elegant chignon at the back of her neck. "And there's Grace. Didn't you date her last year?"

"Oh, God," he groaned.

"There, there, she hasn't noticed you. She's too busy trying to get Danny Barnes to notice her. He just inherited his grandfather's ranch over in Comanche Wells."

"I've had my fill of social climbers," he muttered. He was giving her the once-over with black eyes. "On the other hand, there's you."

"Oh, don't be absurd, I'm not your type," she murmured, her mind on something else altogether. It was a lie. She'd loved him forever, but Ty couldn't see her for dust. And why should he? She was plain compared to the women who chased him. He was absolutely gorgeous. He had jet-black hair and black eyes, and light olive skin that made him look even more gorgeous in that spotless white shirt he was wearing with his dinner jacket and slacks. No wonder women drooled over him. Erin had drooled over him for years and hid it so carefully that not even his sister realized it.

"Why not?" he asked, really curious.

"I don't run around with men."

He blinked. "You run around with women?"

"I don't run around period."

"You're what, now, twenty-five? You'd better run around with somebody or you're going to get left behind."

"You're thirty-one and you're already left behind. Besides, I work for you," she added. "I don't get involved with people that I work for."

"We could make an exception," he pointed out.

She glared at him. "Tyson Regan Mosby," she said, exasperated. "If you keep this up, I'm calling Annie."

"God forbid!" he groaned.

"She loves you. She'll protect you from predatory females."

"I'll give you a great job recommendation if you'll find my sister a husband," he coaxed.

"Annie doesn't want to get married yet," she said. "Any more than you do. And I don't need a job recommendation unless you have in mind firing me tonight."

He made a face. "I don't have enough people as it is. Other San Antonio businesses keep luring our best people away. Even the ones I fire." He didn't like firing people, but he sometimes had to. Even though his company was headquartered in San Antonio, people from Jacobsville worked for it. Mosby Construction Company had grown under Ty's management. He'd taken a little construction company owned by his father and built it into a major contender. He had a degree in architecture. He loved to build things.

He had inherited wealth, he and Annie, and he didn't really need to work. But he loved his job. And San Antonio was the best place for his company headquarters, although he and Annie still lived in Jacobsville. Ty and Annie were direct descendants of the town's founder, Big John Jacobs, who'd talked his father-in-law into putting a a railroad through Jacobsville and built it into a cattle shipping center in south Texas back in the nineteenth century.

"Well, isn't that just like you," she said, exasperated. "I brought you a brand new human resources manager just last week!"

"He drinks vodka," he said irritably. "I don't trust men who drink vodka."

"How do you know what he drinks?" she asked.

"I asked him."

"Oh."

"What are you looking for?" he probed.

"Clarence."

"Excuse me?"

"Clarence Hodges," she muttered, peering over a nearby woman's shoulder. "He's like my personal devil. I can't turn around at a party without running into him."

He didn't like that, but he hid it. "What does he want?"

She looked up at him with raised eyebrows. "He wants me!"

"Why?"

She really rolled her eyes. "Annie needs to get you a book or something about human relationships."

He grinned. "I think I can figure those out without self-help diagrams."

"Can you, now?" she murmured absently, still looking for Clarence.

He'd known her for years. She was as familiar to him as her best friend, his only sibling, Annie. She'd spent weekends with them all through high school and through community college, where Erin got an associate's degree in business education. She was great at cost estimates, which was her position in the company. She had a brilliant mind for math. She could do most anything on a computer, even rework spreadsheet programs that he used in his construction company. She was his right arm at work, perfectly capable of standing in for him at meetings because she knew the business inside out. Of course, why wouldn't she, when she'd worked there part-time through high school and full-time during and after college. He trusted her. Well, on a professional basis. He wasn't keen on thinking about anything more personal. Erin was standoffish. Once, just once, he'd teased her about going dancing with him and she'd mumbled something noncommital and shot out of the room.

He'd never admit it, of course, but it had bruised his ego. Erin wasn't beautiful. She had pleasant features. Nice mouth, pretty complexion, gorgeous figure, sparkling eyes. But she dressed like an old woman most of the time, and she never seemed to date anyone. He'd wondered why. He'd even asked Annie, but all he got was a blank look and a smile.

He studied Erin while she looked around for the man she dreaded seeing. It wasn't so much how she looked that made her attractive, he decided finally; it was her personality. She was warm and friendly to most people, outrageously funny around friends, and she loved animals. That last thing was important to him, because he bred and trained purebred German shepherds.

His dogs were like part of the family. They lived inside with him and Annie in their huge inherited mansion in Jacobsville, Texas. The puppies, when he bred them, had their own room and a caretaker who watched over them and kept their living quarters spic and span and odorless. He rarely had more than one litter a year and by a different female each year, from an outside stud male. No interbreeding at all, because it invited birth defects. He loved the pups when they came and had to be persuaded to give them up for adoption. Even so, he actually ran background checks on potential adopters, right down to requiring photographs of their yards and the pup's living quarters. He was protective.

A recent adopter had taken a leather strap to his puppy when it made a mess on the carpet, and a neighbor had seen and heard what was going on. She'd promptly phoned Annie, who told Ty. He'd gone to the owner's house that very day, accompanied by police chief Cash Grier and the local vet, Dr. Bentley Rydel, along with a search warrant that would give them access to the dog in question.

To say that the man was shocked was an understatement. He hemmed and hawed and tried to weasel them out of looking at the dog. Cash Grier glared at him. That was all it took.

Most everybody was scared of the town's police chief, who was nice enough at public gatherings, but hell on lawbreakers of any kind. Cash loved animals as much as the vet and Ty.

The owner was forced to give them access to the puppy, which had been locked in a closet with bloody marks on its back.

Ty had slugged the man before his companions could react. He picked the pup up, gently, and after Cash took photos to document the abuse, walked out the door with Bently Rydel, to end up at his office where the poor little morsel was treated and sent home after an antibiotic shot and stitches. Cash had promptly arrested the owner. The pup's owner went on trial, was con-victed and sentenced to jail. Nobody in Jacobsville liked a dog beater. The jury had only deliberated for ten minutes, despite the harried public defender's best efforts. All the District At-torney, Blake Kemp, had to do was put up a poster-sized photo of the abused puppy for the jury and the audience to see. It had drawn gasps and the pup's owner had looked around at glares that felt like burns on his skin.

"What's the matter with you?" Erin asked, glancing at his taut face.

"Puppy beaters," he muttered.

Her expression softened. "The man got what he deserved. How is Beauregard, by the way?" she added.

He smiled. "He still whimpers in his sleep. I keep him with me at night. Rhodes isn't enthusiastic about it, but I think he senses that the puppy needs to be spoiled for a few weeks.

Actually," he added on a chuckle, "it's Rhodes's bed that they sleep in, curled up together. For an old dog, Rhodes is amaz-ingly sweet."

"You've had him a long time," she remarked.

He nodded. "Thirteen years. I worry about him. Big dogs don't have the life span that smaller ones do."

"Rhodes is practically immortal," she replied with a smile. "He's pampered."

"I guess so. Dad gave him to me as a Christmas present the year I graduated high school."

"I remember your parents. They were so sweet," she added. "Your mother and mine were best friends."

"Hell of a shame, what happened," he said stiffly.

She nodded. "It's a rare thing, to have a tour bus go off the road and crash down a ravine. But those mountain roads in South America can be treacherous. Your parents were so much in love," she added quietly. "It's hard to imagine one going on without the other."

"That's what Annie and I thought," he replied. "But it's damned tough, losing them both at once."

"I remember. At least you were both grown at the time," she added softly.

He drew in a breath. "Didn't help much," he muttered.

"For what it's worth, I know how it is. It was hard for Dad and me to go on, after we lost Mom."

"Your mother had a hard life," he said.

She sighed. "Yes. Dad's hard to live with. He's not mean or anything, he just makes stupid decisions and runs his mouth when he shouldn't. Jack Dempsey won't even speak to him."

"That must hurt. They're best friends."

"They were," she said sadly. "Dad was repeating some gossip that he'd heard about Jack's wife running around on him. It got exaggerated, by Dad," she muttered, "and Jack's wife divorced him. It wasn't even true. My father has a gift for saying things without thinking first."

"A lot of people are like that."

She grimaced. "I wish they'd had more kids than just me," she confessed, looking up at him. "It would be easier to manage Dad if I had brothers and sisters to share the misery."

He chuckled. "You do pretty good."

She shrugged. "I could do better. I'd have to take away his phone though."

His eyebrows arched.

"This guy called dad and said he could save ten dollars a month if he switched our long distance to their company. Dad said great, let's do it. So I tried to phone one of our colleagues at home in Dallas last weekend and got told that we didn't have long distance anymore. It was a scam. Dad had no idea what he'd done. I tried not to yell," she added on a laugh. "Honestly, he's like a little kid sometimes. Ten dollars a month." She shook her head.

"My mother was like that," he reminded her. "She got a call

telling her the sheriff was coming over to arrest her for a bill she hadn't paid. The man asked for pre-paid gift cards to save her from jail. She was halfway out the door on her way to town when I stopped her to ask what was wrong. Sadly for him, the scammer was still on her phone talking her through the process."

She grinned. "I'll bet his ears are still burning, wherever he is."

"I imagine so. I was really mad."

"Do you still have that jar your mother made for you? The one you had to put money in for every bad word you used?"

He laughed. "Yes. It doesn't get fed, but I've still got it." His eyes were sad with the memory. "She wanted to be a missionary, but Dad came along. She'd lived on a budget for so long that she almost ran away when she saw how much he was worth." That was true. Her father had inherited a lot of money from his late mother, but he squandered it all on get rich quick schemes. He was still doing that, albeit on a very small shoestring. Erin wore herself out trying to save him from himself.

"A unique woman," Ty continued. "She really didn't care about money at all." He studied her quietly. "Sort of like you."

She sighed. "I like being able to buy food and gas and pay bills. That's what money's good for. There are lots of things it won't buy."

He nodded.

"Besides that, I work for this terrific manager who gives me raises," she added with twinkling gray eyes.

"I don't have to think too hard to do that," he said. "I know how hard you work."

"I'm just grateful to have a job. The economy is pretty bad right now."

"It is," he agreed. "Even this company has to be careful. You're working on that bid now, the one we hope will get us the job just outside San Antonio in Bexar County; a whole retirement complex. It's worth millions."

"You'll get it," she said with supreme confidence. "You really do know how to undercut the other bidders. And I know how to price out almost everything," she said, not bragging, just making a statement. She was a good cost estimator.

"We can undercut most of the major bidders," he corrected. "But I've heard that one of them is Jason Whitehall. He and his son Josh have one of the best construction companies around south Texas."

"His son's a dish," she mused.

"And how would you know?" he asked.

"I ran into him at that conference you sent me to, in Dallas, month before last. He looks just like his dad. All three of them were there, Jason and Amanda and Josh." She sighed. "They're just beginning to get over losing Jason's mother, Marguerite. She was a lovely lady. So kind."

"You know a lot about them," he said.

"Well, one of our clients was trying to retool his public image and Amanda still owns that PR firm, so she was there getting information from him. She's very nice. We keep in touch on Facebook."

"Don't keep in touch too closely," he cautioned with snapping black eyes. "They're competitors."

"As if I'd ever sell you out," she said, exasperated, as she stared up at him. "Get real! Annie would have me for breakfast, smothered in jelly!"

He relaxed. "Okay. Just testing the waters."

She ground her teeth together. "Oh, no."

He followed her irritated glance and saw a short, rotund man with thinning hair and a big smile headed toward them.

"I told you so," she moaned. "I'll go hide in the rest room... Ty!"

His arm was around her waist and he smiled down at her shocked expression. "Don't give the game away. Smile."

She did, trying hard to disguise the sudden acceleration of her heartbeat as she felt the strength and heat of his powerful body, smelled the spicy, clean scent of him. She'd danced with him at parties, rarely, and it had been just as problematic, to keep her headlong feelings for him from showing.

He felt a shiver go through her and his brows drew together just for an instant. Surely she wasn't afraid of him?

Then he felt her heart race where her small, firm breasts were pressed close against him, and odd feelings stirred. Her breath was coming too fast. She was trying to disguise it, but he knew more about women than he ever let on in public.

She stiffened and started to pull back, but his arm tightened.

"What are you afraid of?" he asked in a slow, deep tone.

"Noth…nothing," she faltered.

"Lies," he mused. "Here." He handed her his drink. "Liquid courage. Take a sip and we'll ward off your would-be suitor."

She took the glass, sniffed it, and made a face. "It's whiskey. I hate whiskey!"

"Take a sip. It works better than it smells. Trust me."

She took a deep breath, held it, and forced about a teaspoon of the vile-smelling liquid into her mouth. She choked it down, catching her breath.

"You could fuel trucks with this," she muttered as she handed it back.

"This is the very finest aged Scotch whiskey," he defended. "And now I'll know not to share my most precious substance with those same people you don't cast pearls before!"

She glared at him. "I am not a swine!"

"No, you aren't," he agreed. He cocked his head and his black eyes twinkled. "But I'll bet you taste almost as good as a barbequed one," he added in a slow, soft tone as his eyes fell to her pretty, soft mouth.

She actually gasped and her heart ran wild.

"My, my, is that the whiskey or me?" he asked, his eyes dropping to the fluttering of her heart, very visible under the thin bodice of her pale blue cocktail dress.

"Don't you stare at me like that," she said indignantly.

"Like what?" he asked, amused.

"Oh, hi, Erin," Clarence Hodges said as he joined them. He looked crestfallen when he noticed Ty's arm around her. "I was hoping you might like to talk to me about having your company do a remodeling job on my new house…?"

She forced a smile. "I'm truly sorry, Clarence, but that isn't the sort of project we do," she said in a gentle but professional tone. "We do big projects. Shopping centers. Apartments. Housing complexes. That sort of thing."

"It's a big house," he persisted.

"Erin's right, we don't do small projects," Ty told him, and the irritation he was feeling was visible in the tautness of his unsmiling face. "Even if we did, we're already overbooked. Sorry," he added. But he didn't look sorry. He looked oddly threatening.

Clarence swallowed. Hard. His face flushed. "I see. Well…" He smiled hopefully at Erin. "Maybe you might like to come over and have coffee with me one morning?"

Ty's chin lifted. His black eyes narrowed. He glared at the smaller man.

Erin just smiled.

"Oh, there's Billy Olstead," he said, looking past Erin's shoulder. "I need to talk to him about my mother's new car. I'll see you later," he added to Erin and smiled again, nervously, as he made a beeline toward the newcomer.

"Thanks," Erin said with a heavy release of breath. "He's not a bad man, but he can be annoying."

"Annie says he's started calling you two or three times a week."

"He does," she agreed sadly. "I can't make him understand that I just don't feel that way about him. I've never done a single thing that he could construe as encouraging."

"It wouldn't help," he replied. "Men like that don't take hints.

They think they're irresistible and it only needs persistence to wear you down."

"He'd need more persistence than he's got," she said flatly.

He pursed his lips. "You could go out with me."

Her eyes widened. "What?"

He shrugged. "You could go out with me. Jacobsville is small. It would get all around town in no time that we were dating. Clarence would hear it from everybody." He chuckled. "Even Clarence wouldn't be able to convince himself that he'd be any competition for me."

"Well, yes, but..."

"But, what?" he asked quietly, and he looked down into her eyes until she flushed. Her heart was trying to get out of her chest now.

She couldn't even find words. It was like having every dream of her life come true unexpectedly, and all at once. She was breathless, giddy. But it was insane to even think of doing it, of going out with him. The gossip would be terrible. It wouldn't matter that the company where they worked was in San Antonio; too many employees lived in Jacobsville, where Ty and Erin lived. It would be all over town in no time. When he didn't go out with her a second time, it would be even worse. People would start wondering what was wrong with her.

"I don't think," she began.

"Good. Don't. Thinking is responsible for most of the misery on the planet. We can go dancing. There's a Latin club up in San Antonio."

He knew she could do Latin dances. He'd taught her how, for a high school date. How many years ago that seemed now!

"Well..."

Amazing. She was reluctant. He'd never had any woman try to refuse a date with him. It was intriguing, especially considering how fast her heart was going right now. She was attracted to him. Was it new? Or had she always been attracted, but kept it hidden? He wanted to find out.

"Live dangerously. A little gossip never hurt anybody," he teased.

It did, but he wouldn't know, not with his spotless reputation. Well, hers was spotless, too. So spotless that she didn't want to risk staining it, however lightly.

"People will talk. A lot."

He just smiled. "Your friends won't care. What your enemies think won't matter."

"Yes, but I hate gossip."

He cocked his head and smiled at her with those black eyes making sensual promises. "There's a sushi place just down the block from the Latin club," he said. "They have ebi."

Ebi was her favorite sushi dish. It was so expensive that she couldn't work it into her budget. Her father did contribute a little to the family kitty, but never enough. They lived frugally because he was a spendthrift. Ty didn't know and it would kill her pride to confess it.

She loved sushi, especially ebi. She couldn't afford it.

"You're weakening. Think about it. Chilled shrimp with rice. Wasabe and soy sauce and pickled ginger to go on it..."

"Stop! You're torturing me!"

He chuckled. "I love it, too. Come on. Say yes."

She drew in a long breath. "Okay," she blurted out, against her own best interests.

He grinned. "Okay."

When she got home that night, she could have kicked herself for agreeing.

Her father was watching television. A movie on DVD. They couldn't afford cable or satellite. The only reason she had a high-end cell phone was that the company provided it for her, along with a company car. These would have been luxuries, even on her good salary.

"I'm home," she said.

"Hi." He grinned at her while the commercial was on. "Had fun?"

"It was a business party," she reminded him.

"Easy enough to have fun and do business. Speaking of business, I saw this commercial on TV about how to invest in the stock market by doing day-trading..."

"No."

"Now, Erin..."

"No," she repeated. "We're still paying off that course you took learning how to sell real estate," she added pointedly.

He grimaced. "I didn't know I was a bad salesman until I tried it."

"Well, trying things is what got us into this financial mess, Dad," she said, sitting down across from him. "I'm making a good salary. If we live on a budget, we can make it, just. But there's no extra money. None at all. I can't work two jobs."

He studied her with the face of a child. "But it's only two hundred dollars, this course, I mean."

"I don't have two hundred dollars. Not even in savings. That went to the online gambling website you found," she added, trying not to sound as accusing as she felt.

He grimaced. "I guess I'm not as good a gambler as I thought, either. But, listen, this course," he began again.

"I can get an apartment of my own and move out," she said flatly.

He gasped. "Erin, no!"

"I can't live with the way you spend money, Dad. Either you stop trying to spend it on things we don't need, or I'm bailing out." She felt a hundred years old. "I can't keep bailing you out. We already owe more than I make in a year. I'm just one person."

"I do help out," he said stiffly.

"You do odd jobs and you spend what you make as soon as you get it," she replied.

He flushed. He couldn't deny that.

"I'll try to restrain myself. I will." He smiled. "But the man said that this course is foolproof."

She ground her teeth together as she got up. "I'm going to bed."

"If you'd just listen," he said sadly.

She turned. "I've listened since Mom died," she said. "And every single thing you've spent money on has cost us money without returning any. I'm so tired of debt, can't you understand that? I'm being crushed by the weight of it, worried to death about it, and you just can't seem to see what it's doing to me."

He blinked. He shifted uneasily in his chair. "I'll do better next time. You'll see."

"Next time it had better be your own money that you're betting," she replied and toughened her stance. "Or I'm moving out."

"You're being unreasonable, Erin," he retorted. "You don't love me."

"I do love you. And you're the one being unreasonable. Good night."

She went into her bedroom and closed the door, sick at heart. It was like trying to explain to a child. Her father had always lived in the clouds, but her mother had been able to manage him with supreme ease. Erin couldn't.

"I'll spend the rest of my life paying off his bills and then I'll die," she thought miserably. "I'll never get away."

Which was the one reason she could never let Ty Mosby see how she felt about him. Everybody knew her father kept them poor, but not how catastrophically. Ty would never be sure of her. Was she dating him because she cared for him or because he could pay off their debts.

It was an unrealistic thought, but she was almost panicked at the thought of dating Ty. She'd have to find some way to back out of it, a way that wouldn't hurt his pride. All her life, her father had been a stone around her neck. Since her mother's death, it had been much worse.

It would have helped if she had someone to talk to about it, but her only real friend was Annie, and she'd never be able to tell Annie the truth. It would just get back to Ty. Her pride wouldn't take that.

She wanted that date with all her heart. It was just too risky. She was crazy about him. It might show. There were so many reasons that she didn't dare let him see what she felt. Her father was the biggest one.

But there was another. Ty wasn't a marrying man. He kept his liaisons very private, but he'd had relationships in the past. In a small town like this, they wouldn't be able to hide one.

Erin had a spotless reputation. She wasn't having it damaged to keep steady company with a man who only wanted one thing from a woman, and it wasn't love.

So, better not to complicate her life any more than it was already complicated. Which left the problem of her father to solve, if it could be solved. She would never be free of him and his get-rich schemes that never paid off. She'd be in debt until she died.

She put on her gown and crawled gratefully under the covers. She'd think about it tomorrow, she told herself. Tonight, she was going to savor her memory of Ty's arm around her, his deep voice sensuous as he teased her about going on a date.

It could never happen. But dreaming about it hurt nobody. Especially not Erin.

CHAPTER TWO

Erin made breakfast for her father and herself. They ate in silence. Every so often, her father would give her a hangdog look, as if denying him the course he wanted was an evil deed and she was cruel.

Arthur Mitchell wasn't a bad man, he was just a frivolous one. But regardless of his intent, he was making Erin's life difficult. Impossible.

"Well, I guess I'll go back to doing little odd jobs in town, then," Arthur said on a sigh.

"I guess you will," she said, forcing herself not to give in.

He glowered. "It was a good course."

She pulled something up on her cell phone and shoved it across the table. "I want you to read that."

He frowned as he picked up the phone and read the article she'd downloaded during a sleepless night.

As he read, his mouth fell open. It was a tragic story about a man who lost everything through day-trading and killed himself.

It was a cautionary tale, followed with a vivid description of the victim's last note to his loved ones before ending his life. It concluded that day-trading was promising miracles of money but delivering bankruptcy and grief.

Arthur Mitchell handed his daughter back the phone. He bit his lower lip. "The man said it was easy, that anybody could do it. But that poor man…!" He went back to his breakfast. "I guess maybe it's like gambling. You have to know all the little tricks that make it work."

"It's exactly like that. You have to understand the ups and downs so that you don't lose everything you have."

He brightened. "That's why that course is a really good idea."

She sighed. "I'll start looking at apartment listings."

He was doing mental arithmetic. She paid the bills, did all the cooking and cleaning, the laundry and the dishes. If she left, he'd have all that to do. He couldn't cook. He'd never cleaned anything. He didn't even know how to run the dishwasher. He stared at her, debating.

He let out a breath. "I can put it off for a while," he said. "The course, I mean. It will still be there, if I can ever afford it."

She smiled at him. "That's the dad I know," she said gently.

He looked guilty. He grimaced. "I'm not a good father, or I'd be supporting you," he said after a minute. "Your mother looked out for me, all our lives. She was the rock that we built our lives on. Now it's just me, and I'm not like her," he concluded, trying to explain, to apologize, for his shortcomings. "She said I gnawed on things like a dog with a bone. I guess I do."

"You're not a bad father, and I don't mind working for both of us," she said gently. "I just don't want you to put more on me than I can stand. I have a great job, but I could lose it if the economy gets worse."

"No. Ty would never fire you," he said with confidence. "He likes you. Or he'd never have asked you for a date," he concluded with a smile.

She gasped. "How did you know that?"

"Just something I heard," he teased. "And I won't say any more about it. Ty's like family. So is Annie."

"Mom loved their mother," Erin agreed. "They were the best of friends."

"It's a shame that they lost their parents. It's a shame about your mother, too. I miss her something awful," he confessed, staring at his plate. "Maybe it's why I do some of the dumb things I do."

"They're not dumb," she said. "You're just trying to help with expenses. But it would take you a long time, even with a course of study, to be good enough to earn a living at some of these things you want to do," she said gently.

He frowned. "I hadn't thought of it like that. I guess it would. I'm not as young as I used to be," he added with a laugh. That reminds me, I have a physical coming up next week. Will our insurance cover it? Our doctor wants to do some tests."

She frowned, too. "Some tests? Why?"

"He didn't say. You know I had that kidney infection just recently. He sent off a sample for analysis. He said it's not serious, but he likes to check things."

"We'll manage even if the insurance doesn't cover it. I can't lose you," she teased. "I'd have nobody to beat me at chess."

He grinned back. "No worries about that," he said. "I'll live for years yet!"

But it didn't go exactly that way at the doctor's office. Erin was phoned at work to come to the hospital. Their doctor had had Arthur hospitalized and they were doing extensive tests.

She stared at Dr. Worth with her heart in her throat. "But he's only fifty," she blurted out. As if age made any real difference in who got a disease.

He looked at her with real regret. "I know that. It isn't a matter of age. We don't know why people get it. This is a terrible disease. We can treat the symptoms. We can't cure it; especially not when it's gotten to this stage."

She drew in a breath. "How long?" she asked, steeling herself.
"Six months. Maybe."

"Dear God!" She felt sick inside. "He's the only family I have
left in the world," she told him quietly.

"I know that. I'm so sorry. It's hard for me, too, Erin. I've
treated him for a long time."

"You've kept him well. I'm so glad that you have this office
open one day a week, so we don't have to get Dad up to San Antonio to see you. My car, quite frankly, would not make it that
far," she added on a laugh, to lighten the atmosphere of despair.

He smiled. "But you'd try to get it there, if you had to. I know
what a time you're having with Arthur, Erin. I admire the way
you talk him out of these wild schemes he comes up with."

"Losing mom caused something to snap in him," she said.
"He wasn't like this, before. He was levelheaded."

"He was less flighty," he corrected, "because your mother
also knew how to handle him. Can you manage the expense?
He's not old enough for Medicare, and it's going to get expensive if he has to have radiation or, especially, the cancer pill. A
colleague of mine prescribed it for a cancer patient of his and a
month's supply was over four thousand dollars."

"Four thousand…" She felt her knees going weak. She'd never
be able to afford that. Not in a million years.

"There are ways to lower the cost," he said. "One is to write
to the company that manufactures the pill and explain the circumstances and ask for a reduction in price. But you have a good
job. Surely you have insurance?"

"Yes, I do," she said, and felt a little relief. "I had Dad put on
it with me."

"That will help," he assured her.

"I can't tell him," she said, her face contorting. She looked
up at him. "Do we have to? Honestly, if we do tell him, he'll sit
down and die, you know that as surely as I do. He'll just give up."

He drew in a breath. "I can understand how you feel. But if

he's to have treatment, he'll have to know why, Erin. And he's an intelligent man. He'll know there's a reason he's taking expensive pills. He knows people all over town. Honestly, he's the worst gossip I know."

She laughed. "Yes, he is. It's mostly harmless gossip, but he's gotten in trouble a couple of times for passing along things that never happened." She shook her head. "I hope he doesn't cause some terrible tragedy by repeating things he hears."

"Not much worry about that, he's not malicious."

"He isn't. Some of the gossip is."

"True enough. Well, I'll discharge him this afternoon. You can take him home. We'll get started right away. I know a good specialist in San Antonio, and I know Annie will find a way to get you both up there," he added when she turned pale. "Just ask her."

"I hate to presume…"

"She'll go after you with a paddle if you try to do this without her. You've been friends since grammar school."

"I guess I don't have much choice. My car really wouldn't get as far as the county line."

"And let me give you some good advice," he added seriously. "Take it one day at a time. People try so hard to gulp life, to anticipate what's down the road in weeks, months, even years. The secret to having a good life is to live every day as if it's your last."

She managed a smile. "Okay. I'll try."

"You do that. And let me know how Arthur does, will you? Specialists are so busy that they don't have time to inform us about every patient. I like Arthur."

"I'll make sure we keep you in the loop. And thanks, for all you've done."

"Not that much, I'm afraid," he said sadly. "Medicine, even modern medicine, has its limits. You take care of yourself. This is as hard on the family as it is on the patient. Perhaps harder. It's tough to stand and watch somebody go downhill and not be able to help."

"Tell me about it," she replied, and smiled sadly.

★ ★ ★

Arthur wasn't smiling, sadly or not, when she went to his room to get him checked out. He was dressed, sitting in the chair by the bed, looking as if the world had ended.

Erin stood just inside the door, conflicted.

He looked up and saw her. Tears were making his eyes gleam. "I'm dying."

She ground her teeth together.

He smiled then. "But he says I can get treatments that work, and he's sending me to a specialist who can save me!"

It wasn't anywhere close to the truth, but it might keep her father alive past the time medical science considered him done for. She'd take it, she decided, over total gloom.

"Yes, they did say that," she added with a forced smile, while she thought about pills that cost four thousand dollars and how she could afford months of them for her oblivious parent.

"So I'll be okay," he said cheerfully. "I'm glad. I'd miss you."

"Oh, I'd miss you, too, Dad," she replied, and fought down the lump in her throat. "So, let's get you home, and I'll make you something special for supper."

"Scrambled eggs and bacon and toast," he said at once, getting up. "I've thought about it since breakfast." He made a face. "They gave me oatmeal with no milk and sugar. And a piece of toast with no butter, either. You make a great breakfast!"

"Thanks."

"You might go down to the kitchen here, and teach them how to do it," he added, not totally without honesty.

She laughed. "Not a good idea. But I'll cook you something nice!"

"I hate to ask," she told Annie later that day, while her father was napping. "But my car won't go that far. I've got an oil leak. It goes in the shop Friday…"

"No problem, I'll have the car pick you up and bring you

back," Annie said easily, a smile in her voice. "Is it something serious?"

She hated lying to her friend, but it was for a good cause. She didn't want anyone to know her circumstances. Annie might feel obliged to help financially and Erin's ego wouldn't bear it. She'd find the money she needed somehow.

"It can be, but they think they've caught it in time," she said easily.

"Good. I'm so glad. And what's this I hear about my big brother taking you out on a date?" she added gleefully.

Erin flushed, even though nobody could see it. "We're just going to have dinner," she began.

"I've hoped for years and years that he'd look in your direction," Annie confessed. "He doesn't like most women, but he likes you."

"He's a nice man," Erin began.

"Nice? My brother?!"

Erin hesitated to contradict her.

"He set me up with an arms dealer!" Annie exclaimed.

"What?!"

"An arms dealer! The guy actually sold ex-military hardware to insurrectionists in half a dozen countries overseas!"

"Ty did that, to you?" Erin asked.

Annie almost snorted. "He did. And then claimed in all innocence that he didn't know the guy had a criminal record."

"Why?"

"He thought I should get married. I don't want to get married. I'm very happy as I am," she pointed out.

Erin knew why Annie didn't want a man in her life. One had been quite enough. The memories were terrible.

"One day, you might meet somebody…" Erin began.

"That's what I'm telling you, I already did! Ty is lucky he got in the front door! I was going to have all the locks changed. Then I remembered that I can't fix the toilet, the one that keeps overflowing, so I hesitated. Hesitation is death!" she added dramatically.

Erin was having trouble keeping her amusement to herself. Annie was a case when she was upset.

"You're laughing, aren't you?" Annie asked suspiciously. "I can hear you!"

"I'm not laughing. Honest. Not at all."

"Ha! Denial!" Annie said accusingly. "I watched this FBI documentary on criminality and it said that the more you deny something, the more it's true!"

"Then UFOs must be real," Erin replied, "because the government's been denying them for eighty years."

Annie groaned. "Please don't tell my brother that!" she pleaded. "He's already convinced that the government is secretly reverse-engineering flying saucers. He watched three videos about it on that public channel."

"I know," Erin replied. "He told us this morning."

"One day they'll send the men in black after him," Annie assured her.

Erin did laugh then. "Now there's a real figment of your imagination," she pointed out.

"It's contagious! I've caught it from him!"

"No. You're just stressed out from the puppies. How many did Sanja have this time?" she added.

"Six," Annie wailed. "I haven't slept since they were born. They all look just like Beauregard, too," she added, her voice softening. "They're the cutest little things. We're going to go through agonies letting them be adopted, especially after that court case."

"How is Beauregard?" she asked gently.

"Still recovering," Annie replied. "Ty says he'll be at every parole hearing with a picture of the pup after that fool took the leash to him!"

"I don't blame him. It was so awful."

"Poor little guy. He's fine as long as he's here with us, but he's nervous of strangers, especially men."

"Going to keep him?"

"We'll have to," Annie said. "No way Ty will ever let him be adopted. Besides, Rhodes is getting older now. He's thirteen. I do like having a hundred-pound German shepherd dog in the house with us. Beauregard is Rhodes' son, so likely he'll top a hundred pounds when he's grown. And maybe he'll keep my brother from going nuts when he loses Rhodes. Big dogs don't have long life spans. I love having one in the house. Our dogs are gentle, but they don't sound that way when they're upset." She chuckled. "They really sound dangerous. Which reminds me, Ty wants to give you one of the new pups."

Her heart jumped. "What? But he sells those pups for almost five thousand each! I could never accept one!"

"We can afford it, and you know it. He says you need a dog in the house, especially now," she added quietly.

"Oh, Annie...!" She fought tears.

"They told you more than they told your dad, didn't they?"

Erin couldn't answer her. She felt broken inside.

"I'm coming right over," Annie said, and hung up.

The first thing she did was just hug Erin and hug her some more. Arthur was asleep in his room in the back of the house, resting from what had been an exhausting ordeal.

"You haven't told Arthur?" Annie asked when the tears finally stopped.

"No." Erin's eyes were red. She dabbed at them with a paper towel. "I looked it up online, Annie." Her gaze met her best friend's. "It's almost always fatal when it's this advanced. They can treat the symptoms, but not much else. The doctor said it was very advanced. Six months. Possibly not even that much time." Tears threatened again. "I don't have any other family in the whole world...!"

Annie hugged her again. "Yes, you do. You've got me. And my brother."

"Ty doesn't want to be my family," Erin said after a minute. "He's always sarcastic and rude to me."

"That's how I know he likes you," she said on a grin. "He's nice to most women."

"Well, yes, he is, especially at work," Erin agreed.

"And you're rude to him, too, you know."

"If I wasn't, he'd walk all over me," her friend pointed out.

Annie sobered. "It all goes back to that gold-digger he got involved with six years ago. You remember."

Erin nodded. Indeed she had. She'd watched Ty be enveloped in the visiting accountant's spell until he was almost floating at her side. Ruby Dawes had been a traumatic experience that Ty never got over. Annie and Erin saw right through her. Ty didn't. He got engaged and was planning the wedding when the woman's ex-husband showed up in town and told everybody, including Ty, what she'd done to him. She'd married him just for his fortune, which she'd found ways to relieve him of. He was now facing eviction from his own mansion and she'd sweet-talked him out of a fortune in stocks and bonds that she'd gone through like a thirsty woman drinking water.

Ty hadn't believed him until the man convinced him to watch while he confronted his ex-wife in the lobby of the business Ty owned in San Antonio, where she'd been working.

It was unbelievable, witnesses said, still gossiping about it today. The woman had turned into a witch before their eyes, raking her ex-husband over the coals for daring to muscle in on her latest scheme. She had a millionaire dangling right now, she said, unaware that Ty was listening. Her ex-husband was going to make her lose all that nice money. If he did, she'd get even with him, she'd make sure he never got another job, just like she'd done to the man she dumped to marry him!

When Ty walked into the lobby, stunned and furious, she

tried to convince him that she was just lying, trying to make her ex-husband go away. He was stalking her, she said, trying to get what was left of the fortune he'd cheated her out of. She even cried.

Ty called security and had her shown out the door. He thanked her ex-husband for saving him. Then he got drunk and stayed drunk for two weeks.

It had been Erin who kept him from killing himself over it. Ty was the sort of man who loved with everything in him. No shallow feelings, no lukewarm affection. He'd had a loaded pistol on his desk with a bottle of whiskey and he hadn't let Annie near him.

She'd called Erin, who'd just graduated from high school and was taking business courses at the local community college. Erin had gone right over, unlocked the office door with a passkey that Annie had been told blatantly not to use.

Ty, drunk and furious, had told Erin to get out. She'd ignored him, poured the rest of his bottle of whiskey down the sink behind the bar in his study, and paid no attention to the outrageous cursing that followed. After that, she'd calmly emptied the .45 Ruger Vaquero of shells and pocketed them.

He'd told her to go home, using curses she'd only heard in R-rated movies on the movie channels. She'd pulled him into her arms and rocked him and rocked him while he shuddered at the unexpected and largely unwanted compassion that he, nevertheless, didn't protest.

Minutes later, when he was calmer, he jerked away from her, averting his eyes. She led him to the sofa, tugged him down on it, covered him with one of the colorful afghans she'd crocheted for Christmas presents for him and Annie, and then she sat with him all night to make sure he didn't raid the bar again or go looking for more bullets.

Annie, fascinated, had watched from afar with absolute awe. She was afraid of her brother in a temper. Her one experience with love eternal had been almost as traumatic as Ty's, except that hers had involved an alcoholic boyfriend and a bat. Her only other one had been a hopeless infatuation with a man who didn't even see her. But that was before the one with the bat.

Erin had noted once, a couple of years later, that the Mosbys had the worst luck in love of any two people she'd ever known. Annie had agreed. Neither she nor Ty was looking to repeat their bad experiences.

And Erin had never found love eternal, because she'd been in love with Ty since he'd presented her with a bouquet on her sixteenth birthday and a tender kiss on her forehead. She sometimes thought he still saw her as the leggy, awkward teenager who'd almost worshipped her best friend's big brother.

He knew about the crush she had on him, of course, but he just smiled and tolerated it until it finally wore itself out on his indifference. He thought she was cured by the time she was seventeen, when she'd only learned how to camouflage her unwanted feelings. She still had them. She dated occasionally, but she saw her infrequent dates as friends with chest hair. They never got past the front door.

Ty didn't know, and he never would. She knew it was hopeless. But she wondered why he wanted to take her out to dinner. It was out of character.

"He's trying to ward off somebody at work, isn't he?" Erin asked over coffee when she'd made it, black and strong, for both of them and they were sitting at the little kitchen table drinking it.

"What?" Annie asked, all at sea.

"Ty. He's taking me out because he wants somebody else to know about it," she repeated.

Annie made a face. "Oh, darn," she muttered. "I didn't even consider that."

Erin smiled, although her heart was shattering in her chest. "Who is it?"

"It's that Taylor woman he hired last month," she muttered. "She's been wearing seductive clothing to work, invited him over to discuss a report she says needs work. Why didn't I remember that? He's done nothing but complain about her for two weeks!"

"I thought so."

Annie gave her a long look. "I hope that didn't hurt your feelings," she said awkwardly.

"Relax," Erin said, smiling. "I got over Ty years ago," she lied.

Annie let out a breath. "What a horrible thing I would have done to you if you hadn't," she said, relieved. "Honestly, he must not be thinking logically himself. He knew how you used to feel about him. It would have been cruel to do that to you, to let you think he really was interested in you."

"He knows better," Erin pointed out. "I don't mind. She gets on my nerves, too. If she's just staying because she thinks Ty is an easy mark, she's got some shocks coming."

"That damned Dawes woman," Annie said with real venom. Her black eyes snapped with temper. "Because of her, Ty will never get married now. He sees every potential date as someone after his fortune."

"You know, there are a lot of things in life worth more than just dollar signs," Erin pointed out. "Time, for example. When it runs out, money doesn't matter much."

She was staring into her coffee with her heart breaking.

"I'll take care of those pills, if that's what you're agonizing about," Annie told her and made a sound when she protested. "I'm filthy rich. The cost of the meds is pocket change to me. If you don't let me do it, I'll tell Ty and he'll do it…"

"No!"

Annie nodded at Erin's red face and horrified expression. "That's what I thought. So we'll go get the prescriptions together when the doctor prescribes them." She smiled. "Just so you know that you won't sneak off to the pharmacy without me. You're all the family I've got."

"You're all the family I've got, too, except Dad," Erin sighed.

"Not true. You have that sweet elderly cousin in Wyoming."

"I do, but you're family as well."

Annie sighed and smiled affectionately. "Thanks."

"At least I still have you in my life," Erin said softly, and smiled.

"Same here. Well, I'd include Ty in that family thing, but nobody in their right mind wants to be related to him!" Annie said, shaking her head. "Our housekeeper threatens to quit every Friday."

"What happens every Friday?"

"That's when Ty goes out on the ranch to work with the cowboys, after he's gone crazy sitting at a desk the other four days of the week."

"I still don't…"

"He goes out to work on the ranch. Think about it. Red mud? Smelly substances…?"

"Oh!"

"I never even knew that Mrs. Dobbs could curse," Annie said. "Wow, can she ever! She even threw one pair of Ty's jeans away. She said prayer wouldn't get those stains out, and she wasn't about to ruin her brand new washing machine with them."

Erin laughed. Mrs. Dobbs was notorious in Jacobsville for claiming all the Mosby's appliances as her own.

"So far, I've managed to keep her," Annie said. "At that, she's lasted longer than any housekeepers before her, but that's because she loves the dogs."

"I remember the last housekeeper," Erin replied.

"Everybody remembers the last one," Annie said on a sigh. "Honestly, some people just don't like animals, you know? But she should have said something before she walked through the front door. You know how Ty is about his babies."

"A raging, frothy-mouthed fanatic…?"

"Exactly. Anyway, he did at least have one of the boys drive her to the bus station. And he gave her two weeks' salary, which he wasn't obliged to do."

"She shouldn't have called Beauregard names and locked him out of the kitchen and refused to feed him or give him water after he'd been out in the hot sun all day," Erin said on a huff.

Annie cocked her head. "You sound just like Ty did."

"He was right," Erin muttered. "Stupid woman."

"We heard later that she only took the job because she heard Ty was single," her friend said. "I thought at the time that she was too young and attractive to be doing a housekeeper's job."

"And it turned out she was working in a much different profession before she applied to clean your house."

"Very much different. She was a bartender."

"Well, it's a dirty job but somebody has to do it," Erin said, wiggling her eyebrows.

Annie burst out laughing.

Later, when Annie got home, Ty was just finishing with the last pup, cleaning him up after he'd finished nursing.

"How is she?" he asked his sister.

She ran a hand over the little pup's silky fur. "Grieving," she said.

He sighed. "I remember. So do you. It's hard losing one parent. Losing both is a nightmare."

"Yes, but Erin's tougher than she looks."

He chuckled softly. "I'll say."

Annie was remembering, as he was, the night Erin had taken away his whiskey and his bullets.

"I told her if she didn't let me pay for Arthur's meds, I'd tell you. That was enough."

He scowled. "Why?"

"Honestly, Ty," she muttered, taking the pup from him to

cuddle it. "She has a double dose of pride. And we all remember women who wanted money more than…"

"Stop right there," he said and his black eyes flashed.

She shrugged. "Anyway, she'd starve before she'd ask either one of us for help. I don't know how she thought she'd manage to pay for a bottle of pills that costs over four thousand dollars."

"What?!"

"Cancer meds," she explained. "That's what they cost. Per month."

"Good Lord," he whistled reverently. "What do poor people do?"

"They die," she said simply. "It's a sad world we live in."

He took the pup from her and put it back with the others, curled up next to their mother.

"You should have told Erin why you invited her to dinner, though," Annie told him when they were sitting around in the living room.

He scowled. "Told her?"

"About the woman who's chasing you at work," Annie explained, exasperated. "What if Erin still had that crush on you? She might have thought you were taking her out because you were really interested in her. It would have been cruel."

He didn't answer her at first. He was thinking. He had meant to date Erin to give the pursuing woman a hint that he wasn't interested. On the other hand, Erin was familiar to him and he was comfortable with her. But was it really to ward off an aggressive employee? Or was he really seeing Erin in a different light these days? It wasn't a question he was comfortable answering in the privacy in his own mind, much less sharing with his sister.

"I guess it would have been," he said belatedly.

"Never mind," she chuckled. "Erin figured it out all by herself."

"She doesn't date," he pointed out.

"No. She said she got tired of explaining to men that just because women were liberated it didn't mean she was liberated. She goes to church," she reminded him.

"So do we," he replied. "To the same church, in fact."

"Yes, but she doesn't move with the times."

"No sleeping around, in other words," he said, and felt an odd sense of pride that she didn't. Then he wondered why he felt that way.

"Exactly." She yawned. "I'm going to lie down for an hour or two. Mrs. Dobbs is making tuna casserole for supper, by the way. So what did you do this time?" she added, because he hated the dish.

"I just mentioned that I don't like gnomes."

Her eyes widened.

"Well, she didn't have to put gnome towels in my bathroom, did she?" he asked defensively. "You're the gnome fanatic!"

"You mean, you did something before you mentioned that you don't like gnomes?" she exclaimed.

He was glaring now. "I was just making a point that I didn't like gnome towels," he muttered. "Not my fault that they fell on the sidewalk below and Rhodes got hold of them."

"Oh, my goodness," Annie moaned. "Rhodes eats towels if he can get to them!"

"He only shredded them a little. Sort of. Anyway, she never should have done that to my bed. Or put colored sheets on my damned bed!" he added belligerently.

"Colored sheets…?"

"I only said that men shouldn't have to sleep on colored sheets," he added defensively. "I like white sheets. She put pink ones on my bed!"

"Pink ones?" she asked.

"To get even for the gnomes," he said with absolute disgust.

She was trying very hard not to laugh.

"Oh, hell," he muttered, because he noticed. He got up. "I might as well sew lace on my damned bedspread…" he added as he grabbed his Stetson and went out of the room.

Annie gave up and almost doubled over, laughing.

CHAPTER THREE

Erin was all thumbs on Friday morning, because that was the day that Ty was taking her out to dinner. She'd already gone through her meager wardrobe four times, trying to find her best outfit. Even if Ty was only doing it to push away that other unknown employee, Erin was bubbling inside at going on a real date with him, after all the years of hopeless longing. Of course, she had to try to look calm, so that he wouldn't suspect how she felt.

"You've handed me the wrong set of figures three times already," Ty pointed out, lounging behind his massive oak desk. He gave her a long look, going over her trim figure in the neat black pantsuit she was wearing with a draped pink silky blouse. Her long black hair was in a neat bun. She always looked nice. "All nervous about tonight?" he asked, and his twinkling black eyes pinned her gray ones.

She managed not to drop the document she was holding. She even forced a smile. "Not at all." She recalled what was going on at home. She sighed. "I'm just worried about Dad."

He grimaced. "Sorry."

"No problem."

He studied her quietly. "Annie told me. I would have helped, if you'd asked."

She lifted her chin. "I can manage."

"No," he said. "You can't." He got up and she steeled herself as he came closer. Honestly, in that dark blue suit with its spotless white shirt and blue paisley tie, his thick black hair neatly combed, he was as handsome as any movie cowboy. He even smelled delicious.

"Why does it upset you to ask me for help?" he asked aloud.

She lifted a shoulder. "I don't like being obligated to people."

"I know that."

"Annie offered. I didn't ask."

"I know that, too, Erin."

Chills went down her spine at the way he said her name. He rarely used it.

"You never look at me," he said suddenly. "You look over my shoulder or at my chest."

She forced a smile and dragged her eyes up to his. "It's not intentional," she lied.

He scowled. "Annie and I know how is to lose parents," he said.

She nodded, biting her lower lip. "It was unexpected, what Dad's doctor told us."

"I can imagine. We'll do anything we can to help."

She nodded again, afraid to trust her voice.

He tilted her chin up so that he could see the hurt and worry in her eyes. "You don't sleep, do you?" he asked, noting the dark circles.

"Life is hard."

"Yes."

He searched her eyes, still scowling. She smelled of flowers. He liked the scent. It wasn't loud or overpowering. She was neat and trim and pretty, in her way. She'd never be a raving beauty, but she had a kind heart. That made up for so much, in a woman. He wondered if she realized it. She'd told Annie once that she didn't appeal to men, because she wasn't pretty enough. It wasn't true. She'd always been around. He was used to her. He liked her. But just lately...

There was a quick rap at the open door and Jenny Taylor walked in, smelling like a perfumery, with her long blond hair artfully arranged around her lovely face, and too much makeup on. "Sorry if I'm interrupting," she said, her voice almost a purr as she looked at Ty, ignoring Erin. "I need to talk to you about this report I'm typing. I'm afraid it's a little over my head," she added in a cajoling tone. "The terms that are used...?" she prompted with a smile.

"Take it over to Harvey, in legal, and have him explain it to you, Ms. Taylor," he replied, his tone as sharp as the look he gave her. "One more thing," he added as her face fell, "there are notices on the doors about our policy on using heavy perfume. Please read one."

She flushed. "Uh, yes, sir. I will. So sorry..."

She left abruptly.

Erin let out the breath that had caught in her throat. Ty could be very authoritative when he felt like it. She was encouraged by the way he'd spoken to the other woman, but she didn't show it.

"Thanks," she said under her breath. "I was thinking about requesting a purchase order for a gas mask..."

He chuckled, deep in his throat. "So was I," he teased. He cocked his head. "So. I'll pick you up at six. That ok?"

She nodded.

"If you see Ben Jones, send him in, will you? I need to pick his brain on a cost estimate I'm putting together."

She didn't like Ben Jones. The older man had a shifty personality, and there was some gossip about how he made extra money. She'd never told Ty. It wouldn't have done any good. The man had worked with his father, when he'd started the construction company that Ty now captained. Ty would never have believed anything bad about him. Even Annie complained that he was too loyal to a man who'd sell him out for pocket change.

"I will," she said.

His eyes narrowed. "Not one word, Erin."

Her eyes widened. "About what?" she exclaimed.

"I know you don't like him. But he's part of the reason this company exists. Nobody does cost estimates better," he added.

She almost bit her tongue. He didn't know that Ben had taken credit for her last cost estimate, which had been right on the money. She knew it would do no good to tell Ty, because he wouldn't believe her.

So she just smiled. "I have nothing against him," she said easily. "I know he and your dad started the company." She also knew that he'd almost lost Ty's dad the company with his underhanded shenanigans in years past. But it wouldn't do any good to tell Ty that, either.

"Yes, he did," Ty replied. He smiled and the sun came out. "Back to work."

She made a face at him. "I've been working."

"Bringing me the wrong figures. Three times."

She ignored him. "I'll send Ben right in."

He just sighed. He'd never understand her animosity for his father's colleague. Come to think of it, Annie didn't like Ben either. *Women!* he thought to himself and went back to his desk.

Erin chose a simple black dress, no frills, no fads. It was a sheath with a hem that stopped mid-knee and had a fitted bodice with cape sleeves. It was elegant, but it hadn't been expensive. She'd found it on a sale rack when she went shopping at a local boutique. The owner, who did some designs of her own, laughed at Erin's surprise and said that it was a couture piece that a pregnant socialite had bought and hadn't been able to wear. So it ended up for sale at a fraction of its list price. Erin had been ecstatic. They'd once had money, until her father lost it all. Now, even with her good salary, she had to budget to the bone.

She had her hair in an elegant upswept coiffure, and just the lightest touch of both makeup and cologne.

At least she had shoes and an evening bag, left over from a shopping trip two years back. Those, too, had been on a sale rack. There was never much money at home for luxuries, even when her mother had been alive. Arthur kept them poor with his get-rich-quick schemes that cost a lot and never paid anything back. At least, Erin thought, she'd headed him off from the day-trading one. That would have meant disaster.

"You look very nice," Arthur said when she stopped in the living room where he was reading the newspaper.

She smiled. "Thanks, Dad."

"I'm glad you and Ty are finally looking at each other," he said, for once very seriously. "I've thought for many years that you had a great deal in common. But Ty doesn't like most women, and you don't like most men."

"I'm picky," she said, smiling.

"Good. It's the best way to be." He drew in a breath. "It just worries me, how we're going to afford those pills the doctor says the specialist will likely prescribe. He says they cost the earth."

"We'll find a way," she replied, bending to kiss the top of his head. "Don't even think about it."

He smiled. "Okay, then. You have fun."

"Going to do my best," she promised, just as a car drove up. She fought down the excitement. "That will be Ty," she said, picking up her lightweight spring coat.

"I'll see you when I see you," he said.

She just nodded as she opened the door.

Ty looked spectacular, she thought, in a dark suit and white shirt and tie. He really paid for dressing. He was looking at her, too, with appreciative black eyes.

"Nice," he murmured, wondering if she'd robbed a bank,

because he knew couture when he saw it. Annie was a walking dictionary when it came to clothes. She'd educated him.

"This old thing?" she teased. "I found it in the closet!"

He laughed, as he was meant to, but a suspicion lodged in the back of his mind. He turned it off. "Ready to go? Hi, Arthur. How are you feeling?" he asked her father as they paused just inside the door.

"I'm doing well, thank you, Ty," he replied with a smile. "It's nice of you to take my baby girl out," he added. "She's been too worried about me lately. It's not good for her."

"I'm looking forward to tonight," Ty told him. "And you're going to be fine. We'll help in any way we can. You know that."

"I do, and thanks."

"Well, let's go," he told Erin, and paused to help her into her coat, his big, beautiful hands lingering just briefly on her shoulders. "Good night, Arthur."

Her father grinned and waved.

"He's going to spend the night watching game shows," Erin told Ty as they climbed into his big luxury car and headed toward San Antonio. "It's his passion. And at least it keeps his mind off day-trading!"

"What?"

"Oh," she said. She hadn't meant to blurt that out. "He wants to take a course to teach him how to do day-trading. I showed him a news story about a man who lost everything he had trying to do that and ended up taking his own life. I think it made an impression."

"With all due respect, your father has no head for handling money." He shook his head. "My mother used to worry about your mother, because she said one day Arthur would lose the very house right out from under them with one of his unlucky schemes."

Erin sighed. "I know. I can barely talk him out of things, especially now. He's bull-headed."

"But blood is blood, so we do what we can for our kin, no

matter how warped they may be. In which case, may I just mention my great-uncle Phil…"

She groaned. "Oh, please don't!"

He chuckled. "Well, it was a memorable scandal, and it took Annie's mind off grieving for our parents. It helped me, too."

Phil was a rotund little man with a genius for getting into trouble. He'd been married with a lovely, sweet wife and two little boys, when he met a woman on the internet who promised to get him into show business as a comedian. It was the dream of his life. But Phil had no sense of humor and his idea of it was insulting anyone he could think of, especially his own relatives. So Phil left his wife, went to Hollywood to meet this woman. She was very enthusiastic about his new career. But, she said, it would take a lot of money to make his dream come true. Luckily, she knew people in show business who could be enticed to help him for some cash. He believed her. He handed over thousands of dollars, every penny in his savings account, and his wife knew nothing about it. She thought he'd gone on a business trip for the company that employed him.

Then, four months later, the sheriff came to her door with an eviction notice. She and the little boys had no house. Phil had sold it and given the money to the woman when his savings account ran dry. All that he got for his investment was ten minutes at a comedy club where he was booed off the stage. Despondent and apologetic, he tried to come back home and start over.

His wife had already started divorce proceedings, out of the meager sum she made at her own job, clerking for the local phone company. Phil was left with a guilty conscience, no money, nothing. Ty, his only close relative, had bailed him out and gotten him back the job he'd lost due to his escapade. Phil was still working there. He got to visit his sons, but his ex-wife wouldn't even speak to him. It was a painful lesson in how gullible some men could be.

"Do you think Lucy will ever take him back?" Erin asked.

Ty sighed. "I have serious doubts about that. She'd worked so hard to keep up those house payments. She had no idea that her husband had sold the house out from under her; easy to do, as it was in his name only." He glanced at her with twinkling eyes. "So if you ever get married, make sure your name is on everything of value, as well as his."

"I'm too old to get married," she laughed. "Besides, I've got Dad to take care of."

He was silent the rest of the way to the restaurant he was taking her to. It was a five-star affair, only the best.

"You're not too old, Erin," he said after he'd parked, and they were walking toward the door.

She looked up. It was a long way. He towered over her. "I feel a hundred sometimes," she said quietly.

He paused and looked down at her. "I can imagine why," he said softly. His hand reached out and brushed back a wisp of black hair that had come loose from her coiffure. "You haven't had an easy life."

She searched his black eyes. "Neither have you, Ty," she replied softly. "But neither of us are quitters. We put one foot in front of the other and keep going," she added with a smile.

He got lost in her eyes. She was unique among the handful of women who'd graced his life. He smiled back. She made him feel as if he'd had champagne. Which was a hoot because he never drank anything stronger than iced tea. The effect was the same, though. A kind of sweet euphoria. It was new and heady and exciting.

Laughter from behind them as a group of people headed toward the door, talking to each other, moved them apart. But as they walked, his fingers tangled with hers and brought them close.

Her heart was doing jumping jacks in her chest. She hoped he wouldn't notice.

"I hope you like beef," he remarked as they walked in behind the group of people. "This restaurant is famous for it."

"I like it." She was lying. She loved fish. She wasn't fond of beef or even chicken.

And Ty knew. It warmed his heart that she was lying for his benefit. He felt her cold little hand in his and felt suddenly protective. She was nervous in his company. He recalled random remarks Annie had let slip about her best friend. Erin didn't date. She was hung up on some man who couldn't see her for dust. Was it—could it be—him?

His heart skipped. He looked down at the top of her head. She was always around, especially at holidays at the house, because all three of them were without mothers, so Erin was included in festive family meals, along with Arthur. The two families had always been close. But Erin didn't date. Could he be the reason she never dated? She said it was her father. Taking care of him gave her no time to go out. But here she was going out with Ty. He felt a jolt of delight.

He was pretty much heart-whole, too. There had been one bad experience with a woman that had soured him on romance, although it hadn't kept him from a few passionate interludes. But he kept to himself. Now he was wondering if there wasn't someone close at hand who was more to him than he'd realized. He wasn't rushing into anything, though. He had time. Plenty of time.

The waiter handed them menus and Erin sighed sadly. It was all in French. She looked up to find Ty watching her, but the smile on his face was gentle.

"You don't really like beef, Erin, and you don't read French. This was a bad choice on my part. I'm sorry."

"It's fine," she said at once. "It's a great place to eat."

"And that's like you," he added. "You never complain. Not even when our cook served you liver and onions for supper one night at home, and you ate it. Your mother told our mother later that you loathed the dish."

She laughed softly. "It was one of your mother's favorite

dishes, and I loved her almost as much as I loved my own. I'd never have said a word."

He leaned back in his chair with a sigh. "You're not demanding, even when you should be." He frowned slightly. "I've said this before, but you don't listen. You need to stand up for yourself more."

She smiled back. "It's just not me," she said simply. "People are pretty much what they seem, Ty. You can't remake someone to suit yourself."

He shook his head. "You misunderstand me. I mean that you shouldn't give in sometimes, just because you might hurt someone's feelings."

"Oh, that's rich," she mused, grinning. "I can just see you doing that when some tycoon wants a house built and you tell him the design he wants is gaudy."

He chuckled. "Well, maybe sometimes it's not politically savvy to do that. But in your case…"

"In my case," she interrupted gently, "I do what I please."

He raised an eyebrow. "That was more like it."

"What?"

"That's what I meant, Erin. You need to learn to stand up to me."

Her eyes widened. "I don't understand."

"I had a friend in high school who was like you. Gentle," he said, smiling, "easy to get along with, undemanding." The smile faded. "She married a football hero. He was charming and funny and popular. Except that he used drugs and nobody knew. One night he lost his temper and hit her. She didn't call the police, of course. She was too nice. She told herself that he was just angry and he'd get over it. But he didn't."

"That was the Smith girl," Erin recalled, grimacing.

"Yes. The newspapers had a field day. Football hero kills pregnant wife. What a headline. Did you ever wonder what would have happened if she'd just called the police the first time he hit her, or even one of the times that followed?"

"I did," she said, sighing. "But, Ty, you're never likely to kill me in a drugged-up rage," she pointed out.

"I don't drink or do drugs," he replied. "But a woman's spirit can be damaged even by words."

"You only yell at me once a week," she replied.

He rolled his eyes. "I'm trying to get a point across."

She held out a hand, palm up.

"You can't let a man walk all over you," he said. "Not for any reason."

She frowned. She didn't understand what he was trying to say.

He looked into those pretty gray eyes and got lost.

She was having the same problem. He had bright, black eyes, and they were playing havoc with her emotions. She couldn't manage to drag her gaze from them and her whole body felt as if it was vibrating.

"Uh, sir, are you ready to order?"

The waiter was smiling.

Ty ground his teeth. He forced a smile. "Give us about five more minutes, if you will."

"Yes, sir."

The waiter left.

Ty opened the menu, startled at his own reaction to Erin's pretty eyes. "What would you like?" he asked.

She opened her menu and stared at unfamiliar letters. "Something with chicken?"

"You hate chicken. How about a nice filet of fish?"

She looked up, startled.

He smiled. "The chef is also famous for his fish dishes."

She almost cried. He'd considered her love for fish when he brought her here. It was so flattering. "Then I'd love the filet. Thank you," she added softly.

He chuckled softly. "I know what you like," he teased. Then

he added, deliberately, "You've been part of my family for years, you know."

She did know, although she'd been hoping for more tonight, a lot more. But she forced a smile in return. "Yes, I did know," she replied without resentment. After all, what good would it do to resent the fact that he wasn't interested in her romantically? It did kill a few dreams.

Just as they started to eat, a familiar voice came from behind them.

"Well, well, taking the family out to dinner, are you?" Ben Jones asked.

He was a big man, husky and overweight, in his fifties now and not very attractive. He was married, to a nice little woman who always looked harried.

"Yes," Ty replied with an easy smile. Everybody knew that Erin was like family. "What are you doing here?"

"Treating the wife," Ben said, jerking a finger toward her. "It's her birthday."

"That's nice of you," Ty said, wondering where he was getting the money. The restaurant was largely beyond Ben's pocket. Maybe he'd inherited something from the rich aunt who'd recently died. It wasn't his business.

"By the way, Erin, you left your desk unlocked this afternoon," Ben said. He pulled a key out of his pocket and handed it to her. "I locked it back. You need to watch that. You have access to proprietary documents. Wouldn't do to leave those accessible."

"Yes, I know. Thanks, Ben," she said, and tried not to look as irritated as she felt. Way to go, Ben, announcing my failings to the boss in that condescending tone. And where had he gotten her key? She remembered putting it in her purse and leaving it on the desk just briefly while she went to the ladies' room. It wouldn't do to mention that now.

"She was a little distracted this afternoon," Ty told him. He grinned. "This restaurant is five-star."

"Way beyond her pocket and mine normally," Ben chuckled. "I won a little bet."

"A little one?" Ty prodded.

"Okay, a pretty good one. I'm getting good at poker," he blurted out, and then colored, because it didn't sound the way he meant it to. "Not that I'm into gambling. No, sir. No way. It was just a friendly game. I got lucky."

"People usually don't," Ty said genially, "so don't get in too deep."

"I'd never do that. Good to see you."

"Good to see you, too, Ben. Eva," he added, smiling at the gray-haired little woman beside Ben. She smiled back, but didn't speak.

"Does he have her trained, you think?" Erin blurted out before she could help it, after they were eating dessert.

"Who, Eva?"

"Yes."

"That's a case in point," he told her. "You could end up like that, married to some forceful man who keeps you on a leash. I love Ben. I owe him a lot. But I don't like the way he treats his wife."

"I know." She forced a smile. "But I don't have plans to marry. My dad takes too much looking after."

He gave her a long look. "I know you were nervous about coming out with me tonight. But you have to be careful about locking your desk."

"I know. I'm sorry. I was sure that I locked it," she said worriedly.

"It's all right. Ben took care of it. Just keep your eyes on the job while you're doing the job, okay? In this economy, every business has to watch its steps. Even this one."

"I'll be careful. I promise," she replied.

"More coffee?" he asked.

"Yes, please."

He signaled the waiter.

* * *

When he took her home, it was breezy, but the night was clear and stars twinkled overhead. There was even a half-moon to give light, beyond the streetlights at the end of Erin's gravel driveway.

"I envy you this porch," Ty said as he walked her to her door.

"But it's tiny, compared to yours," she pointed out.

He turned to her in the light from the small overhead night-light. His big hands rested on her shoulders, making her tingle all over. "It's small, but it's homey," he explained, his deep voice soft like velvet in the stillness. "You sewed cushions for the chairs and the porch swing and you put potted plants everywhere. It has a warm atmosphere. If you didn't work for me, I'd advise you to get a job as an interior decorator," he teased. "You really do have the talent."

"More years of study," she protested, wrinkling her nose. "Besides, I like doing cost estimates for you."

"Ben did the last one. Weren't you assigned to do it?" he asked gently, because she had a boss who oversaw her work. Not Ty, who sat at a desk as company manager. Well, he sat at a desk when he wasn't on site, pointing out corrections or assigning jobs. He was very muscular for a businessman. It was because he was just as likely to be out with his men moving lumber or fitting river stones together for a huge fireplace in some new million-dollar-plus home he was constructing.

"Well, Ben got in first with his estimate," she said, because Ty got militant if she said anything against his friend, even if it was something bad, and deserved.

He put a gentle hand on her face and turned it up to his. "This time, get yours in first," he advised.

"Okay," she said in a husky tone. "I will." She smiled.

His black eyes dropped to her mouth. It looked soft and sweet and delicious. He wanted it with a suddenness that shocked him. He took a steadying breath and dropped his hand. He didn't know what was happening to him, but it was something he was definitely not ready to face. Not yet, anyway.

So he forced a smile, with both hands in his pockets. "I had a good time. I hope you did, too," he said gently.

She just smiled back. For just a few seconds, he'd wanted to kiss her. She knew it. It was in his eyes. But just as quickly, he'd moved away and he was the brother of her best friend. Just like that. Nothing to regret, nothing to hope for. He'd taken her out...why?

She cocked her head and looked up at him. "Why did you take me out?" she asked softly.

He didn't know. So how was he supposed to answer that question. He shrugged. "Impulse," he said, and that was the truth. He sighed. "Besides, I thought you could use a night on the town, away from home." His face grew solemn. "It's easy to lose your focus when you're faced with someone's life-threatening illness. You have to get away sometimes, even for just an hour or two, so that you don't get overwhelmed."

Her whole expression softened. That was the Ty she'd always known, kind and thoughtful and always looking for the best in people.

"You're the nicest boss around," she told him, and meant it.

"I do my best. I'd rather run cattle, but we don't have room for much more than the horses and the house." He pursed his lips. "Maybe one day I'll build a house for myself, and leave Annie with the mansion, while I grow a cattle empire. They could write books about me. Compose songs..." He looked down to see how she was reacting to that.

She was laughing her head off. It felt good, to see her that happy, even briefly, to remove her from the almost certain loss of her only remaining parent.

"I could so do it if I wanted to," he continued haughtily.

"I think you're about two hundred years too late, and in the wrong place," she pointed out.

"Go ahead, kill my dreams of an empire out West," he lamented.

"Those days are long gone, killed by reality and the income tax laws," she reminded him. "Besides, building houses and businesses is honest work, and building gigantic apartment houses in San Antonio is even better!"

It probably was—that was an empire-building open door of its own, a project Ty had dreamed of getting. He was putting in a bid for the job soon; the bid Erin was working on now, in fact. It might be the only chance he'd get in the next few years, and he needed it. Business had fallen off after the most recent tax law changes, not to mention the downswing in the economy. Even a business as big as Ty's had to be careful. He needed this job badly, to keep the company solvent.

"Ok," he said. "I guess I can settle for being a famous architect."

She laughed. "That, you already are."

"That was my dad's dream," he said, shifting his long legs. "He loved to draw and he was good at it. He taught me the fundamentals. I went to college to learn the rest. I do love it. But part of me would love to run cattle and raise champion German shepherds."

"You already do one of those things, too."

He sighed. "I suppose so. It's the scale that matters, though."

She wrinkled her nose. "Your scale is plenty big."

"For now, at least." He studied her for a moment and smiled again, but it was that social smile she'd seen him use at parties time and again. "I had fun."

"So did I," she said. "Thanks for the night out, boss." She curtsied.

He chuckled. "On that note, I'm leaving. See you Monday."

"See you."

And he was in the car and gone before she got the second word out. She went inside, surprised to find her father in the living room. He gave her a big smile. He looked guilty as sin.

"Have a good time?" he asked.

She laughed. "Yes, I really did. We went to a fancy restaurant downtown and Ty had to read me the menu. It was all in French."

"High class stuff," he remarked.

"Truly. We both had fun. Did you run out of game shows?" she asked, because the TV was off.

"Yes. I've been reading a murder mystery."

She didn't see a book, but he pulled one up from the other side of the couch. It was written by a well-known crime author.

"Nice," she said. "It's the newest one. I haven't read it yet."

"I ordered it from the book club last month," he said, and managed to look guilty. "I know it's not in the budget…"

So that was why he looked guilty! She laughed with relief. "It's just a book," she said gently. "No worries."

He let out a big sigh. "Okay. Thanks for not fussing."

"How could I fuss? You're my dad and I love you."

He grimaced. "I love you, too. I wish I had more to leave you than just this house and our savings."

"Don't talk that way," she chided. "I have a great job and I'm happy."

"You'd be happier married with a family," he said.

She made a face at him. "I'm too antisocial to find a husband. Can I get you anything before I go to bed?"

"Not a thing. You sleep good."

"You, too." She kissed the top of his head and went on to her room. For a big, exciting date, it fell a little flat. So much for hoping Ty had taken her out because he was suddenly noticing her. No such thing. And another, worse thought, too root. He did this sometimes to throw off other women, Annie had said. Dating one woman to put himself off limits to another. Was that why he'd taken her out? Had it been to ward off their pretty new blonde employee, Jenny Taylor? She went to bed and slept badly all night, shattered dreams pricking her skin.

CHAPTER FOUR

Erin went to work Monday after a troubling weekend. Her father had said very little, but he still looked guilty, and it wasn't because he'd ordered a book. Yes, they had a tight budget, but a book wouldn't break it.

She couldn't trick him into admitting anything. There was no visible evidence that he'd done anything he shouldn't. But that guilty look was disturbing.

Erin went to her desk and searched in her purse for the key that unlocked her drawers. Everything was in its place except the new cost estimate she'd been working on, the one vital to Ty's bid for that high-rise apartment complex contract. It had only been moved a little, but Erin remembered with textbook accuracy where everything was in her drawer of important documents. It might look chaotic to an outsider, but to Erin, it was just creative chaos.

She wondered if she should mention it to Ty, but only for a minute. He'd think she was nuts. Besides, it had probably been disturbed when Jones locked it for her. He had access to most of her work because his job, estimating building materials, was compatible with her own. Ty trusted him so she had to. But that last cost estimate had been hers to do, and she'd locked the drawer. She had the only key. Except Ben had handed her the key, this very one, in the restaurant last night. It was very disturbing.

She put her purse in the bottom drawer and locked it before she went to work on new figures to compile for the project.

She had a good head for math, which had landed her this job just out of high school. She went simultaneously to business school in San Antonio, where Ty's office was located, and got her degree along with on-the-job training. She knew that her close relationship with Annie and Ty had gotten her the job, but she worked hard to earn it. Like them, she lived in Jacobsville, an easy commute of twenty-five minutes.

Now, in her neat secondhand blue sedan, she was earning enough money to pay off the mortgage on the house her parents owned. Only about two more payments, and it would be theirs free and clear. She was so happy to be able to do that for her father. With Annie's financial help, they could afford his medicine, and her insurance covered most of his cancer treatments. Things were looking good.

But even with those worries gone, she had plenty left. Her father's health began to deteriorate. He went downhill faster than she'd dreamed that he would.

At his next treatment, she asked the specialist what had gone wrong. It was the way of cancer he said quietly. Sometimes for no apparent reason, even with treatment, it advanced rapidly. There was nothing more they could do than what they were already doing. His particular form of cancer was deadly and claimed many lives.

It didn't help that he wasn't eating, and that he still looked guilty. She'd made potato soup for supper and he ate with little appetite, even though the soup was his very favorite.

"Dad, what's wrong?" she asked softly.

He gave her a blank look and then forced a smile. "I'm getting worse," he said. "I'm so sorry, honey."

She got up and hugged him, rocking him in her arms as she felt tears on the fabric of her sleeves. "It's okay," she said, when she was screaming silently in terror at the loss she was going to face sooner or later. "It's okay, Daddy. Everything will be okay. Really."

"Okay," he said in a wobbly tone.

She dabbed at her eyes. "Come on, eat your soup. These poor potatoes sacrificed themselves so you could have a nice meal."

He laughed, as he was meant to, and they dropped the horrible subject to replace it with one about a television serial they were both watching.

Ty was feeling more and more uneasy about Erin. He found himself watching her, for no apparent reason. She was familiar to him. He'd known her since she was a child. So why was she suddenly more interesting than ever before?

She wasn't beautiful, as many of his earlier flames had been. But she had a big heart and she was honest, two traits he valued in anybody.

He was getting a little tired of Miss Taylor's pursuit of him. She was overperfumed overcoifed, and frankly a nuisance. She flirted with all the men, but particularly with him. He didn't like being chased.

"All I need are damned antlers," he muttered to himself as Erin was coming in through the door he was exiting.

She blinked. "Excuse me?"

He took in the outfit she was wearing. Black. Black skirt, black shirt and a filmy pink silk duster that fell around her to her knees. She paired it with a scarf that echoed shades of pink. Her long black hair was down today, thick and soft and feminine. She smelled of wildflowers. She looked good enough to eat.

"Well, well," he murmured, studying her with warm black eyes. "Aren't you a sight to behold? Very nice," he added.

She cleared her throat. "I like to experiment with colors," she said.

He looked over his shoulder. Miss Taylor was in pursuit. He took Erin's arm, turned her around, and steered her right out the front door of the office building.

"Ty!" Erin exclaimed as he caught her hand and led her to the car park.

"Hush, or you'll give the game away."

"What game...?"

They were in a shaded part of the underground parking garage. He turned, pulled her against him, and bent to kiss her with impassioned hunger right there next to his car.

Erin went under like a drowning victim, too shocked and delighted to even try to save herself. Ty gathered her in, riveting her to his long, powerful, muscular body. He smelled of spice and soap, and his arms were warm and hungry around her. His mouth ground into hers as she gave in to the most extraordinary, delightful episode of her whole life. Dreams came true, there in the cool semi-darkness, to the sound of car horns and sirens and people talking.

He wrapped her up against him finally, with his mouth at her neck, his heart beating hard and heavy at her ear. She was floating, soaring, like wind, lost in the moment.

He took a deep breath and stepped back. He grinned down at her. It was forced, but she was too shaken to notice.

"Thanks," he said.

She stared up at him like an accident victim. "What for?" she managed.

"Saving the buck from the hunter's bow and arrow," he said.

She blinked. "Did I miss something?"

"Yes," he said as he released her and stepped back. "Miss

Taylor, minus a bow and arrow. The damned woman's driving me nuts!"

"Oh." She was still disoriented. Paradise had suddenly been turned back into a drab city street with traffic noises. She stared up at Ty, trying to force her starved senses to forget their momentary feast.

He was feeling something similar and trying to hide it. She was absolutely delicious to kiss. Her mouth was soft and warm and tasted like honey. He stared at it for a few seconds before he pulled himself back from the abyss.

"I'd fire her if I could type," he said at last, and forced a chuckle.

"You could literally accuse her of sexual harrassment," Erin replied, and managed a smile of her own. "I know two men in the office who would buy you dinner as a return favor."

He shook his head. "My, how times have changed."

"Equal opportunity," she defended her coworkers.

"Of course." He drew in a breath. "How about dinner at my place two weeks from Saturday night?" He grinned. "I have to make two trips out of town, or it would be sooner."

"With you and Annie?"

"With me," he said, his voice deep and husky, his black eyes piercing. "At the cabin. I'll have it catered."

Warning signals went off in the back of her mind. The cabin was deserted. She'd been raised by an old-fashioned mother, and one red flag stood out. No nights alone with men in secluded locations. Even with the best of intent, it could result in disaster. This was true. Ty didn't want to get married and had been vocal about it. Erin, on the other hand, wasn't going to become a convenience for any man. If she ever married, she planned to save her innocence for that man, not give it away to the first person who asked for it.

"You really are too predictable," Ty said on a sigh and smiled, not even sarcastically. "Suppose I give you my solemn promise not to seduce you?" he added and held up three fingers.

"You're making me a promise with the Girl Scout salute?" she queried, wide-eyed.

He made a face. "Okay. I'll give you the other salute…"

"Don't you dare!" she exclaimed as he started to actually do it.

He burst out laughing at her flushed face.

"You're just compounding guilt!" she grumbled.

He drew her close and just hugged her. "Honestly, you're the sweetest female creature I've ever known. I'm sorry. I really will promise. Just food and good company. I'll even tell Annie where I'm taking you."

That made her sigh with relief. If Annie knew, Ty would have to keep things straight. His sister would nag him to death.

"Okay," she said, drawing back. "Sorry. I just don't move with the times. And you're, well, worldly."

He shrugged. "I'm a man. We're mostly worldly at my age."

She nodded.

He caught her arm, turned her, and they walked back to the building. "What do you want to eat?"

"Now?" she asked, flustered.

"Two weeks from now on Saturday."

"Oh." She thought for a minute. "Fish," she said, just as he echoed it with her.

They both laughed. She was, as he'd said, too predictable.

Friday, two weeks later, was almost a repeat of the earlier Friday, with Erin nervous and all thumbs, even though she wasn't having supper with Ty until the next day.

"All thumbs today, again, huh?" Ty teased as she put a report on his desk.

"I'm actually very calm," she protested, with twinkling gray eyes.

He laughed. "Today, I might join you. We put in the bid two

weeks ago and they promised an unusually quick answer. But I haven't heard a word yet." He leaned back in his chair with a long sigh. "The business can survive without the contract on that high-rise, but the economy is in a famous slump. Even this one could fail. I worry."

"You're really the best at what you do, and when you make a bid, you stand by it," she replied. "No hidden charges, or accidental upgrade fees, nothing like that. Your reputation is spotless. Not so for at least one of the competition."

"Yes. Harold Bradley." He made a face. "The man cuts too many corners. He's been called down for it at least twice, and once he faced charges. He managed to sleeze out of them, but his record is far from clean. I hate it that he's even allowed to bid with the rest of us."

"Surely the planners know that," she protested.

"They're looking for the lowest bid. And they're not too careful about where they look. Out-of-town owners with out-of-country execs."

"I begin to see the light."

"One of the foreign owners is in town tonight, which is why we're having supper tomorrow night," he told her. "I'm hoping to encourage him a little more in my direction. We're having cocktails after dinner."

"You be careful to snack on something before you drive," she blurted out.

He glared at her. "Erin, that was six years ago," he pointed out.

She flushed again. "I know, it's just..."

He raised an eyebrow. "It's just that you worry about me," he said quietly, admiring the color the soft flush put into her face. She was really pretty like that, he thought, and then clamped down hard on the images he was getting.

"It was a bad wreck," she said in her defense.

"And not completely my fault. The other driver was a lot

more intoxicated than I was," he reminded her. "I got off with a stern warning from the judge. I haven't forgotten."

"Annie and I were devastated, and it wasn't long after you'd lost your parents…"

"Such concern," he said, shaking his head. He grinned. "It was nice that so many people cared."

"Everybody, in fact, except for that woman…"

His face tautened. "And we won't discuss her."

"Sorry!" She pretended to zip her lips.

He shook his head as he held the door open for her. "You drive me nuts sometimes."

"I know somebody who does it better," she said under her breath as the blond and beautiful Miss Taylor came gliding toward them like a poisonous adder. "See you later, boss."

She took off for her own office while Ty muttered to himself something about desertion under fire.

When Erin got home, her father looked even more ashen than he had the day before. She put up her purse and jacket and went to him at once where he was seated in his recliner.

"Dad, are you okay?" she asked.

He took a deep breath and looked up at her. He grimaced. He took a long breath. "Erin…"

"Yes?"

He searched her worried face and felt guilt all the way to his soul. Time, he thought. There was still enough time to fix what he'd done. He should have listened to her, as he should have listened to his wife years ago. They were both right. He was wrong. He wanted to confess, but there was still time to make it up to her. He had a friend who would help him. He was sure of that. It would be all right. No need to confess. Not yet, at least.

He forced a smile. "Just a bad day, honey, that's all."

"Are you sure?"

"I am absolutely sure," he assured her.

She drew in a long breath. "Okay, then. I was just worried. More worried," she added.

"About what?"

"Oh, we're bidding for a big job in the city and Ty's meeting with one of the owners tonight. For cocktails," she added.

"I hope he's careful," he said.

"I know. He promised he would be," she assured him.

"This job, I guess it's worth a lot of money, huh?"

"A whole lot."

"Then I hope he gets it. Not that he really needs it. His family's always had money."

"Anybody can lose it all tomorrow," she pointed out.

"Ty won't. He's resourceful, and really smart."

"I guess so," she said.

He cocked his head. "Anything you want to tell me?" he asked, because she had a strange, happy look on her face.

"Just...well, Ty's taking me out to supper tomorrow night."

His eyebrows rose. "That's two weekends in a row."

"Just friends," she said quickly, and then blushed, to disprove her words.

He chuckled. "Maybe you'll get lucky," he said gently. "I know how you feel about him."

"He doesn't feel that way about me," she countered. "There's this woman at work who's after him," she added. "She's a real dish, but he just doesn't like women these days."

"Because of that Dawes woman," her father replied with a sigh. "I can't say that I blame him. Her ex-husband really did him a favor, although I don't imagine he appreciated it at the time. The gossip was bad."

"Nobody around town ever forgot," she said, "even though the incident happened in San Antonio. Too many people from here work at Ty's company."

"It wouldn't have been quite so bad, if she hadn't started screaming at Ty from the top of her lungs after he caught her bragging to her husband that she had a dumb cowboy like Ty on a string."

"It killed his pride," she recalled. "He didn't date anybody regularly after that. He told Annie that women always seemed to be after him for what he had, and that he'd already been sold out too many times."

"Poor guy."

"Yes, he is," she replied. "I'd never sell him out. Not for anything."

Her father averted his eyes. "I know that, sweetheart," he told her. He grimaced. There was no way she could find out. His friend wouldn't sell him out, he knew that. Still, it hurt to do it to her. But he had to make up for what he'd done. This was the only way. He'd tried and tried to think up things he could sell, but there wasn't anything left. If he didn't get his hands on some cash soon…

"Why do you look like that?" Erin asked.

"Like what?" he asked, and forced a smile.

She studied him for a few seconds and then laughed. "Never mind. I'm just not thinking properly. I'll go start supper. Want anything special?"

"How about scalloped potatoes and ham?" he asked.

She smiled gently. "Sure."

He watched her leave the room with a miserable sigh. He'd never felt so guilty.

She washed the car and made a cake and cleaned every room in the house on Saturday, because she was too nervous to sit still.

Her cell phone rang loudly while she was vacuuming. She turned off the vacuum and picked it up.

"Don't tell me," Annie said in a laughing tone. "You've already remodeled the house, painted the car, repaved the sidewalk…"

"I would have, but I don't have any cement," she interrupted with a laugh. "Ty told you?"

"Of course he did. He said that you felt like a sheep headed for the shearing pen and if he didn't tell me, you might call up and refuse to go."

"Well…" She sighed. "He's right, in a way."

"Ty wouldn't dare seduce you," Annie pointed out. "I'd filet him on the kitchen table. It's safe. You can go with him. Honest."

She laughed. "He didn't wreck the car last night, then?"

Annie laughed, too. "No. Not even given a warning by the state police. He told me you'd been worried."

"I was. It was a bad wreck."

"None of us ever forgot, so bless you for being uneasy and telling him. I can nag him, but he listens to you. He just ignores me."

That was news. It made her glow.

"You do know why he's taking me out lately?" Erin asked.

"Because he likes you?"

"There's this pretty blonde barracuda who works in our office…"

"Oh, no," Annie groaned. "And I thought romance was blooming!"

"Don't be silly. Ty's known me forever. He even says I'm like one of the family," Erin reminded her and managed not to sound as heartbroken as she really was.

"I did know about the blonde. I hoped it was just Ty being himself."

"Not so much. She's made a play for every rich, eligible man she can find. Even some only moderately rich ones."

"Dreams die," Annie said on a sigh.

"Oh, tell me about it. I'm sure Ms. Taylor's are dropping dead as we speak," she added gleefully.

"Well, anyway, you be careful tonight and keep him away from any liquor bottles," Annie said. "He doesn't drink to excess, ever, but because of that, he's more susceptible to it."

"I'll just refuse to drink anything except water or coffee," Erin teased.

"It might take more than that."

"Why? What happened?" Erin asked.

Annie sighed. "He went to have dinner and cocktails with the main owner of the property, the one who has final authority over the contract. It turns out that he'd heard some gossip about Ty that he didn't like."

"What gossip?" Erin exclaimed.

"For one thing, that Ty used cheap materials and he'd had run-ins with building inspectors because of it."

"That's a lie! And it's easy to disprove...!"

"This guy was foreign and he didn't care. He told Ty that he'd already given the bid to a contractor who underbid him."

"That couldn't be possible, not without using really inferior materials," Erin protested. "I know, because I compiled the information that Ty used in the bid."

"He said the bid was hand delivered by one of Ty's executives," Annie replied gently. "And that it was much higher than the other company's." Annie quoted the overall amount of the bid.

"But that's wrong! I know what the figures were!" Erin protested. "Those are not my figures!"

"Did you see them before Ty turned them in? Maybe they were mistyped."

Mistyped. Ms. Taylor did the forms. Was there a chance that she'd been furious about that kiss in the parking lot and she'd deliberately retyped Erin's work to show a higher figure?

"Well, don't worry about it," Annie said. "Ty said he was bidding for another job up in Dallas, and he had hopes to get it. It's not as big, but..."

"I just don't understand this," Erin groaned.

"Things go wrong. Bids get undercut, you know that. Unless you're psychic, you have no idea what the other guy's going to pull out of his hat," her friend replied.

"I suppose not."

"You stop worrying and go put on something pretty. And have a nice dinner. Ty ordered that fish you like so much."

Erin beamed. "That was nice of him."

"He can be nice. He can be a beast, too." Annie sighed. "Especially if he thinks he's right, whether he is or not. You can't argue with him. It's like debating a stone wall."

"I hope not to have that problem."

"Just don't let him try to drown his woes, is all," Annie said.

"That, I can promise," Erin replied.

She looked worried even as she picked out her dress. She only had one choice really, a black cocktail dress that Ty had seen once before, at an office party for a retiree. It wasn't especially sexy, but it was couture—another of her bargains from shopping at the consignment shop. It fit her like a glove, outlining a slender but perfect hourglass figure. The black dress was a striking contrast to the string of pearls her mother had given her long ago for a birthday present. She fingered them gently and admired the simple stud pearls that were barely visible under the fall of her long, black hair.

Ordinarily, she kept it up in a neat bun or a complicated twist, but she knew that Ty loved long hair. So she left it down. It would get windblown and tangled but she kept a small brush in her purse. It wouldn't matter. Anyway, Ty had seen her disheveled often enough when she and Annie had gone riding with him on the ranch.

She recalled so many perfect days that he'd been part of. Her heart had worn itself out on his indifference. Not that he was unkind; he was always gentle with her. But he hadn't felt what she did, and it was obvious. Eventually she learned to control her nerves when she was around him, and she disguised her awkwardness with humor. Annie often said that the only time Ty really laughed was when Erin was with them. He was serious most of the time, always involved in some new idea about construction projects or busy with his German shepherd brood. When the puppies were born, it was Ty who stayed up with them all night for as long as it took, until they were well on the way to healthy growth. He babied their mother, and them, as if they were human.

Ty had brought a casual date home with him one weekend when Annie and Erin had just come in from riding down to see a new foal. The woman was shouting at Ty because one of his new puppies had urinated on her best pair of shoes.

He hadn't said a word. He smiled at the girls, pulled out his car keys, and motioned his date out the door. They heard later that he'd actually purchased her a pair of designer shoes to replace the ones that were damaged, in pea green and orange. Annie still laughed about it. He was the soul of politeness usually, but he was protective about his animals. Erin would have laughed it off and asked for a cloth and some cleaner. But people were different.

She used very little makeup. Her complexion was exquisite, peaches and cream, a perfect backdrop for big pale gray eyes and black winged eyebrows. Ty didn't like makeup, but Erin didn't use it for a different reason. She hated the goop on her face that had to be washed off at night. A light touch was easier to remove. And on her, it looked better.

Picking up her evening bag, she came out of her room with her spring coat over one arm, smiling as she looked into the living room where her father was in his recliner, watching a game show.

"You have fun," he said gently.

She frowned. He was very pale. "Are you going to be all right?" she asked worriedly.

He sighed. He started to speak and then just smiled. "Yes. We both are," he said oddly.

She laughed, thinking that he referred to her upcoming date. "Okay. If you need me, you can call or text me," she added.

"I won't," he promised. "I'm just going to watch my shows and go to bed. You turn on the porch light so you can see to get in, okay?"

"I will," she replied. "Dad, you really are pale. Do you want me to stay home with you?"

"Heavens, no," he said at once. "I'm just feeling a little weak from the infusion," he added on a sigh. "Same old, same old," he chuckled, quoting a familiar old-time saying.

"At least it's only that, and nothing worse," she agreed. "But you call if you need me. Ty will bring me right home."

"I know that." He looked past her as car lights penetrated the front curtains. "Your ride's here," he teased.

She jumped and almost dropped her purse. This wouldn't do. She took deep breaths before she forced a smile and went to open the door.

Ty was wearing a black turtlenecked shirt with a blazer and jeans and a black Stetson and boots. He looked as handsome as a movie cowboy and Erin was hard-pressed not to swoon like an old-time movie heroine. He was the stuff of dreams.

"You look fantastic," he said, admiring her with a slow smile.

"Thanks. So do you."

"How's it going, Arthur?" he asked with a smile.

"Doing all right, Ty, thank you," her father replied in a faintly strained tone. Once again, Erin had that odd feeling of guilt that emanated from her parent.

"I won't keep her out late. I bought her a whole fish. Now I'm going to feed it to her," Ty teased.

"I'd share it, you know," she teased back.

He just chuckled. "If you need her or me, just text her, okay?" he asked her dad.

Her father just smiled. "I'll be fine. No worries. You two have a good time!"

They were halfway down the driveway when Erin glanced at Ty. "Dad looked guilty about something," she began.

His eyebrows arched. "What?"

"Sorry. I was thinking out loud. He's been acting that way for days. It's like he's got something on his conscience and he's afraid to tell me," she murmured.

"He's probably worried about the cancer, Erin," he said gently. "It's a hell of a thing to go through. Remember Bud Hollins and how he died?"

She grimaced.

He glanced at her and winced. "I'm sorry, honey," he said gently, and one of his big hands came down over hers resting on her purse. "That's the last thing I should have said."

"It's true, though," she replied quietly, feeling tremors at the warm strength of that hand on hers, however briefly. "He knew Bud, too."

"I wish we could do more for your dad," he said on a sigh. "I know how you must feel. I've been there."

"You and Annie," she agreed, because the Mosbys were parentless also.

"But life goes on. We cope. Sort of."

"Annie told me about the bid," she ventured. "I don't understand. I ran those figures three times to make sure I kept them as low as possible without using substandard materials!"

He made a sound deep in his throat. "We won't talk business tonight," he said curtly. "I just want to forget the whole damned thing and have a nice supper. Then we can sit on the porch and listen to the frogs sing."

She laughed involuntarily. "You have singing frogs?!"

"Honey, all frogs sing," he drawled. "We just can't appreciate how talented they are."

She just shook her head.

CHAPTER FIVE

The lake house was made of wood. Ty had designed it himself. It had a dock and a boat house behind it, and the house was cozy but open and beautifully situated. On a clear day, he could sit on the back deck and watch sailboats on the lake. On a less busy day, he was on the lake sailing in his own boat. He loved the water.

Erin, on the other hand, was terrified of it. She couldn't swim and she got seasick. So when Ty went sailing when they were younger, kind Annie would stay behind to keep Erin company.

She thought about that and laughed.

"What?" he asked lightly when they'd pulled up at the front door, amid a stand of flowering trees.

"I was remembering poor Annie having to keep me company while you sailed. She was always so sweet. I tried to get her to go, too, and she wouldn't. She loves the water."

"Why are you so afraid of it?" he asked and was really curious.

She took a breath. "One of my church friends drowned when we went on a trip up to Dallas and the Sunday School teacher took us swimming."

He frowned. "You were in that group? I don't remember that, although I remember the story in the papers."

She sighed. "You were off at college when it happened. I was very young. I didn't make a big deal of it, especially around Annie. But it kept me away from water. It still does. I was up to my waist in water and headed out to shore because I was really scared. She was a sweet girl. We were church friends. She teased me about being afraid to swim. I laughed and said I sank like a log. She'd show me how to do it, she said, so she took off toward the middle of the lake. But she got a cramp in her leg and started going under," she gritted. "And I couldn't swim, so I couldn't save her. By the time my screams brought the lifeguard, it was too late."

"What a hell of a thing to happen!"

"So I never went swimming again," she said. "It's true, you know, about sinking like a log. I can't float. I never could."

"Oddball," he said, but in a soft, teasing tone.

"That's me," she sighed.

The table was set, food was on it, and the kitchen staff was just about to leave. While Ty saw them off, Erin looked over the dishes. Everything looked mouthwateringly good.

A bottle of wine sat in a holder on the table, already chilled. He popped the cork and poured it into wineglasses. A pot of coffee was in a warmer, also on the table, and a tray of cream and sugar sat beside it. Bowls of food, including ham, fish, scalloped potatoes and a huge salad took pride of place. There was an enormous chocolate cake in a cake holder and a sweet potato pie.

"All my favorites," Erin exclaimed, her eyes going to the big smile on Ty's handsome face.

He chuckled. "You've had a hard time lately, with your dad," he explained gently. "I thought a little pampering wouldn't hurt."

"A little!" she scoffed. "You're spoiling me!"

"Not so much." His black eyes searched hers. "I don't think you can be spoiled. You've got too much common sense."

"That's my mother's influence," she said, smiling as he took her coat and then seated her beside him at the cherry wood table with its expensive linen tablecloth and matching napkins.

She grimaced at the starched whiteness. "Goodness, I'm glad you got white wine," she said. "The first thing I'd do with red would be to knock it over and ruin the tablecloth. I'm clumsy."

"No more than I am," he said. "White goes best with fish."

"You don't like fish."

He raised both eyebrows and his eyes twinkled. "I like it well enough. This is the chef's specialty." He put his napkin in his lap. "Say grace, Erin."

She did, a brief, sweet little prayer, a tradition in both families for generations.

"Dig in," he invited.

They ate in a pleasant silence. The wine was like drinking flowers. She had little taste for it as a rule, but she was nervous and excited. For years she'd dreamed about having Ty take her anywhere, even just driving. Here she was on her second real date with him. It made her warm all over.

"Cake or pie?" she asked when they got to dessert.

"Need you ask?" he chuckled.

No, not really. His passion for chocolate cake was known far and wide. She loved it, too, although sweet potato pie was her great favorite.

She got up and cut slices of the rich cake and put them in the delicate china dessert plates.

"No pie?" he asked when she put his serving down and poured him a second cup of coffee to go with it.

"I'm sort of in a cake mood tonight," she replied, sitting back down. "And this looks delicious!"

"Our mothers made cakes like this one, years ago, to take

on picnics here at the lake," he recalled sadly. "They were both great cooks."

"Yes," she agreed, sipping coffee with her slice of cake. "But your mother made the best fried chicken and potato salad."

"Yours made the best cakes," he replied. "Although I'd never have said that to my mother while she was alive."

"She was such a sweet woman," Erin sighed. "Your dad was very nice, too. And he had a good business head. Nothing like my poor father, with his constant get-rich schemes." She shook her head. "His latest thing has been this mania for learning how to do day-trading."

"Dangerous stuff, for an amateur," he replied. "If you want to invest, the best way is to find a reliable stockbroker."

"Exactly what I told Dad," she agreed. "I managed to talk him out of the so-called training course he wanted to take. Heavens, it was hundreds of dollars, and when I researched it online, there were a lot of complaints from people who'd tried it and lost thousands of dollars! We could never afford that sort of investment, much less pay a stockbroker. Not that I'm complaining about my salary," she added on a laugh. "I get paid too much just to push numbers around."

"Don't sell yourself short. You're good at math."

"Thanks."

He was studying that dress. He'd seen it before. It was couture and he wondered just briefly how she'd managed to afford something so expensive.

He refilled the wineglasses.

She eyed hers warily. "You don't usually drink this much, and I shouldn't," she told him. "I don't have any head for alcohol."

"Don't fuss," he said easily. He put the wind back in its cradle and sat back down, sipping more of the pale beverage. "I've had a hell of a couple of days."

"I heard from Annie," she said sympathetically. "I just don't understand it," she added. "I know what our figures were. The cost estimate was down to the last nail. The only way anybody could have undercut us would be by using substandard materials, nothing any reputable business would have considered."

"I know that," he muttered. He took another big swallow.

"We're not really in trouble, are we?" she wondered out loud.

He shrugged. He loosened his tie. "We could be, unless I can land a project I'm bidding on up in Dallas," he confessed. "Even a company as well-grounded as mine can run aground. The economy is in a slump."

"Pay us all less," she suggested with twinkling gray eyes. "Nobody would complain."

He laughed shortly. "Want to bet?" He took another big swallow and sighed. "Sometimes I get tired of the rat race and I think about just tossing it all, selling the company and going off on a long sailing trip around the world."

She knew how much he'd have loved that. He'd crewed on one of the ships in the America's Cup race years ago when he was in college up north. "You really love sailing, don't you?"

He nodded. "It's in my blood, I guess. We had ancestors who were sea captains back in the 1800s and early 1900s. And, so the rumor goes, a pirate or two in the 1700s down around Jamaica."

"Our ancestors were landlubbers. One fought for the Swamp Fox, Francis Marion, during the Revolutionary War. Another was a horse thief," she teased.

He chuckled as he leaned back in his chair, studying her. "Pirates and horse thieves," he mused. "What a combination."

She drew in a breath and took another big sip of her own wine. She was feeling very good. She studied him with helpless appreciation. He was a dish. She'd never been so attracted to anybody. She'd had a crush or two on boys in school, but always the wrong ones who never returned her feelings. From the time she was sixteen, there had been no secret passions except the one for this gorgeous man sitting across from her. Nobody else in her heart, not for years.

"You're staring," he accused.

"You're really gorgeous," she said, her tongue running away. "It amazes me that you don't have to plow up your driveway to keep eligible beauties from flooding your yard."

He chuckled. "I've had an occasional issue like that," he confessed. His eyes darkened. "But mostly it was the money they were after. Not me."

"I've never had that problem," she sighed. "I'm neither rich nor beautiful, so I don't have to beat off crazed admirers. Speaking of which, how are things going with Ms. Taylor?"

He rolled his eyes. "If I could find a legitimate reason to let her go, I would," he muttered, getting up to fill his glass again. He topped off Erin's glass as well.

"I'm drinking more than I should," she protested weakly.

"We're eating with it," he reminded her. "No big deal. Besides we're only two miles out of town and I can get us home safely. Stop worrying. I'll call a cab if I think I'm not competent to drive." He sounded just a little irritated, and she flushed.

"Sorry," she said at once. "I don't mean to nag."

He sat back down. "Damned project," he said gruffly. "I was sure we had the winning bid. The partner I had cocktails with last night was surly and frankly insulting about my business and my family."

"Why?" she asked, shocked.

"I don't know. He said he'd heard things about me that he didn't like, and he wasn't about to give the bid to someone whose reputation he doubted."

"You said he was foreign," she began.

He nodded. "I didn't like him either," he replied. "The man was discourteous and disrespectful. I've been in this business for a long time. My reputation is sound. I can't imagine where he got the idea that I'm sloppy on my projects. Not from anyone who's done business with me. I'd bet money on that."

"Well, if he'd take some stranger's word for a businessman's reputation, maybe you're better off without the project, Ty," she said gently. "He could really damage your reputation if he started gossiping about something he didn't like. And some customers are very hard to please. Like the Smiths…"

"Oh, God, don't remind me," he groaned.

She sighed. "Well, they found something to complain about twice a day while you were working on their condominiums. The doors were the wrong kind of wood, the glass in the windows wasn't clear enough, the elevators were in the wrong places…"

He shook his head. "That was a job with little profit, after they got through demanding changes. And then they had the gall to come back a year later and invite me to do another project for them."

"Which you refused. Politely, though, and I imagine you bit your tongue almost through saying it."

He grinned. "I did."

"Building has its drawbacks. But you do great work. And your designs are wonderful. You did win an award for one, for that home you built over in New Mexico that incorporated so many green ideas. It was beautiful."

"My one claim to fame," he said. He finished his wine. "I like building things. But when I get old, I'm just going to raise champion German shepherds."

"You already do," she said.

"Yes, but I don't go to the actual shows with them. I have to have Randy do that. It's an international thing, when you want champion bloodlines to sell, and I don't have the time. He enjoys it. His wife keeps them groomed and he runs them through their paces on the field. I'd love to do that myself," he added with a sad smile. "But I only have two breeding champions, at that. I'd like to have a kennel of them. I'd still breed them in small batches, though. I'm not running a puppy mill with my babies."

"Nobody would ever accuse you of that," she pointed out.

He studied her across the table. "You look good enough to eat."

Her eyebrows arched and her lips fell open.

He laughed at her expression.

"How many glasses of that have you had?" she asked, indicating his wineglass. She was feeling foggy, too.

"I lost count. Let's go sit on the porch and insult the frog opera."

She laughed. "Okay. Let me put up the food first."

"I can call the caterers back…"

"Nonsense. It's five minutes' work." And she got to it.

He was sprawled in a rocking chair on the porch with his tie off and his shirt unbuttoned down the front. It was a warm night for spring. Erin tried not to stare. His chest was beautiful, lightly covered with curling black hair over bronzed muscle. He had an amazing physique to go with his equally amazing good looks.

"What happened to the frog opera?" she asked as she came onto the porch.

"They shut up when you walked out the door," he laughed.

"Well, if they can't take criticism, that's their problem," she replied.

She sat down in the chair next to his and closed her eyes, drinking in the night air. Flowers were blooming and the scent was light and delicious.

"I've always loved it here," she said on a sigh. "It's not so far out of town, but it's like being in another world. So peaceful."

"Except for the frogs."

"What frogs?"

"I told you. They shut up when you walked out here."

"I had nothing to do with it. I didn't even criticize their singing."

"A likely story."

She laughed.

He got up from his chair, lifted her out of hers, and sat back down in the rocker with Erin in his lap.

"That's better," he sighed, folding her close, so that her cheek was against his bare chest.

Better? She felt her whole body catch fire at the proximity, in a way it never had before. Her heart ran away. Her breath caught in her throat. He smelled of soap and spicy cologne. He was warm and hard-muscled, and she felt as if all her bones had melted at once.

His big, beautiful hand smoothed over her long hair. "How long have we known each other?" he murmured deeply.

"Years. Forever."

He sighed. "I remember you with pigtails and a big mouth."

"I still have a big mouth," she said, trying not to sound as flustered as she was.

"I don't mind. You're honest, at least."

"Mostly."

His head bent. His nose rubbed against hers. She could feel his breath, smell the wine on it as his mouth poised just over hers.

Her nails bit into his shoulders involuntarily. This was new territory.

"Don't panic," he whispered. "I'm just exploring."

"Oh, is that what it is?" she tried to joke.

His hard mouth brushed her lips. "Mostly," he whispered, echoing her earlier comment.

She felt her slender body shiver. It was like dreams opening from hopeful buds into full grown flowers in an instant.

"You're nervous," he teased. "Are you afraid of me?"

"Of course not," she lied.

"Lies."

His lips slowly parted hers. He didn't demand. He coaxed. He teased the upper lip apart from its companion and moved between them in a tender exploration that sent shock waves all through her body.

He shifted her, turning her toward him. His mouth grew

slowly insistent until hers opened and gave him access to the warm, sweet darkness inside it.

She felt his tongue go slowly inside and she made a sound, a soft, surprised little cry that echoed her sudden, helpless response.

"You taste like honey," he whispered.

While she was trying to think sanely, his thumb began a teasing exploration at just the edge of her small breast. It wasn't intrusive, or blatant, and it did something very odd to her nerve endings. She found herself shifting helplessly toward it, wanting it to move closer, to become more intimate.

She knew very little about men and intimacy, but Ty was a past master at bedroom arts. He knew exactly how to get through her defenses, and he was intoxicated enough not to mind very much about whether or not it was ethical to shoot pretty fish in a barrel.

Slowly, her arms went up around his neck, inviting him to do more than tease. Both hands were under her arms, now, both thumbs working gently under her bra through the layer of fabric until she was on fire from the touch.

Her dress had a zipper in back. She felt it going down. She should protest. She should resist. But by the time her sluggish brain processed the thought, her bra was unclipped, and two big hands were smoothing the fabric down, down, down to her waist so that the warm night air felt so good on her bare skin.

He eased her back into the crook of his arm and while his mouth teased her lips, his fingers teased over her breasts, making the nipples go hard, making her arch up toward them and moan piteously as pleasure washed over her in waves.

His head lifted and he looked down at her in the light coming through the windows. "Glory," he whispered just before he bent his head and his mouth slowly covered one small breast and took it inside.

She cried out, her head thrown back, her body bursting into flames as he explored her.

"Yes," he whispered roughly.

He picked her up, his mouth still on her breasts, and carried her inside, kicking the door shut behind him.

She wasn't thinking at all. The wine had robbed her of sanity; the wine, and that drugging mouth on her breasts so intimately. There was an ache in her body that she'd never felt before, and a building tension that pleaded for relief.

The room was dark. She felt a cover under her back and Ty's weight half over her body as the dress was eased away, along with her slip and her brief undergarments. She should protest, she told herself. This was too much. She should never have let him bring her in here...!

He touched her in a way that no man ever had. It was a shock that grew into such pleasure that she had no hope of stopping him. She moved her legs apart to accommodate that sweet, sweet probing, arched to encourage it.

Something was happening to her, something incredibly new and sweet and exciting. She cried out as pleasure shot through her like a bolt of lightning, arching her, making her boneless and without the will to do anything except moan like the damned.

He paused just long enough to peel off his own clothing. She felt bare, hair-roughened skin against her own, heard a moan as poignant as the one coming from her own arched throat.

He was touching her again. She cried out and she heard her own voice pleading with him not to stop, not to stop...

His mouth was all over her, finding new places to explore, new ways to increase her restless movements, her soft cries. He felt her shiver as he built the tension to almost painful levels. She was sobbing now, pulling at him, pleading.

When he was certain that she was ready for him, he went into her. It was a little difficult at first and he felt her body stiffen, but his hand moved between them and coaxed her into passion, into acceptance, into willful compliance.

She sobbed as his powerful body moved on hers, moved into

hers, as he thrust down into her aching, inviting emptiness and filled it.

"Ty...!" Her high-pitched cry was accompanied by an endless moan and fingernails digging into his back as she went under.

He groaned as well, his body wracked by a new and staggering fulfilment that surpassed anything he'd ever experienced. He shuddered over and over as the tide washed him, exhausted, to shore.

She felt his weight over her with a sense of shocked, delighted horror. She hadn't counted on the wine and her own lack of resistance. She was so sated that her body felt boneless. It had been the most exquisite pleasure she'd ever known. But it was over, and what in the world were they going to do...!

He moved. He was still inside her, swelling, growing, as his hips moved gently from side to side.

Her nails bit into him and she moved, too, moaning, pulling, her legs lifting to curl around his and encourage him. She wanted him all over again, just that quickly, just that helplessly.

She sobbed as he moved and the pleasure not only returned, but to a degree she hadn't anticipated. She cried out as they moved roughly against each other, both hungry to experience again a pleasure that was almost pain.

He wrapped her up tight and pushed and pushed until she convulsed and moaned endlessly.

He let out a shocked cry of his own at the culmination, his own body going into rigor at the end, into degrees of pleasure he'd never known.

At last, freed of the agonizing tension that had fallen into passionate satisfaction, they fell asleep in each other's arms.

"Erin."

She heard his voice at her ear, deep and slow and ridden with guilt. Guilt?

She moved and felt the new discomfort. The sheet was rough against her sensitive skin. Skin?!

Her eyes opened. She was naked under the sheet. Ty was dressed, looking down at her with both hands in his pockets and a look of dazed anguish on his tanned face.

"Oh...!" she gasped.

Her expression said it all. He could almost read her mind. She was a virgin. She'd been a virgin, he corrected mentally, as he recalled the difficulty of the first encounter. He'd taken advantage of her. He hadn't meant to. He'd been devastated at losing the project's contract, irritated by Ms. Taylor's headlong pursuit, and he'd had too much to drink. None of which would absolve him from this sin.

"I am truly sorry," he said heavily. "I didn't bring you here for this."

She swallowed, hard. That wasn't the look of a man who was newly in love and delighted at their new intimacy. That was guilt and remorse.

"I had too much to drink," she said through her teeth.

"Me, too."

They just stared at each other for a minute.

"Bathroom's free," he said. "I'll sit on the porch." He turned and left the room without another word.

Erin had a shower, hating herself, feeling such guilt. She wasn't on the pill and she was fairly certain that he'd been too far gone to think of any sort of protection. But here were alternatives, she told herself, including that morning-after pill thing. It would be all right. Of course it would!

But the bigger problem was that she'd just let herself be seduced by her boss. The fact that she was in love with him didn't help, because he wasn't in love with her. That was painfully obvious. Where did they go from here?

It wasn't a question she was comfortable with. She had terrible problems at home. Her father was in bad shape, dying, and she had him to consider. This was a problem, too, but not a life or death one. Not yet at least.

She put her clothes back on and brushed her long hair into some sort of order and used a little powder and lipstick. It wouldn't do to go home and have her father think she'd been reckless. He never needed to know. It would break his heart. He and her mother had raised her to certain beliefs. This went against all of them, and even alcohol wouldn't excuse it.

She went out into the living room and picked up her coat and purse. She went out onto the porch, not meeting Ty's guilty eyes.

"You're sure you're okay to drive?" she asked in what she hoped was a normal tone.

"Yes. Erin…"

She just held up her hand. "Just…take me home, okay?" she asked and forced a smile. She turned and walked ahead of him to the car.

It was a quick, silent trip home. Ty pulled up at her doorstep.

"You don't need to walk me to the door, it's okay," she said, smiling in his general direction. "I'll see you at work Monday."

While he was trying to find the right words to apologize, she was out the door and onto the porch. Before he could consider cutting off the engine and going after her, she'd already unlocked the door, gone inside and turned off the porch light.

He cursed under his breath. After a minute, he pulled back out into the road and drove home.

Erin put her purse and coat up. The house was quiet and dark. Her father must have already gone to bed, she reasoned.

She went to his bedroom. The door was open. The light from the bathroom revealed his body on the floor.

"Dad!" she screamed.

She ran to him, felt for a pulse. He was still alive. She pulled out her cell phone and called 911.

The waiting seemed to take forever. She sat like a statue in the emergency room waiting area with a couple of elderly people and a man who paced constantly.

She barely noticed. It had been the worst night of her recent life. She refused to think about Ty and what had happened. She had to keep her mind on her father. There would be time for re-criminations and worry later, when she had the luxury of time. Right now, the only thing that mattered was her father's health.

Finally, a nurse came to get her and take her back to the treatment room where her father was lying quietly with a doctor making notes into a computer.

The doctor, a young man, looked up. "Miss Mitchell?" he asked.

"Yes. How's my father?" she asked, with a worried glance at her parent, whose eyes were closed.

"He's had a stroke," he said gently.

Her face paled. "A stroke?"

"Yes. I have his medical records here." He indicated the computer. "He's being treated for cancer, I see, and his general health is not good. He has two completely blocked arteries in his heart…"

"What?!" she exclaimed. "But nobody told me!"

He grimaced. "I phoned your primary care physician. It was your father's wish that you not be told. He refused surgery for it. He said the cancer was burden enough."

"Will he live?" she asked frantically.

"I can't promise you that," he said gently. "I'm sorry. There's been a good deal of damage. We'll do an MRI and run more tests, then we'll have a better picture of the road ahead. My advice to you would be to go home and get a good night's sleep and come back in the morning. Leave your phone number at the desk so that we can contact you if we need to. Your father won't know you're here," he added gently, "and he'll be in ICU in any case."

She drew in a long breath. "I was out on a date," she began miserably.

"This is not something anyone could have predicted," he said softly, "so put that guilt away. You have a job, yes, you work outside the home?"

She nodded, tears in her eyes.

"It could have just as well happened when you were at work. You can't be with him every minute. Don't punish yourself. Okay?"

"Okay. Thanks."

"I'll be in touch the minute I know something. Your own physician will be here in the morning to make any decisions that need making."

"I'll be here early."

"Fine. Try to get some sleep. It does help."

"I will."

She went to her father and kissed his forehead. "I'll be back in the morning, Dad. You hang in there, okay? I love you." She turned and went out to the nurses' desk.

CHAPTER SIX

But Erin didn't sleep. She tossed and turned, agonizing about what she'd done with Ty, about leaving her father alone at home. He'd had a stroke. How long had he been on the floor like that before she got back? It tormented her.

She got up finally and made coffee and grabbed a biscotti out of the container. It was better than nothing. She didn't feel like cooking.

She forced herself not to think about the night before. She had to think about her father now. She dressed and went to the hospital.

Her father was in ICU. He hadn't regained consciousness. Their family doctor came out to the waiting room to talk to her.

"I wish I could give you a better prognosis," he said. "His cancer has spread. Tests indicate that it's metastasized into his liver and lungs." He grimaced. "The fact of the matter is that pancreatic cancer is deadly. Even if we'd gotten to it when it first appeared, it's hard to treat."

Her heart fell. "He's dying."

He nodded. "The stroke is a major complication. If he recovers, I'd send him to an intervention cardiologist to see if the blockages could be opened with stents. Failing that, it would mean open heart surgery. In his condition, he wouldn't survive it."

She drew in a breath and felt as if the weight of the world was sitting on her shoulders. "I see."

"I'll do everything I can for him, you know that. I've already contacted specialists, including his cancer specialist, to confer. But you need to know exactly what he's up against."

"Yes. I appreciate your honesty."

"I don't enjoy telling people hard facts," he confessed. "Your father is one of my favorite patients. But he and your mother always insisted on the truth, no sugarcoating. You're like them," he added with a gentle smile.

She smiled back. "Yes, I am. When can I see him?"

He told her. "And you can talk to the nurses in ICU about the rest of the time," he added. "Visits are limited as you already know."

She nodded. She sighed. "I remember when Mama was here," she said.

"So do I. A good woman."

"She truly was. And Dad is a good man." Sadness overwhelmed her.

"One day at a time," he advised. "Just put one foot in front of the other. If you need help sleeping, let me know. I'll prescribe something. You're going to need your strength in the days ahead."

"I'll take you up on that right now," she said honestly. "I've been up all night."

"No problem." He took out his phone.

She took advantage of brief visits to look at her father's still, quiet face in the hospital bed. Machines beeped, fluid seeped into veins from the drips. So much equipment surrounded him that it was hard to get close to the bed.

She held his hand and talked to him during the visiting periods. But there was no response. None at all.

Monday morning she called in from the hospital and told a coworker why she couldn't come to work for a few days.

A few minutes later, Annie came into the waiting room. She didn't say a word. She just hugged her friend close and let her cry.

"Why didn't you call me?" Annie muttered.

"I haven't been quite sane since this happened," she replied, choking on tears. "He was lying on the bedroom floor when I got home Saturday night. I called an ambulance. The rest of the time, I was crazy with fear."

"Well, I'm here now," Annie said stubbornly. She looked her friend over. "Have you slept?"

She nodded. "Dr. Harris gave me a sedative to take. Oh, Annie, first the cancer, now this," she groaned. "It's just so much…!"

"I know how it is," Annie replied gently. "You went through it with me when Ty and I lost our parents."

"I remember. Both at once. It was horrible for you."

Annie sighed. "At least I had Ty, though. He took care of everything." She glanced at Erin's pale face. She wanted to ask her friend why Ty had been so withdrawn since that supper at the lake, but it would have been cruel. Erin had enough to worry her without Annie bringing up a subject that seemed to have complications. Ty looked guilty as sin. Mrs. Dobbs, who was their housekeeper, had gone to the lake house to clean it up and came home tight-lipped and refused to talk about it. That was a huge red flag to Annie. The housekeeper was usually talkative, and Annie had been very curious about that supper at the cabin. She'd hoped for years that Ty would notice Erin. Something must have gone terribly wrong.

But this wasn't the time to pry. Erin needed comforting and sympathy, not probing questions.

"Let's get a cup of coffee in the cafeteria," she said. "I didn't even stop for breakfast."

"Okay," Erin said. "Let me stop by the nurses' station first."

They had a nice breakfast and black coffee while Erin recalled her parents' strange recent behavior.

"I don't know why he looks so guilty lately," Erin said. "He hasn't even been anywhere to get into mischief." She laughed. "Dad and his get-rich-quick schemes. In some ways, he's so naïve. Honestly!"

"I remember one of them that almost landed him in jail. That so-called land development idea he had…"

"Yes, he actually bought ten acres in a flood plain without checking first, and then couldn't get any builder to partner with him," she sighed. "He's impulsive. He leaps and then looks." She sipped black coffee. "At least I talked him out of the day-trading thing," she said. "He wanted to take some course he'd found. He said it was a sure thing. I handed him an article to read about how one man had tried it and ended up killing himself after losing everything he owned."

"Why did he need money?"

"For the day-trading." Erin sighed. "I told him that there would never be enough to make up the losses. He finally listened." She shifted. "At least I almost have the house paid off," she said, smiling. "Mom's insurance money buried her and paid down the mortgage. Two payments left, and the house will be free and clear."

Annie shook her head. "I've never had to worry about mortgages. Ty's always taken care of the finances, ever since we lost Mom and Dad."

"He's got a great head for business."

"Not so much for women," Annie replied, shaking her head. "He can sure pick them."

"I noticed."

"Now it's that Taylor woman at work," Annie groaned. "He says he may have to fire her. She's stalking him."

"Hence my dates with him," Erin lied with a convincing smile.

Annie's eyes widened. "No! No, it can't just be a means to make that woman leave him alone. Say it isn't so!"

"Sorry. It is."

Annie groaned. "And here I was hoping he was falling in love with you!"

Erin shrugged. "That would be a nice fantasy. But it's not realistic, Annie. If he was going to notice me, he'd have done it already." The words hurt, but they were true. If Ty hadn't gotten drunk, chances were good that he'd never have touched Erin.

"So much for all my hopes, dash it," Annie muttered.

"One day he'll find a nice wife," Erin comforted her.

"One day Ty's dogs will learn to read and write," she countered.

"How are the piano lessons going?" she asked to divert her friend, because Annie, at twenty-three, had just started taking lessons.

She groaned. "My fingers tangle on the keys. I can't remember which pedal to use. My piano teacher grinds his teeth and smiles like a skeleton. It's an agony." She sighed. "But I want to learn, so I'll persevere."

"That's the spirit," Erin told her.

"It's not fair. Ty plays like a master and I can't hit two keys without making a discord."

"He just has a better ear for music than you do. It doesn't mean you can't learn."

"I suppose so. Well, if persistence is key, I'm persistent."

"I'll drink to that," Erin replied and finished her coffee.

That night, Ty came to the hospital with Annie to sit with Erin. She wished he hadn't, because she felt guilty and he looked guilty. Annie was giving them both overly curious glances as they sat in the waiting room.

"This is really nice of both of you," Erin said. "But it's not necessary. I know you have other things you need to be doing."

"If it was our dad, you'd be here," Annie pointed out.

"Dead right," Ty added.

Erin sighed. "I appreciate the support." She shook her head. "It's just that he's not coming out of it. Dr. Harris said he might not. Even if he does, he's facing either stent placement or open-heart surgery. If there's light at the end of the tunnel, it's a faint light and very far away."

Ty studied her in the jeans and pullover green short-sleeved sweater she was wearing. Her hair was in a long braid. He remembered it long and silky and soft in his hands in the bed at the cabin. He ground his teeth trying not to think about the pleasure she'd given him.

He knew her conscience was probably flogging her over what had happened. He felt bad about it, too. He'd had too much to drink and he'd made a convenience of her. She was a person of faith. That would make it harder on her, and she had enough worry with her father in a desperate condition.

He was still trying to figure out who'd sold him out. He knew what the bid had been from Erin's figures. Either someone had changed them or someone had told his competitor what those figures were. The man who'd gotten the contract was a lowlife who used substandard materials. He'd been prosecuted once, but a little artful bribery had gotten the case dismissed. The foreign client would be lucky if the project didn't fall down around their ears and subject them to lawsuits. It was an accident waiting to happen.

He kept remembering Jones telling him that Erin had left her drawer unlocked with the final bid for the job lying in it. He was also remembering her couture garments and her father's new car and that trip her father had made to a business that loaned money. The business was rumored to have mob ties, and it dealt in quick cash. He wondered if Erin knew? Surely she did. Her father didn't keep secrets from her. Was that how she could afford couture, on her salary?

Of course, she still drove that secondhand car. But then it wasn't really his business. She was passionate in bed and he'd enjoyed her more than any woman he'd ever had. He kept remembering how difficult it had been at first. He'd wondered if she was really as innocent as Annie believed her to be. She hadn't resisted him, and she'd given him a response that still fired his blood. Would a virgin be so responsive?

It was just a step from that to believing he'd imagined it. Some women tightened up when they were passionate, he knew that from his own experience, and that made first encounters with a woman difficult. It didn't mean she was innocent. And if she wasn't, she was probably on some form of birth control. Most women were these days, even if they abstained. He wasn't worried about that. Children weren't ever going to be a part of his life. He loved his freedom. Annie might have some one day. He wouldn't mind. He loved kids as long as they belonged to other people.

"You're deep in thought," Annie told her brother while Erin was back in ICU with her father for a few minutes.

"I'm still brooding about losing that contract," he muttered.

"Ty, just let it go. We won't starve. The ranch pays for itself."

"I could lose the business," he pointed out. "A lot of people depend on me for food on the table."

"I know that," she said warmly. "But there will be other jobs."

"Not like this one. And if gossip has made the rounds that I'm sloppy, what new jobs will we get?" His face tautened. "I'll find out who did this. And when I do, they'll pay and keep on paying," he added coldly.

Annie shivered inwardly. She'd seen her brother pay back people. It was never pleasant to watch. He had money and power and a nasty temper and he knew how to use all three.

Erin was back, looking pale and even more worried.

"Any change?" Annie asked.

Erin met her eyes. She just shook her head.

They walked out with her when she was reluctantly persuaded to go home.

"You could ride with us," Annie suggested.

"Thanks, but I'll take Dad's car."

"Your father has a car? That's new," Ty remarked, because he couldn't let on that he'd had her father checked out.

"I know. It's a late model and he paid cash for it," Erin sighed. "I asked him where he got the money, and he said he'd found a second life insurance policy on Mama that he'd forgotten he even had. He called the agent and sent them a copy of the death certificate. They sent him a check." She shifted her purse. "I'd hoped he'd finish paying off the house, but he bought the car before I had a chance to mention it."

"Your father has issues with money management," Annie commented affectionately.

"Big ones," Erin agreed. "So thanks, but I can drive." She glanced at Ty. "I'm sorry, I'll miss work for a few days…"

"Nobody's worried about that," he said quietly. "Take all the time you need. And let us know how we can help."

"Thanks. But the only help I need at the moment is divine," she added, looking upward.

"Call me," Annie said.

"I will."

"Go ahead to the car. I'll be right along," Ty told his sister.

"Okay. Good night, Erin."

"Good night," she called, wishing that Ty would just go to his own car.

They paused beside the sporty little gray car her father had bought. He looked it over. "Nice," he remarked.

"Dad likes it."

He stuck his hands in his pockets. "Erin, about what happened…"

"It was a moment out of time," she said through her teeth,

and forced a smile. "Really. It wasn't the first time I had too much to drink and went overboard," she lied.

He felt a pang of anger at that. He'd thought her innocent. But then, why had he? Very few modern women were. "I see," he said coldly.

"So, no worries," she assured him. "I have to get home."

"I hope your father does well," he said stiffly.

"Yes. So do I. Good night. Thank Annie for coming tonight. Thank you, too."

"You work for me," he said indifferently. "It was the least I could do. Good night."

He walked away without a backward glance and she felt her heart shatter in her chest. She hadn't wanted him to know how innocent she was. It didn't matter to him, anyway, from all indications he was full of regrets. She had enough guilt for both of them.

But her primary concern right now was her parent. That was when she remembered that she hadn't done anything about the morning after pill that would have assured she had nothing to regret from her interlude with Ty. But she was unlikely to get pregnant from one night, and it was too late now anyway. She went home and to bed.

"You're going where?!" Annie burst out when Ty announced an overseas business trip. "But why now? And what about the puppies?"

"Randy's got all that in hand. The business will go on without me for a few weeks."

"Ty…"

"I just need to get away for a while and do some thinking about my life," he said shortly. He paused. "Let me know how Erin's father gets along, though, will you? And help her out if she needs it. Not that she does. She's wearing couture garments and her dad just paid cash for a new car. I don't know of any insurance that pays so long after a death, Annie," he added.

"Well, really, neither do I," she confessed slowly. "You don't think her father's done something illegal…?"

"Or she has."

"Erin? Oh, come on!" she exclaimed. "We've known her forever!"

"Have we, really?" he asked with a cynical smile. She'd certainly gone to bed with him quickly enough. What did that say about her scruples. "You never know people unless you live with them."

"Erin's as honest as the day is long," she protested.

"You're entitled to your opinion. I can't forget her leaving her desk unlocked with that bid inside, before we sent it over."

"Ty, Erin would never sell you out for money," she said at once. "Please, don't class her with other women you've been involved with. Don't make that mistake. She's my best friend. I know her very well, even if you don't."

He started to say that he knew Erin far better than his sister realized, but he wasn't opening that can of worms.

"It's still suspicious," he said. "I'm going to put a private detective on it and see if he can get at the truth. We can't let malicious gossip cost us the company that our father spent a lifetime building."

"You do have a point," she gave in.

"I'll get on it. Meantime, I'm going to take some time off."

"You need it," she agreed. "You've had a lot of pressure lately."

"Too much," he replied, and smiled. "I won't be away long."

"I'll hold you to that," she replied, and smiled back.

Meanwhile, Erin's father began to slip away. She could see it for herself during the brief intensive care visit.

"Oh, Dad," she moaned softly as she held on to one of his hands with a canula in place, feeding him from a bag on the pole beside the bed. "I hope you can hold on. I would miss you so much!"

His hand moved just barely, but she felt it. "I think you can hear me," she said, her voice breaking. "If you can, I love you very much. If you have to…let go… Mama will be waiting for you," she whispered as tears rolled down her cheeks.

Incredibly, her father's eyes opened, just once, and a partial smile bloomed just barely on his lips before his eyes closed. They didn't open again.

She told the doctor what had happened. He went to check on her father. Minutes later, while she chewed a fingernail, he returned. She got up from her chair, eyes wide with hope. But he wasn't smiling. He was sympathetic but he couldn't offer hope.

"I'm truly sorry, Erin," he said gently. "Sometimes people seem like they're going to rally, but it's more often a signal that there isn't much time left. I'm happy that Arthur responded to you, even that little bit. It's something to hold on to. But you have to keep in mind that we've done everything humanly possible to keep him going. It's just a matter of time."

She drew in a long breath. It had seemed like a sign that her father might live. She'd had a hollow feeling these past few days, as if a catastrophe was at hand. Not even just her father's serious illness. It felt…like the end of everything in her young life. She tried and failed to put the feeling of foreboding out of her mind.

"I guess I knew that. I've been clinging to hope."

The doctor smiled sadly. "Everyone does that. It's human nature."

She nodded. "Thank you for all you've done, just the same."

"I wish I could do more."

She went back to her lonely vigil in the waiting room. Less than thirty minutes later, the doctor came back out to tell her, very gently, that her father had lost his battle.

She thanked him. A few minutes, and many tears later, she went to the nurses' desk to tell them about the arrangements she'd just made with the funeral home. Then she went home, took the sedative the doctor had already prescribed, and slept until the next morning.

She hadn't called Annie, who was standing on her doorstep when she went to make coffee.

Annie didn't say a word. She just hugged her best friend while she cried.

They sat over cups of black coffee and discussed what came next.

"You'll have enough food to keep you for a month," Annie said with gentle humor. "The prayer group at our church started cooking already. They'll bring dishes by this afternoon."

Annie was part of that group. So was Erin. They both cooked for other families who had loved ones pass. It was something that was done in small towns.

"We'll have visitation tomorrow afternoon and tomorrow evening at the funeral home," Erin told her. "I'll arrange it when I go over the details with them this morning. Dad had a policy with them, so the funeral cost won't be an issue. The house will be mine. I'll have to go see our attorney and get letters testamentary…" She broke down and mopped up tears. "I knew it was coming, but it's still so awful, Annie!"

"I remember," Annie said, patting her hand. "I've been there."

"I know you have." She took a breath and another sip of coffee. "I'll be back at work Monday. I called the office and told them. Ty wasn't there."

"He's off somewhere," Annie said. "I don't know where. He was very upset at losing that bid," she added.

"I don't understand why the company didn't get the bid," she replied. "You can never know how much another company will bid, but we had ours as low as it could get without cutting corners and using substandard materials. I know that no other company could have undercut us on that!"

"I don't know, either," Annie said.

"I didn't dare suggest that Ben Jones might have been responsible," Erin said with some heat. "He was in my drawer, where I had the bid. He said it was unlocked, but I'm certain that I locked it. And if I did, how did he get it open?" she added with cold gray eyes. "I've never trusted him. He's showing wealth he shouldn't have, on his salary, but you can't talk to Ty about him. He won't listen."

"He was Dad's best friend," Annie pointed out. "They started the company together. Ty trusts him."

"I wish he trusted me," Erin sighed. "As if I'd ever sell him out for money!" She looked at her friend with tormented eyes. "I've loved him since I was in my early teens," she confessed huskily, "for all the good it will ever do me. He likes me. But I'm just one of the guys. There's nothing else. There never has been." It was a lie, but she couldn't bear to share her downfall with her best friend.

"I know how you feel," Annie said gently. "The way you look at Ty says it all. The man is blind, if he can't see it."

"He doesn't want to see it," Erin replied quietly. "He's not a white picket fence sort of man. He likes variety. And I'm not like that."

She wasn't. She'd slipped, just that one time. But it was enough that Ty would never believe she didn't sleep around. He probably thought she was like every other woman now, out for pleasure with no guilt. The way he'd looked at her at the hospital had hurt. It wasn't the look of a man who loved a woman. It was a worldly sort of dismissal, as if he now classed her with all the other women who'd passed through his bed. If only she'd kept her head that night!

As she tormented herself, she remembered something else. Annie's housekeeper, Mrs. Dobbs, would have gone to tidy up the cabin. And the sheets hadn't been changed…

Erin drew in a breath. "I'm so glad we came home early from the cabin that night," she said, her eyes on her coffee cup. "Ty seemed in a hurry to get back there." She made a face. "I think he had plans for the cabin later, if you know what I mean," she added, and managed a teary smile.

Annie's eyebrows rose. That would explain a few things. She'd have to have a word with Mrs. Dobbs when she got home. But it made Annie sad. If Ty had compromised Erin, he might have been involved enough to lose his heart. It was possible. Not probable, however. He'd had years to fall in love with Erin. It hadn't happened. He treated her like a second sister. What a bummer!

"Considering the condition your father was in, I imagine you were very glad to be home early," Annie said. "It must have just happened."

"That's what the doctor said," she agreed. "We were lucky to get him to the hospital so quickly. But a massive stroke like that…our doctor said there hadn't really been much of a chance that Dad could have survived. And if he had, he would have been so compromised that it would have been a living death. So I guess things happen as they're meant to," she added.

"Of course they do," Annie replied. "We're people of faith. We accept that our days are numbered."

"Yes, but the last time I spoke to Dad, his eyes opened and he tried to smile at me. I thought it was a great sign, that he was coming back, that he could make it." She closed her eyes. "Then the doctor told me that people often rally like that, just before they let go."

"My aunt was like that. She'd had a heart attack and she was unconscious. She came to very suddenly and smiled at us. She told us she'd be coming home very soon. That night, she died. The night nurse told me that she looked toward the doorway and just said one word: Howard. And she let go."

"Who was Howard?"

"Her husband, whom she'd lost three years before," Annie said. "She loved him so much. We thought she'd mourn herself to death. Nobody even knew she had a bad heart until she had the attack." She sighed. "It's kind of nice, thinking that someone who loved you would come back to take you over when you pass."

"It is," Erin agreed. She drew in a breath. "I dread having to do all this," she said.

"I'll be with you every step of the way," Annie replied. "That's what family does."

"Oh, Annie," she wailed.

Annie hugged her and rocked her. Of all the times for Ty to be away, this had to be the worst. She pondered messaging him to come home, but considering the mood he was in when he left, he'd be of no help. In fact, he'd probably make things worse, brooding about the lost bid.

The company would stand, regardless of one lost bid, and he'd eventually find out who sold him out. She was betting on Jones. Like Erin, she'd never trusted the man. He smiled too much.

Visitation brought people from Comanche Wells and Jacobsville, and far flung communities. Jacobs County wasn't so big that people didn't know each other, and most of them were distant kin as well. The funeral home was full for the two hours of visitation.

Erin sat by her father's coffin. It was closed, per his instructions. He'd often said that he didn't want a lot of people staring at him after he was gone. The casket was beautiful, a rich mahogany color, and it was surrounded by baskets of flowers and sprays and wreaths.

So many friends and neighbors came by to express sympathy. There was one notable exception. Ben Jones. He and his wife sent a small basket of flowers, but they didn't come for visitation. Ms. Taylor, predictably, did nothing. Ty apparently had his secretary send flowers, because an enormous spray came from the company, and a huge basket of flowers came from Annie and Ty.

"We sent those," Annie told her as visitation was winding down, indicating a basket of gorgeous yellow orchid plants, "so you'd have something to bring home with you. And don't worry, you don't have to have a light table for them like I have for mine. These are phalaenopsis orchids. They'll do fine with filtered sunlight, an occasional spritz, and weekly watering. Just remember they don't like wet feet," she said with a smile.

"They're beautiful," Erin said, hugging her friend. "Yellow is my favorite color."

"I noticed."

"I'll give you orchid pots for your birthday," she added with a smile.

"I'll take good care of them," Erin promised. She noticed another basket of flowers, smaller than Annie's, with two exotic blooming plants and a small fern. Not as expensive as orchids but very pretty and in her favorite colors of maroon and pink. She looked at the tag. Surprisingly, it was from Jones and his wife. That was a surprise. She didn't know anything about Mrs. Jones, but the flowers indicated that she knew something about Erin's preference of colors. It was touching.

She looked at the casket with sad eyes. "Now all I have to do is get through the funeral tomorrow. I'll miss Daddy," she said huskily.

"He's off with your mother, hiking," Annie said gently. "They're holding hands and laughing."

Erin looked at her. "You said that about your parents when you lost them," she recalled with a sad smile. "It helps. It really helps to think of it like that."

Annie shrugged. "I'm notorious for hanging out on NDE sites."

"Excuse me?"

"NDE. Near death experiences," she explained. "There are lots of them. Most say the same thing, that someone you love comes back for you when it's your time. And that all your pets meet you running when you arrive. It's a great comfort."

"Yes," Erin said. She hugged Annie again. "Thanks."

"I'm sorry Ty can't come," she told her friend solemnly. "I don't even know where he is! Honestly, I got one text message and now he doesn't even answer them. I've got half a mind to call a detective agency and send them after him."

"You could get Ms. Taylor to do that for you," Erin laughed without humor. "Her father is a detective. He has a small agency in town."

"If he's anything like his daughter, no thanks," Annie said curtly. "She's started even calling the house looking for Ty."

"You could block her," Erin suggested.

"What would I tell him, if I did?" she replied. "I don't know if he's ignoring the woman or if he's involved with her. He keeps his cards close to his chest. You never know exactly how he feels about people because he's so secretive."

"I suppose so."

Annie shrugged. "I had high hopes for your supper at the cabin."

"So did I," Erin said, and managed to look as if nothing at all had happened. "It was a nice supper, but he saved dessert." That was a lie, but nobody would know except Erin and Ty. "So maybe he was saving it for somebody else." That fib might save her reputation if the Mosbys' housekeeper gossiped with any friends.

"That would have been awful of him," Annie said shortly.

"Just keep that to yourself, please," Erin pleaded. "He'd know who told you."

"Yes, I guess he would. I'll keep it quiet. Darn," she added with a grimace. "What a sister-in-law you'd have made."

"We all have dreams. They die for lack of love, eventually."

"Don't I know it," Annie said solemnly.

"Sorry. I didn't mean to bring up painful subjects."

"Just as well," her friend replied with a sad smile. "I was like you, hungry for someone who couldn't see me for dust. That's life."

"That's life."

The next day was rainy and cold, even for late spring. Erin and Annie sat together on the front row at the burial plot in the church cemetery where generations of their people had worshipped, wearing raincoats and clutching tissue in their hands.

The other chairs were occupied by friends and neighbors and one very distant cousin from Wyoming—Maude Ryder, an elderly woman who had a ranch in Carne County, Wyoming, a few miles from the ranch where a cousin of Annie and Ty had lived before she moved to Texas with her husband.

"You should come and live with me," Maude said. She was in her early sixties, tall and willowy, with silver hair and sparkling blue eyes. "I've got kittens in the barn and baby animals of all sorts, along with some of the best Black Angus cattle in the state. Plus it's a big house. Since I lost my husband, it's way too big. Would love the company, any time you want to visit, if you won't come to live."

Erin hugged her. "I may take you up on that during summer vacation," she promised with a smile. "I could use some time away from here."

"Come now," Maude coaxed.

"I wish. But I've got all Dad's financial stuff to get through, including probate of his will. That will take time."

"So it will. You have my phone number. Just text me any time you want to come. Or just text me," Maude added with a smile. "Gets lonely up there all on my lonesome."

"I'll do that. I promise. You be careful going home!"

"Tell that to the pilot of the plane I chartered," Maude chuckled. "But he's good. I fly with him all the time. Take care. Sorry about your dad. He was flighty, but I always liked him."

"So did I," Erin said, and they both wiped away tears.

Erin started going through her father's papers two days later, on a Monday. What she found was not only shocking, it was staggering. She stared at the computer screen with eyes so wide they looked like saucers. She couldn't believe what she was seeing!

CHAPTER SEVEN

The document she'd pulled up on her father's computer was devastating to read. It showed his transactions on a day-trading website. He'd lost thousands and thousands of dollars. As she looked at it, she wondered where in the world he'd managed to get his hands on so much money.

She thought about the nearly new car in the driveway for which he'd paid cash. That had been an additional thousands of dollars. No way he'd cashed in an insurance policy on her mother, because it had been years since she'd died. And he'd never had more than just burial expenses, even so. That wouldn't be enough to buy a car and spend thousands more on a day-trading site.

While she was puzzling over the transactions, there was a knock on the door.

Absently, she opened it, her mind on money matters. But she came back to the present with a jerk when she saw that a deputy sheriff was standing on her porch with a piece of paper in his hand.

"Miss Mitchell?" he asked politely.

"Yes…?"

He grimaced. "I'm really sorry to have to give you this," he said heavily. He handed the paper to her.

She read it with shock evident all over her face. "This…this can't be happening," she choked. "He didn't…he couldn't have done this!" She looked up, her eyes plainly begging him to say that it was a cruel joke.

"I'm sorry, ma'am, but it came straight from the courthouse in Jacobsville," he replied. "Apparently Mr. Mitchell borrowed a lot of money on the property. The people he borrowed it from are wanting their money back and they wouldn't wait. Sheriff Carson even asked them to. But it didn't do any good. To be honest with you, the company Mr. Mitchell got the loan from is, well, they charge real high interest and they want the money back quick."

She understood what he was saying. It was most likely a company that did business barely legally.

She pushed back her hair. "I was going to work in the morning," she said blankly. "When do I have to be out?"

"Today," he said.

"Today?! But I just buried my father…!"

"Call a storage company and just put everything in there until you get another place to stay," he suggested. "I'm pretty sure they won't ask us to throw you in the street. It's very bad for business," he added gently.

She drew in a breath and nodded, her mind whirling. "Okay. Yes, I can get a storage unit. I'll get right to work. Should I call my lawyer?"

"Yes," he said at once. "He might be able to buy you a little more time with the loan company."

"Okay." She drew in a breath and managed a smile. "Thank you," she said.

"I'm sorry," he replied. "I don't like serving these things."

"We all do our jobs," she pointed out.

"Yes, ma'am, we do, but some are really hard."

She watched him drive away. Then she went inside and called their family attorney.

It was no use. The attorney contacted the loan agency and tried to work out a deal, but it was no go.

Erin had already come to that conclusion, so she'd booked the storage unit, and the moving company, for the next morning. She went through what seemed like years of papers that night, getting together any that she might need and putting them in a storage box. They would have to go with her while probate was underway.

The big question was where would she live? What about her father's car…! Finally, a joyous thought. She could sell his car. The money wouldn't pay back the loan, but it would give her a little grubstake. She'd already noted that her father had spent every penny in their joint checking account, and even the savings account. All she had was her week's salary and her credit card to which, thank God, he didn't have access. She'd secretly hidden his credit card weeks ago to keep him off Amazon. The house was overloaded with things he didn't need or use.

She looked around and wished she'd had time to hold an auction. Some of the furniture was antique. Maybe she could leave the storage unit key with Annie and ask her to get the older pieces appraised and sell them. It would give her a little extra money at least.

She cleaned out her closet, only taking the clothes she wore to work and church. The rest of them, and her father's, could go to the county's charity shop. The pots and pans and appliances would go into storage. When she found a place to rent, she could come and fetch them. She had her car, at least. However, as she considered things, it would be easier to keep her father's car and give up the one she made payments on. His car was practically new. At least he hadn't had time to sell it yet or she might be walking to work!

She did still have her job. That was a blessing.

She looked for rentals in the local paper and felt her jaw drop. The cheapest thing she could find was over a thousand dollars a month. She would still have bills to pay and food and gas and groceries to buy. It was shocking. How had prices gone so high, so quickly?

Finally she found a little ad tucked away in the local paper, advertising for a tenant for a family home. The applicants were warned that the family would be very selective about their choice. Erin was hopeful that she might fit it. And the apartment was in San Antonio, not more that six blocks from her job. That would save on gas for sure!

She called the number and spoke to a nice-sounding woman who only asked two or three questions and then asked if Erin could come to see her the next afternoon. Erin explained that she worked until five, and asked if she could come after work. The woman agreed. When she hung up, she felt much better.

But in the meantime, she had to find a place to stay. Or maybe not. She could spend the night in the house and oversee the removal of the furniture and accessories in the morning. Then she'd go to work, and then to apply for the apartment in person. If she got it, her problems were solved. If not…well, there were always motels. She breathed a little easier.

Her cell phone rang just before she went to bed.

"How are you?" Annie asked.

"Doing okay," she replied, trying to sound cheerful. "It's just a lot to get done, that's all. I'm going to have to skimp on expenses, so I'm applying for an apartment in San Antonio, near the company. It will save on gas."

"I hate for you to move," Annie said, sounding miserable.

"I can still come visit," she replied. "So can you."

"Apartments can be dangerous," Annie persisted.

"Yes, but this one is in a private home. I'm going to see the landlady tomorrow after work. So cross your fingers for me. It sounds really nice. She sounds nice, too, on the phone."

"Well, that's something at least."

"I'm putting my furniture in storage for the time being," she told Annie. "Later, can I get you to have someone appraise that antique furniture mama had and let them make me an offer for it?"

"What's wrong?" Annie asked at once.

She took a deep breath. No way was she admitting how bad things were to her best friend. "Dad ran us into debt," she said. "He was doing day-trading and hiding it from me. He lost a lot of money. So I'm going to have to sell some things."

"Like the house? Oh, no!" Annie wailed.

"It's just a house," she replied. "There's a saying, that you can't go home again. Despite his faults, and he had some, the house wouldn't be the same without Dad, you know."

Annie hesitated. "I guess not."

"Dad was childlike in some ways. We had some fierce arguments about day-trading. I'd hoped that I convinced him how easy it was to go broke doing it. He didn't listen, but I didn't know. Not until he was gone."

"I'm so sorry."

"Me, too," Erin sighed. "But life goes on. I'll miss him." She had to choke back tears, because his loss was just starting to hit her. "I'm going to keep his new car and let mine go."

"That's sensible."

"Yes, it is. I've been cleaning out closets until I'm almost blind," she laughed.

"Why are you doing it in the middle of the night?"

Uh-oh. She thought fast. "If I get the apartment, I'll move in as soon as possible, so I'll need to move my work stuff up there."

Annie sighed. "Of course. I wasn't thinking."

"It's been a long day. I'm going to take one of the doctor's sedative tablets and go to sleep. I'll talk to you tomorrow. And, Annie, thanks for everything!"

"You know I'd do anything I could for you," she replied gently. "We're sisters in every way except blood."

"Isn't that the truth? You sleep good."

"You, too. Night night."

"Night."

She did sleep, but not for a long time. She got up and made coffee and then cleaned and packed the coffee pot. She wanted to be ready to move the little appliances if she got the apartment.

The moving people arrived and she went with them to the storage building she'd rented. It was a tight squeeze, but they managed to get the sofas and chairs and the headboards of the beds into it. She'd had to leave the mattresses and box springs because no way would there be room for them. The coffee pot, a waffle iron, and a couple of pots and pans went into the trunk of her father's car. The paperwork to sign it over to her would have to wait a day or two, but she had the registration papers in its pocket.

Ms. Taylor was all mock sorrow when Erin was seated in her office.

"We were all so sorry about your dad," she said.

"Thanks," Erin replied. "Everybody's been very kind."

"Mr. Jones was going to send a big wreath, but we all took up money for a wreath so I suggested a small basket of potted flowers that you could keep at home," she added.

"That was very nice of you," Erin said and meant it. "I love flowers."

Ms. Taylor smiled. "Lots of people do. Not me. I have awful allergies."

Erin laughed. "So did my mother, but she planted stuff everywhere."

"Must be nice, having a family," she said with real wistful-

ness. "I came up in a series of foster homes." She made a face.
"Back to work, I guess."

"Thanks again," Erin told her.

She shrugged. "No problem."

Ben Jones stopped by her desk an hour later.

"I'm truly sorry about your father," he said solemnly. "He was
a good man. A little frivolous at times, but a solid human being."

"Thanks, Mr. Jones," she replied.

"And I'm sorry about the day-trading," he said through his
teeth.

She blinked. "Excuse me?"

He drew in a breath. "We used to go to the same coffee shop
around the corner a couple of days a month. He came up to do
business with some company he worked for part-time. We met
a couple of year ago. We had a lot in common. We got to know
each other and then, we'd meet to get cappuccino together. I'd
just discovered day-trading and I was a fanatic about it. I made a
good deal of money at first, but I soon realized how easy it was
to lose. So I quit. But he'd gotten into it and liked it a little too
much. I hoped I'd dissuaded him." He gave her a pained look.
"I hope I did, before he lost too much. I never should have en-
thused about it so much."

It was a shock that he'd started her father on the path, but a
bigger one for him to confess that he was sorry for it. Then she
reminded herself that even serial killers sometimes loved their
dogs.

She forced a smile. "He did stop eventually," she lied. After
he lost everything he owned, she added silently. "Thank you
and your wife for the basket of flowers. I loved them."

"Should have been something bigger, but Ms. Taylor said the
company as a whole was sending a big wreath and I should just
get you something more personal. Your mom loved flowers,"
he added with a wistful smile. "She used to come up with your
father to the coffee shop once a week. She was a lovely person.

So I figured if your mother liked flowers you would, too. So I got you some you could plant. My wife called a florist in Jacobsville to get them, and the florist knew your favorite colors," he added.

She was surprised and touched. "That was a lot of trouble to go to. Thank you," she added softly.

"It wasn't much," he said. "I'll miss your dad. Every other Thursday. Cappuccino will never be as much fun ever again," he added.

He went back to his office, leaving a puzzled Erin behind. She'd never really talked to Mr. Jones before, certainly not to that extent. She had no idea that he and her father even knew each other. No wonder her dad never said anything. He was probably afraid that he'd slip and let on that he had a friend who knew about day-trading.

Ty was studying a prize quarter horse stallion on a ranch in Montana. His heart wasn't into it. The more he thought about Erin, the more depressed he got. He'd been certain that he was her first man. When she told him offhandedly that it wasn't the first time she'd gotten drunk and slept with someone, it depressed him beyond measure.

She'd had a crush on him once, in her early teens. It had amused him at the time, but he knew it hadn't persisted. Erin was friendly, but nothing more. And then he'd asked her out, and everything had changed. He found himself thinking about her, a lot. Funny, to feel a new hunger for a woman he'd known most of her life.

He'd hired Ms. Taylor's father's private detective agency to find out who'd slipped the information about his bid to the other major bidder. He didn't like Jenny, but her dad had a reputation for being honest and thorough. He was hoping to discover the culprit. If it was someone who worked for him, heaven help them. He was burning for revenge.

"What about it?" the rancher asked him.

He snapped back to the present and smiled. "I like his conformation," he said. "Let's go talk prices."

The rancher grinned. "Happy to!"

Annie drove by Erin's home on her way to lunch at Barbara's Café. She could have cried when she saw the For Sale sign out front. She was surprised that Erin was able to get it posted so quickly, but of course, it was necessary. It still made her sad. Life in Jacobsville would never be the same without Erin.

Ty had phoned and said he was having a champion quarter horse shipped back to the ranch. He hadn't asked about Erin, but then, Annie knew by now that he wasn't interested in her. One sadness after another, she kept thinking.

"You're all sad today," Mrs. Dobbs noted as Annie sat listlessly in a rocking chair on the porch.

"Erin's moving up to San Antonio."

"Why?"

"Her father did day-trading and lost everything they owned," Annie sighed. She glanced at the housekeeper. "Oh, you know that Erin came home early from the lake house when she had supper with Ty? She said he was going back." She glowered. "Do you think he had another woman on tap to come up there? Erin said he'd only asked her out to keep Ms. Taylor at bay."

The housekeeper let out a sigh. "That's welcome news."

"Why?" Annie asked, frowning.

"No reason," she replied with an innocent smile. "But Miss Erin isn't cut out for wild parties. She's not the sort of woman your brother likes, and that's in her favor. He's a rounder, Miss Annie. He won't settle. Not for years."

"I know," Annie replied. "I'd hoped it was the beginning of something beautiful. But Erin said she'd been hoping, too, but that he was in a rush to get her home. They didn't even eat dessert."

"Maybe that's a good thing, too," the housekeeper told her. "Mr. Ty had been drinking. You never know what men will get up to with a little alcohol in them. He probably hadn't had time to drink much before he brought Miss Erin home."

"And a good thing he did, because her father was on the floor unconscious. He'd had a stroke. Imagine if it had been hours later. He might have been dead. Erin would never have forgiven herself."

"That's true. Poor old man." She shook her head. "But it's like they say, you know. When your time's up, it's up. No matter where you are, what you're doing, that's it."

"So they say," Annie agreed.

Erin parked in the driveway at the address she'd taken from the advertisement. It was a nice part of San Antonio, mostly old houses with front porches and lots of trees. They stood a little apart and there was a paved sidewalk. Erin loved it at once.

She rang the doorbell. There was a pause, and then a slightly overweight lady with bright blue eyes and silver hair in a bun opened the door. Erin almost laughed because the woman was wearing a golden cross identical to the one Erin always wore. She usually kept it inside her blouse, but she'd dropped her keys and it had fallen out.

The other woman's eyes fell on the cross at once. She beamed. "I'm Mrs. Mallory," she said, extending a hand.

Erin shook it. "I'm Erin Mitchell. Thank you for letting me interview so quickly."

"Oh, I'm on my last legs," she explained, offering Erin a seat in the living room on the big, plush sofa.

She perched on an armchair. "You see, I lost my husband a few months ago."

"I'm so sorry," Erin said genuinely. "I've just lost my father. Believe me, I know how it is."

Mrs. Marlowe smiled. "Thank you. I'm sorry for you as well.

But the problem is that I'm in debt up to my eyes and probate is taking a long time. I need the rent money to pay my bills, so I need to rent the rooms soon. That sounds mercenary and I'm sorry. But it's the honest truth."

"I don't mind honesty," Erin laughed. "I'm in something of a bind myself. But never mind that. What would you like to know about me?"

"I already know most of what I need to know," the landlady said mysteriously. "Where do you work?"

"At a construction company over on Melrose Street," Erin replied, and named it. "I do cost estimates."

"Oh, you're one of those brainy people," Mrs. Marlowe laughed.

"Not me. I'm just good at math." She smiled.

"How long have you worked there?"

"Since I was in high school," Erin replied. "The owner's sister and I are best friends."

"I see."

Erin laughed. "It only got my foot in the door. Ty wants people who can do the job, he doesn't play favorites and he only hires on the basis of ability. I had to go to school to learn how to do the job I have now."

"How very strange," the landlady laughed. "It seems to me that these days we hire for an agenda and we punish ability."

Erin shook her head. "It does indeed seem that way."

"Can you cook?"

"Yes, I can," Erin said. "I have my coffee pot and my sauté pan and my waffle iron and my Crock-Pot in my trunk."

Mrs. Marlowe's eyes widened.

"I'll explain later. It's rather a complicated story."

"I can hardly wait!" She laughed. "So." She told Erin how much she was asking for the apartment, which was much less than the house payment she'd been making for her father's house.

"That seems a bit low," Erin said.

Mrs. Marlowe's eyebrows arched. "Well, I don't really need a lot of extra money, and so many people are living on the streets that I thought I could offer some kind soul a nice place they could afford." She leaned forward. "But I've already interviewed twenty people. And oh my goodness, I'd be afraid to turn out the lights at night if any one of them was inside here with me!"

Erin burst out laughing. "I can tell you that my boss interviewed several people for a job opening, and he said the same thing."

"It's a dangerous world, now, to be sure," she agreed. "Do you want the apartment?" she asked then and smiled.

"I do indeed. And you can have the first month's rent in advance. Plus, do I pay for utilities?"

"No, they're included," Mrs. Marlowe said gently. "May I ask, do you go to church?"

She nodded, smiling. "My great-grandparents founded our local methodist church in Jacobsville, Texas. Both my parents taught Sunday school."

"My great-grandmother was one of the first members of our local Baptist church. But that's okay," she added. "We were never prejudiced against Methodists!"

And they both laughed.

The apartment was big and had its own bathroom. It was nicely furnished as well, and the window overlooked a birdbath and a bird feeder.

"You have a birdbath!" Erin exclaimed. "Oh, my poor birds back home. I hope the people who buy dad's house will feed them!"

"You had to sell your home?"

Erin turned with a sigh. "My father was frivolous. He was a lovely man, but not street smart. He got into day-trading without my knowledge. He lost everything, including our house. The sheriff's department came yesterday with an eviction notice. I had no idea. I had to get everything out by this morning, which I did, barely. It's all in storage. It was…something of a shock," she added on a sigh.

"Oh, my dear," Mrs. Marlowe said, shaking her head. "I am so sorry for you!"

"It's all right," Erin assured her. "Because I now have an apartment with a view and no more high mortgage payments and utility bills. And I also have a birdbath right outside my window," she laughed.

Mrs. Marlowe just smiled. "We are going to get along very well indeed," she said. "Oh, I forgot. I have Clarence…!" she added worriedly.

"Clarence?"

"He's my cat…"

"I love cats!" Erin said. "We had one several years ago, named Ducky. He was twenty-one when he died and we were all so sad that we didn't want to risk getting another one."

"You can share Clarence," Mrs. Marlowe said. "He loves women."

Erin smiled. "Thank you for letting me have the apartment."

"Oh, I knew I was going to do that when I spoke to you last night," she said. "I'm not a bad judge of people." Those blue eyes twinkled. "I was a policewoman in San Antonio for twelve years."

"I feel ever so safe now, and I promise never to speed in town." Erin grinned.

Mrs. Marlowe laughed.

Erin settled in at Mrs. Marlowe's house. They shared cooking chores and got along beautifully. In the evenings, Mrs. Marlowe got out her knitting and they watched a program with dragons that they both liked.

When she was younger, Erin's mother had taught her how to crochet. So she stopped by a craft shop on the way home one evening and bought yarn and needles. That night, she and Mrs. Marlowe both had something to do with their hands while they watched television.

Erin got her father's car changed over into her name and renewed the license. She got probate underway as well. The ad ran in the county organ for any creditors to come forward, and Erin held her breath, praying that her father hadn't run up even more debts that she didn't know about. But as time passed, nothing new came in. Existing debts were paid, and death certificates sent to the appropriate authorities. She cried less.

It was almost two months after the funeral when Ty got back to town. Annie had been watching the same series on pay per view that Erin and Mrs. Marlowe watched, because she loved dragons, too. So she was in the middle of the latest episode when Ty came in the front door.

He paused to pet old Rhodes and young Beauregard before he stalked into the living room where Annie was sitting.

"How are you?" she asked.

His eyes were sparking like broken electrical wires. He looked livid. "Don't ask."

"That bad, huh?"

"I just got off the phone with the detective agency. I know who sold me out."

"Who?" she asked, worried that it might really be his friend Mr. Jones.

"Your best friend."

"Erin?!" she exclaimed, turning off the television. "Ty, that's not possible!"

"I have sworn statements," he said shortly. "If she wasn't your best friend, I'd have had her arrested."

"But..." Annie was all at sea. It was such a shock. "But why would she need to sell her house and her car and move to an apartment if she made money by selling you out?" she asked bluntly.

He stared at her. "What?"

She drew in a breath. "Her father died," she said.

"Yes, I read about it in a San Antonian newspaper. I had the office send flowers."

She glared at him. "I sent flowers and went to the funeral."

He averted his eyes.

"Anyway," she continued, "Erin had to sell the house and let her car go back to the dealer because her father lost everything they had at day-trading without telling her. He even looted both their savings and checking accounts."

He felt a twinge of regret for that. "But it doesn't change the fact that she sold me out," he said, turning. "Mr. Taylor was shocked as well, but his agent had signed statements from both the company that put out the bid and the owner as well," he said. "They both said that Erin passed the preliminary bid along to them before my actual bid went out."

Annie just looked at him.

"I know what you're going to say, that she's your friend and she'd never do anything like that," Ty said coldly. "But I know more about your friend than you do. And there are a lot of things she'd do that you don't know about." He got up. "She's getting fired tomorrow. I won't prosecute, although I probably could, for industrial theft."

He went up the staircase two steps at a time. He was feeling raw. It hurt to think that Erin would have betrayed him to such an extent. But then, she'd slept with him, hadn't she? A woman with so-called sterling morals would hardly have done that while betraying him at the same time. And she'd admitted to him that it wasn't the first time she'd done it. So, no, Annie didn't really know her best friend that well. And he wasn't having Erin in his office one minute longer than he had to.

Erin, meanwhile, had thrown up her breakfast on Sunday morning and felt weak and sick all day. Her landlady had suggested a doctor, but Erin was sure it was only a virus.

Until the next morning, when she stopped by a twenty-four-hour pharmacy to get a pregnancy diagnostic kit. She dreaded using it. It had been two months since her reckless encounter with Ty. But it was necessary. If she really was pregnant, she had to get out of San Antonio.

She went into the restroom when she arrived, several minutes early, to work. She used the kit. The little field that colored was the right color for certain pregnancy. She read it again and again, with the same result. She was pregnant. What did she do now?

She tucked the kit into the bottom of the trash bin, where, hopefully, it would go unnoticed by anybody except the cleaning staff. And there were plenty of women, married and single, in the company. No way would it point to Erin.

She went to her desk and turned on her computer. But when she put her password in, nothing happened. She tried again. The system must be glitched, she decided. But five minutes later, her intercom sounded and she heard Ty's deep voice for the first time in two months.

"Miss Mitchell, come to my office, please."

"Yes, sir," she said professionally.

She got up from her desk, a little dizzy, and took a deep breath. She knew when Ty was angry. His voice got deeper, and slower, and that tone usually preceded an explosion of some magnitude. She wondered what she'd done that had caused it.

His office seemed larger than ever. He was sitting behind his desk, leaning back in his chair, his powerful body displayed beautifully in a gray suit with a spotless white shirt and blue paisley tie. His hair was trimmed, he looked sexy and handsome and it hurt Erin to remember how tender he could be, how expert…

She stopped the thoughts at once. "Yes, sir?" she asked, because he didn't smile.

"Sit down."

He indicated the chair in front of the desk. She perched on the very edge of it.

He pushed some papers toward her and indicated that she should look at them.

She pulled them to her, picked them up, and prayed that she wouldn't pass out when she read them.

"I didn't sell you out," she said quietly as she finished reading and pushed the papers back to him. She lifted her chin proudly.

"Really?" he asked, and he smiled coldly. "You wear couture clothes and your father paid cash for a late-model used car. Where did the money come from?"

"Dad sold our house," she said.

"I noticed the For Sale sign," he said. "So you spent all the money already, did you?"

"My father lost it, doing day-trading."

"After getting all that money for giving my bid to the opposition, and your father spent every penny of it?" he asked, his voice deep and grating. He lifted the papers and shook them. "This is positive proof that you sold me out!"

His voice was like a whip. He took a deep breath. "Positive proof." She just looked at him. "I've been like part of your family since I was in my early teens. And you think I could do this?"

"Why not?" he asked, his eyes narrow and piercing. "You slept with me, didn't you? Where were your sterling morals then?"

She had no defense, short of telling him she loved him. And that she was carrying his child. Neither fact would have moved him, because he wouldn't have believed them. His face was like stone. He was furious and barely able to contain it.

She got to her feet slowly, staggering a little because the nausea was ever present. She noticed his sudden glance, but she pulled herself up and fought to control it. "Do I work two weeks' notice?" she asked, almost inhumanly calm.

His face tautened. "You can go. I'll have your check waiting for you at the front desk."

"It isn't necessary," she said with what pride she had left.

"It's company rules," he said shortly. "I made them myself."

He got up. "I hope it goes without saying that you're no longer welcome at the ranch, regardless of what my sister tells you." He smiled coldly. "You wouldn't want me to tell her about our little escapade at the cabin, and blow her image of you to bits, now would you?"

"Annie wouldn't be judgmental," she said weakly.

"Show up at my front door, and you can see for yourself." He meant the threat. It was in his eyes.

"I won't ever do that," she said. She studied his hard face. "One day, you'll know the truth. But it will be too late."

"And what's that supposed to mean?" he drawled.

"Exactly what I said." Her teeth clenched. "If our positions were reversed, I'd know you were innocent, and I'd defend you to the death. There's a reason for that. But you won't understand it, I know."

He frowned. "You're talking in circles," he said shortly. "But it won't save you. I know you're guilty. I have proof. If you and Annie weren't best friends, I'd haul you into court for industrial espionage."

"Do it," she said quietly. "I dare you. Do it. And whoever wrote up that report, and falsified it, will go to jail in my place."

"A respected detective agency doesn't falsify information!" he said and slammed his hand down on the desk.

Erin caught the back of her chair and held on until the dizziness passed. Apparently she was going to have to avoid shocks. Well, at least she'd never have to avoid this one, again.

"What's wrong with you?" he asked angrily and with a gram of guilt for startling her. "Drinking so early in the day?"

She straightened and took a deep breath. "Of course. I drink, I sleep around, and then I go to church every Sunday and sing in the choir." She said the last with a droll look that caught him off guard.

She turned and walked to the door.

"Why did you do it?" he asked, exasperated.

She turned and looked at him sadly. "The only bad thing I've ever done was to…" She bit down hard on the rest. "Goodbye, Mr. Mosby."

She went out and closed the door.

He stared at it, infuriated. Why wouldn't she confess? It wasn't as if the detective agency would lie to a client. The agency would lose all its business!

He called down to accounting and had them issue her two weeks' pay and told them to have it ready at the front desk as soon as possible.

He leaned back in his chair and grimaced. He shouldn't have thrown Erin's passionate response to him back in her face. Yes, she'd always been clean cut, above wild parties and drinking. She was in church every Sunday. She lived her faith. So how had she fallen so far so fast? The detective agency said that she'd been paid thousands for the information about the bid. Where was it? If she was having to sell the house…

Well, her father had lost it all day-trading, he surmised. So much for any evidence that she wasn't guilty. Anyway, it was over and done with. Annie would nag him about it, but he wasn't letting Erin get away with selling him out. If it hadn't been for her friendship with his sister, he'd have had her prosecuted. So why did he feel so guilty? She should feel guilty! Perhaps she did. She'd almost fainted when his hand hit the desk. He felt bad about that. She'd looked unwell. He should have controlled his temper better than that. He was disheartened and angry that he'd trusted Erin. It had poured out of him like water. But he did feel unsettled about her reaction when he'd banged on the desk. He shouldn't have done it. In spite of everything, she'd just lost her only parent and her house. And now her job.

He cursed under his breath. He'd fired her when she was sick. It made him feel worse. He got up and went downstairs to the accounting office. He wanted to make sure that Erin had gotten her check.

CHAPTER EIGHT

Erin was shell-shocked. She sat in her car, staring at the check for two weeks' pay, wondering what in the world she was going to do now. She had a nice apartment and no job. She was pregnant. She couldn't afford to stay in San Antonio, but she would have to, while probate was going on, and she had to do something about the furniture.

She wanted to call Annie, but that would cause big problems for her friend. Ty was relentless when he went after people who cheated him. He thought Erin had. It wouldn't matter that she and Annie had been friends for years. He wouldn't relent.

Well, there was the Perrin Agency. They'd tried a couple of times to get her to quit Ty and come to work for them. She didn't dare ask Ty for a reference but maybe she could get a job there without one. Mr. Perrin knew her.

She went to his office and asked to see him. She only had to wait a few minutes before he ushered her into his office with a big smile.

"Erin Mitchell. I'm delighted to see you," he teased, the light making his white hair silvery as he sat down behind his desk.

"Dare I hope that you've had a tiff with Ty and you want to come to work for me?"

She burst out laughing. "My goodness, does it show that much?" she asked.

"I'm afraid so. But even if you only stay briefly, I'll love having you here. When can you start?"

"Right now?" she asked hopefully.

He was taken aback. But then he grinned and got up. "Right now is excellent! Come along with me and I'll get you a desk and some assignments!"

"Thank you!" she said.

"No need. And no need to explain why you're here," he added on a chuckle. "I just pray that Ty doesn't come to his senses soon."

So did Erin.

So she went to work for Mr. Perrin. And for three whole weeks, she enjoyed her new job and got through with probate, including being assigned executrix of her father's will and getting legal documents that were required, such as death certificates and letters testamentary. It was a tiring process and she was happy to have it done.

Her house had already been sold. She lamented its loss, but it wasn't unexpected. She'd called Barbara at Barbara's Café to see about it.

"Why aren't you living there?" Barbara asked. "And why didn't you call Annie and ask her? She's your best friend."

"Because I'm on the outs with her brother," Erin said on a sigh, "and Dad lost the house playing at day-trading. He lost everything."

"Oh, you poor kid," Barbara said softly. "I'm so sorry."

"Me, too, but it was just a house, you know. Memories are portable."

"So they are. You're still working for Ty's company, aren't you?"

"Well, no, that's part of the problem. We've had a difference of opinion. I'm working for Perrin Enterprises now."

"Ty's loss," Barbara said at once. "And serves him right! That womanizer," she added on a huffy note. "Any sensible woman would run from a man like that. Thank goodness he never had his eye on you! Your poor late mama would have had a fit. She loved Ty, but she said he'd do nothing but break hearts, and he'd never marry."

"That's probably true," Erin said softly. "Thanks for the information about the house. Any idea who bought it?"

"Not really. It was some out-of-town Realtor. There's nobody living in it yet, though."

"Will you call me when they do? I don't want to go down to Jacobsville right now. I'd put Annie in a bad spot with her brother. I don't dare even call her right now." That was true. She wouldn't even answer text messages from Annie. She just sent heart emojis instead of words.

"I'll call you," Barbara said. "You take care of yourself."

"You do the same. Thanks."

Her pregnancy was slowing her down just a little bit. At least she was able to keep it hidden from her landlady. She went to a doctor and bought vitamins she would need and a prescription nausea medicine at a pharmacy where she wasn't known.

At least she had a job, she told herself. She'd be able to provide for her baby. She wanted it very much, from the day she'd discovered she was pregnant. She could never have Ty. He would never love her. But she would have a baby, a gift from heaven, someone to love with all her heart who would love her back. She was overwhelmed with joy. And not able to tell a single living soul about it. That was the saddest part.

It was her third week at Perrin Enterprises when she was called into Mr. Perrin's office. He wasn't smiling.

"Erin, why were you let go at Ty's company?" he asked point blank.

"Because he had a private detective dig out information about a bid he lost, and I was accused of giving it in advance to the company that won the bid for the job. I did not do it," she added with quiet pride. "But the detective agency had sworn statements that said I did." She smiled sadly. "I would have cut off an arm before I'd have betrayed Ty," she said. "I've loved him since I was thirteen years old. Not that it's ever helped. He likes variety."

Perrin scowled. She didn't talk or act like a guilty person. And what she said about her feelings for Ty wasn't false. It had been a rumor around the local construction companies ever since Erin had started work there.

"Nobody believes me," Erin told him quietly. "I know it looks bad. If you want me to resign, I will." She took a breath. "It might be a good idea to just get out of San Antonio for a while, until things cool down. Maybe when Ty has time to think about it rationally, he'll dig a little deeper into his so-called positive information from the detective agency. He said he wouldn't prosecute me for industrial theft, but I should have insisted that he do it. I'm not guilty. His attorney would have to prove that I was, and under oath, he couldn't."

She looked innocent to him. He knew a lot about her, because his parents were from Jacobsville and still had ties there. She wasn't the sort of sleazy person who sold out people who cared about them. Not that Ty did, or he'd have believed her. Perrin did.

"I don't mind keeping you on," he said, and was thinking how difficult that could be if Ty passed around the information Ty had given him over the phone that morning.

"I'd just make trouble for you, maybe cost you clients," she replied. "Ty called you, didn't he?"

He nodded.

She sighed. "He has breakfast most mornings at Barbara's

Café. She must have mentioned where I was working to him. But he'd have called you sooner or later," she said philosophically. "He's very thorough when he pursues people. He called every single auto shop in south Texas about a mechanic who did a sloppy job on his Jaguar. It probably saved lives, but the mechanic couldn't get work. He moved out of state."

"Probably won't help a lot," Perrin sighed. "I've seen some results of Ty's impatience with people who cheat him or hurt people close to him. Chilling."

"It is. I just never dreamed I'd be on the wrong side of his temper, and for something I didn't even do." She got up. "Thanks for believing me," she said simply. "My word used to be enough to defend me. Not anymore. Not with Ty."

"Where will you go?" he asked.

"I have a distant cousin in Wyoming," she said, smiling. "She lives on a ranch, way out in the country. She's invited me to stay, because she's all alone now. I'm going to take her up on her offer. I've never needed to get away from things more than I do right now."

He got up and offered his hand. She shook it.

"I've enjoyed having you here. And you'll get a month's advance wages, Ty can stick that in his…well, never mind where," he chuckled. "I wish you all the best."

"Same to you, Mr. Perrin. I've enjoyed working here."

"Maybe in a few months you could come back to work for me," he said with a grin.

"Maybe in a few months, I just might," she laughed.

She picked up her check and sat in her car. Ty was vindictive. He would never stop getting her thrown out of jobs as long as she was in Texas. So the best thing for her right now was to get out of Texas.

She took out her cell phone, looked for Maude's number, and

texted her. The reply was immediate. Come now. Do you need an airplane ticket?

She laughed and texted back, No. I have enough. But I'm going to need a job.

Not a problem. You can keep the books here. The ranch is going under without my husband's keen math skills!

Erin hesitated. She had to tell the truth. There's just one more thing. I'm a little bit pregnant. And I don't want anybody here to know it.

Ty Mosby, damn it! came the reply.

Erin caught her breath. Maude knew her almost too well.

Does he know? Maude texted back.

No. And he won't. Ever. It's my baby.

There was a pause. You'll need a fictional husband.

I was just thinking that, she replied. It would be necessary to keep Ty from making connections in case Annie found out about the pregnancy and told him.

How about a husband in the military who didn't make it out of Afghanistan?

Perfect. He had my same last name except we weren't related, Erin fabricated. So I don't have to change my name in a dozen legal places.

Pure genius, Maude texted back, and Erin could almost hear her laughing.

Come tomorrow, Maude said. Text me when you're at the airport and I'll send one of the boys to pick you up.

Will do. Thanks, Maude, she typed.

You're my very favorite distant cousin, came the reply. Besides, I'm lonely and going broke for lack of an accountant.

I can solve both problems, Erin typed, smiling. See you tomorrow.

The hardest thing was telling her landlady that she was leaving town. She wanted to be honest with the sweet lady, so she told her everything, including about the baby.

"You poor child," the older woman said sorrowfully. "Is there no chance that you can prove you're innocent?"

"I could if I could make him prosecute me," she said. "The detective who put out that false information could face some jail time. But I can't let Ty know about the baby," she said, putting a hand protectively over her tiny baby bump. "I don't know what he'd do," she added, her eyes tearing up. "He might insist on an abortion, he was that mad at me for what he thought I did. I can't risk it. I want my baby so much!"

"What will you do?"

"Invent a husband in the military and pretend to be married. It's the only way," she said on a sigh. "Plus I have to leave town. I can't risk having Ty see me."

"I'll miss you," the older lady said solemnly, tearing up.

"I'll miss you, too. But you'll find another renter," she said gently. "There are scores of nice people in the world, and you only have to find one!"

"I already did. But she's moving to Wyoming," came the reply.

And they both laughed.

After a tearful farewell, and a long hug, Erin got into a cab to take her to the airport. She'd sold her car, which gave her a little ready cash. She'd left her pots and pans, the Crock-Pot and the waffle maker and coffee pot with her landlady, plus an extra week's rent to help her along. It was such a sad world, with prices so high and fixed incomes so low. She hoped the landlady would find a nice renter soon.

She got on the plane without looking back out at San Antonio. It was a wrench to leave the place where she'd worked since high school. Not only was she leaving the job behind, she was leaving a history behind. Both her parents were buried in the Methodist Church cemetery down in Jacobsville, along with both sets of her grandparents and great-grandparents. She had a long history in Jacobs County. She didn't want to leave it, but she had no choice. Her immediate need was to get away from anybody who knew her, who might tell Annie or Ty how her waistline was expanding. Annie would know at once why and who. In fact, so would Ty. But if she got to Wyoming and broadcast about her poor late husband, and wore a wedding ring and pretended to mourn the nonexistent mate, perhaps word would get back to Texas through people who had relatives around Catelow. There were several, including the sheriff of Carne County, Wyoming, who had relatives in Jacobsville. Word would get around. Even men gossiped.

All Erin had to do was get through her pregnancy and not worry about being seen as a traitor in the eyes of the only man she'd ever loved. One day, he'd know the truth, she told herself. And he'd pay for the misery he'd caused her. He'd pay dearly.

Maude had sent her foreman to the airport to pick up Erin. He was a tall, solemn-looking man in his mid-thirties, muscular without it being obvious, with dark eyes set deeply in a handsome face with an olive complexion. A pretty woman was giving him the eye nearby, but he never even looked in her direction. Justin TwoBears was apparently impervious.

As Erin came down the ramp from the plane, into the concourse, he seemed to recognize her at once.

"Miss Mitchell?" he asked politely, tipping his hat. The hair under it was black and thick. He had a face that resembled the one on old silver nickels.

She smiled. "Yes. Do I look that obviously out of place?" she asked.

He pulled out his cell phone and showed her a picture of herself that Maude had snapped at Arthur Mitchell's funeral.

"I see," she said.

"Do you have luggage besides this?" he asked, taking the rolling bag from her gently.

"Yes, I'm afraid so. I had to bring my whole wardrobe. There are two suitcases…"

"No problem. I threw a nine-hundred-pound bull just this morning," he said, tongue-in-cheek and without breaking stride.

She grinned. Maude chose her employees well, it seemed.

"This is glorious," she said as they whizzed down the long highway in a new truck equipped with everything, including heated seats. But she was looking out the window, not at the truck.

In the distance were snow-capped mountains.

"There's snow on the mountains in summer?" she exclaimed, looking toward the driver.

"There's snow every month of the year, up that high," he replied. "I've seen tourists parked on the side of the road in July, playing in the snow."

"We don't get much snow where I live. Where I lived," she amended sadly.

"I heard about your dad. I'm sorry."

"So am I. He was naïve about money, but he was a wonderful father."

"It hurts when we lose the old ones in our families," he said. "They carry our history. Very often, we save important questions until it's too late to ask them."

"Yes, we do," she agreed.

He felt her eyes and shrugged. "My people are Lakota," he

said. "My parents are dead, but my mother still lives on the Wapiti Reservation up in Montana."

"Your history must be eloquent," she said quietly.

Both eyebrows rose. She'd shocked him. "What do you mean?"

She turned a little in her seat. "What I mean is that your culture suffered a major defeat. So did mine. I come from south Texas, but my ancestors came there after the Civil War, from Georgia. We both come from cultures that suffered defeat."

He took a breath. "That never occurred to me."

"It doesn't, as a rule. My father was stationed in Okinawa when he was a teenager, just inducted into the military. He said he got on well with the Japanese because they also had that common history. It was tragic in one respect and inescapable in another."

"I've been to Japan," he said, surprising her. "And I wanted to go to China," he said. "Mostly because of the language. I wanted to see if there were any similarities between my native tongue and theirs." He chuckled. "I found an internet site that taught Chinese, so I enrolled. There are many similarities."

"Chinese is tonal, isn't it?" she asked. One of their former employees had been Chinese and taught her few words.

He glanced at her as they turned onto a long, winding dirt road. "Yes, it is. Do you speak it?"

"Oh, no," she said. "We had an accountant who was Chinese. She taught me a few words." She chuckled. "I'm not sure if any of them could be used in mixed company. She had a vicious sense of humor from time to time. But she was a lovely person. She loved flowers."

"She loved flowers." He thought about that. "Is that a character reference?"

"It is to me," she said with a smile. "People who plant things are nurturing people for the most part."

"Yes, they are," he replied. "My mother plants hibiscus every spring when the weather warms."

"Hibiscus?" she exclaimed. "But they can't live this far north, surely…!"

"Oh, she digs them up and puts them in a pot and brings them inside before the first frost," he said easily. "She has a sun spectrum light for them, in their own room." He chuckled. "It used to be my room. Now, when I visit, it's the flowers' room and mine."

"Well, if sun spectrum lights make things grow, it certainly explains your height," she said, laughing.

He shook his head. "I guess so. There's the ranch."

It was breathtaking. What seemed like miles of fence with pastures full of black cattle. There was a windmill, which made her homesick for Texas already. As they pulled up into the yard, she got a good view of the house. It was like a giant log cabin, but with modern touches like double window panes. It had picture windows in what might be the living room, and there was a huge porch where a rocking chair and a settee took pride of place. There were pots of flowers growing there as well.

"That's Maude, all right, all those flowers," she sighed.

"Yes, and you should see the men carrying them inside before the first frost, groaning all the way."

Before she could answer him, Maude came out onto the porch. "I'm so happy to see you!" she exclaimed, coming down the steps carefully as Erin held on to the handle inside the truck door and stepped down carefully to the ground, smiling politely at the foreman as she declined help. His eyes were on her left hand, the one she was holding onto the handle with.

"You married?" he asked.

She grimaced. "I was," she said softly, and averted her eyes. "He was in Afghanistan…"

"Sorry," he bit off at once.

"No worries. You didn't know. I can't talk about it just yet."

Maude ran up and hugged her. "I'm so glad you decided to come!" she exclaimed. "You can heal here." She looked at the tall man.

"Justin, the washing machine is dancing in the laundry room and I think the belt is loose in the dryer..."

"No sooner said than done. I'll get Tandy up to fix it right now." He smiled at her, tipped his hat to both women, and started carrying in Erin's luggage."

Maude pulled her to one side. "Did you tell him about your 'husband'?" she asked.

"He spotted the ring," she replied. "I bought it in San Antonio before I left town."

"What are we going to call your late husband, so I'll know..."

"Benedict Arnold...?"

Maude pretended to hit her. "Stop that. We have to have a name."

"Oh, how about Richard? I had a crush on a boy named Richard in third grade. He wouldn't mind. He moved to Maine with his family when I was in fourth grade."

Maude laughed. "Okay. We can call him Dick, can't we?"

"He's career military," Erin said, making it up as she went. "We have to call him Richard. Richard Mitchell."

"Ok. That works. How are you?" she added with some worry. "You've had a very rough time and you haven't even gotten over losing your dad yet. All that stress," she groaned.

"I'm tough when I have to be," Erin said. She sighed. "But I must admit, I'm very happy to be here. It's like another world. Another life. Another chance," she added quietly.

"I know it's hard for you, losing your husband with a baby on the way," Maude said just as Justin came back to the truck. "But you'll be safe here. I'll take good care of you."

"Stop that, mother hen," Erin laughed. "I can take care of myself. And I'll take care of your books!"

"She doesn't read," Justin said with a snarly look at Maude.

"At least I would read in English, if I read! And I do read! I just do it with real, actual, paper books!"

"Poor damned trees," Justin muttered.

"Poor damned ex-foreman looking for a new job," Maude shot right back.

"Wouldn't bother me," he said nonchalantly. "Was looking for a job when I found this one, wasn't I?"

"Reprobate!"

"Muleskinner."

She threw up her hands. Justin just grinned, glanced at Erin with a raised eyebrow, and climbed back into the truck. He was gone before Maude stopped muttering.

"He seems very nice," Erin told her over coffee—decaf for Erin—at Maude's little kitchen table while she made supper. "Your foreman, I mean."

"He's a good man. A little naïve about women," she said with a sigh. "He had an episode that I know he'd rather forget. They actually got engaged. Then he overheard what she said to a girlfriend. He was a novelty, she told her girlfriend. She was spending the summer with her grandad here in Carne County, and she liked to flirt with men. So when she was ready to go back east to Princeton to work on her degree in social studies, what she'd learned from him would stand her in good stead with her professors. She had firsthand knowledge of how native people felt about the world and how they expressed their culture and religion among themselves. It was a look into a very secretive culture. It was too bad that she had to involve herself with one of them to do it, and she'd had to make sure she wasn't seen with him at any place she was known." Maude drew in a breath. "Can you imagine how he must have felt?"

"I'll bet he was out of it for days," Erin replied.

"Two months," Maude corrected. "He almost went over the edge. One of the local girls who comes here to help with branding and tagging saw him with a revolver in his hand—that big .45 double action Colt that he wears on his hip when the men are working in areas where they've found snakes. She knew about the failed romance and went looking for him. He actually had the barrel in his mouth when she jumped on him and pushed it away. There's still a bullet hole in the barn where it happened."

"Thank goodness he was seen in time!"

"The bullet grazed the girl's arm. She had to be taken to the emergency room. He was too impaired to drive but he insisted on going with her and one of the ranch hands. She told them she'd been practicing with a pistol and accidentally shot herself." Maude shook her head. "It was a real incident. The sheriff got called in because it was a gunshot wound—they have to report those. So Justin pulled Cody Banks to one side and told him the truth. No charges were ever filed. But Justin was furious that she'd risked her life to save his. She got a lecture. She just smiled and went on with her job, despite the bandage and the pain."

"There are so many miserable people in the world who love the wrong people," Erin said sadly.

Maude gave her a knowing look as she turned steak on the griddle and then bent to take her potato casserole out of the oven. "Smart, aren't you?"

"He's a nice man," Erin said quietly. "It's good that somebody cares if he lives or dies."

Maude left the steaks for a minute to finish her coffee. "Speaking of the wrong people, what happened that sent you up here so quickly. Besides the baby," she added.

She took a breath. "Ty accused me of selling him out to another company that bid for a big job in San Antonio. I didn't do it, but he hired a private detective agency that had notarized statements from two people who swore that I'd given them an advance look at Ty's bid, which he lost."

"Could they prove it?"

"No way," Erin said icily. "I should have made Ty take me to court. They'd have been in some big trouble if they'd tried to prove those documents were real."

"That's what I thought. But you were working for another company…?"

"Ty called my boss and told him what I was alleged to have done. Mr. Perrin didn't believe him either, but it was going to affect his business if he kept me on, with rumors flying that I'd sold out Ty's company for money." She smiled. "He offered to let me keep my job anyway. He didn't believe I'd done anything wrong." She looked up. "Isn't that something? A man I loved and would have died for thought I was guilty of selling him out. And a man I barely knew believed me and supported me." She shook her head. "Life is strange."

"It is," Maude agreed. "Well, you're here and safe and we'll all take care of you. Most of the people who work for me are second generation cowhands. Justin has been here since he was a teenager. He ran away from home. His father was a terror."

"He drank?" Erin asked.

"Far worse. He had serious mental issues. He hated alcohol. But he loved beating his son. He never believed that Justin was his son in the first place. He was brutal to the boy. So Justin got tired of seeing his mother cry her eyes out, and he drifted down here, looking for work. My Sam hired him at once. We never were able to have kids, so Justin sort of filled that spot for us. He still does. We go back and forth, but it's all in fun. I'd do anything for him."

"The reverse is also true, I imagine," Erin replied, smiling. "I like him."

Maude raised both eyebrows.

Erin shook her head. "I'll die loving Ty Mosby. Not that he deserves it." Her hand went to her stomach. "He'll never know his own child. But I'll know. And I won't tell."

"I know you're bitter. A few months here and you'll start to mellow. I'll bet by spring you'll even be able to smile like you mean it."

Erin forced a smile. Maude went back to oversee the steaks.

★ ★ ★

Justin was a walking encyclopedia of Wyoming. He knew all the native plants and pointed them out to Erin when he walked with her down the long paths on the ranch as the baby grew.

"You never talk about your husband," he said out of the blue.

"Hurts too much," she replied.

"How did he die?" he asked bluntly.

She hesitated. This was something she and Maude hadn't discussed. She'd have to remember whatever she told Justin so that she could tell Maude in time. "He was in a military vehicle. It ran over a…a bomb."

"And IED?" he asked.

She looked at him blankly. Had she said something wrong?

"Improvised explosive device," he replied. "We had them in Iraq when I was there in 2010."

She stopped walking and turned to him. "Iraq?" she asked gently.

He drew in a breath. "I don't talk about it," he said with a sad smile. "Nobody who was in combat there talks about it, except maybe with other veterans. It's not for civilians' ears."

"Oh." She started walking again. "Were you in the army?"

"Yes. Sort of," he added.

She looked up at him with raised eyebrows.

He just smiled, that faint echo of a smile that was a hallmark of his restrained personality.

"I see," she teased. "Not for civilian ears."

"Got that right," he said. "How much farther you going to walk?"

"Not far. Why? You got something important to do?"

"Depends."

"On what?" she asked, pausing.

"On whether or not she forgets what she asked me to do."

"Maude?" she asked.

"No," he said, looking over her shoulder as the sound of a horse's hooves came closer. "Her."

CHAPTER NINE

The girl who rode up on the sleek bay mare wasn't beautiful. She had pleasant features, though, including her long thick light blond hair and her pale gray eyes. It was obvious that she didn't wear makeup. And as far as Erin could decide, she didn't need it. She had a complexion that rivaled anything seen on television heroines.

"Gabby, I've warned you about that mare," Justin said, looking up at her sternly.

The girl grimaced. "I know, but Baddy's got Bess and Johnson just took out Harley, so Jessie was the only horse left."

"You're too soft for a spirited horse," he continued, unabated. "She'll throw you and walk back to the barn."

She lifted her chin. "I can handle her."

He just sighed.

She shifted in the saddle. "Hi," she added belatedly as she looked at Erin, and smiled. "I'm Gabriel Dane, except everybody calls me Gabby. Aren't you Mrs. Mitchell?" the girl asked her gently and smiled. "We heard about you coming up to live with Maude. I'm sorry about your husband."

Erin put a hand on her slightly swollen waistline and drew in a sigh. "Thanks," she said. "I'm sorry about it, too." She wasn't kidding. She was still furious at Ty for believing lies about her, but she couldn't stop loving him. That would take more strength than she had.

"Did you ask her?" she asked Justin.

He lifted an eyebrow. "Since you came anyway, you can ask her yourself."

Erin looked from one face to the other. "Ask me what?" she wanted to know.

Gabby Carlson grimaced. "Well, you see, Daddy wants to build a new house. I do, too, but I'm not sure we have enough in the bank to do it. Daddy, well, he doesn't handle money well. Mama did, but she's been gone for two years." She looked up. "You worked for a contractor and Maude said you knew how to figure a job's cost down to the penny. So I was wondering...hoping..."

Erin just smiled. "Of course I will. Just get me some basic information about the materials you want, a plan of the house, the name of the business where you buy your building materials, and I'll do the rest."

"That would be super!" Gabby exclaimed, and her somber little face lit up like a butterfly's wing in bright sunlight. She was really pretty when she smiled. Something, Erin noted with suppressed humor, that her somber companion seemed to notice as well.

"Can you come over late tomorrow morning?" Erin asked. She smiled ruefully. "It's just that I stay tired all the time, so I sleep late to compensate."

"Should you be walking?" Gabby asked, all concern.

"Yes, that's what the obstetrician recommended," she said, because she was seeing one in Catelow who was highly recommended. "Exercise, exercise, so I can have the baby naturally." She grimaced. "He wants me to take Lamaze classes when I'm about five months along and I don't want to. It's something you do with husbands..." If only Ty had believed her. If only Ty had loved her. She'd be taking the classes with him, sharing every minute of the baby's growth. It hurt. A lot.

"Oh, no, not just husbands," Gabby said quickly. "My older sister—she lives up in Maine—got me to do them with her because her husband was active military. That was before he got out. Now he works in a bank." Her eyes widened. "Would you like me to take them with you? I wouldn't mind. I'm Dad's secretary, so my hours are flexible. He says I'm too spacy to be let loose on the world outside the ranch." She grinned. "I'm mostly obnoxious."

"She is," Justin agreed without cracking a smile.

"Not to you," she protested. "I even knitted you a cap to wear in the snow!"

"Cough…wrong size…cough," he returned.

"Well, if I'm obnoxious, you're reprehensible!" she tossed at him.

He smothered a laugh.

"So, I'll see you in the morning, Mrs. Mitchell," Gabby told Erin.

"Erin, not Mrs. Mitchell," she was corrected.

"Okay, then. Erin. See you!"

She turned the mare, who wasn't happy to go farther away from her stable.

"I told you…" Justin began.

The mare took off. "Bye!" Gabby called back as she held on to the reins. The horse was headed right back toward her father's ranch as if its tail was on fire. She was clinging to the mane and the reins, her long blond hair flying behind her.

"Oh, damnation!" Justin swore and slammed his hat down on the ground. "Why won't she listen?! She's going to get herself killed, riding horses she can't control!"

The show of passion from such a stoic man was surprising, and amusing. He had a temper that didn't frighten her. On the other hand, she recalled Ty slamming his hand down on his desk. She'd jumped. But she really hadn't been afraid of him, not even when he was furious. He'd never raised his hand to any woman. Certainly he wouldn't have hit Erin. Thinking about him hurt so much.

She forced a smile. "How old is she?" she asked Justin as he picked up his hat and brushed it off, still grumbling.

"Twenty-two going on thirteen," he muttered.

"Twenty-two isn't that young," she pointed out. "Not these days."

"It's young when you're thirty-six," he said with a wry smile. "Let's turn back. I've got to get the guys out to check on the breeding bulls. It's almost time to drive them north to new pasture."

"Suits me. Walking is good, but it's tiring."

"Only if you're pregnant," he said.

She just laughed. It was becoming clear to her that Gabby had feelings for Justin, and that he was fighting having any for her because he thought she was too young for him. She knew how that felt. She just hoped poor lovesick Gabby wouldn't get herself into the same predicament that Erin had. It would have been kinder if Ty had never asked her out at all. But knowing there was a tiny life inside her, she couldn't regret that impulse. The more the baby grew, the more she hungered for it to be born. She didn't know which sex it was, because she didn't want to know. She'd just make her crocheted baby things all yellow.

Annie had just found out that Erin had left Texas, from a Wyoming visitor who mentioned casually that a Jacobsville girl who'd married a man in the military was living with Cousin Maude in Carne County, Wyoming.

She was so stunned that she was quiet for thirty whole seconds. "Married? Pregnant?" she exclaimed, almost overbalancing the older man as she held him by the coat sleeves in Barbara's Café.

"Oh, yes," the man said, catching his breath. "She keeps the books for Maude. She doesn't talk much about her husband. He was in Afghanistan," he added quietly.

"I see." And Annie did. It had been a disastrous withdrawal.

"But she got married and never told me. Got pregnant and never told me." She was almost crying.

It was a slow afternoon. There was nobody in the place except Annie and this nice Hamilton man from Wyoming. Barbara overheard the conversation and came out from behind the counter.

"I hope I didn't get her in trouble," Barbara said. "I mentioned that she was working for the Perrin man in San Antonio. I heard from a girl who works there that your idiot brother," she said with some heat to Annie, "even called over there and told that tale about her stabbing him in the back and got her fired. That was two months, almost three months ago. So no wonder she hasn't been in touch with you. She probably figures you hate her, too."

Annie sat down heavily, fighting tears. "My brother did what?" she exclaimed.

"Got her fired," Barbara said flatly. "So I guess he put all the other contractors on notice that hiring Erin was a risk they shouldn't take."

"He never said a word to me," she said almost to herself. "Not one word. I thought she was still working in San Antonio. Every time I text her, I just get an emoji heart back. I thought maybe she was mad at me, too, because Ty fired her. But married, pregnant, Wyoming...!"

Barbara drew in a breath. "I'm sorry. But not for calling your brother an idiot. Everybody in Jacobsville except Ty knows that Erin's in love with him. Or she was. She's the last person who would ever have sold him out."

"I know that, too," Annie said heavily. "And no, I don't mind if you call my brother an idiot. Because he is an idiot!"

"You didn't know about her husband, either?" the Hamilton man asked. "They had the same last name, but they weren't related. They say she talks about him a lot these days. Still wears her wedding ring." He chuckled. "One of Maude's men is really soft on her, but all she talks about is her husband and the baby. It's due around Christmas. What a present she'll have!"

"Yes, indeed." Annie felt the sorrow all the way through her. What should have been the most joyous period in Erin's whole life was being shared by other people, not by her best friend, almost-sister, in Jacobsville. And all because of Annie's brother. She felt flames bursting in her head. But she smiled at the other two people and kept them hidden.

But not for long.

Ty was just back from walking Beauregard when she came in the door.

He looked at her and raised both eyebrows. "I can see that you've been in it with somebody. Who?"

"Not yet, but I'm about to! I'd like to speak to you in the living room." She looked past him at Mrs. Dobbs, the housekeeper. "With no witnesses."

"If you kill him, try to do it on the linoleum and not on the wood. Stains, you know," the older woman said with twinkling eyes.

"I'll keep that in mind," Annie promised.

Ty sighed and gave Beauregard over to the housekeeper. Then he followed Annie into the living room and waited while she closed the door. She also locked it. Audibly.

"Remember what Mrs. Dobbs said about the blood staining the wood floor," he reminded her.

She glared at him. "You got Erin fired from Mr. Perrin's company in San Antonio."

He closed his eyes for an instant. He'd flogged himself mentally for that for weeks. He hadn't meant to cause Erin so much grief. It was just he'd trusted her, more than he trusted anyone outside of family. She'd let him down and he had to work it out of his system. Maybe he'd gone a little too far.

"Yes, I did," he confessed, dropping down into his favorite armchair. "It was a low thing to do, when I'd already fired her."

"Well, your loss was someone else's gain, I guess," she said slowly.

"What do you mean?"

She smiled coldly. It was nice, administering poison drip by drip. "I mean, she got married."

His face paled by at least one shade. "Married," he exploded. "When? To whom?"

"I don't know, because she won't talk to me, thanks to you. But she's moved to Wyoming to live."

"Wyoming?" He was sitting up straight now. "Why?"

"Maybe because she feels safer there," she replied. "I mean, especially—" she lowered her eyes "—since she's pregnant," she added with a malignant smile.

If he'd been standing he might have fallen. Emotions that he hadn't felt for years shot through him like bullets. Erin had gone into his arms as if she'd waited her whole life to feel them around her. She'd given in to him at the cabin. He'd faulted her for that, ridiculing her morals, when she'd never put a foot wrong before in her life. He'd treated her like an enemy, when she'd been part of him, part of his family, for so many years. Had he gone totally mad, to believe a report that could easily have been falsified, to have thrown Erin away like a piece of garbage? To have hurt her so badly that she'd married someone else and even left the state so she wouldn't have to see him again.

He couldn't believe the things he'd done. He didn't understand why he'd done them. Erin had never hurt him. She'd always been on his side, even when he was wrong and everybody knew it. Why had he believed a stranger and not believed the one person who would have defended him to the death? It was like coming out of a daze into painful reality. He was seeing things in a whole other light, and at the worst possible time.

"Married," he choked out. "Pregnant!"

Annie wasn't enjoying this as much as she'd thought she would. She sat down on the edge of the sofa. "Her husband was killed in Afghanistan," she said after a minute.

He looked up, his anguish undisguised. "I blamed her before I ever had the detective agency go digging for the traitor." He stood up, hands in his pockets, and walked over to the window, where the curtains were pulled back. "I shouldn't have taken one detective agency's word for it. I should have had another one recheck the information."

"Why don't you do that?" Annie asked coldly. "A day late and a dollar short, but why not?"

He turned. "You're really upset."

"Of course I'm upset! I've lost my best friend in the whole world. But Erin's lost her father, her home, her job, and her husband! And she's pregnant! How would you like to be in her shoes? If it wasn't for Maude, I guess she'd be living in her damned car!"

His lips fell open. Until that moment, that very moment, he hadn't thought about how bad things had gone for Erin. If he had, he might have thought she deserved it. But what Annie said hit him right in the heart. Even a murderer would feel pity for what Erin had gone through.

"That's not all," Annie said.

"What else?" he asked dully.

"Her father lost everything. She was evicted from her home and given one day to get out and get her stuff in storage."

"What?!" He turned on his heel, shocked to the core. "Who did that to her?" he demanded.

"A fly-by-night loan company with ties to some very bad people," she replied. "Her father sold the house for more money to try and get back the thousands he'd lost on the day-trading website. It was how he could afford to pay cash for a late model car."

"And Erin's couture clothes...?"

"What couture?" Annie demanded. "She found a nearly-new shop that had several couture pieces that a suddenly pregnant debutante couldn't wear. Erin wore that exact size, so she was able to afford them!"

Now he felt about two inches high.

"The one thing I'm grateful for is that you brought Erin home early from the supper in the cabin," she said coldly. "She told us that you'd been expecting other company after you brought her home. Mrs. Dobbs washes the sheets at the cabin, you know," she said meaningfully and with a knowing stare.

He was very pale. "I see." It was something he hadn't thought of. But Erin had. She'd protected him, even from that suspicion. His eyes closed. He felt guilt like bile in his mouth.

Annie was still glaring at him. "I don't ask about your private life. I don't care. But I swear, if you'd seduced Erin, I'd move out of this house today! She loved you so much that it was painful... Ty!" she exclaimed, because his grip on her arms was over tight.

"Sorry!" He loosened his grip. "What did you say?"

She drew in a long breath. "You're the only man in Jacobs County who doesn't know that Erin's been in love with you since she was thirteen years old. She'd have sold out her own parents before she'd have sold you out." She shook her head. "I still can't understand why you didn't believe her when she told you she was innocent. Her word is her bond. She never lies."

He let go of her arms and sat back down in the recliner, hard. So many puzzle pieces fell into place. So many questions he'd never wanted to ask were suddenly answered. Erin had loved him. She'd as much as told him so when she yielded in the cabin. He didn't need to ask if she'd been innocent. She'd waited for him, all those years. Only to be sold out herself, after he accused her of selling him out.

"I should have listened," he said at last. "Oh, God, I should have listened!"

"Yes, you should have," she replied. "But it does us no good now, does it?" She brushed back her hair. "I'm going up to San Antonio to have lunch with an old friend. I probably won't be back until late."

"Okay."

He wasn't really hearing her. He was hearing himself berate Erin and threaten her with litigation, with the loss of her job, with taunts about her morality. She'd been dizzy…she'd almost passed out when he startled her by slamming his hand on his desk.

He caught his breath. She was pregnant! Had she been pregnant that day? The baby. Was it, could it be, his?

He got up and found a calendar and only then realized he didn't remember the date when he'd taken Erin to the cabin. He pulled out his phone and scrolled down the messages. He remembered sending a text to his sister, whom he'd asked to send a caterer up with Erin's favorite dishes at the cabin. He noted the date and put it in "notes."

This would take some detective work, some very discreet work. He knew where to find it, too, and it wasn't in San Antonio. It was in Houston, where the Lassiter Detective Agency was headquartered. While they were at it, he thought, pulling up the agency's website up on his cell phone, they could recheck who gave that bid under the table to the construction company that won the bid. It didn't hurt to get a second opinion. Just in case he was wrong.

He closed his eyes. God, if he was wrong, he'd just ruined not only Erin's life, but his own as well. She would never speak to him again, not after what he'd done to her. His heart dropped in his chest. She was also married, and pregnant. That was really his first priority, the baby. He had to know if it was his. But her innocence was the second most important thing. He wanted to know the truth. He would worry about how to deal with both issues afterward. Not now, when the pain was so fresh.

It was too important a matter to discuss over the phone, so Ty flew to Houston and sat down with Dane Lassiter. The man was a legend. First a Houston cop, then a Texas Ranger who almost died in an exchange of gunfire. After that, unable to assume the physical demands of police work because of his injuries, he founded a detective agency and made it a watchword for the profession.

Even now, in his middle years, Dane Lassiter was impressive. His wife worked with him, as a skip tracer. So did their daughter. Their son was off in Colorado on a case of his own. It seemed very much a family business.

Ty said so.

Dane chuckled. "It seems to have become one," he said, smiling. "So, what can I do for you?"

Ty handed him a folder that contained the bare bones of the case, along with the sworn statements of the people who'd won the bid for the huge complex in San Antonio.

"Yes, I remember these people," Dane said coldly. "Harold Bradley's construction company. I handled a case involving them. There was a young woman who worked for another similar company. She stole a file key, had it copied, and took out the bid before it was submitted. She gave it to the contact and was paid twenty grand for it. Her employer, of course, never knew she did it. Not until the culprits were finally pulled into court and tried for a disaster caused by their shoddy work. They managed to sleaze out from under the charge. I'd love to see them go down, before lives are lost." He looked up. "I'm amazed that they can still get work. I'll never believe they could handle a project of this size without casualties."

"Erin Mitchell was accused of selling me out," Ty said, not adding that he'd been the accuser. "She lost her job over it. I saw all the evidence against her. You're holding it. But now I've had second thoughts. I want to be sure she was responsible."

"Is she the sort of woman who'd sell a man out for money? I'm assuming you know her."

"Our families have been friends for two generations," Ty said, hating himself. "Erin was my sister's best friend."

"Was?" Dane asked softly.

Ty took a breath. "Erin won't speak to her."

"I see." And he saw a lot more than Ty realized. His background made sizing up people an easy task. "What do you want me to do?"

"Find out who gave that bid to the project owners before I sent over the actual bid. And," he added, taking another breath, "there's one more thing."

Dane just waited patiently.

Ty looked at his boots. "Erin's pregnant. They say it's her late husband's." He looked up, with regret tautening his features. "I think it's mine."

"And she hasn't told you?"

"She wouldn't," he said, averting his eyes. "I was…pretty hard on her. She'd think I had ulterior motives if I even asked."

"She'd think you wanted a termination."

His teeth ground together. "Yes."

Dane, who'd had his own rocky road to married bliss, felt for him. His own wife before their marriage had become pregnant and hidden it from him. When he found out, he'd been less than kind. It had taken a near-tragedy for him to realize how much she meant to him. He hoped this tormented man didn't have to pay the price he did for his own lack of trust.

"I'll need dates," Dane said.

"I don't have many. Just the day we went to supper at my cabin and the county where she's living in Wyoming. It's Carne County. The sheriff there has relatives in Jacobsville, where I live…" He stopped.

"Okay. I can dig out the rest. If she's in Wyoming, she'll have an obstetrician."

"He won't talk to anyone about her, I guess," Ty said.

Dane just smiled. "There are ways. Never mind what they are. I'll get to work on this today. But we're overburdened with cases at the moment, so it may take a week or two before I can get to this one."

"No problem," Ty said. He stood up and shook Dane's hand. "It will give me that much more time to avoid the truth."

"You won't believe it, but I know exactly how you feel," Dane said, smiling as he walked him out. "I'll be in touch when I have something."

Ty shook hands. "Thanks."

Gabby's father's house, which she was doing the cost estimate for, kept Erin's mind joyfully occupied for days. It was nice to be able to use her skills, even in this small way. But it reminded her painfully of how her career had ended. She put it to the back of her mind and went on with her chore.

By the second week, she had what Gabby needed.

The younger woman actually whooped with glee. "We can afford it!" she said, and impetuously hugged Erin. "Oh, thank you so much! I'd never have been able to get my father to do this without actual figures. Honestly the roof is about to cave in, the well house needs rebuilding, the stalls need repairs, and that's all that concerns Daddy," she groaned. "The best building on the place is the stable where he keeps our horses, for goodness' sake!"

Erin laughed. "Well, he should build a house while he has the capital for a home improvement loan."

"I agree wholeheartedly!" She looked around, to make sure nobody was within earshot. She leaned closer. "Can I ask you something, well, sort of personal?" she asked almost in a whisper.

"Of course you can. What is it?"

"It's Justin." She bit her lower lip, still looking around nervously. "I mean, he's around you a lot and he smiles more than he used to." Her pale gray eyes were glistening like silver. "You don't… Are you, I mean." She stopped suddenly and colored.

"I'm not," Erin replied gently, and smiled. Then the smile faded and her own gray eyes began to glitter. "And you want to know why? It's because I'm stupid! Because I'm still in love with the miserable backstabbing son of a swamp rat who's the father of my baby!"

Then she started crying.

Gabby got around her and hugged her, rocking her in her arms. "I'm sorry. I'm so sorry. I know how it feels."

"I know you do," Erin sobbed. "I'm so sorry, too."

"I'm just a fly speck in the swamp."

Erin leaned up and whispered in her ear. "He thinks you're too young."

Gabby's whole face lit up. "What?"

Erin wiped away tears and took a breath. "You don't see the way he looks at you," Erin said simply. "Two words. Be patient."

Gabby looked almost ethereal. "You see things that other people don't," she said.

"Yes. It's a nice skill. Pity it didn't work for me when I really needed it to. That miserable rat…!"

"Now, now, you'll upset the baby."

"He needs to know the truth about his other parent," Erin said doggedly. "He's not going to grow up to be just like him!"

Gabby chuckled. "You said, 'him.'"

Erin shrugged. "Well, Ty has a sister," she said. "But Ty's grandfathers on both sides had only sons. It's sort of a fifty-fifty split, but it leans toward a boy."

"Ty. Was that your husband's name?" she asked, all at sea.

Erin sniffed and mopped at tears. "No. It's the name of the man I've been in love with since I was thirteen, who fired me and accused me of selling him out. So here I am pregnant and alone and I hope he falls in a pit and gets eaten by worms!"

Gabby's eyes almost popped. "But your husband…"

Erin sighed. "I don't have one. But that's top secret," she added, smiling sadly up at the girl. "I ran. It was the only thing I could do."

Gabby nodded. "Running. I'm thinking of that myself," she

said, sighing. "Sometimes retreat is a good idea, especially when things seem hopeless."

"Exactly." She patted her stomach gently. "It's probably a boy, but I'd love a little girl," she said softly.

"You'll love what you get," Gabby teased.

"You bet I will. It's just that if I had a girl, she'd never grow up to be a distrustful, vicious man who fired people he should have trusted!" Erin muttered.

"Girls can be headstrong, too," Gabby pointed out.

"Exactly," came a deep voice from the doorway. "Like riding a mare they can't handle!"

Gabby gave Justin a haughty look. "I'm riding Belle today. That shows good sense."

"No, it proves the other horses have already been taken out," he returned. He glanced at Erin. "Headed for the post office. Need stamps?"

"Why would I need stamps?" she asked. "I have a phone."

"You might want to write somebody. About the baby."

She shifted in her chair and glared at him. "I don't want to write anybody about the baby."

"Pity. A kid has two parents."

"He's better off without his father," she huffed, not realizing that Justin had indicated he knew the father of her child wasn't dead or in the military.

"Not the case. Well, not usually. Mine should have stayed in North Dakota with the Hunkpapa instead of marrying my mother, who was Oglala Lakota, and coming to live in Montana with her Crow grandparents. But as bad as he was, at least I knew him."

"I'm not writing a letter."

He shrugged. "Texting isn't a bad idea, either."

"Aren't you going to the post office?" she asked with a glare.

He tugged his hat over his eyes. "I am now." He turned and left them.

Gabby stared after him with her heart in her eyes. Erin noticed.

"Don't do that," she whispered. "Never let a man know how you feel. You'll be sorry."

Gabby grimaced. "I guess so. But he's so gorgeous."

"He's not bad-looking," she conceded.

"Got a picture of the baby's father?" she asked Erin. "Just one?"

Erin didn't want to see him. Yes, she did. She opened the photo app on her phone and showed the picture to Gabby. It had been taken at a party last year. Ty was wearing a somber dark blue suit with a striped navy and blue tie. He was glaring at her. It was the way he usually looked when she tried to take a picture of him.

"He never liked to be photographed," she told the other woman. "I insisted. His sister helped me."

"He's really handsome. The baby will be gorgeous," she said wistfully.

"He's good-looking," Erin said, putting up the phone. "I'm just ordinary."

"Not when you talk about him, you're not," Gabby told her gently. "You glow."

She drew in a long breath. "The dirty rat."

"Oooh, can you do a Jimmy Cagney accent when you say that? I watched an old movie on YouTube that had him in it, and he said that. It sounded really menacing!"

That made Erin laugh. "I'll find it and watch it," she said.

"Good for you. I'm going. Thanks again for the figures! I'll have to owe you…"

"Friends don't charge friends," Erin said firmly. "And don't you forget it."

"I'll find a way. Thank you."

"He was really worried when the mare took off with you," Erin told her before she left.

Gabby's eyes lit up. "He worries about all the people he

knows," she said. "But maybe he worries a little more about me. It would be enough. I'm not asking for the moon."

"One day you may get it," Erin told her.

"One day I may live in a cavern on Mars, too." She shrugged. "Dad wants me to go back to college. If things don't get better here, I might do it," she sighed.

"Patience."

"Doctors have those," Gabby reminded her. "Regular people can go mad waiting for things that never happen. And I can be patient at college as well as here. See you!" She stopped and turned around. "And thanks for the pep talk, too. I really needed it."

She was gone before Erin had time to reply.

Ty hadn't heard from Lassiter, but he did finally tell his sister that he'd hired a detective to dig a little deeper.

"About time," Annie said curtly.

He stuck his hands in his pockets. "He might not find anything more than the first ones did," he reminded her.

"You can bet your best German shepherd that he will," she said, and went off to the kitchen.

He was secretly dreading Lassiter's report, because he had a sick feeling that he was going to be on the wrong side of the issue when the truth was known. But what the truth was knocked him winding.

He'd just gotten home from the office when his phone rang. He knew from the caller ID that it was Lassiter.

"What did you find?"

"Enough to cause some serious problems for several people, the main one being the so-called private detective agency you used," Lassiter said curtly. "To put it bluntly, the agent on your case was bribed to falsify both information and signatures of persons involved in the case. He was arrested two hours ago and he faces some serious jail time. His employer swears he didn't know about it. That will be for the courts to decide. And since the detective's daughter is directly involved, working for you, that will make his case more difficult to adjudicate."

"Wait a minute." Ty sat down in his recliner. "His daughter? She works for me!"

"She also has a profitable sideline of selling information to interested buyers," he continued. "Her last boss, up in Dallas, has just been contacted to testify as a witness for the prosecution in her case. She's being charged with industrial espionage. Of your company, by the way. I was informed by a contact that she admitted stealing the key of a Miss Erin Mitchell out of her purse, making a copy, and using it to gain access to a drawer containing a bid so that she could make a copy of it. She gave it to the company that won the bid you were competing for."

Ty felt his heart go cold in his chest. "Erin didn't do it," he said absently.

"No, she did not. If she wants to charge the said Ms. Taylor with character assassination, she should speak to an attorney."

Ty was sick to his stomach. "She's not like that," he said quietly. "She's the least vindictive person I know."

"Pity," he said. "Considering what she's been through, it amazes me that she isn't vindictive. In her place, I would be."

"I'll deal with this later. But the other matter…"

"Yes. The baby. We were able to ascertain that Ms. Mitchell has never married. Her so-called husband is a construct. As to the other…yes, the baby is most definitely yours. A doctor in San Antonio could verify that there had never been a lover before you. So there's no question of paternity."

Ty felt wetness in his eyes. He shook his head to clear his vision. "I can't thank you enough," he said.

"I don't like other detective agencies doing sloppy work," Dane said. "Any more than I'd like other contractors doing slipshod work, if I were you. By the way, the company that won the bid for that complex in San Antonio—a wall collapsed two days ago and killed two workers. They'll discover after a little probing that the materials used were substandard. The contractor is going to be in a world of hurt. I know one of the investors. I just happened to mention that I suspected there might be some skullduggery afoot."

"There might be," Ty agreed with a hollow laugh. "I'm grateful."

"I'd love to see that company go out of business. You can read about the tragedy in the San Antonio paper, by the way. It's pretty detailed. The owner of the conglomerate that's paying for the construction expressed shock and regret about accepting the bid. I expect charges to follow, and Mr. Bradley may be in prison soon, if not on the receiving end of several lawsuits from survivors of the victims. If I can be of any more help, let me know. I'm sending the documents out today, overnight. They'll be on your desk first thing in the morning."

"I'll look forward to them," Ty lied.

Annie, who'd been hovering but not interfering, walked into the room. "Well?"

He took a long breath. "She didn't do it," he said, pain in every word. "She never sold me out. It was Jenny Taylor. She bribed her father's agent to falsify the information I was given about the leak."

"I remember telling you, several times, that Erin was innocent."

"It's worse than that," he told her. "When she got another job, in the industry, I called her boss and got her fired."

"Thank you," she said with malice. "How kind of you. Do you also kick lame dogs?"

His face was frozen with anguish. "It gets worse, Annie."

"How?"

He looked up at her with dead eyes. "The baby. There is no husband. The baby is…mine."

CHAPTER TEN

Annie just stared at her brother. "I tried so hard to tell you. I didn't want to give her away, but it broke my heart to have you accuse her when I knew why she'd never sell you out for money."

"She loves me," he said quietly, and lowered his eyes.

"She's always loved you. Or, she did," Annie said quietly. "After what you've done to her, Ty, I have serious doubts that she still feels that way."

He drew in a long breath and leaned forward. "So do I." He shook his head.

"So something did go on at the cabin," Annie said delicately.

He moved restlessly. "I even taunted her for that. She told me it wasn't the first time she'd had too much to drink and gotten…involved…with a man."

"And she lied," Annie said. "Because I knew that she'd never even been out with another man, much less out to drink with one. For God's sake, don't you even remember me telling you that she'd never been in a bar in her life?!"

"I do now," he said. He leaned back in the chair. "All that time, Jenny Taylor was stalking me and I took it for infatuation. When it was really to throw me off the track and put Erin on the firing line."

"Sweet girl. I hope she slips on a banana peel and…!"

"Jenny Taylor." He made her name sound like a curse. "Why am I not surprised? But I couldn't have known she'd bribe an agent to falsify a report. He's in jail, by the way," he added. "Lassiter has his own issues with detective agencies that cheat on clients for any reason. He turned the man in."

"Good for Lassiter. How about Ms. Taylor?"

"Arrested for industrial espionage. They've got another victim up in Dallas who'll testify, because she got caught doing it to him and talked her way out of it. She won't this time. I'd bet money that the construction company was involved in that bid as well. By the way, a wall of their new construction project in San Antonio collapsed two days ago. Five lives were lost. So they're going to have some serious problems as well," he added quietly.

"Yes, but none of this solves Erin's problem."

"I could send flowers," he said wistfully. "Maybe offer her the puppy I promised her back before I destroyed her life."

"Keep them for yourself," Annie advised. "She won't even talk to me, so what does that tell you about the reception you'll get?"

He scowled. "She won't talk to you? Not at all?"

"I've tried. I get heart emojis back. Not a word. And she never answers her phone."

"But she gets the texts," he persisted.

"I suppose so." She sat down. "Maybe if I'd pushed harder, if I'd nagged you into questioning that so-called evidence…"

"It wouldn't have made a difference. I'd already blown up too many bridges by then." He looked down at his boots. "Well, I guess I'll try texting her."

"If you do, don't mention the baby," Annie advised.

"I wouldn't dare," he replied. "She'd think I either wanted to insist on a termination or find a way to take possession when it's born."

"Exactly."

"I never thought I'd get into this kind of situation," he said solemnly. "I've avoided it all my life, with a procession of women who saw dollar signs and diamonds."

"And you end up with a child who won't know you because you turned your back on her mother when she was the most desperate. I suppose it's occurred to you that Erin was already pregnant the day you fired her?"

He grimaced. "She got dizzy in the office and almost fell. I was furious. I slammed my hand down on the desk and startled her. I've never felt so bad about anything." His throat was full of pins, choking him. He took a minute to regain his composure. "I doubt she'll talk to me. But I have to try."

"Ty, think about why you want to do it," Annie said gently. "Don't contact her if you aren't sure how you really feel about her. You shouldn't involve yourself with anyone out of pity or guilt. Not even my poor best friend."

"Pity." He laughed coldly. "I pity myself, for being so blind. I knew she had a crush on me in her early teens. I thought she'd grown out of it."

"She just learned how to hide it," Annie said simply. "She knew you didn't feel anything for her."

"I didn't. Then." He drew in a long breath. "What was that song about the big yellow taxi our grandad used to sing?"

She shook her head. "The 'Big Yellow Taxi' song? You really don't know what you've lost until it's gone," she agreed.

"I'm going to try texting her later on. I'll go along with the dead husband thing. I'll tell her I heard about it in Jacobsville, that she'd married."

"Good idea. I hope it works. I'd really like to have my best friend back," she added icily.

"I'll do my best," he promised.

She gave him a long look and shook her head. "It will be the worst time in the history of our family if I can't even see my niece or nephew." She didn't add that she was already missing the excitement of Erin's pregnancy, which Erin was most likely loving, even if she'd given up on Ty. She'd always loved children. So did Annie.

"Maybe I could go up there," he said, almost to himself.

"I wouldn't," Annie said, and meant it. "You don't know Maude, but I do. She has a twelve-gauge shotgun. You don't want to see the end of both barrels."

"I guess it's not a good idea," he conceded. "I don't think I've had any good ideas in the past few months, though. None at all." He shoved his hands in his pockets and went into his study.

Annie looked after him with sorrow. She knew already what Erin's response would be to any contact from Ty. After what he'd put the poor woman through, he'd be lucky to get her to answer him with any sort of emoji. And Annie had a sneaking hunch which one she'd use, too.

That night, Ty finally worked up enough courage to message Erin. He still had her phone number and she'd apparently not thought to block it. She wouldn't expect him to try to get in touch with her.

He'd spend hours thinking what to say, to melt some of the ice between them. He missed Erin. She haunted him at work, at home, even in town at places where they'd been together. The church where both their families had worshipped, Barbara's Café where they always had lunch after church. The baseball field where they'd cheered their home teams. The river where they'd played as children. Well, where his sister and Erin had played. Ty had been older than them, off in the military and then college. But the memories were strongest in this very house, where Erin had spent so much time over the years.

He'd driven by her father's house on the way home today. It was still vacant, although the For Sale sign was gone. She'd lost her father, her home, her job, everything, and most of that was his fault. He hadn't trusted her. He recalled what she'd said to him the last time she saw him. She'd said that she'd have defended him to the death, if their situations had been reversed.

And that wasn't all. The rest of what she'd said chilled him to the bone. She'd said that he'd learn the truth one day. But that it would be too late. Prophetic words.

He turned the phone over and tried to explain all he felt, in a few words. It was impossible. He needed to see her, talk to her, hold her. He thought of the tiny little life growing inside her, and he melted. He loved children. He'd never expected to have any of his own, but he'd spoiled the children to whom he played godfather. How would it be to have a child of his own to cuddle?

But that wasn't likely to happen unless he could get Erin to trust him again. How hard was that going to be? He'd blamed her from the beginning. She didn't like Jones, and he revered the man. That had started him suspecting her. But then Jones was hard to get close to. Few people knew what he was really like. He wasn't the sort of person who would ever do something under the table.

Neither was Erin, though, and he hadn't even questioned the report when he got it. He'd known Erin most of her life, knew that she was religious and pristine, and then was so ready to believe that she slept around, that she was underhanded, that she would cheat him.

He was wrong, on all counts. Wrong, and guilty, and guilt-ridden. He didn't know if there was even a way to make it up to her, but he wanted to try. The road ahead was bleak and bare. She'd only been out of his life for a few months, and the emptiness he felt was choking him to death. He hadn't realized how much a part of his life she'd become, until she wasn't there anymore.

Well, hoping wasn't doing any good with acting. He punched

in a few terse words. I was wrong. I'm sorrier than you can imagine. Can we talk?

He pushed Send and waited. And waited. And waited. Finally, thirty minutes later, he got two responses. The first was an angry red face with its mouth taped and bad words obviously being blanked out. The second was that his number was blocked, so that he couldn't try again.

He hefted the phone and almost threw it at the wall. But what good would that do now? He'd already known how she'd react to any queries from him. And he knew that it would be futile to try again. Maybe Annie could contact her in a month or so. Maybe she'd talk to Annie.

In the meantime he had something to occupy him. Getting ready for Ms. Taylor's day in court. He was going to enjoy it. Really enjoy it.

Autumn in Wyoming was glorious, but brief. The days went by lazily while Erin kept Maude company, knitted baby things while they watched television at night, took long walks around the ranch, sometimes with Justin, sometimes with the ranch wives whom she'd gotten to know.

Erin had told Maude about Ty's brief text message the day it came. "Some nerve, isn't it?" Erin had asked angrily. "After all he did to me, he wants to know if we can talk."

"Compromise prevents wars," was all Maude said, with a wry smile.

"I'd rather roll naked in poison ivy than even speak to him!"

Maude had drawn in a long breath. "Well, I had days like that with my late husband," she reminisced with soft eyes. "We had tiffs, but the making up was fun."

"This one isn't going to get made up."

"So what do you tell your child when he comes home from first grade and wants to know all about his daddy in the military for show and tell?" Maude asked. "A baby has two parents,

Erin. It's not fair to keep that to yourself. Ty may be every sort of a heel, but he loves kids. Look at how he babies those pups he sells."

Erin did remember. Ty had promised her one. That brought back memories of losing her home, her father, her job, the love of her life… Tears started rolling silently down her cheeks.

"Oh, now, don't do that," Maude said gently and went to hug her. "Don't. It will all work out, you'll see."

"He should be with me," she said on a sob. "He should be with me while the baby grows, when he's born, when he says his first word…!"

"How do you punish a man without revealing his crime?" Maude asked softly.

Erin's eyes were red. "I guess you can't."

"Keeping the baby a secret from him only hurts you," she reminded her young relative. "If he doesn't know, it certainly doesn't hurt him."

Erin had looked at Maude with pure terror in her eyes. "What if he wanted a termination?"

"Ty? The way he loves little things?"

And that was true. He was tender with everything from puppies and kittens and colts to baby humans. Always. He helped out with expenses when his ranch hands needed things for their children that they couldn't afford. He was godfather to at least seven of them. He did love little things. And he saw to it that people who hurt them got punished. Severely.

That started her crying again.

"Okay," Maude cooed. "Okay, I won't say another word. But you think about this very carefully. Very, very carefully."

She'd drawn in a steadying breath and wiped her eyes. "I'll think about it," she promised. "Right now, I'm just grateful to have a home and a job. I don't know I'll ever repay you."

"No need to think of any such thing," Maude told her. She sighed. "I wish I'd known you better before I made my will," she muttered. "I left everything to a great-niece who lives in Wyoming. She won't want to live here. Has her own place there, in town somewhere. I'd already made the place over to her." She looked up. "She's nice," she added regretfully. "Just as nice as you are, and she doesn't have anybody, either."

"That's sad."

Maude nodded. "I lost both my parents when I was just in my twenties. Then Dean came along. I married him and we were so happy. Then year before last, out of the blue, he had a heart attack while he was leading a horse out of the barn. It was just that quick. The ambulance came immediately, but the doctor told me at the hospital that it wouldn't have mattered if it had happened in the emergency room. It killed almost all of his heart muscle. No way could he have lived."

"I'm so sorry."

"So was I, but we all have trials. We get through them, somehow." Maude smiled at her. "They make us stronger, you know."

Erin agreed. "But they make us sadder, as well."

"That's also true." She cocked her head over her embroidery as she sat back down. "Don't ever assume that you have tomorrow," she added quietly. "You don't. Nobody does. Yesterday is a memory. Tomorrow is a hope. All we're really promised is right now, this moment. It helps to think of things like that. Especially when you're hurt."

"I'll remember," Erin had said. "But I'm not ready to talk peace. Not by a long shot."

"That time will come," was the reply, said with a twinkle in Maude's eye.

It hadn't just yet. As autumn turned the leaves red and gold, and Christmas decorations went up all over the ranch, Erin was lost in memory of other Christmases, almost all of them involving Christmas Eve at the Mosby home, before and after Ty and Annie lost their parents.

It had been a time of great joy. Jacobsville always had a cattlemen's ball, and a fundraiser for the local animal shelter, plus one for various other causes. From time to time, Erin would go with Annie and Ty to some function or other. Ty never noticed her in those days. He wasn't much for women, as a rule, but in the past few years, he'd become restless. Annie said that at his age, heading toward the mid-thirties, he was looking for things he hadn't found.

Sadly, he'd found a woman he thought he wanted to marry. She'd cheated on him, ridiculed him, and finally dropped him like a rock and gone home to California. Annie and Erin had discussed the woman at the start of the so-called romance. Both of them had pegged Ty's heartthrob as an adventuress, out for thrills and romance, but not a white picket fence at the end of them.

Ty, for the first time, was thinking in that direction. He was crazy over the woman. Erin watched and moaned to herself. She'd just graduated from high school and Ty still thought of her as a kid. She knew but mourned silently at the thought of Ty giving up Jacobsville for a new home in California, one where his monied would-be forever partner had her estate.

But as things turned out, she had more money than Ty did, and she wasn't keen on having a cowboy architect around her neck like an albatross. She'd even made mention of the fact, plus she'd blown up her hunger for Ty's money—a lie if there ever was one. She could have bought a new Rolls every year on her stock holdings alone, as Ty found out much later. But he took her at her word that he wasn't rich enough or exciting enough to suit her.

After that, he'd gone a little wild on the subject of women. He had a reputation these days as a rounder. Which meant that virtuous women around Jacobsville—and there were some—wouldn't go near him. Even in modern times, there were women who revered the idea of being a wife and mother, rather than a captain of industry. Especially if the man was independently wealthy and presentable in parlor company.

It tickled Erin to think of Ty like that. He was much more the renegade than the conservative. He would never settle down. Not now, after he'd been sold out by the one woman he'd ever wanted for keeps.

Erin would have loved living with him. But she could settle living for her baby. It was the most exciting thing that had ever happened to her. She loved every little flutter in her belly, and later, the feel of a little fist or a little foot pressing against it. She talked to the baby at night and sang lullabies to it. She dreamed of holding it in her arms and cuddling it, feeding it, being a mother.

She thought of how loving and kind her own mother had been, a simple, sweet woman who loved her family more than anything on earth. There had been hard times, thanks to her father's naïve get-rich-quick schemes, but her mother had gently guided him out of dangerous things and back into normal, routine ones. He'd had many jobs. He was more of a handyman than anything else until he grew tired of going here and there at odd hours to fix things. That was just about the time her mother died. After that, he was tired of any routine jobs. That was when he thought about day-trading and eventually ruined his life and Erin's by doing it without expertise or advice.

Then she remembered Mr. Jones apologizing to her, because he and her dad had been friends and he'd made money day-trading. He was sorry he'd interested her father in it. She saw a side of her colleague that she hadn't even known about. Her father had never mentioned that he and Mr. Jones had coffee every other week, or that Mr. Jones knew her mother. Truthfully, Erin had been too wrapped up in her job to think about such things, or even to ask questions. If she hadn't been so moony over Ty since she'd started her job, perhaps she'd have paid more attention to what was going on at home.

And she'd actually praised her father for offering to take over the checkbooks for savings and bills and manage them. That had been a stupid move. If she'd once called the bank and questioned the figures in her checkbook that never seemed to change, or if she'd paid attention to the bank statements—if she'd even asked her father why he had to ask her for lunch money one day. If she'd looked at the mortgage, which he'd offered to pay and she'd agreed. She just moaned. She'd helped them both into misery by not paying attention.

It was just that each new day was another day that Ty would be in the office or on the phone and she could look at him, listen to his deep voice, indulge her anguished unrequited love for him. Not once did it occur to her that she was wasting her whole life hoping for a miracle. Ty didn't love her. He never had. And just at the end, he'd made a convenience of her, just another roll in the hay. It hadn't helped that she'd made him think she was a rounder, too. She'd ruined her spotless reputation with that blatant lie to save his feelings, so that he wouldn't feel bad about seducing her.

She must have been out of her mind, she decided. But she was in Wyoming now, safe and happy, and she might stay here forever. She'd gotten to know some of the people in town, at the drugstore and the café and the post office. Even at the doctor's office. She had invitations to visit and every so often, Maude would come home with a quilt or a crocheted blanket or even baby clothes for the coming child. It wouldn't be so bad, living in Catelow.

Except that she missed Annie. She wouldn't admit that leaving Texas had torn her heart out. She'd never admit that she missed Ty as well. Certainly, he felt guilty about accusing her for something she hadn't done. Judging from that curt text, somebody had finally told him the truth. She wondered what it was, but not enough to get in touch with either Ty or Annie. Oh, no.

She was only safe so long as Ty was nowhere in her life. That meant even sacrificing Annie, her only friend. It broke her heart.

It was a week before Christmas. Erin and Maude were making cookies in the kitchen when a wash of water fell onto the floor under Erin. She actually screamed.

Maude patted her on the shoulder, calmly retrieved two bath towels, dropped one on the floor, one in a chair, and sat Erin down.

"Stay right there," she said, pulling out her cell phone to call 911.

The ambulance was very quick. So was the delivery. Erin had only had little twinges for the past twenty-four hours, nothing really indicative that the baby was due. But when they got to the hospital, the pain was like sticking a wet finger into an electric socket. She ground her teeth together to keep from screaming.

Then there was test after test, including a scan of her belly to make sure the baby was in the right position. That was when the trouble really started.

"Okay," Dr. Tanner said quietly. "Here's the thing. One, you haven't dilated even one centimeter. Two, the baby's in the wrong position. I want to do a Cesarean section. And it needs to be done very soon."

"Cesarean…" She looked at him, horrified. "I don't have insurance…!" she gasped.

"We can talk about that after we get the baby safe and sound. Okay?" he asked and smiled. "Don't worry. Let me do my job."

"All right, then," she said. "Whatever you…" she ground her teeth to stifle a scream, because the pain was bad.

"Let's get you prepped," he said.

He went outside to call a nurse.

Maude, meanwhile, had Erin's phone and she'd scrolled through messages. Ty's number was blocked and hidden, but Annie's wasn't.

She sent a text.

It's Maude, she typed. Erin's in Carne County Medical Center. They're about to do a Cesarean. Don't tell Ty or she'll kill me when she comes out of surgery.

The reply was within seconds. He's out of the country anyway, Annie texted back. I'm having our pilot warm up the plane. I'm coming, whether she wants me to or not!

Maude chuckled as she sent a text back. Good for you. I'll have Justin meet you at the airport. Text me when you get here.

How will I know who Justin is?

Six foot two, two hundred and twenty pounds, big booted feet, big white cowboy hat. You can't miss him.

There was a laugh emoji and a smiley one. Then silence.

Maude was on pins and needles until Dr. Tanner came out into the waiting room.

"She's fine," he said at once, and smiled as Maude laughed and shook her head, delighted at the release of tension.

"She'll be in recovery for an hour or so until we can get her into a room," he said. His dark eyes twinkled. "Want to see the baby?"

"Oh, yes!" She got up. "Is it a boy or a girl?"

"Boy," he said. "A strapping eight pounds and two ounces, healthy and hungry. I'll lead you to the nursery."

"What a relief!" Maude said as they walked. "We were all afraid that she'd go into labor when she was out on one of those walks she likes to take." She grimaced. "I wish she'd gone to Lamaze classes, like you wanted her to."

"Not everybody likes that," he said. "She had a hard time the past few months. I didn't want to press it."

"A hard time…but she's so healthy!" Maude exclaimed.

"I'm not allowed to tell you," he said. "But you might ask her if she has any minor heart conditions that need watching." He glanced at her with a solemn expression. "Nothing dangerous, at the moment, but we had a cardiologist on standby, just in case."

"She never said a word!"

"She didn't know," was the quiet reply. "We did a routine echo before the surgery."

"I see." Maude felt the floor shake under her. Heart problems ran in her side of the family. Even Erin's mother had died of a heart attack. "There might be some weakness that passed down through the generations..."

"She'll tell you about it, when she's ready," Dr. Tanner said. He stopped at the big glass window and motioned to a nurse and pointed to the only blue blanket in the place.

Maude laughed. "Oh, my, all girls."

"Except for that one," Dr. Tanner said on a sigh. "I know. I delivered three babies today. Dr. Hammond delivered two. All the others, every single one, was a girl."

"Erin said she'd love a girl. But she knitted everything yellow," she teased.

"Nothing wrong with yellow," he chuckled. "Well, I'm off to the delivery room again. Take care."

"You, too, and thanks very much!"

He waved, but Maude's eyes were now trained on a puckered-up little red face in a soft blue blanket. His eyes were open and he was glaring at her. Shades of Ty Mosby, she thought to herself. And grinned.

CHAPTER ELEVEN

Erin's eyes were barely open. She felt drugged. The nurse came in and said something that she barely heard, patted her on the shoulder, and smiled at her. Erin winced and moaned softly.

"No worries, I can handle that," the nurse told her gently.

She was back very soon with a syringe, which she shot right into the cannula at Erin's elbow. "That will take care of the pain."

"My baby," Erin whispered.

The nurse smiled. "A little boy. A strapping little boy, I might add," she said. "And the only one in the nursery."

"A boy." Erin managed a smile and drifted away again.

When she came to the next time, they were getting ready to put her into a room. "Can I see my baby when you get me into the room?"

"Of course you can," the nurse assured her. "And you have visitors waiting as well."

"Is one of them a tall man?" she asked, still groggy.

"Well, Justin is more of a bear..." she said, tongue-in-cheek.

Erin managed a weak laugh. "Is Maude here, too?"

"Of course. Just a few more feet."

They wheeled her into the room and one of the assistants helped ease her from the gurney onto the clean sheets. They tucked her up and then connected her to fluids on a rolling pole.

"Need anything?" the nurse asked when they'd finished.

"This…thing," she murmured, looking embarrassed.

"The blue canoe?" The nurse grinned. "When you have to go, you just go naturally. It ends up there," she indicated a clear jug with a tube attached. "For the other thing, you call us and we'll get you a bedpan. Don't you dare try to get out of that bed. It's wired," she whispered with a grin. "If one of your feet gets to the floor, it sets off an alarm you could hear in Cheyenne," she promised.

Erin just sighed. "I can barely move without groaning. I won't move. Honest." She hesitated, glancing down at the sheet over her thighs. "That thing really works?"

"It really works. Now just relax. And look who's here," she exclaimed as another nurse walked in carrying a blue blanket.

"Oooooh!" Erin exclaimed as they laid the baby beside her and she groaned as she managed to turn over onto her side so that she could see him. "He's so…beautiful," she whispered, tears stinging her eyes.

"Do you have a name?"

Erin nodded. "My father's middle name was Callaway. My… well, another name is Regan. So, Callaway Regan Mitchell."

"The Regan part would be for your late husband, I imagine," the nurse said matter-of-factly.

Erin smiled sadly. It was Ty's middle name. "Yes," she said.

"Those are nice names," she replied.

"But I'll call him Cal," Erin said softly.

"I like that."

"Me, too. I wanted to breastfeed, but I'm sick at my stomach and it hurts so much…"

"We thought about that. You can talk to Dr. Tanner before you decide, but we brought a bottle, just in case. Here you go."

Erin took it with thanks and held it to the tiny little mouth. "He's so small," she exclaimed. "I never thought babies were so tiny!"

"Oh, he'll grow," the nurse chuckled. "I have three. All teens." She shook her head. "I miss the days when they were just born. They were portable then!"

Erin laughed with her.

She was lost in the delight of motherhood when the door opened tentatively and Maude stuck her head inside.

She laughed and turned back toward the door. "It's a bottle. You can all come in!"

Erin was expecting the ranch people. But when the door opened wider, one of the people who rushed in was Annie.

Erin burst into tears. "Oh, Annie," she sobbed.

Annie hugged her gently, around the baby so that she didn't disturb his feeding. "You didn't tell me," she whispered. "I'm sorry about your husband, sorry I wasn't here, sorry…!"

"Don't. It's all right," Erin whispered, trying and failing to hug Annie back because it hurt to lift her arm. She settled for patting Annie's hand. "Isn't he beautiful?" she asked, indicating the little boy.

"So beautiful," Annie laughed, wiping away tears. "The nurse says he weighs over eight pounds. Do you have a name picked out?"

"Yes. Callaway, for my father," she replied, praying that the nurse who'd heard the baby's middle name wouldn't overhear her and mention his middle name. Annie, of all people, wouldn't be fooled.

"Callaway. It's nice," Annie said.

"How did you know?" Erin exclaimed.

Maude came closer and raised her hand. "Sorry," she added.

"But you didn't have Annie's number and it's unlisted," Erin said, all at sea.

"Yes, but I had your phone, and it's listed there." Maude

grinned. She pulled the phone out of her pocket and discon-
nected it from the battery charger. "I made sure it was charged,"
she added as she put it on the bed beside Erin.

"I've got an extra charger in my purse. I'll leave it with you,"
Annie said and went digging for it. She found it and plugged it
into the wall and looped it around one of the little posts on the
raised side of the bed. "Good thing I like long cords," Annie
remarked. "Can you reach this?"

"Yes. I've got a little phone bag in my purse, wherever it
is…" she said.

Maude found it in the locker near the bed. "Right here," she
said. "And it has a string. How nice!"

Maude looped it around the arm on the side of the bed and
secured it. Then she dropped the phone into it. "That's not going
anywhere," she said with a chuckle.

"Thank you both," Erin said. She was still looking at the
baby, enthralled.

Justin was standing at the door, fascinated by the baby. "I don't
think I've ever seen one up close before," he said with twinkling
eyes. "Handsome little devil."

"Thank you," Erin said. "Do you know Annie?"

He tipped his hat. "I met her at the airport. She has a wicked
sense of humor," he remarked with a smirk.

"He has a wickeder one," Annie riposted.

"They got along nicely except when she tried to pour ginger ale on him," Maude said. She held up a hand when Erin
started to question them. "A minor incident. No need to bring
it up again."

"Absolutely," Annie said.

Justin just nodded.

"Well, I need coffee and I'm not likely to get any in here,"
Justin huffed. "You coming, Maude?"

"Yes, just enough time for coffee. Then we three should head
out to the ranch."

"Three?" Erin asked.

"I'm not leaving you, so don't ask," Annie said. "Besides, I sent the pilot home to Jacobsville so the only way home is to walk."

"Baloney," Erin shot back. "You own stock in two airlines. Buy a ticket."

"I'm broke and I shredded my credit cards. Besides, I can't cook."

"You can, too."

"Maude's feeding and lodging me until I decide to go home."

Erin bit her tongue wondering about Ty.

"We'll be back," Maude said, sensing the tension. She shooed Justin out before her and closed the door.

Annie sat down beside the bed, her eyes on the baby. "I can't get over how precious he is." Her expression saddened. "I know it's hard to be here with just us and not the baby's father. I was sorry to hear about your husband." She winced. "Oh, Erin, how could you have gotten married and not told me?"

"It was pretty rushed," she confessed, lying through her teeth. "I met him in San Antonio, but he was headed back to Wyoming on leave. We dated for a week and he asked me to go home with him and meet his sister, but before that could happen he was recalled urgently and sent back to Afghanistan. So we got married, really quickly." She left the sentence hanging to make the point that she might need to be married.

"When did you know, about the baby?"

Erin sighed. "Very soon. I was working for Mr. Perrin. It was a good job…" Her face tautened.

"I know what happened. If it helps, Ty's miserable. He hired a private detective out of Houston, who discovered that our Ms. Taylor had done the same thing to another construction company in Dallas. Her former boss is testifying against her, along with Ty, when the case comes to court."

"The documents," Erin began slowly.

"Ms. Taylor enchanted one of the agents at her father's detective agency and had him falsify documents blaming you for the leak. That's actionable, if you want to press it. But she's in so much trouble that she'll likely end up in jail. I just feel sorry for her dad. He's an honest man, but the reputation of his agency is in shreds. You see, the same agent was also charmed by Ms. Taylor to do a number on the construction company in Dallas."

"Poor man." She sighed. "I always thought she smiled too much."

"Me, too." She was looking at the baby and her eyes were soft and loving. "He's just fascinating to me."

"To me, too. Remember when we were in our teens, we thought about marriage and babies. We even had hope chests." She grimaced. "Mine's in that storage building in Jacobsville. I had the fee put on my credit card, so I wouldn't risk losing any of my stuff."

"You've had such a rough time. I'm so sorry," Annie said gently.

"Not your fault," she replied.

"I hope you don't mind that I came. Maude sent me a text and she was worried. Me, too. I came as soon as I heard."

"I'm happy to see you," Erin confided. "I never wanted you to get caught in the cross fire, if you know what I mean."

"But you didn't trust me not to pass information on," Annie said with a half smile. "It wouldn't have mattered. Everybody in Jacobsville knows that you were married and widowed and pregnant. Well, except for me and..." She cleared her throat. "People sort of left us out of the loop after you mentioned to Barbara that you were working for Mr. Perrin and I repeated it and got you fired." She grimaced. "I'm so sorry!"

"I know you didn't do it deliberately," Erin said softly. "You're my best friend. I'm so glad you're here." She fought tears. "I kept thinking this is all wrong, I should have called you or texted you. I only had Maude and Justin."

"Two pretty straight shooters, though," Annie said. She smiled. "I like them."

"Me, too."

Erin watched the baby finish his bottle. "Oh, dear, he'll need to be burped, how will I burp him when I can't sit up?" She thought for a second. "I know." She rolled him over gently and rubbed between his shoulder blades until he burped. Both women laughed at the sound.

"He's spit up on the cloth. Just a sec."

Annie went out of the room and came back with a nurse's aide who saw the problem and solved it quickly.

"Does he need burping?" she asked.

Erin grinned. "Necessity is the mother of invention. I just turned him on his tummy and rubbed his back."

"Excellent!" she said and gave Erin a thumbs-up.

"You need to rest," the nurse, coming in behind the aide, said, noting the strain in her face. "And I have some meds for you as well." She had the aide take the baby back to the nursery, after he'd been soundly kissed by his mama.

"I know, you want him with you all the time. But you've had surgery, and you need rest right now. In a few days, you'll feel much better," the nurse assured her.

"Okay, then," Erin said. She sighed, her light eyes bright with joy. "It's magic."

"Babies are," the nurse sighed. "I love working in the maternity ward. I get to cuddle them." She chuckled. "Late at night, if I'm here and I have a free minute, I go to the nursery and rock the ones that are crying. Puts them right to sleep."

"That sounds nice."

"It feels nice, too."

"When Justin and Maude come back, I'm going home with them. Unless you want me to stay? I wouldn't mind. Really."

Erin sighed. "Thank you. But I really do need to rest. I haven't slept well the past couple of weeks."

"No wonder," the nurse said, handing her a small cup of pills and a cup of ice water. "Take these. You'll see a big difference in a few days."

Erin smiled. "Thanks."

Annie was getting some odd flashes. There was something wrong with her friend, and not just the aftereffects of surgery. She was going to do some sleuthing. Maude would take care of her, certainly, but Annie had deep pockets and that child was her nephew. Erin didn't have to know that she was aware of that, for her to help out. They'd been friends for many years. Erin wouldn't suspect anything, not after the groundwork she'd laid.

She used the camera on her cell phone to take pictures of Erin with the baby, and then showed them to her.

"That's an excellent camera," Erin said, smiling. "Will you share the photos with me?"

"Of course I will. I'll text them to your phone right now." Which she did. "I'm going home with Maude so you can rest," she added, gathering up her things. "But I'll be back bright and early tomorrow. You get some rest," she said firmly.

Erin smiled. "Yes, mother hen." She studied Annie's lovely face in its frame of long, curling blond hair. "I'm glad you ignored me and came anyway."

"So you should be. As if I'd miss the birth of my only…" She changed it mid-sentence and it sounded natural. "Of my only best friend's baby boy," she concluded without missing a beat.

Erin didn't catch the hesitation. "It wouldn't be the same without you."

"I'm just sorry about your husband," Annie said with mock sadness. "I know it's even harder for you, having the baby without him."

Annie thought of Ty and almost burst into tears. He'd never see his child, never know that he had a son. Serves him right, she thought angrily, and just as quickly tried to imagine the look on his face if things had gone along naturally. If he hadn't had that bad experience that turned him against marriage. If he'd loved Erin the way she'd loved him. If he'd courted her, cared for her, wanted to marry her, and the baby had come along then.

But regrets would do no service. She had to be strong for her baby. It was unfortunate that they'd found a heart condition during her pregnancy that had required treatment by a cardiologist. She was doing well, all the doctors said so. It was just…she worried about the baby's future. He was just born, and Maude was old. If anything happened to the two of them…but then, there was still Annie.

Yes. There was still Annie.

A hand on hers brought her out of the mist. "I'm going now. Don't brood, okay?" Annie asked with a smile. "Everything is going to be okay."

"You think so?"

"I do." She patted the hand. "I'll see you tomorrow. Sleep well."

"I'll do my best," Erin sighed. "Thanks."

"You'd have done it for me," her best friend pointed out.

"Dead right," Erin assured her.

Thank God for Maude, she thought, and she said it when all three of them were crammed into the front seat of Justin's ranch truck on the way home.

"She wouldn't answer my emails," Annie said sadly. "I tried so hard. If it hadn't been for you, I'd never have known."

"I had a feeling it was a good time to intervene." She hesitated. "There's something going on. The obstetrician hinted at it, but he said I'd have to dig it out of Erin. He's giving her medication and they had a cardiologist on standby in the delivery room."

"Oh, dear God," Annie groaned. "Her mother died of a heart attack, you know."

"All my people did," Maude replied. "It runs in the family. Listen, Annie, if anything ever happens to me, that poor child will be all alone in the world. I long ago left my estate to a great-niece who lives here in Wyoming. She agreed, in writing, that she'd never sell the ranch and she'd keep Justin as manager. She'd never live here and Justin would never leave here. So it's ideal. But Erin will be left without a home or a job."

"I'll manage all that when the time comes," Annie said simply. "No worries." She smiled at the older woman. "Honestly, I almost had the pilot fly me up here a dozen times and I chickened out. She wouldn't answer emails. I was afraid she'd slam the door in my face. You worked magic."

"Dead right. She keeps the pointy hat in her closet," Justin added, deadpan.

"You can just hush," Maude told him. "You're in enough trouble. Pouring ginger ale all over our houseguest…!"

"She was hotter than a pepper. Just wanted to help her cool down," he replied.

Annie laughed out loud. "I mistook him for my brother," she said in her defense.

"Nobody's that bad except Tyson," Maude drawled, rolling her eyes.

"He's not so bad right now," Annie replied on a sigh. "I've never seen him like this. He worries me."

"About the court case?"

"About Erin," she replied. "He tried to text her."

"I noticed. She blocked him."

"He's been miserable. Not that he doesn't deserve to be. He should have listened. I told him she'd never betray him. He went off half-cocked."

"His usual state," Maude laughed.

"Not anymore. He knows how badly he's treated her. He wants to make amends. I told him to keep his distance."

"You did?" Maude said. "May I ask why?"

"You know how she feels about him, Maude."

"Of course."

"Well, I don't think he really knows how he feels about her.

I don't want him to give her false hope. It's kinder to just stand back and let things settle down. I'm not sure that it isn't guilt. You know?"

Maude nodded. "It's a wise decision, all things considered," she agreed.

"Yes, it is." Annie fiddled with her purse. "I think Callaway's a nice name."

"It is. So is Regan…" Maude stopped short.

Annie gave her a long, knowing look. "I knew. I know my best friend inside and out. She's been in love with him since she was thirteen. It wasn't ever believable that she'd have let another man touch her."

"No. But you can't let her know," Maude insisted.

"I won't."

"Or him," Maude emphasized.

"Or him," Annie lied. "I know better."

"Okay. Just so you do. It's never wise to meddle in other people's business," she added. She glanced at Justin. "Especially in matters of unrequited love. Because sometimes people run away from it."

"Wise choice," Justin said curtly.

Annie listened without understanding that they were speaking on two different levels.

"She likes college, I hear," Maude said conversationally.

"Lots of nice young men for her to pick through."

"Yes, she found one already. Look out, Justin," she said quickly, because the wheel jerked, just a little.

"Who is he?"

"A medical student from South America," she said. "Brilliant, too. He helps her with labs."

"Our neighbor's daughter, Gabby," Maude explained to Annie. "She's training to be a vet. She already had some of her core courses completed. She's in the veterinary medicine program. Her new friend is doing many of the same courses before he switches over to human anatomy and other necessary courses of study."

"A brainy guy," Annie laughed. "Ty was like that. He graduated in the top ten percent of his class in math."

"I can count up to twenty if I use my fingers and my toes," Justin interjected.

"You nut," Annie laughed.

"But I have to take off my socks first," he informed them.

"In which case, you can do your math on the porch," Maude replied.

Annie laughed.

Ty had just come home from another long business trip, to find the house empty and Annie gone.

Mrs. Dobbs just shrugged when he asked where his sister was. "I have no idea," she lied. "She left me a message saying she was going shopping in New York. That's all I know. But there's something else for you to deal with," she added, muttering to herself as she led him into the room he used for an office at home.

"What?" he asked.

"There!"

He moved closer to his desk. The carpet was in shreds behind his leather desk chair. Part of the chair had been gnawed and there was stuffing on the floor. One of the feet that held the desk up had gnaw marks. To top it all, most of the baseboard looked like shredded wood.

"Oh, God, not again," Ty groaned. He turned and looked as the German shepherd puppy, Beauregard, came rushing in to meet him, tail wagging, barking, all loving joy.

The puppy sat at his feet, since he'd been trained not to jump on people, and looked up with pure love, his pink tongue hanging out one side of his mouth as he panted.

"You horror," Ty said with mock outrage.

Then he reached down and picked up the puppy and hugged it to him, nuzzling his chin against the top of its head. "You're going to bankrupt me. This is the third time this month!"

"I try to keep him out of here, but it's just impossible when I'm cleaning," Mrs. Dobbs defended herself. "Besides that, he's miserable when you aren't here. I'm no substitute. He only loves me when I have food for him in my hands."

"Beau," he sighed, putting the puppy down, "too much love is unhealthy."

"It is not," Mrs. Dobbs replied. "But too much absence is."

He glowered at her. "I'm a businessman. I have to go where business is."

"Ha! You're just running away from your problems and you know it, young man!"

"I'll fire you," he threatened.

"I'll quit!" she threatened right back.

He drew in a breath. "White flag," he replied.

She nodded with a jerk of her head. "Now that we've got that settled, I've a nice latticework apple pie with ice cream, and some strong coffee in the kitchen."

"Say no more." He grinned at her and followed her out of the room. "I'll send some of my construction people out here to undo what Beau did. Yes, I'm talking about you," he told the young dog, still wagging its tail and trotting beside him. "Who told you that you could tear up my office, huh?"

"If he ever answers you, I'm really quitting," Mrs. Dobbs told him.

"He's smart," he replied.

"Too smart," she returned. "He's learned how to open the refrigerator."

"Oh, good grief, not him, too! Rhodes did that until the trainer finally was able to break him!" He put his hands in his pockets. "Well, I'll call the trainer and have her come down to work with him. I'd better do it before Christmas Day or there'll be a disaster!"

"You'd better believe it! If my Christmas turkey ends up in that furry child's mouth, you're toast!" Mrs. Dobbs informed him.

He chuckled. "I'll call her right now."

"Good for you!"

He was looking at figures in the office downstairs, with a Christmas tree sparkling with colored lights and the gas logs putting out warm flames when his cell phone rang.

He picked it up absently and muttered his name.

"It's just me," Annie said.

"Where the hell are you?" he asked. "I thought you were shopping in New York City."

"I'm in Wyoming."

His heart jumped. "Why? Did Erin relent and let you come up to visit?"

"No," she said heavily. "She still wasn't answering her phone. Maude got my number from Erin's phone and called me, just after the ambulance came."

He almost overturned his chair. "Erin!" he exclaimed. "Something's happened to Erin?"

"Calm down," she said, encouraged by his involuntary show of fear for her best friend. "It's all right."

"How can it be all right if she had to be carried off in an ambulance?" he demanded. "Is it serious?"

"No. It's eight pounds and two ounces, and twenty inches long," she replied.

He drew in a quick breath. "She had the baby!"

"Yes." There was a smile in her voice. "But there was a complication. They had to do a Cesarean section."

"Good God," he whispered reverently. "Is she all right?"

"Yes. They say she'll be fine. It will just take time for her to recover. It's major surgery, you know."

"And the baby?" he asked softly.

Annie wanted to rage at him for what he'd done to her best friend, but this really wasn't the time.

"A boy," she said gently. "Erin named him Callaway, for her father."

"Callaway." He felt warm all over. "It's a good name."

"I thought so, too. He's beautiful." The wonder was in her voice. "I never knew babies could be so exciting. I didn't want to leave the hospital."

"Callaway," he repeated, his voice softer than his sister had ever heard it.

"How's Beau?" she asked hesitantly.

"How did he get into my office?" he asked, his tone changing suddenly.

"I'm sorry. I had to write a check, so I did it at the desk and forgot to close the door. Listen, you either have to board Beau when you go off places or take him with you. He only does it because he misses you. It's revenge."

He chuckled. "I noticed. I'll figure something out. Meanwhile, one of my crews is coming out Friday to repair the damage."

"Second time this month," she pointed out.

"I'll manage it," he replied. "How long are you going to stay in Wyoming?"

"A few days," she said.

"Where is she? What hospital?"

"Catelow only has one," she pointed out. "What do you want to do? If you send flowers, and she knows they're from you, she'll either have them trashed or she'll give them to somebody."

He felt those words, felt them hard. "I'd deserve it, too," he said. "I guess that's not a good idea."

"Not now, at least. Give it time," she advised softly.

"What have you told her?"

"Nothing. I'm playing along with the poor late husband thing."

"What last name is she giving him?"

Annie stared at the phone for a few seconds. Good heavens, men were dense! "Her 'late' husband's name. It's Mitchell, the same as hers. As she tells it, they have the same last name but weren't related."

"Better for official documents, so she wouldn't have to change any," he got the idea at once.

"Yes," she said. "I don't dare tell her that we know. I'd be back on the no-call list."

"I see. Well, take her some flowers, at least," he said.

"I'll have a big bouquet sent. But your name isn't going on it."

"I knew that. Be safe. Talk to you soon."

"Okay," she said. "Love you."

"Same."

He hung up. The next thing he did was call the pilot of his baby jet and book a time.

CHAPTER TWELVE

It was snowing when Ty got to Catelow. He'd told nobody where he was going, or what he planned to do. It was dark, just at the end of visiting hours, and he'd laid his plans very well.

He was going to sneak into the hospital, when there would likely be fewer people around, and look in the nursery. Surely he could mingle with the numbers of people milling about as visiting hours ended and go largely unnoticed.

And it might have worked, if he hadn't gotten off the elevator on the second floor and run straight into his own sister.

"Oh, no," she groaned.

He drew her to one side. "I just want to see him," he said gently, and there was misery in his whole look. "That's all. I won't go near Erin. Is she okay?" he added.

"She's having a lot of pain today. The pain medicine makes her sleep, so I haven't talked a lot. I've just been here."

"Good." He drew in a breath. "I couldn't just sit at home," he added quietly.

"The baseboards will be completely chewed to dust by the time you get back," she groaned.

"No, they won't. I put him in his crate."

"What crate? He's never been in a crate. You won't use them." It was an accusation.

"His trainer is teaching him. You'd like her. She's tiny but she can make him stand around," he chuckled. "Just out of high school, smart, snarky, and top of the line at dog training. Her name's Perri."

"I like her already. He'll still mourn while you're gone. Want to bet on whether Mrs. Dobbs will let him out in self-defense?"

He grimaced. "Probably," he had to agree. "It's early days for crate training."

She looked around. "Justin and Maude are in the canteen having coffee. We'll go this way."

She led him down the hall to the nursery. One of the aides who'd been in and out of Erin's room all day was there. She recognized Erin and grinned. A minute later, she brought out a baby wrapped in a blanket.

"My nephew!" Erin laughed, peering inside. "Thanks, Tina! Oh, this is my cousin from Cheyenne," she improvised. "Chester," she picked out an unlikely name. She grinned. "I called to tell him the news and he flew up to see the baby."

Ty was wrapped in wonder as he stared at the small face so like his own, or he'd have questioned Annie's choice of fake names. As it was, he beamed at the child, reaching out a big hand to touch the little hand. It suddenly caught one of his fingers and curled around it, opened its eyes and looked straight into his.

"My God," he whispered reverently.

"Want to hold him?" the aide asked, amused by the big man's fascination with the tiny baby. Odd, she thought, he didn't look like a Chester. But you never knew.

"Yes, please," Ty said.

She put the baby in his arms, carefully, instructing him how to hold it.

Ty was in heaven. He'd never dreamed that a child would look like this, feel like this. He hadn't known that there would be such an instant connection between him and a baby that he'd fathered. He felt himself on fire with joy, blazing with it. His eyes betrayed that joy.

Annie moved closer. "Isn't he adorable?" she asked.

"Callaway," he whispered, smiling at the child.

In all their lives together, Annie had never seen a smile like that on her brother's face. Before she had time to think about the wisdom of it, she pulled out her cell phone and took a couple of quick photos, grinning all the while.

But a few minutes later, Annie looked around. The crowd was thinning. "You need to get back to Cheyenne, Cousin Chester," she prompted. "You have that meeting tomorrow with the bank manager."

"What?" Ty wasn't hearing her.

"We really need to go. It's a long flight home."

"Not so far," the aide laughed.

"Well, it's not, but he needs to get some figures ready for the meeting."

"I see." The aide nodded.

Ty reluctantly gave the child back to the aide. "He's really something," he said, and it was an understatement.

"Yes, he is. My first nephew," Annie sighed. "Thanks for letting us see him."

"No problem." She smiled at both of them. "Have a safe trip home."

"We will. Take good care of Cal for us."

"You bet!"

"You have to get out of here before Maude sees you," Annie said, almost dragging him toward the elevator.

"You said they were in the canteen," Ty reminded her. "I want to see Erin. Just to see her," he added quietly.

She drew in an anguished breath. "She'll go nuts if she sees you!"

"You can check and make sure she's not awake first," he conceded. "Please, Annie." That look could have melted ice.

She couldn't resist him. "Okay. But we have to hurry!"

They made it to Annie's room without being seen by Maude or Justin. Annie peeked in the door. The drugs had done their work. Erin was sound asleep.

"Just for a minute," he whispered, and went into the room despite her desperate pantomime urging him to come back out.

He went to the bedside and looked down on the woman he'd mistreated so badly. He felt the guilt like a hot brand in his mind. He'd failed her, in so many ways. She'd loved him for years, and he'd never noticed. She'd given him a son, after all he'd done to her. He felt humble.

His big hand went to her dark hair and he touched it very lightly. "I'll make it up to you one day," he whispered, as he bent and kissed her tenderly on her forehead. "I swear I will, Erin! I..." He tried to say the words. But he'd never said them to anyone except his parents and Annie. He couldn't get them out. But he meant them. Every single syllable of those three words he couldn't speak.

"Just get well. Don't worry about anything." He heard her soft breath, her sudden movement, as if she'd heard him. But she hadn't. She was still asleep. "My beautiful girl," he said, almost choking on the words. "I lost you before I found you. Why didn't I know how I felt? I'm so damned sorry, Erin. My life is like a painting with all the color gone, since I ran you off. I should have trusted you. Now, I can only hope that someday you'll forgive me. Be safe." There was so much more that he wanted to say, that he couldn't get out in words.

But there was Annie, gesturing wildly toward the door.

He looked at Erin one last time. So pale, so stressed, so fatigued. He'd put her in this position. He felt so much guilt that he could hardly bear it. Someday, I'll have another chance, he promised himself. I'll work hard at it.

He moved to the door. "What?"

"I just told Justin and Maude to go on ahead, I had to use the ladies' room," she said quickly. "Give us five minutes and then you can leave."

"Okay. She looks terrible," he added as they walked toward the elevator.

"She's just had a Cesarean," she replied. "Even with the bikini cut they do these days, it's still surgery. She'll be okay soon, but it takes time." She glanced at him. "She said the pregnancy itself was easy. She went for long walks with Justin on the ranch, and it kept her strength up."

"Justin?" he asked, and his face tautened.

"Maude's foreman."

"Married?"

"Nope."

The tension in his face got worse.

Annie wasn't going to enlighten him. She was still furious at him for the way poor Erin had been treated, and it didn't matter that he was her brother.

"I'll see you back home in a few days," she said.

"Sure." He glanced at her. "Take care of her. Whatever she needs."

"I knew that."

He nodded. He looked lonely and sick at heart and miserable.

Well, blood was blood. She moved closer and hugged him. "One day, things will work out."

He hugged her back. "One day we'll all be dead and gone," he muttered.

"You stop that," she said, drawing back. "Times get hard. We get through them."

"Tell Erin you're sending her something for Christmas. I'll have it overnighted to the ranch." He looked away. "Don't tell her it's from me."

Annie felt his pain. "Okay," she relented.

He managed a smile. "Thanks. I'll go home and fuss at Beau."

"Pet Rhodes. He gets lonely, too."

He nodded. "Be careful."

"You, too."

She gave him a quick kiss and went out the door. He watched as she climbed into the ranch pickup and it pulled out of the parking lot. Only then did he go outside, pulling his Stetson down over his eyes as the snow rained down. It was only a short walk to his rental car. The jet was waiting for him at the airport.

He wished he had a photo of his son. He'd been too overwhelmed to take a picture. He texted his sister. Did she have one?

There was a smiling emoji. A couple of minutes later, the photo came through. It was Erin, as she always was, smiling and beaming into the camera with the baby close in her arms. She was smiling down at the little face, one hand touching his cheek. It was the most beautiful photo he'd ever seen. Erin and his child. He moved it into his photo file and then selected it as the lockscreen photo. That was before he saw the other photo she'd sent—one of him with his son. His heart jumped up into his throat. That photo he added to his phone's screen as well.

He texted Annie back and thanked her.

You're welcome. Don't flash them around, she cautioned, and there was a laughing emoji.

I won't, he promised.

The minute he got home, he went in search of Mrs. Dobbs, who was just locking up for the night.

He showed her the photo.

"Oh, isn't he beautiful!" she exclaimed. "I wonder how big he is...?"

"Eight pounds, two ounces," he said, repeating what Annie had told him. "And twenty inches long."

Mrs. Dobbs looked up at him with one eyebrow raised. "I'm not stupid, you know."

He grimaced. "I've made a few mistakes," he conceded.

"This—" she indicated the photo "—wasn't one of them." She grinned.

He chuckled softly.

"But for all practical purposes, Miss Erin is a widow."

The smile faded. "Yes. For now," he added quietly.

The housekeeper just nodded. There would be a reckoning, sooner or later. She knew that her boss would be crazy to get that child in his possession, one way or another. She was equally sure that Miss Erin wouldn't budge. Payback was a sad thing. Mr. Ty was going to learn it the hard way.

The next day, Annie presented Erin with a jeweler's box.

"Now, it's just a little thing," she said as she gave it to her friend. "So don't go bonkers over it, okay?"

"I promise. But you shouldn't have..." She opened the box and just stared at the thing inside. It was a ring. A dinner ring. A huge beautiful ruby in the center with sparkling diamonds around it in a yellow gold setting. She'd loved rubies her whole life, but never owned one. This had to be at least three karats!

"It's just a trinket," Annie argued.

"It's priceless," Erin wailed. "How could you!"

"Don't be like this," Annie said. "You know very well I could buy a dozen of these and call it pocket change. Don't you like it?"

"I love it. I've wanted one for years, but I can't, I just can't accept it!"

"Bull feathers," Annie replied. "You certainly can. I'm your best friend. There's no reason I can't give you a dinner ring. Now try it on and stop muttering."

Erin was forced to laugh. "Oh, all right." She slid it onto her finger, but it would only fit the ring finger, not her pinky.

"That's okay," Annie replied when she was told. "Lots of women wear them on any finger, even the thumb."

"But it's so expensive," she wailed. "And so beautiful!"

"I'm glad you like it," Annie replied, thinking how pleased her brother would be to hear how his present was received. He'd wanted to give Erin something precious to mark the equally precious birth of their first child, their son. This was the only way he could do it, he'd told Annie over the phone, with some anguish in his voice. He knew how much Erin loved rubies. This one was from a designer he knew, and he'd been sure that she'd love it. But she had to think it was from Annie. It was the only way she'd have accepted it.

"I love it. But you shouldn't have," Erin said and hugged her friend around the baby on her shoulder.

"I should have," Annie replied. "Here, I'll take it to Maude and let her keep it until you come home."

"Ok. Thanks."

Annie put it back in the box, just before Maude came in, without Justin.

"He's gone to the feed store," Maude told them. "Do you like the ring? Annie showed it to me this morning. It's beautiful!"

"I love it," Erin said. "I'll never take it off! But I can't give you something of equal value when your birthday comes up," she added to Annie with a chuckle.

"Crochet me a hat and I'll love you forever," Annie replied. "My ears get cold, even in Texas!"

"I'll put that on my to-do list as soon as I get home," Erin promised her.

Erin had never been so happy. The baby filled her life. She ignored the lingering pain from her surgery and breastfed him. It was hard going at first. She didn't have enough milk to satisfy him, so he had to have a bottle at feeding time as well. But some new meds and her own stubborn will soon fixed that.

"I had the oddest dream night before last," she told Annie while she was burping the baby.

"Oh, did you?" Annie asked innocently.

"Yes. I was in this room, asleep, but there was somebody

here. He was talking to me." She laughed. "It must have been my dad, watching over me. He'd have loved Cal."

"Yes, he would have," Annie said, not daring to mention that her friend's dream had been real, that Ty had been in the room. That would never do. Not now.

"It's so sad that neither of my parents lived to see their first grandchild," Erin whispered, fighting tears. "It's just so sad." She didn't add that it was even sadder that Ty would never see his child, would never know that he had a son.

"Now, now," Annie said, gently soothing her back, then reaching to smooth her hand over the baby's small head. "The baby is a darling! It's so exciting!"

Erin laughed. "Yes, for me, too. I never knew what it would be like to have a child, to actually have one. It's so different from what I imagined."

"I wish I had one," Annie said.

"No problem. You can share Cal with me," she replied, smiling.

"I'll hold you to that," Annie promised. She hesitated. "I hate to go, but I must get back home. The construction gang is coming tomorrow, and Ty has a business meeting in Montana, so I have to be there when they arrive."

Erin's heart jumped at just the mention of Ty's name. She hated the reaction she couldn't help. The man had betrayed her and she couldn't hate him, even now. Heaven knew, she'd tried to!

"Construction gang?" she asked suddenly, frowning.

"Beauregard," Annie sighed.

"Beauregard...?" Erin queried.

"You see, Ty's been travelling a lot lately, and Beauregard really misses him. So far, he's scored part of the carpet, all of the baseboard, and a good bit of Ty's leather desk chair. Plus the leg of the desk."

"Oh, my gosh!"

"He misses Ty. It's revenge."

"Didn't Rhodes do the same thing when Ty was at college?"

"Exactly the same thing." Annie shook her head. "When I remember all the incredible damage those fur babies can do, I'm amazed that Ty keeps having more of them."

"He loves puppies," Erin recalled, and felt warm inside. "Especially Beau, because he was so badly abused." Her face tautened. "I hope the man who beat him never gets out of jail!"

"There will be a parole hearing eventually," Annie said. "I hear that Ty plans to attend it, with photos of what he did to Beau."

"Good enough for the man!"

"Exactly what I thought," Annie said. "So, when I go home, you won't just send me heart emojis now?" she probed.

Erin flushed. "Of course not. I was so happy to see you!"

"No happier than I was to see you," Annie said softly. "It's been hard, not even being able to text you."

"I'm truly sorry. I just…didn't want to know anything about your brother."

"I can understand that. You've had an awful time, and it was mostly his fault."

"He didn't trust me," Erin said sadly. "I don't know why I expected him to. Love is the basis of trust."

"Ty has had a hard time with women. You know that."

"A hard time." She laughed bitterly. "Sure he has. Mr. Playboy. And why not? He's single and handsome and rich. What woman wouldn't jump at the chance to be his woman of the month?"

"Not nice," Annie said.

Erin shrugged and winced, because she was still sore. "I guess so. I'm just bitter."

"That will pass, in time," Annie said, and mentally crossed her fingers.

Erin looked down at her son. "He's missing so much," she said in a moment of weakness, and she smiled sadly. "So is my late husband, of course," she added quickly. "He'll never get to see his son."

Annie didn't dare mention the fictional husband, or the fact that Ty had already been to the hospital to see his son, without Erin's knowledge.

"That's sad." Annie went along with the fiction. She got up. "Well, the jet's waiting for me at the airport. I have to go." She bent and kissed Erin and the baby. "Maude and Justin will take care of you. But text me often, okay? And I'll text you."

"Don't tell Ty you've been here," Erin pleaded.

"Would I sell out my best friend in the whole world?" Annie asked solemnly, lying through her teeth.

"Of course you wouldn't," Erin agreed. "Sorry."

"No problem."

"Text me when you get home," Erin said when Annie was at the door, "so I know you got home safe."

"You bet I will. Take care."

"You, too."

Annie smiled. "Love you both," she added, blowing them a kiss.

"Love you back."

The door closed. Erin stared at it for several minutes, feeling hollow as her best friend left. But the baby stirred, and she turned back to him with lingering wonder.

Annie went back home with dozens of photos of Erin and little Cal, which she shared with her morose brother.

"He's amazing, isn't he?" Ty asked as he flicked through them on the phone app. "She's doing okay?"

"Yes. She has new meds. I had to fight her, but I paid for them."

"Not surprising," he said on a sigh. He glanced at her with one eyebrow raised. "Any new photos?" he added.

She nodded, laughing. He was becoming predictable. "Yes. A ton of them."

She pulled up her photo app and showed him the new additions.

He sat down behind his desk with her phone and looked through them at the baby, his eyes soft and warm and loving. Until he came to the last few pictures.

The dark scowl on his face gave him away.

"That's Justin," she said before he could ask. "He's Maude's foreman."

He was openly glaring at the man in the broad Stetson. Not bad looking. Tall, muscular, dark-haired and dark-eyed.

"He runs the ranch for Maude." Annie rubbed it in.

"He looks like a roughneck," Ty muttered. "Did Maude do a background check before she hired him?"

"He isn't a roughneck, and it was Maude's late husband who hired him. Justin is a former reservation cop. Not a roughneck."

"Oh." He glared at the photo even more.

Erin smothered a laugh. Ty's jealousy was so obvious that it was almost funny.

He handed her back the phone. "You take good photos," he said.

"Thanks."

"How is she?" he asked.

"Still hurting, but much better."

There was an undercurrent there. He looked up. Annie had a poker face, but he knew her. There was something more, something else worrying her.

"Is she really all right?" he persisted.

She lifted her eyebrows, feigning surprise. It wouldn't do to let Ty know what she suspected, especially with Erin in this condition, unable to fight him. If he went tearing back to Wyoming, trying to force her to go to specialists, she'd dig her heels in and refuse to do anything. It wasn't time to tell him. At least, not until she could persuade Maude to persuade Erin to go to a heart specialist and find out exactly what was wrong. No need to involve Ty until she had facts, not suspicions.

"You look worried," he persisted.

"Of course I'm worried! She's had surgery! She's just had a baby, and she's weak and worn out."

"Okay, I get it," he said, relaxing with a sigh. He leaned back in his chewed desk chair, his eyes on Beauregard, now lying across his boots on the floor.

"She'll be okay. I know because Maude spoke to the obstetrician," she added. That much was true.

"Will she come back to Texas, do you think?" he wondered quietly.

"Ty, she's made her home in Wyoming with Maude." She said it gently. "Why would she want to come back now?"

He glowered at her. "Because that's my son," he said curtly.

"Okay. Go up there and tell her you know it," she invited, holding out a hand, palm-up. "And insist that she come back to Jacobsville, where everybody knows what you accused her of, and what you did afterward!"

He grimaced, averting his eyes.

"Dug your own grave, old dear," Annie said with cold relish.

"I know I did," he ground out. He got up, displacing Beauregard. He picked up the pup and held him over one shoulder, petting him. The pup was still half asleep. He didn't budge.

"You're spoiling that puppy," Annie pointed out. "Nobody is going to get to buy him, because he's bonded to you."

He turned around and smiled. "I noticed."

She studied him, her heart melting. "You never intended to sell him after you got him back, did you?"

He shook his head. "He's had a fraught puppyhood," he explained. "I'd never be sure that whoever got him wouldn't do the same sort of thing that slimy reptile did to him," he added, his face going hard with anger. "Anybody who'd beat a puppy would beat a child," he added coldly.

"I agree," she said softly. "I didn't say I blamed you for wanting to keep him."

He managed a smile. "He's just a baby, still," he said, disregarding the fact that Beauregard was already the size of a five-year-old child.

"A very big baby," she corrected.

He chuckled. "Rhodes weighs over a hundred pounds. I expect this furry child will even exceed that. He's bigger than Rhodes was at this age." He put the puppy down in the soft dog bed he kept in the office and watched it circle and then lie down and go right back to sleep.

"He's very sweet."

"He's a shepherd," he pointed out. "Sweet is a good personality trait. I don't raise dogs to be bodyguards, although the way they look would deter most criminals," he added. "Aggressive dogs are dangerous around kids, and I sell to families."

"Beau wouldn't hurt a fly," she teased.

"Not unless somebody attacked one of us," he agreed. "Rhodes is the same. Remember that disgruntled cowboy I fired who came in here threatening to punch me?"

"And before you could draw back your fist, Rhodes bit him." She winced.

Ty grinned. "He didn't sit down for a while. Even tried to sue me and have Rhodes taken away as a danger to the public."

"Yes, and then Cash Grier had a nice discussion with him about the dangers of provoking a sweet house pet."

He chuckled. "Our police chief is eloquent at times."

"It helped that he has one of our pups at home with his wife and two kids," she added.

"And his young brother-in-law, who takes the dog fishing with him."

"I remember when Cash married Tippy," she sighed. "Nobody believed that he'd ever marry. He was one tough customer."

"I remember." He turned back to her. "Isn't there some way we can get Erin to come back to Texas?" he asked quietly.

"It will take time," she said. "Maude is good to her, you know that."

"I know." He sounded sad and resigned. "I'd love to get to know my son, is all," he confessed.

"It's too soon."

He stared at the floor. "It's been months since she left," he replied.

"Months, during which she lost her father, her home, her job—two jobs," she amended, giving him a glowering look.

He winced. "I know what I did. You don't have to rub it in."

"That Mosby temper will be the end of you yet," she pointed out.

"I guess it will." He glanced at her. "Did you tell her what happened, about Ms. Taylor?"

She nodded.

"What did she say?"

She shrugged. "That she always thought Jenny smiled too much."

He thought about that for a minute. "I guess she did."

She went to him and hugged him. "Be patient," she said. "She'll come back one day. Meanwhile, it's best to just relax and let life happen. If she's meant to come home to Texas, she will. Something will happen."

Those were prophetic words. The very next day, Maude went out to the barn to look at a sick calf and dropped dead in the doorway of the barn.

CHAPTER THIRTEEN

Justin was running for all he was worth. Maude was lying in a heap at the door of the barn. He had his cell phone in his hand, calling 911 as he ran.

He gave the address. When the operator asking what was the emergency, he went down on one knee beside Maude and felt for a pulse. There was none. She was blue. She was also cold. He had no idea how long she'd been lying there. He and the cowhands had been out on the ranch rounding up stock to bring closer to the ranch house because heavy snow was predicted.

He ground his teeth together. "I don't know," he said honestly. "I just found her. She's blue and stone-cold. I've seen death overseas in the military. There's no hope. Better send the coroner, Jill," he added, because he knew her from her other job at the coffee shop in Catelow, which she held part-time.

"I'm so sorry, Justin," she replied. "I'll get Dan Burton right out there."

"Thanks."

He hung up. He drew in a long breath. "I'm sorry, Maude," he said quietly. "Wouldn't have had it happen like this for the world. I should have been here!"

He thought he heard faint laughter. He could imagine Maude being amused at his temper, as she always had been.

"Safe journey, old friend," he said, patting the hand lying beside her, gloved and still.

The coroner examined her and said he expected it was a massive heart attack. "We'll have to do an autopsy to be sure, but I'm already sure. Just have to prove it to everybody else," he told Justin. "Where's she going?"

"Landon's," he said, naming the funeral home in town that Maude's family had always used. "Hell of a thing. She was kidding with us this morning when we rode out. And now this."

"Well, it was quick," the coroner said. "That's a blessing. It was the way she would have wanted to go. Just like her husband did." He smiled sadly. "I expect they're both on horseback about now, out hunting heavenly strays."

"No doubt about that." He ground his teeth. "I'll have to go to town and tell her houseguest. Her young cousin from Texas has just had a baby, with a Cesarean. Not sure they'll let her out just yet."

"That might not be a bad thing. What's going to happen to the ranch?" he added. "Will her heir sell it?"

"No, of course not. She has a great-niece besides the cousin who's had a baby. Great-niece inherits. Lives in Cheyenne. It's already been discussed. I'll stay on as ranch manager. The niece doesn't want to let the ranch go, it's part of her family history, but she doesn't want to live here. She's a town girl."

"Couldn't give me town on a platter," the coroner scoffed. "Too crowded."

Justin chuckled. "That's how I feel. I like a lot of room."

"I'll get back to work," the coroner, who was also a dentist in town, said. He glanced toward his van, where his helpers had just loaded Maude. "I hate to see her go."

"No less than I do," Justin agreed. "She was a grand old lady. Hard as nails and softhearted to boot. She'll be missed."

"Better call Gabby Dane's dad. He can call Gabby."

"I will." He grimaced. "She'll be devastated. She was like a granddaughter to Maude."

"Who's going to break it to the young lady in the hospital?"

Justin rolled his eyes. "Definitely not me. She's got health issues." He scowled and pulled out his phone. "She's got a friend in Texas. I'll see if she can come up and do the dirty work."

"You could just have her doctor do it."

He shook his head. "Maude loved her. That's no way to treat a woman in her condition." He pulled up the information that Maude had given him and dialed.

Annie was just finishing lunch. She and Mrs. Dobbs were discussing what sort of baby stuff they could send up to Wyoming for Erin's baby when her phone rang.

It wasn't a ring tone she'd assigned, so she looked at it with disinterest, sure that it was a scam or a politician robocall. But when she saw the number displayed, she punched Accept.

"What's happened?" she asked at once. She didn't know who it was but she knew Maude's area code by heart by now.

"It's Justin." He hesitated.

"Something's happened to Maude," she replied. "Tell me, Justin."

He took a deep breath. "I found her at lunchtime," he said heavily. "She was cold. The coroner said it must have been very quick. She wouldn't have felt anything."

"Poor Maude," she said on a sigh. It had been only a few days since she'd come home. Maude had been fine. So quickly, things could change.

"You coming up?"

"You bet I am, as soon as our pilot can get the plane juiced." She paused. "Has anybody told Erin yet?"

There was a pause. "I didn't think I should be the one to do it. Or the doctor either. Gonna hit her hard."

"Okay," she said gently. "I understand. Can you meet me at the airport?"

"Sure. Call me about ten minutes before you land."

"I will. Thanks."

He hung up.

"What is it?" Mrs. Dobbs asked.

"Maude died."

"Now what?" the housekeeper asked. "If Miss Erin's just out of surgery, she won't be able to do much."

"I know. She was supposed to come home from the hospital tomorrow." She grimaced. "I don't know how to handle this," she confessed, looking at the housekeeper. "If I tell Ty, he'll go roaring up there demanding that she come home with us, and she'll dig in her heels."

"It's his baby," Mrs. Dobbs pointed out.

"He's not supposed to know that," she was reminded.

"I know."

Annie wrung her hands together. She hesitated. "There's some big deal being set up in England. A building project in London that they want Ty to consult on." She nodded slowly. "It will keep him out of the country for at least two or three weeks."

"What a nice coincidence," Mrs. Dobbs exclaimed.

"Tailor-made to help our situation," she agreed, smiling. "I'll tell him I'm going up to see Erin, that she's due to come back to the house tomorrow. That much is the truth. I just won't tell him anything else!"

"Miss Annie, you were born to be a secret agent," the housekeeper chuckled.

"All I need is a trenchcoat," she murmured. "I'll go talk to him right now."

Ty was headed out to lunch with Mr. Jones. He paused as Annie came in the front door.

"Go ahead, I'll catch up," Ty told his friend with a smile.

"Sure thing. Hi, Annie."

"Mr. Jones," she replied, smiling.

"What are you doing here?" Ty asked.

"I'm going to fly up to Wyoming tomorrow, so I'll be there to go with Maude and Justin to bring Erin home from the hospital. What do you think I should get her?" she asked innocently.

He frowned. "How about a car seat, or one of those cribs with all the mobiles?" he asked. "Something that she couldn't afford," he added softly.

"A car seat," she said at once. "I'll have Justin drive me into Catelow and look around, after we get Erin and the baby settled. Maude already bought her a baby bed," she added, biting down hard on the thought that Maude wouldn't be there to see the homecoming. "That's a good idea," she said, "about the car seat. Good ones are expensive."

"I wish I could go," he said quietly.

"You've got that thing in England, though," she said in all innocence. "When are you leaving?"

He sighed. "Tonight. I might as well get it over with."

"Poor Mrs. Dobbs. She'll be stuck with Beauregard and his furniture appetite."

He chuckled. "She'll manage."

"He really misses you."

"I won't be gone that long," he said, and Annie almost held her breath. He grimaced. "Well, not all that long. Two or three weeks."

A good thing, Erin thought. It would give her time to decide how to help Erin. Even with the new situation at the ranch, Erin wasn't going to want to stay and impose on the great-niece's hospitality, because she was no longer employed by the ranch. Maude had let her keep the books, but Annie had been told that there was already a bookkeeper whose job it was. He was temporarily let go so that Maude would have a job to offer Erin.

It had been a kind gesture, but Erin would find out the truth and her pride wouldn't let her stay on. What would she do? She'd have to have a place to stay and money to keep herself and the baby, and a job. How would she work? She wasn't in good health. If what the doctor had told Erin was true there might be even worse things in Erin's future.

"What's wrong?" Ty asked, sensitive to his sister's expression.

"What?" She looked blank. "Oh. Sorry. I was thinking about car seats…"

He chuckled.

"Anyway, you have a safe trip. I'm going home to pack."

"I already did," he said smugly. "And the suitcase is in my trunk. All I have to do is drive to the airport. Have Jake pick up the car in the morning."

"I will."

"And you fly safely," he added.

"You do the same."

"Pictures," he said firmly.

"I'll take lots," she promised, smiling.

"Okay. I'll see you when I get back."

"Absolutely."

Late the next morning, she stepped off the plane in Catelow and Justin was waiting at the gate. He was solemn.

"How is Erin?" she asked.

"Not good," he replied, going with her to baggage claim. "You know how small towns are. Gossip gets around fast. Somebody told her about Maude."

"Oh, no," Erin groaned.

"So we'd better go by the hospital on the way home," he added. "She'll need reassurances. You know Maude's great-niece isn't going to throw her off the place. She's nice. She'll come for the funeral."

"I know of her," Annie agreed. "I'll talk to her. If nothing else, I'll try to persuade her to let Erin keep the books for another month or two and I'll pay her salary without her knowing."

"Nice." He glanced at her. "Ever think of going into crime as a profession? You've got prevarication down pat already."

"Don't start," she threatened. "I know where to find some more ginger ale!"

He chuckled.

When Annie walked into the hospital room, Erin burst into tears.

Annie put down her purse and coat and hugged her gently. "I'm so sorry," she said softly. "I didn't want you to know until I got here. I just forgot how small towns are. I know how they are, I live in one. I didn't think you'd find out so soon."

"She was like a second mother," Erin bawled. "I can't believe it! She was so healthy!"

"Heart disease isn't always predictable," Annie said, trying to calm her. "But I'm here now. It's going to be all right. We'll talk to the great-niece at the funeral and see what we can do next, okay? You know she won't toss you out into the snow," she added, trying to sound calming.

Erin drew in a breath. She sat back up and wiped her eyes. "I know. I just panicked. It's so sudden!"

"Life is like that," Annie said sadly.

"I can't stay on at the ranch," she replied. "One of the nurses said there's a bookkeeper who was kind enough to give up Maude's work so that she had a job for me. He keeps books for several ranches, so he's not starving, but I'm taking work away from him."

"And he won't mind," Annie said firmly, "or he wouldn't be doing it. People in Catelow are kind, just like people in Jacobsville. Now you stop worrying and concentrate on getting better. This will all work out. You'll see."

"You really think so?" Erin asked, her silvery gray eyes wide and red and wet.

"Yes, I do."

Erin took a long breath and laid back down. "I'm not usually so wimpy," she sighed. "It's just that I'm not over the surgery, not nearly well enough to support the baby and me if I have to get an outside job and find an apartment and a car...!"

"Stop that. I'll help. You'd do the same for me," she pointed out. "It's just a hand up, not a handout, you know," she chuckled.

Erin relaxed. "Okay. A hand up." She studied Annie. "What about Ty? He still doesn't suspect...?"

"Of course not!" Anne replied. "You know me better than that."

She relaxed a little bit more. "Yes, I do."

"Besides, he's out of town," she added. "For at least a month." She mentally crossed her fingers.

"I see," Erin said, but she felt the separation. Ridiculous. She didn't miss him!

"Justin's going to see to the funeral arrangements. The great-niece is flying in tomorrow. She'll stay at the ranch with us."

"You're staying?"

"Idiot. Would I leave you at a time like this?" She saw the suspicious look. "Ty's in Europe," she told her worried friend. "He'll be there for weeks. He's consulting on a job in London."

"Thanks."

"I love my brother, but I know what a pain he can be. If he knew your circumstances, despite everything he'd be up here trying to browbeat you into coming back to Texas. So he knows nothing." That much was true. Ty was a complication Annie didn't need right now.

"That's a relief."

"Justin and I will come get you and take you out to the ranch tomorrow. Gabby's coming home for the funeral. Justin called her dad, who called her. She loved Maude."

"She's so sweet. Justin never sees her, you know?" Erin said softly. "She went off to college to get away from her hopeless situation. Sort of like me," she added sadly. "It's hard to go nuts over a guy who can't see you for dust."

"One day…" Annie began.

Erin looked at her with an expression of such pain that she stopped in mid-sentence.

"False hope is no help," Erin said. "I'm sure Gabby knows that, too. You just put one foot ahead of the other and go on."

"We do what we have to," Annie agreed finally.

"So. One day at a time," Erin said. She smiled. "Want to see Cal?"

"Do I!" Annie exclaimed.

Erin laughed and called the nurses' station.

The ranch hadn't changed but it was so sad to sit in the living room by the beautiful lighted Christmas tree and not hear Maude humming as she made coffee or worked on meals or puttered around the living room.

"It's so quiet," Erin said.

Nan Demaris, the great-niece from Cheyenne, agreed. She was dark-haired, with blue eyes and an elegant carriage, the result of years at a finishing school and then a European university. Her people, related to Maude's late husband, were wealthy. Old money. She was nice, but she made Erin uneasy.

She made Justin uneasy as well. He found plenty of excuses not to go near the house.

She caught Erin looking at her and smiled. "I'm not an ogre," she said softly, and with a smile. "I'm not about to toss you out into the snow. Especially when you have that adorable little elf in the next room that I get to cuddle!"

Erin burst out laughing. "Is that how I looked?" she asked self-consciously. "I'm sorry. I feel like I'm taking advantage, just being here."

"You kept books for Maude and did a far better job than her

usual bookkeeper, although I hope you won't repeat that," the other woman said. "You earned your place here."

"You aren't going to sell the ranch?" Erin asked.

She shook her head. "It's very profitable, and Justin does a great job as manager. It was a stipulation of the will that he stays on in that capacity. Although," she added, "I'd have kept him on anyway. He's really good at what he does. My late great-uncle lost money hand over fist because he was sentimental about stock. Justin isn't. He buys and sells without regard to sentiment. It's why we're making money these days." She smiled sadly. "Maude was like that, too. She fell in love with certain bulls and dug her heels in about keeping them. Justin just let her work through it until she arrived at the same conclusion he did. It's an art, managing people without riding roughshod over their feelings."

"You seem to have inherited it," Annie teased.

She smiled. "I think it runs in the family. You have a brother, I seem to recall," Nan said.

Annie grimaced. "Oh, yes."

"I ran into him at a party a few months ago. He's…" She spread her hands.

"Yes," Annie chuckled, getting the inference.

"He loves women, but not singularly. Only in numbers."

Annie's eyebrows went up.

Nan shrugged. "I got mixed up with a man like him in my late teens. I followed him all over Europe, certain that I could make him love me." She smiled impishly. "Isn't it amazing how stupid women get when their hormones take control. All it took was one very sophisticated woman—far more sophisticated than I was at the time—to show me what an idiot I was. I packed my bags and came home."

"My brother has some issues when it comes to women," Annie allowed.

"He has a lot. It's a sad, sad woman who'll take him at face value and start building imaginary picket fences." She shook her head. "She'll never convert him. A bad love affair in the past, I expect?" she added to Annie, unaware of the quickly concealed tragic expression in Erin's averted eyes.

"Very bad," Annie conceded. "It turned him sour on the whole female sex."

"I'm much the same way," Nan replied. "If I ever marry, it will be for a sensible reason, not a sentimental one. I love children," she added softly. "But I've seen too many marriages falter on them. There are men who can't be housebroken."

"That is a sad fact of life, and we're all victims of the wars, in one sense or another." Annie laughed deliberately, so that her scars didn't show.

"But back to business," she said, turning to Erin, "I hope you'll stay on for a while. I've gotten used to being profitable here. And I'd love to drop in from time to time just for a quick cuddle with that gorgeous little man," she chuckled.

Erin sighed with relief. "You're a lifesaver," she said quietly. "I'm most grateful. I do want to go back to Texas, perhaps in the spring. But it would help me very much to be able to stay here while I get back on my feet. I have to be able to work outside the home when I get back."

"No problem," Nan said easily. "We'll be helping each other."

Gabby came rushing in late that afternoon. She went straight to Erin and hugged her and hugged her.

"I'm so sorry that I wasn't here," she said miserably.

"Bless your heart," Erin replied. "We were doing very well. But Maude...well, none of us guessed that she had a hidden heart condition." She drew back. "It was very quick," she added. "She never knew what was happening."

"That's a relief, at least." She sat back on the heels of her boots, kneeling at Erin's feet. "Who is she?" she added with icy venom.

Erin couldn't help it. She burst out laughing.

Gabby flushed. "Sorry."

Annie came into the room carrying her coffee mug. She stopped, looking from Erin's amused face to Gabby's embarrassed one. "What's going on?"

"Me," Gabby muttered, getting to her feet. "Being stupid again." She studied the older woman. "Are you Erin's friend from Texas?"

Annie grinned. "Yes. I'm Annie."

"I'm Gabby. Your brother is a cad!" She flushed even more. "Sorry!"

"No need. He is a cad," Annie chuckled. "But I'm sure we'll redeem him in the end." She glanced at Erin. "Where's Justin?"

"Being charmed by the family cobra," Gabby muttered, sticking her hands in her jeans pockets.

Both women laughed.

"Sorry again," Gabby moaned. "I'm just hopeless."

"But nice," Erin said with a smile.

"Very," Annie agreed.

"Well, where's this amazing baby Daddy told me about?" Gabby asked, brightening.

"I'll bring him," Annie said, motioning Erin to stay in her chair. "Stitches still pull," she told Gabby with a grin. "Or what passes for stitches in modern medicine, at least. Be right back."

"Your friend. She's nice," Gabby told Erin.

"Very nice. We've been friends since grammar school."

"I had a friend like that, but she drowned," Gabby replied. She was looking out the window. "She's pretty and she's rich..."

"And Justin treats her like furniture, but you grit your teeth while she's here," Erin advised softly. "Don't let him see. It won't have a good result."

She grimaced. "I guess not." She drew in a long breath as she turned back to Erin. "If I could just find some lovely man who wanted me for keeps..."

"I thought you had?" Erin replied.

She smiled. "He's gay. He's so sweet. We hang around to-gether because the guy he's got his heart set on is into women."

"Is anybody in the world happy?" Erin groaned aloud.

"I seriously doubt it," came a deep voice from the doorway.

Gabby averted her eyes as Justin walked in beside Nan. He gave Gabby a long look that she didn't see, and it wasn't im-personal.

"You home for the funeral?" he asked Gabby in a gruff tone. "Won't the college boy mourn?"

Gabby turned her head around and glared at him. "Probably. What's it to you?" she asked curtly.

Both eyebrows went up while two sets of feminine eyes spar-kled with amusement.

Gabby turned her attention back to Annie, who was just walk-ing into the room with the baby in his blanket.

"Awww," she said, quickly diverted. She went to peer into the blanket. "He's lovely. Just like his mom," she added with a glance at Erin, who beamed.

"I haven't had a look at this fellow myself." Nan laughed and joined Gabby to look at the baby.

"Isn't he a little doll?" Nan said softly.

"He sleeps all night," Annie said. "I've heard that babies mostly don't."

"That's what the obstetrician says," Erin sighed. "I guess I'm truly lucky."

"Daddy says I cried all the time until I was three, and then he threatened to send me off to school and I shut up," Gabby laughed.

"You've still got your dad?" Nan asked. "You're so lucky. I lost my dad to a car wreck and my mom to cancer years ago."

"Me, too," Annie said.

"And me," Erin said sadly.

"All of you?" Gabby exclaimed. "I'm so sorry!"

They smiled at her.

"I guess I really am lucky," she conceded, trying not to look too hard at the man standing just apart from them, and the pretty debutante from out of town.

Erin watched the younger woman exclaim over the baby while Justin glowered at Gabby. It was amazing how jealous he was, and Gabby didn't seem to notice. She wanted to tell her. But, then, that was probably a very bad idea. If Gabby got too forward, Justin would probably knock her back again, thinking it was for her own good. Her best bet was patience.

Justin left shortly afterward to settle his men for the night, and Nan went to sleep. She'd had a tiring two days with her attorneys trying to settle everything with Maude's estate. She had to get back to Cheyenne. There were two parties that she was hosting for out of town guests, and she couldn't stay long.

That was music to Gabby's ears. She went home after Justin left, with a satisfied smile.

"Justin was jealous of Gabby's college friend, did you notice?" Annie chuckled while Erin nursed Cal.

"I did." She shifted the baby. "But we shouldn't make her aware of it."

"I agree." She shook her head. "Justin is blind."

Erin gave her a look. "No. He's not. He sees things that she doesn't yet. She's very young. All she's known is Catelow. It's a big world. He's seen a lot of it. She hasn't. Maybe he thinks she won't settle for this town. A lot of young women want to travel, have professions, enjoy their freedom."

"I didn't," Annie replied with a faraway look. "I wanted to stay in Jacobsville after I got out of school. Get married. Have kids." She lowered her eyes. "It didn't work out for me."

"Join the club," Erin sighed. "We have so many dreams that never come true. I'm sorry for Gabby. She's really nice."

"And really jealous," Annie chuckled.

"Well, Nan's very pretty and she's sophisticated and well-traveled. I imagine Gabby feels a sense of inferiority, compared to her."

"She probably does," Annie said. "But she doesn't see the big picture. Justin has a humble background. He's part of this place, this lifestyle. This is where he'll be, maybe until he dies. He's seen some of the world and apparently didn't find it to his taste." She leaned back in her chair. "But Gabby is just getting a sense of freedom, of her own gifts. She's not ready to settle down."

"In other words, she's infatuated, not in love, and Justin may be playing a waiting game, until he knows what she really wants."

"Exactly." Annie laughed. "And isn't it a good thing that men aren't quite as perceptive as we are?"

"For which," Erin agreed, "we should all give thanks."

CHAPTER FOURTEEN

Ty had just landed at Heathrow, worn to the bone by holdups and the myriad inevitable obstacles of international travel in the present age. He dodged people who weren't paying the least attention to where they put their feet, not to mention trying to spot the driver who was due to meet him here.

He ground his teeth together. He'd agreed to this consultation, but where he wanted to be was in Wyoming, with Erin and his new son. The child fascinated him. He'd barely noticed the passage of time as he traveled, his eyes on his child in the dozens of photos Annie had texted him.

The boy was going to be tall, he thought. His hair was dark, like Erin's and his own. His eyes were a very pale blue. He had long fingers. He was perfect, Ty thought. He'd never wanted kids. He'd never even considered that he might have them. Well, years ago, when he was engaged to the woman who'd turned him away from commitment. But not in any recent time.

Now it was all he thought about. He wanted desperately to be in his child's life, to be part of the family that the child and Erin comprised. But he'd done stupid things and now he was paying for them. Erin wouldn't let him near her.

He deserved it. He'd been callous, and cold, and unfeeling. As Erin had said, when he threw her out of his office that day he'd accused her of stabbing her in the back, he'd accused her without proof.

Erin would have defended him to the death, without proof. He'd found her interesting all of a sudden, although his motive had been to use her to get Jenny Taylor off his trail. But it hadn't turned out like that. When they'd gone to the cabin, and she'd responded to him so completely, so wholeheartedly, he'd gone in headfirst, without questioning the gift Erin gave him that night.

But he'd gotten cold feet almost at once. What did she want? Was she playing him? She had nothing and he was rich. He'd already been burned on that front. Was Erin eyeing him for what he could give her?

His suspicions had grown until she'd as much as told him that she'd had encounters before after drinking too much. That had set him off, made him doubt her. She'd been wearing couture garments—he hadn't realized she'd gotten them at a consignment store. She'd looked guilty when Jones had braced her about leaving her drawer unlocked with the bid inside. Then her father had a new car. He could be forgiven, surely, for being suspicious after all that.

But he recalled what she'd said, over and over, that she'd never have doubted him. Of course she hadn't. She loved him.

He hadn't loved her. That was why he'd doubted. It was why he'd accused her. Erin had been around most of his life, his sister's best friend. At first a pest, then a part of the furniture. Finally, a worker that he wasn't sure about. She worked for him, but he'd paid her little attention except when she was doing things for the family, especially during the grieving process when he and Annie had lost their parents. Erin had been their rock.

They'd done what they could for her, when her mother died. Then, also, when her father had died. But Ty had lost the bid for the big job in San Antonio. He'd gotten drunk, seduced Erin, and almost at once he'd been eaten up with suspicion.

It hadn't occurred to him to feel guilty that he'd taken advantage of her while he was under the influence. He was used to women giving in. But Erin wasn't that sort of woman. She didn't move with the times. She was religious. She had principles, morals. She was like his sister, principled.

So why hadn't he taken that into consideration, instead of blaming her and making her feel so guilty about what happened that she'd liked about her own past indiscretions. He recalled the blood on the sheets. He hadn't thought that it might have been proof of an innocence he'd discounted. Women sometimes were just starting their periods at the end of an encounter. But Erin wasn't like that. And he hadn't even considered it.

The guilt had made him cruel. Not only had he fired her, when he found out that she was working for another company in town, he'd made sure her new boss knew what he'd accused her of. He'd cost her the job.

She'd been pregnant when he did that. Her father had died. She'd lost the only home she ever had. Pregnant, and Ty had upset her that day in his office and then driven her out of the building. He'd driven her all the way out of Texas.

Had that been necessary? Or had he been trying to assauge his own guilt by making sure he didn't have to see the result of it? Had he chased Erin out of the city to make sure he didn't see her, feel her eyes accusing him. Had it been to accommodate his own feelings, without having to account for hers?

The baby, seeing the baby, had caused something inside him to explode with feelings he'd suppressed for years. Now all he could think about was Erin and the baby, his son, his little boy. He ached for them both. It was like losing an arm. Worse.

And unless he could come up with some good reason, Erin was going to stay in Wyoming. He'd never get near her, or the child, when she was wide awake.

He groaned inwardly. Well, he'd finish this job then he'd go back home and start thinking up ways to get her back. No way was he going to give her up. Not Erin or Callaway. He was going to find some way to bring his family back home.

The funeral home had been covered up, standing room only. Maude had been much loved in Catelow and Carne County, and many people came to pay their respects.

Now, walking gingerly around the house, alone except for the baby and Annie, Erin was feeling the loss more keenly. Worse, she was worried about what she was going to do.

While Cal was sleeping, Annie drew Erin into the kitchen and made them both cups of strong decaf.

Erin looked up at her friend with horror. "You hate decaf," she said slowly. "You know I hate it, too. But you made decaf...!"

"Maude told me," Annie said quietly as she sat down at the table with her friend.

"But I didn't tell Maude!"

"Small towns. Gossip. People who work in hospitals aren't immune," Annie lied, not liking to give away the obstetrician who'd told Maude. "So. What is it?"

Erin hesitated for a minute. Then she grimaced and sipped coffee. "I have a leaky valve," she muttered.

Annie's eyebrows went up. "Which valve?"

"Which...?"

"Yes. Because if it's called Barlow's syndrome, or mitral valve prolapse, you'll be fine," Annie added. She smiled. "I have it, too."

Erin's mouth fell open. "But they had a cardiologist in the operating room!"

"Just as a precaution," Annie replied. "It's not a big deal, honest. Sometimes they go critical and require surgery, but the condition itself is not that uncommon. It's not a bad idea to see a cardiologist occasionally. But you're going to be fine. Just fine."

Erin sat back in her chair and blotted tears. "I was so scared! Yes, that's what they called it, mitral valve prolapse."

"Did the cardiologist talk to you?"

"No. They made me an appointment, but it's not for two months. He's pretty busy."

"And it didn't occur to you that if it was dangerous, they'd have made you an appointment right away?"

Erin let out a long sigh and smiled. "Well, for heaven's sake. I didn't think about that. I didn't even think about it!"

"So you'll be around for a while. Certainly, long enough to raise that adorable young man in the guest bedroom."

Erin laughed to herself as she sipped coffee.

"One problem solved. Now, there's another." She put down her cup. "Do you really want to stay in Wyoming forever?"

Erin's face was a study in tragedy. She lowered her eyes to the table. "I miss home," she said at last. "But I can't go back…!"

"There was a story in the paper. Front page news, not only in San Antonio, but in Jacobsville as well," Annie said. "I have a copy in my suitcase. Ty let them interview him. He told pretty much everything that happened and put the blame for your dilemma squarely on himself. He even apologized for being so wrong and blaming you."

She studied Annie curiously. "Ty doesn't apologize."

"Yes. I know. But he did."

"Oh." She turned her coffee cup around and around. "Did you make him do it?"

Annie shook her head. "You can't make the stubborn man do anything," she pointed out. "He's been eaten up with guilt ever since Lassiter gave him the report about what really happened."

Erin frowned. "Lassiter? Dane Lassiter?" she asked.

Annie's eyebrows arched. "Yes."

"Dad had a friend who knew him, in Houston. He has a solid reputation for honesty and results. They say he's the best in the country."

"He's got my vote," Annie replied. "Ty wouldn't listen to me, but he sure listened to Mr. Lassiter."

She sipped coffee. "I'm shocked that he'd get a second opinion," Erin said sadly. "He was so certain that I sold him out."

"And I was so certain that you didn't," Annie said firmly.

Erin drew in a breath and wrapped both hands around the coffee cup. "I would never have believed him capable of doing something like that, because I loved him," she said. "That's how I knew how he felt about me, really felt, I mean," she added with a hollow laugh. "If you love someone, you know them. You believe in them. I told him that day, when he fired me, that he'd know the truth one day, but that it would be too late." She looked up. "It is."

Annie just stared at her, smiling.

"It is!" Erin insisted.

Annie sipped coffee.

"You have no idea how much I wish I could hate him," Erin said with pure venom.

"You have no idea how much he wishes you wouldn't," Annie replied. "He's been tormented. He still is."

"Good!"

"It would be a perfect world if we could stop loving people just because we wanted to," Annie said, her voice very quiet. "It would have saved us both a lot of heartache."

Erin was remembering what her poor friend had gone through, with the one great love of her life, and the one who'd almost taken her life. Two different men. One had never loved her. One had pretended to, because she was rich.

"I guess we've both had our trials," Erin agreed.

"Ty is different lately. I won't ask you to believe it. But it's true. He hasn't been the same since you left. And when he found out about your husband, and the baby, he went wild."

Erin hated the sudden leap of her heartbeat. Her hands on the coffee cup had contracted just enough to prevent a spill. "Oh?"

"He was livid. Then he blamed himself for that, too," she added. "He thought you'd rushed into marriage because you hated him."

Erin averted her eyes. She didn't dare tell her friend the truth. "It wasn't like that," she said after a minute.

"Why don't you come home with me?" Annie asked gently. "Ty won't be home for a month. I'm all by myself. You can look around for a house and a job..."

"I can't be in the same town with him," Erin bit off.

"Why not? He works in San Antonio," she was reminded. "You'd almost never see him. He's out on jobs a lot, traveling a lot. If you hadn't worked for him, you could have gone for weeks without ever even seeing him."

Erin had to admit that was the truth. She finished her coffee. "I suppose so," she said finally. She grimaced. "I can't work at a profession I know, though," she added. "And I'm not recovered enough yet to hold down a full-time job. I'd have to have a babysitter..."

Annie raised her hand. "Mrs. Dobbs and I volunteer."

"You should ask her first," Erin laughed helplessly.

"Already did," she replied. "Even Barbara volunteered. Not to mention Tippy Grier, who loves anybody's babies."

"Wow."

"You have more friends than you know," Annie said. "Don't let Ty spoil it for you. I'll make sure he keeps his distance. Please come home. I'm selfish. I have nobody to talk to since you left. Besides," she added, "it's going to be Christmas. You can spend it with me. The tree's up, there are presents under the tree for you and Callaway..."

"Already?" she exclaimed.

Annie grinned. "I'm an incurable optimist. Come on. Say yes. I'll have you out of my house, working, and in an apartment and out of sight before Ty comes back. Please?"

Erin was weakening. She wanted home. She wanted familiar surroundings. She wanted…no, she didn't want Ty! Her face tautened.

"Forgiveness is divine," she was reminded gently. "It's why wars end."

"I can forgive him. I just don't want to see him," Erin said shortly.

"And you won't. If he comes home sooner than expected, we'll improvise. Okay?"

Erin grimaced. "Let me sleep on it."

Annie beamed. "That's a deal!"

All of Erin's things didn't amount to a lot. They were packed into two suitcases and she was driven to the airport with Annie by a broody Justin.

"Place won't be the same without the sprout," he muttered, glancing toward the baby in Erin's arms. The truck didn't have a back seat, so he was held instead of strapped in, but Justin was a very careful driver and the small airport was only five minutes from Maude's house.

"You can come visit," Annie told him. "It's a huge house. We even have guest rooms."

"Might take you up on that. Maybe in the spring."

"Spring is roundup," Annie remarked.

He wrinkled his nose. "Maybe in summer."

"Bull roundup. Storms."

"Autumn."

"Weaning, tagging, breeding."

He glared at her. "Winter."

"Fixing equipment, plowing for spring planting, taking care of first-time mothers and checking on them constantly," Annie replied.

"Smarty pants," he said.

"I know all about cattle ranching. Jacobs County has almost nothing except ranches and nice people."

"So does Catelow."

"I'll come back and visit," Erin promised. "When Cal's a little older."

"I'll make sure she does," Annie added.

"Better than nothing, I guess," Justin chuckled.

"You bet," Annie told him.

Justin saw them onto the private jet.

"Tell Gabby goodbye for me, and that I'll write to her," Erin told him. "I didn't plan to leave before she came home on Christmas break."

"She's not coming," he said shortly. "Got a job in the town where the college is. To be near her new friend."

Erin had to stifle a really stupid remark, not to mention the truth about Gabby's friend. "College is expensive," she said. "Gabby must need the money, especially since she convinced her dad to build a new house. He won't have a lot of ready capital."

"True enough, I guess," he said. He ruffled Erin's hair. "Behave yourself."

"I'll do my best. You do the same."

He grinned at Annie.

"I won't, so don't ask me to behave," Annie told him firmly. "And if you keep grinning, I have ginger ale on the plane."

He held up both hands. "I'm sweet enough."

They all laughed.

Erin stared down at the landscape of Catelow growing smaller and smaller as the private jet whined and climbed.

"I'll miss it," she told Annie.

"You'd miss Jacobsville more, if you stayed there," Annie said softly. "You're a Texan. You won't transplant easily."

"I guess now. I just hope I'm doing the right thing," she said, almost to herself, as she cuddled the sleeping baby.

"Believe me, you are," Annie said. "The absolute best thing."

Erin leaned back in her seat and closed her eyes. She wasn't positive that it was, but she didn't feel right staying in Catelow and taking someone else's accounting job in such bad financial times. Besides that, it wasn't home without Maude. It would never be the same again.

Maude had been so kind to her. Erin had remarked about it once, and Maude had grinned and said, "Pay it forward." And she would. Sometime in the future, she'd help someone else over a bad place. She'd pass on that great kindness. She hoped Maude was safe and happy with her late husband, strolling through fields of wildflowers where cattle grazed. It made the grief sting less.

CHAPTER FIFTEEN

Mrs. Dobbs was crazy about Callaway. The other two women had to fight her just to get to hold him. Erin had the advantage there, of course, because she was breastfeeding.

"Not fair," Dobbs muttered.

"He does get the occasional bottle," Erin pointed out with a smile.

"I guess he does, darlin'," she agreed with a smile. "You look better already."

"Yes, she does," Annie agreed, lounging across from them on the sofa with a newspaper in her hands.

"Why don't you read that online and stop messing up my nice sofa with newsprint?" Dobbs muttered.

"Now, now, if I stop taking the physical paper, what will you line cabinets with?" Annie asked reasonably.

"I'll buy something with flowers on it!"

"This has flowers. Look." She showed the housekeeper a black-and-white rendering of a lily on the church page.

Mrs. Dobbs huffed and left the room.

Both women chuckled.

"She's right, you know, you do look better," Annie remarked.

It was true. Just in a few days, Erin's dark hair was softer, her body was gaining strength and just a little weight, and she looked pretty. Really pretty.

"I feel better. But I have to find a job pretty soon," she added.

"I know. You won't find much during the holidays, though. It's Christmas in a week."

"Gosh. We wait all year for it, get all excited, and then it's here and gone," Erin said. Her eyes were on the tree. "It's so beautiful."

"I love decorating it. I never thought…"

"Heads up!" came a voice from the library. Beauregard came dashing into the room, all frenetic energy and lolling tongue.

"How are the baseboards?" Annie called.

"Splintered, thank you," came the resigned reply. "And he's eaten part of the leather on the chair!"

"Ty can afford repairs. Remember, Beau's had a troubled childhood. Puppyhood. Whatever."

Erin, laughing, shifted Cal and reached a hand down to pet the pup, who rubbed against her fingers.

"He's so sweet," she said. "How could anybody hurt such a precious baby?"

"There are evil people in the world," Annie said on a sigh.

"Oh, my goodness, and they're everywhere!" Mrs. Dobbs said in a haunted voice.

She was staring toward the front door, which had glass panels on either side that went all the way up.

"What are you looking at…?" Annie began.

Just then, the door opened and a weary and irritable Ty grumbled, "Why the hell was the door locked? You try getting to a key with this lot in your hands!" He shook the suitcase, garment bag, and a huge bag from a toy store at Dobbs.

There was a pregnant silence.

Ty looked toward the living room. There was his sister, looking horrified. Across from her was Erin, nursing Callaway, and her expression was even more horrified than his sister's.

He let go of all his encumbrances, ignoring Dobbs's cry of dismay as she bent to pick up the mess.

He moved into the living room, his black eyes riveted to Erin, to the beautiful tableau of her nursing their firstborn. The little black-haired boy was suckling at her breast, one tiny hand propped against her in his yellow blanket.

"So this is why you wanted me to stay in London for the holidays?" he asked his sister and glared at her.

"It was just a thought," Annie said in a squeaky voice while she stared with anguish at Erin.

But Erin's eyes were on Ty. She lifted her chin. "Annie offered me a room while I look for work..."

"You're more than welcome here," Ty said quietly. He searched her face with quick, soft eyes. "You look better."

"Better?" she asked blankly.

"Than you did in the hospital," he replied.

She was all at sea. She just stared at him while Cal suckled.

He smiled gently at the child. "He's got more hair, too."

Beau sat looking up at him and whining.

"Jealous baby," Ty murmured, bending to pick up the puppy and cuddle it.

"He's eaten the office again," Dobbs muttered, returning.

"Anything he tears up can be fixed, don't sweat it," he said simply.

"How do you know how we looked in the hospital?" Erin persisted.

He shrugged. "I wanted to make sure you were all right," he said simply. He smiled gently. "I wanted to see the child, too. You're part of our family, Erin. I don't deserve to have you in it, after all I've done to you, but you belong here as much as we do."

He'd stolen her thunder. She wanted to rage at him, yell, accuse, hurt him as he'd hurt her. But all she could do was stare at him. He'd been at the hospital? Why?

"I hope you're going to stay in Jacobsville," he added, moving into the room to drop down into his own recliner with Beau in his lap. "You can have a puppy of your own. He'll be company for the baby as he grows."

She was searching for words and failing miserably.

"Why are you home?" Annie asked, finally finding her voice. "You said you'd be gone until January, and you didn't call!"

"Dad spent enough Christmases away from us," he said simply. "I didn't want to carry on the tradition. Besides, I closed the deal."

"Well!" She glanced at Erin, hoping she wasn't going to be in a lot of trouble. She hadn't expected Ty.

But Erin didn't look vindictive. She finished feeding the baby and handed him to Annie while she fumbled under the blanket to fasten the nursing bra and button her blouse.

"Look at all that hair," Ty exclaimed as he watched Annie carry the baby. He glanced at Erin. "Was your husband dark-haired?" he asked, trying to sound convincing.

"My hus…oh. Yes. Yes, he was," Erin said, taken aback. She held out her arms for Cal, took him and burped him gently.

"I was sorry to hear about Maude," he replied quietly. "She was a good woman."

"Yes," she replied.

He glanced at Annie who got the message and stood up. "How about sandwiches? Are you hungry?"

"I could eat," he told her. "They gave us peanuts on the plane. Next time I'll take my own."

"Peanuts or transportation?" Annie teased.

"Both!" he returned.

She chuckled. "I'll help Dobbs make some sandwiches. Erin, are you hungry?"

"Yes," she replied. "I'm going to rock Cal to sleep first, though." She got up slowly.

Ty watched her as if she were a jeweled bird flying close by. Erin had never seen that exact look on his face. It was strange.

Tender and quizzical, all at once. She averted her gaze and carried Cal down the hall to the guest room.

"Why didn't you warn me?!" Annie demanded, whacking her brother with a dish towel.

"I didn't think I needed to," he replied reasonably. "I didn't expect… How did you get her to come?" he asked.

"I told her you'd be away for a month," she shot back and then winced when she saw his expression. She grimaced. "Sorry. I could have put that better."

He shoved his hands into his pockets. "No need. The truth doesn't need any apologies."

"Are you staying?"

He drew in a long breath. "I guess I could move into a hotel for a few weeks," he said.

"Not yet," Annie said.

He started to speak.

"Not yet," Dobbs added her two cents worth.

He sighed. "Okay." He hadn't really wanted to go in the first place. But he didn't want to make Erin any more uncomfortable than she must already be.

"Have a sandwich and some coffee," Annie offered, putting a plate on the table. He sat down and she poured him a cup of coffee.

Erin was sitting outside on the patio, drinking in the sound of Christmas music coming from inside the house while the baby slept. It was cold, but the house and grounds were decorated beautifully, and everything was lit up. She had on jeans and a sweatshirt and a denim jacket.

"You'll catch cold," Ty said from behind her.

She jumped but caught herself before it was too apparent. "No, I won't. I like the cold. I went walking every day until Cal was born."

"I like walking," he replied.

"I remember. Hello, Beau," she said gently as the puppy trotted over to her and sat on her foot. She laughed. "Just like Rhodes. He likes feet."

"He seems to think they're warm stools," he pointed out. He dropped down into a chair beside hers and stretched. "I hate overseas flights. Jet lag kills me."

She was still petting Beau. She didn't answer him.

"If you're uncomfortable with me here, I can move into a hotel for the time being," he offered.

She glanced at him, appalled. "Heavens, no, not at Christmas!" she burst out. "It's just you and Annie. How do you think that would make me feel?"

His black eyes searched hers. "I deserve everything I get, Erin," he replied very quietly. "You were right. I accused you on the flimsiest evidence, even cost you a second job." He turned his face away. "I should be shot."

She drew in a long breath. "I didn't blame you," she said after a minute. "You didn't know me."

"What?"

She smiled sadly. "I'm Annie's friend, not yours, Ty," she replied. "To you, I'm an occasional guest, a coworker. That's all I ever was." She lowered her eyes, missing the pain that fell over his face. "You have to care about people to ignore blatant evidence of wrongdoing. Even then, sometimes you're wrong, and you defend someone who's really guilty."

"Yes, but you'd have defended me to the death," he said through his teeth, "even if I'd been guilty and you knew it for a fact. That's the difference."

She looked at the colored lights strung around the fence near the street. "I was living in dreams," she said. "Fantasies. I needed something to snap me out of it, and back into the real world. You can't live on dreams."

He was staring into the distance as well. "Is that what it was? A dream?"

She turned and looked at him. "You had your heart broken six years ago," she said, ignoring the faint wounding in his eyes. "That did it for you. You didn't want anything permanent again. You gave up on dreams and settled for sensible things."

She turned away. "I should have realized that you were just taking me around to discourage Jenny Taylor, but I didn't." She laughed. It had a cold, hollow sound. "I thought…well, I hoped…" She couldn't say the words. "But it was just a means to an end, for you. We both had too much to drink and things… happened." She took another breath. "But that's in the past. I married and lost my husband, and now I have a child to raise. So I'm done with dreams as well."

He frowned. He wasn't understanding what she meant.

She leaned forward. "I didn't come back for any other reason than to find a job and raise my son, in a town where I grew up and feel safe," she concluded. "So if you're worried that I'm here to harass you about what happened, or make any claims on you, it's not that at all," she said, gathering speed because it was embarrassing to say the words. She flushed a little. "I don't want…anything from you, is what I mean."

"Erin," he said softly, "that's the last thing I thought!"

"Oh." She swallowed. "Well."

"I came home for Christmas," he said quietly. "Isn't that why you came home, too?"

She lifted her eyes to his and fought down the sense of loss, of grief, that she felt. He was so handsome, and she'd loved him most of her life. But he was the dream, and she had to adjust to reality now. She forced a smile. "Yes," she said. "I came home for Christmas."

He smiled back. "We'll make it a good one."

She hesitated. Then she nodded.

He'd brought a bag full of toys from a toy shop near the airport, including a soccer ball and several toddler toys.

Erin laughed when she saw them. "But, Ty, he's just a baby…!"

"He'll grow," he assured her. "Besides, there's this…"

He pulled out a mobile in a package. "It's got music," he said, handing it to her. "Light and sound and music. It's a developmental toy, just for newborns. It goes in the baby bed." He frowned. "Do we have one?"

Erin colored. "Well…"

He got up, pulled out his phone, and started making calls. Later that same day, a beautiful white baby bed arrived, along with a state-of-the-art car seat, several sets of little jumpers and socks and shoes, all sorts of baby clothes, even a fuzzy coat with a hood.

"But, Ty," Erin protested.

"You hush," Annie said firmly. "We're going to spoil the baby and if you try to stop us, we'll have Beau lick you."

He was already doing that, propped against Erin's leg over her jeans. She gave up and just laughed.

Ty saw that. His whole face changed. He smiled, loving the expression on her lovely face. It had been so long since he'd seen her happy. It made him feel as if he were flying. But he averted his gaze before she saw it. It was too soon for such things.

His only ambition at the moment was to make it the best Christmas any of them had ever had. Especially the baby.

Erin had been worried at first that Ty might be uncomfortable with her living in his house, but he didn't seem to mind her presence. She found him often in the baby's room, just watching the little boy sleep. His fascination with her son touched her. She didn't understand why he was so interested in the little boy, but she recalled that he rarely had been around infants. He loved kids. He had several godchildren, whom he spoiled rotten, but none of them were newborns.

He found everything the baby did interesting. He tried not to stare when Erin fed Cal, but he couldn't help it. She was beautiful like that, soft and pink with the tiny little boy cuddled against her as she bent over him.

"Does it hurt?" he asked suddenly.

She looked up, surprised. "What?"

"Does it hurt when he suckles?" he asked.

She drew in a breath. "Well, just at first, it feels like labor pains. But only for a few seconds. It doesn't hurt."

He just nodded, as if the answer satisfied him.

"You watch him all the time," she remarked.

He smiled slowly. "I've never been so close to a baby before," he said simply. "He's beautiful."

Her eyes smiled with her lips. "I think so, too. We never had any relatives with babies, so it's new for me, as well."

"I wanted kids once," he said slowly and winced.

She knew what he was talking about. That awful woman, five years earlier. He'd wanted children with her, before he found out what a lying, pitiless woman she really was.

"I should have realized that a woman who was so wrapped up in her own appearance wouldn't want to risk her figure to have a child," he said coldly. "She even said so, after her husband set her up and let me hear her brag about what she was going to do with all the nice money when she married me."

She sighed. "We never really know people. She was very beautiful."

"Yes, but Annie couldn't stand her. That should have been a red flag. Annie loves most people."

"Women can usually spot a phony. Maybe men can, too—other men, I mean."

"Who knows?" He was smiling at the little boy. "When he gets older, we can build him a fort out back."

She just stared at him.

He grimaced. "Sorry. You won't be here then." He looked away. "Well, I can build it anyway. You might like to bring him over once in a while. I need all the godchildren I can get, so they'll look after me in my old age," he joked.

She felt sad for him. He'd never trust another woman, not enough to want marriage and kids. It was such a waste.

Cal finished drinking and she was trying to fumble her bra closed when Ty stood up. "Here, let me have him while you do that."

"They spit up…"

"Honey, clothes clean," he said very softly, and with a smile, as he held out his arms.

The endearment, which he never used, was like fire inside her. It hurt, to hear it and wonder how many ears he'd whispered that word into without meaning it.

He didn't seem to realize what he'd said. He picked up the little boy and put him over his shoulder, rubbing between his shoulder blades. A huge burp came afterward, along with some Olympic-style spitting up. And he laughed.

"What a sound!" he exclaimed, nuzzling the baby's head with his cheek.

"You'll be soaked," she said, offering him the diaper she'd used to conceal her blouse while she was nursing Cal.

"I have shirts," he pointed out.

She watched him rocking the baby against his broad shoulder.

"He's a sturdy child," he mused. "Will he be tall, do you think?"

She lowered her eyes. "I think so," she said. "It's hard to tell, at that age."

"His hair will be dark. How about his eyes?"

"They're blue right now, but they'll change in a few weeks. Brown is dominant…" She stopped short. She hadn't meant to say that. Ty had black eyes—at least, very dark brown ones.

He didn't react to the slip of the tongue. "His father had dark eyes, then?" he asked conversationally.

"Yes," she said at once.

He turned so that he could see her averted face. She was flushed. She didn't lie. He imagined it was difficult for her to tell him things that weren't true, to keep up the masquerade. But if he let on, if she even guessed that he knew who the father of her child really was, she'd be gone like a shot. He couldn't risk it.

"You lost so much, all at once," he said quietly. "Your father, your job, your home. Then your husband. Now Maude." He drew in a breath. "I'm so sorry, Erin."

She fought tears. "We all have hard times. They make us stronger."

"I suppose so."

He dropped down into the recliner and looked down at the little boy in his arms. He smiled slowly. "Hello," he said softly, watching the child watch him. "What a handsome little guy you are."

The baby just looked at him, wide-eyed and cooing.

Erin laughed. So did Ty.

She sat down, wincing a little. "Stitches still pulling?" he asked as he noticed that.

She shrugged. "Just a little. It's much better now."

He was watching her. "If you need help with the baby, just tell me. We can get a nurse if you need one. You can choose her."

"I'm not that bad," she said. "I can do what I need to."

"I'm not pushing," he said, smiling. "But you can have whatever you need while you're here."

"You've done enough already," she said, and smiled.

His face tautened. "I've done nothing, except make trouble for you," he said, averting his eyes to the baby in his arms.

"Ty..." She felt guilty. She shouldn't have. He'd caused her no end of grief. But he seemed unusually contrite, and she wondered why.

He drew in a sharp breath. "You could have lost the baby. You were pregnant the day I fired you. I frightened you when I lost my temper."

She'd almost forgotten that. "I was...just startled," she faltered.

"Me and my damned black temper," he murmured icily. "It's cost me so much. Far too much." His eyes closed. "If I could go back and start over again..."

"Nobody gets to start over," she interrupted. "We put one foot in front of the other and go on. That's all any of us can do. We can't undo the past."

He looked up at her with tortured eyes. "I would, if I could."

He said it with such passion that she felt the words all the way to her toes. She didn't know how to answer him. She'd been sure that he got off scot-free, that what he did to her didn't bother him. Sure, maybe he was sorry that he'd fired her. But this was something far more passionate than regret. She didn't understand it.

He averted his eyes before she could read too much in them. He smiled at the little boy, who was moving his arms and legs and staring up at him.

"Does he always move like this?" he asked her.

She smiled. "Most of the time. Except when he's sleeping."

His head was cocked. "Okay, now he's puckering up like he wants to cry, but he's not crying."

"Oh, dear."

She got up. He looked up at her as she held out her arms.

"Oh, dear?" he asked.

"What goes in must come out?" she prompted.

He gave her a wicked smile.

"Let me change him," she said.

He got up. "I'll carry him for you. We bought a changing table, didn't we?"

"Yes. It's very nice. I don't have to bend over the bed to put on a new diaper."

"I can imagine that it would be pretty uncomfortable, after a C-section."

"It is," she agreed, following him into the guest room.

He put the baby on the changing table, moving aside to let her work. He handed her the things she asked for and watched the process with fascination. It amused her. He seemed to find anything to do with the baby fascinating.

"Imagine you, learning how to change diapers," she teased.

"I expect I could get good at it," he said. "Of course, nursing would strictly be your part of the bargain," he added, tongue-in-cheek.

She burst out laughing. So did he.

The baby watched them both and suddenly gurgled.

"Wow!" he exclaimed.

She glanced at him. "They do that," she said.

He shook his head. "Every minute is an adventure."

She sighed and smiled. "Yes. It really is. I had no idea what it would be like to have a child. You read about it, watch movies about it. But when it's your baby…it's a whole other world."

He nodded, without realizing it. He felt a surge of love for that tiny boy that almost staggered him. It was unexpected. Like what he felt, standing next to Erin. She'd been part of his life for most of hers, but it was different now. She fascinated him as much as the baby did. It was a new reaction, a new feeling that she engendered in him.

For years he'd avoided any hint of domesticity. Now here he was elated because he'd learned how diapers were changed. He was almost glowing because that little boy, his son, had gurgled at him. He felt as if his feet weren't touching the floor.

There was a high-pitched little bark from under their feet. And there sat Beau, with one ear standing straight up and the other one flopping, pink mouth open, pink tongue hassling, dark eyes as bright as black diamond as he looked up at his humans.

"Jealous baby," Erin teased the pup.

"I think he's curious," Ty said. "He's never been around babies either."

"It's a learning curve."

DIANA PALMER

"Yes. For all of us," Ty teased, glancing down at her.

She laughed, too.

Erin loved to cook. Ty and Annie took turns watching the baby while Erin and Mrs. Dobbs worked in the kitchen, making cakes and pies and fresh bread. These would go in the walk-in freezer, to be taken out on Christmas Day. There was more than enough to do before the big day. There were eggs to boil and devil, there was stuffing to make—which had to have biscuits and cornbread as ingredients, and neither woman was willing to buy it already cooked. No, it had to be done fresh. There was the turkey to thaw, which took three days by itself. Then there were the candies that were a tradition at the Mosby home, from three generations back—pralines and divinity fudge. It was a lot of work and worth every minute.

"You're all sweaty," Ty chided when Erin came out of the kitchen shedding her apron to reach for the baby. "You'll get him wet," he accused, holding him away from his mother.

"Oh, yeah?" she taunted. "Well, let's see you breastfeed him!"

He glared at her.

She raised both eyebrows and held out her arms.

He made a face, but he gave her Cal.

She laughed and sat down in the chair to feed the baby.

"I'd help in the kitchen, if I could," he said, crossing his long legs as he sat back in his chair.

"No. Anything but that!" Annie pleaded as she joined them.

He glared at her. "It was a small fire," he pointed out.

"The curtains went up," she replied.

"And so did the cat's tail," Erin added. "It was so lucky that he had such a big fluffy one that he didn't feel it!"

"He bit me when I was trying to put it out," Ty muttered.

"In his defense, he didn't know he was on fire," Mrs. Dobbs interjected as she joined them. "Well, Erin, I think we've got it underway far enough for one day. That's a lot of work!"

"It's fun, though. I used to love working with Mama in the kitchen," she said, watching the baby nurse. "Especially at Christmas. She taught me all I know about cooking."

"God knows, I've tried to teach those two," Mrs. Dobbs muttered, glaring toward Annie and Ty. "He caught the kitchen on fire and she blew up my oven!"

"The heating element," Annie defended. "The unit was old and on its way out anyway!"

"And the kitchen curtains were a disgrace," Ty said haughtily. "They deserved to die."

Erin was laughing by now. So was Mrs. Dobbs.

"Excuses, excuses," the housekeeper said, shaking her head.

"I can make biscuits," Annie said in her own defense.

"Out of a can," Mrs. Dobbs said under her breath.

"It's still a biscuit!" Annie huffed.

"And I don't leave dish towels on the burners anymore," Ty defended himself.

"No, you don't, but you've taught your dog to eat furniture!" Mrs. Dobbs accused.

"He needs a little fiber in his diet," he muttered.

Erin burst out laughing. It was like old times. For the first time in months, she really felt like she was home and part of a family again.

CHAPTER SIXTEEN

Ty was around the house most of the time during the days leading up to Christmas. One night, he got everybody in the big touring car and drove them around Jacobsville to see the Christmas decorations.

One of the prettiest ones was a Spanish-style house on a back street, owned by the Ramirez family, Rodrigo and Gloryanne. They had a little boy in first grade, and their yard looked like a toy factory. There were moving decorating rocking horses, and Santa Claus complete with reindeer, and all the trees were decked out in colored lights.

"That's so pretty," Erin exclaimed.

"They always do such nice displays," Annie agreed. "How about the Pendleton place?"

"They're in San Antonio this Christmas," Ty told them. "But the Carson ranch is really something. We'll head out that way next."

"The sheriff's ranch?" Erin asked.

"Yes. He and his wife moved there with the kids when her aunt passed away."

"Did the giant iguana go with them?" Annie asked.

He chuckled. "Of course. He follows the kids around like a puppy."

"Lizards." Mrs. Dobbs gave a mock shudder.

"Lizards are very nice," Ty told her. "I'm thinking of getting one myself."

"I'll quit!"

"I'll fire you!" Ty shot back.

"Peace," Annie said. "It's Christmas!"

"Not yet," Ty said with a menacing glance in the rearview window.

"You better be nice to me," Mrs. Dobbs retorted. "I know where Santa Claus lives the rest of the year."

"Oh, yeah?" he said. "Well, I know where he is right now."

He turned the car onto another back street and pulled up in front of a house where a huge sleigh and realistic reindeer were lit up. There was a line of kids all the way to the road.

"See?" he told Dobbs. "You mess with me, you'll get coal in both stockings!"

She made a face.

"Peace on earth?" Annie tried again.

They gave in.

"We can't!" Erin protested when Ty pulled up at the curb. "They don't know we're coming!"

"Yes, they do," Ty told her. "I called Cash earlier."

"They heard about the baby," Annie laughed. "Tippy's called me twice already to make sure we were coming. It's not us they want to see," she added.

"Oh." Erin was well aware of the Griers' fascination with babies. He might be a former government sniper, now police chief, but he loved kids. So did his ex-model, ex-movie star wife, Tippy.

And in fact they were coming down the steps even as Erin was helped out of the car by Ty, who had the baby in his arms.

"We couldn't wait," Tippy laughed. "Please?" She held out her arms.

Cash Grier stepped nimbly in front of her. "Get in line," he said haughtily, and took the baby. "He's perfect," he cooed, while Tippy hung on to his arm, laughing, to look at the tiny boy wrapped up so cozily in the cold.

"I want to see, too!" came a plaintive wail from the porch.

"My baby brother," Tippy laughed. "He's nuts about kids. Tris loves him to death. So does our son."

"I never realized how much fun kids were," Ty said, watching the Griers enthuse over the child he couldn't acknowledge.

"They're addictive, too," Cash chuckled.

"How are you?" Tippy asked Erin. "We heard about the C-section."

"I'm still a little sore, but doing much better, thanks," she said with a smile.

"If she'd stay out of the kitchen, she'd be even better," Annie chuckled as she joined them, followed by Mrs. Dobbs.

"Well, if it wasn't for her, darlin', there wouldn't be Christmas dinner to look forward to. I can't do it all."

"They don't cook?" Tippy asked her, indicating the brother and sister.

"Only if the fire department stages in the front yard," Mrs. Dobbs said, tongue-in-cheek.

"It was only one fire," Ty said, exasperated. "One little bitty fire."

"And one burned up oven element that would have burned if I wasn't even in the kitchen," Annie added.

"I lock the door when I'm cooking, in case they try to get in and help," Mrs. Dobbs said in a fake whisper.

Everybody laughed.

The last stop was the Jacobsville City Park, which put on a fantastic light show during the holidays. It was a feast of color and cars and trucks lined up to go around the circle, very slowly, so that the kids didn't miss a single exhibit.

"This is just awesome," Erin sighed. "I never had time to come and look at it."

"I know," Ty murmured, watching the narrow drive as he followed the vehicle ahead. "I kept you working overtime."

"I didn't mind," she replied, turning to Cal, who was lying wide-eyed in his car seat, looking around. "See the pretty colors, baby?" she teased softly. "Oh, and he loves that mobile you bought him!" she added to Ty.

He grinned. "I noticed."

She looked puzzled as he glanced at her in the rearview mirror.

"Sometimes he wakes up in the night," he explained, faintly embarrassed. "So I turn it on and watch him."

Erin was touched, and heartbroken. Ty thought her child was another man's. He'd never know that the little boy he was becoming so attached to was his own son.

He saw that expression on her face and scowled. He averted his eyes to the display around them.

"Sorry," he said gruffly. "I probably should have told you earlier."

"I don't mind," she replied at once, faintly surprised.

He frowned. "Then what made you look like that?" he asked softly.

She met his eyes in the mirror and felt like crying. She was hurting inside, and not from her recent surgery. She tore her eyes away and swallowed, hard. "Aren't the lights beautiful?" she asked.

"They are indeed," Annie agreed from beside Ty. "Isn't it a shame we only get treat like this once a year?"

"You'd get bored if it happened every day," Ty teased, erasing the frown.

"I guess so."

"Who wants to go home and drink hot chocolate?" he asked as they pulled back onto the main road.

Three hands went up.

"The car is warm, but I'm chilly," Annie laughed.

"Me, too, and somebody needs to have his supper and go to bed," she laughed, tickling the baby under his chin.

"I wonder if babies remember things?" Ty wondered aloud as they headed back home.

"That's a good question," Erin replied. "I'll ask the pediatrician… Oh, gosh," she groaned. "I don't have one!"

"A problem easily solved," Annie assured her. "We have several specialists who come down here from San Antonio once or twice a week. We'll go look at reviews first. Nothing but the best and nicest doctor for this baby!" she added.

Erin laughed. She didn't mention that she'd need an installment plan, because she had no insurance. Her policy that had come through work at Ty's business had expired.

"I reinstated your policy, by the way," he said, almost as if he sensed her concern.

"Wh…what?" she faltered. "But, Ty, I don't work for you anymore."

He looked at her in the mirror. "That's something we can talk about later," he told her. His eyes went back to the road. "I've got an idea."

Erin worried about that. She fed Cal and burped him and kissed him and rocked him to sleep.

She was watching him close his eyes when she felt Ty standing beside her.

She looked up at him without wanting to. He was the most gorgeous man she'd ever known and as far out of her reach as the moon. She lowered her eyes, drinking in the warmth and power of his fit body, the faint spicy scent of his cologne.

"He looks a lot like you already," he said softly. "Especially his eyes. I don't think they're going to be dark like…" He stopped himself just in time. "Like your late husband's," he said without missing a beat.

She drew in a breath. "My father had gray eyes. My mother's were pale blue." She smiled. "But eye color does change. He could still have dark eyes, down the road."

He turned to her and tilted her face up to his. "I'm sorry we can't go back a few months," he said very quietly. "I was wrong about you, all the way."

"You didn't know me…"

"But I did," he interrupted. He searched her eyes. "I knew you from the ground up. That's why I kept backing away."

She frowned. She didn't understand.

"I got taken for a hell of a ride five years ago. It wasn't even love, it was something far less noble. She played on my senses until I was desperate for her. Her ex-husband did me a huge favor. If he hadn't intervened, I'd have gotten what I probably deserved."

"Nobody deserves to be hurt like that," she countered quietly.

His big, lean hand lifted and brushed a wisp of dark hair away from her eyes. "Especially not you, Erin," he replied. "I was running, didn't you notice?"

"Running?" That hand was maddening. Now it was tracing her mouth and she almost moaned. It had been so long since she'd been touched, held, wanted.

"I knew that if I walked toward you, I'd never be able to walk away," he said tautly. "You weren't a good-time girl…"

"You said I was," she bit off.

"I listened to you, which was one hell of a mistake," he said curtly. "Why did you lie and tell me it wasn't unusual for you to drink and lose control?"

Her eyes went to the front of his pullover shirt. It was dark, like his eyes. "You felt guilty about what happened. It wasn't all your fault. I should never have had a drink at all."

He drew her close. His big hands framed her face with warm strength. "Yes, but, honey," he whispered, "if you hadn't had that drink, we wouldn't have this beautiful little boy."

Heat rushed through her body like liquid fire. She just stared at him, without even a comeback, as horror sat in. He was guessing. She had to throw him off the track, she didn't dare let him know…!

"Lassiter was very thorough," he whispered. "And I had actual dates."

She went pale. She started to pull away, but he brought her right back and wrapped her up in his arms, rocking her.

"I don't deserve your trust. I'm not the man I wish I was. But I'll take care of you and Cal as long as I live. And I'll love you," he added, lifting his head to stare down into her shocked eyes, "until I draw my last breath."

Her lips were trembling. Tears stung her eyes. "But you don't want…" she began.

He bent and kissed her, very tenderly. "I want you and my son, more than I want to go on living," he said.

"You're just guessing," she sobbed.

He reached into his pocket, pulled out his cell phone, and handed it to her.

There, on the lock screen, was Ty holding little Cal in his baby blanket, in the nursery at the hospital in Catelow, Wyoming.

She caught her breath. She looked up at him. "That's why you were there!"

He nodded. "I had to dodge your mother hen and the foreman, but Annie helped me sneak in." He leaned his forehead against hers. "My son. My firstborn. How in the world could I miss that? How could any human being stay away?" His mouth brushed hers again and again. "I was worried about you as well. Things can go wrong with a C-section. I had to make sure you were both all right."

"Annie never told me," she murmured.

"I made threats." He kissed her more insistently. "Really nasty threats. Like never letting her pet the puppies again."

"Very nasty," she agreed, involuntarily following his mouth with her own. She was only just beginning to believe he meant what he said.

"You have to forgive me," he added softly.

"Why?" she asked, but she smiled.

"I want more babies," he said simply, and he grinned.

She laughed helplessly. "Oh, Ty!"

He wrapped her up carefully in his arms and kissed the breath right out of her body. She held on for dear life, ignoring the faint pull of the incision, drowning in pleasure and joy and love and happiness. It was like walking out of a nightmare into the light. She'd never known such passionate belonging. Not even that night at the cabin.

Just before they crossed a line that would have proved embarrassing, there was muffled laughter from the doorway. They turned together. Annie and Mrs. Dobbs were standing there with their hands over their mouths.

"Peeping Toms," Ty said haughtily.

They burst out laughing. So did Erin.

"Please forgive him," Annie pleaded. "If you do, he'll marry you and I'll have somebody to talk to besides Mrs. Dobbs."

"And I'll have somebody to help me cook," Mrs. Dobbs added.

Ty smiled down at her with his heart in his eyes. "We could have a Christmas wedding, right here in the house. We can email invitations and you can wear a lacy dress and a veil and carry a bouquet of holly and white roses."

She drew in a long, sweet breath.

"After all, you're already wearing the engagement ring," he pointed out.

She gaped at him. She lifted her hand. The ring was, after all, on her ring finger. And now that she considered it, the ring didn't look at all like the dinner ring Annie had said it was.

"I lied," Annie told her. "It was from him. He was afraid you'd flush it down the toilet if I told you where it really came from."

"Yes, and besides, it has a mate," Ty added, pulling out a ring box. He opened it and placed it in her hands. It was a wedding band with the same beautiful ruby motif as the ring she was wearing. He cocked his head and studied her, smiling. "So. I can go down on one knee if you want me to?" he added. "I've been practicing."

"Yes, he has," Annie agreed.

"Practicing by cleaning up Beau's little presents all over my nicely mopped floor...!"

"He can't hit the paper every time," Ty defended the puppy.

"We'll both work on that," Erin said.

He grinned. "Yes, we will." He pursed his lips. "Well?"

She sighed. It was like being handed the moon, and despite their rocky beginning, she had high hopes for the future. He loved kids and dogs. What was left to worry about?

"I will," she said.

He whooped, as he swooped and kissed her hungrily. The whoop woke the baby who started bawling.

"Now look what you've done," Mrs. Dobbs wailed, because as the baby cried, Beauregard and Rhodes came into the hallway and started howling.

Ty looked at a beaming Erin and grinned. "Home sweet home," he said.

She just hugged him for an answer.

They were married on Christmas Eve, with half of Jacobsville crowded into the living room as witnesses while the Methodist minister, Jake Blair, married them. Erin wore a lacy wedding gown—Ty had insisted—and a veil, but her bouquet had holly and white roses and white orchids. The room was festooned with poinsettias—which had to be quickly removed after the service because they were poisonous to dogs and cats.

And so, they were married, with a gurgling Callaway Regan Mitchell Mosby, as he was soon christened, as a participant.

"It's Christmas," Ty murmured sleepily as they lay in each other's arms under the covers.

It was just after midnight, and one enthusiastic bout of passion had been followed by two more, until they were both far too tired to continue.

"You need to take more vitamins," she sighed, laying her cheek against his damp, hair-roughened chest.

He kissed her hair. "I'm old. Don't make fun."

"You're thirty-one, not eighty," she chided.

He chuckled, rolling her over to look down at her lovely body. His hand smoothed over her flat stomach. "I didn't hurt you?" he asked with genuine concern. "It was an overenthusiastic beginning, I'm afraid." He shrugged. "I haven't indulged since that night at the lake," he added sheepishly.

"What?" she exclaimed.

He brushed back her damp hair. "I guess I knew even then," he said quietly. His eyes searched hers. "There was never a woman like you in my life. Not even one. And it wasn't until I'd turned on you that I realized how much I loved you." He kissed her tenderly. "It didn't help that Lassiter told me the truth about the baby just after that." He shook his head. "Talk about retribution. I wanted you back. I wanted to see our son. And I was afraid to go near you. I knew you hated me."

"But I didn't," she replied softly. "The evidence was all against me…"

"When you love, you don't accuse," he interrupted. "I didn't understand that until you told me that you'd have defended me to the death, if our situations had been reversed." He nuzzled her nose with his. "But the kicker was when Annie told me, finally, how you felt about me. Why you never dated." His eyes closed. "Coals of fire," he whispered.

She pulled his head down and kissed his eyes closed. "Hush," she said softly. "We've both walked through fire. Now it's gone. We have a little boy. We have a life to look forward to."

He nodded. He glanced down at her stomach and raised an eyebrow. "And maybe another one in the not-too-distant future?" he teased.

She smiled. "Even that."

He sighed. "I wonder if a man can die of happiness?"

"I'm not sure, but we can…"

He groaned.

She groaned.

In the distance, a little voice was raising fury. And two German shepherds were howling right along with him. Worse, from farther down the hall, where the other three puppies had their own room, even more howling started up.

Erin and Ty looked at each other.

"Want to flip a coin?" she asked.

"Nope," he replied, moving the covers aside. "He's our baby, not just your baby. We both get up."

She was absolutely delighted. She laughed. "I can see that you're going to be a hands-on dad from the beginning."

"You can bet the house on that," he replied, laughing with her.

And now the squalling and the howling was joined by plaintive voices from downstairs.

"Make it stop!" two voices drifted up the staircase.

Ty made a huffing sound as he and Erin, both in bathrobes, padded down the hall. "Pay them no mind," he said, drawing Erin close beside him. "They'll adapt."

Erin reached up and kissed him. And she laughed.

★ ★ ★ ★ ★

SPECIAL EXCERPT FROM

CANARY STREET PRESS

Was she his dream come true…or a dangerous love?

Driven by his new undercover job, DEA agent Rodrigo Ramirez isn't sure if his attraction to the oh-so-tempting Gloryanne Barnes is just about completing his mission— or something more. But as Gloryanne's bittersweet miracle and Rodrigo's double life collide, they decide if there's a chance for the future they both secretly desire.

Read on for a sneak preview of the classic
and exciting romance Fearless *by Diana Palmer.*

CHAPTER ONE

"I won't go," Gloryanne Barnes muttered.

Tall, elegant Detective Rick Marquez just stared at her, his dark eyes unyielding. "Hey, don't go. No problem. We've got a body bag just your size down at the medical examiner's office."

She threw a wadded up piece of paper across the desk at him.

He caught it with one lean hand and raised an eyebrow. "Assault on a peace officer…"

"Don't you quote the law to me," she shot back, rising. "I can cite legal precedents from memory."

She came around the desk slowly, thinner than she usually was, but still attractive in her beige suit. Her skirt flowed to midcalf, above small feet in ankle-strapped high heels that flattered what showed of her legs. She perched herself on the edge of the desk. Her high cheekbones were faintly flushed from temper, and something more worrying. She had very long, light blond hair which she wore loose, so that it fell in a cascade down her back almost to her waist. She had pale green eyes and a wide forehead, with a perfect bow of a mouth under her straight nose. She never wore makeup and didn't need to. Her complexion was flawless, her lips a natural mauve. She wouldn't win any beauty contests, but she was attractive when she smiled. She didn't smile much these days.

"I won't be any safer in Jacobsville than I am here," she said, trotting out the same old tired argument she'd been using for the past ten minutes.

"You will," he insisted. "Cash Grier is chief of police. Eb Scott and his ex-mercenary cronies live there, as well. It's such a small town that any outsider will be noticed immediately."

She was frowning. Her eyes, behind the trendy frames of the glasses she occasionally wore in place of contact lenses for extreme nearsightedness, were thoughtful.

"Besides—" he played his trump card "—your doctor said..."

"That's not your business." She cut him off.

"It is if you drop dead on your desk!" he said, driven to indiscretion by her stubbornness. "You're the only witness we've got to what Fuentes said! He could kill you to shut you up!"

Her lips made a thin line. "I've had death threats ever since I got out of college and took a job here as an assistant district attorney," she replied. "It goes with the work."

"Most people don't mean it literally when they threaten to kill you," he returned. "Fuentes does. Do I really have to remind you what happened to your coworker Doug Lerner two months ago? Better yet, would you like to see the autopsy photos?"

"You don't have any autopsy photos that I haven't already seen, Detective Marquez," she said quietly, folding her arms across her firm, small breasts. "I'm not really shockable."

He actually groaned out loud. His hands moved into his pockets, allowing her a glimpse of the .45 automatic he carried on his belt. His black hair, almost as long as hers, was gathered in a ponytail at his nape. He had jet-black eyes and a flawless olive complexion, not to mention a wide, sensuous mouth. He was very good-looking.

"Jason said he'd get me a bodyguard," she said when the silence grew noticeable.

"Your stepbrother has his own problems," he replied. "And your stepsister, Gracie, would be no help at all. She's so scatter-brained that she doesn't remember where she lives half the time!"

"The Pendletons have been good to me," she defended them. "They hated my mother, but they liked me."

Most people had hated her mother, a social-climbing antiso-cial personality who'd been physically abusive to Glory since her birth. Glory's father had taken her to the emergency room half a dozen times, mumbling about falls and other accidents that left suspicious bruises. But when one bout of explosive temper had left her with a broken hip, the authorities finally stepped in. Glory's mother was charged with child abuse and Glory tes-tified against her.

By that time, Beverly Barnes was already having an affair with Myron Pendleton and he was a multimillionaire. He got her a team of lawyers who convinced a jury that Glory's father had caused the injury that her mother had given her, that Glory had lied out of fear of her father. The upshot was that the charges against Beverly were dropped. Glory's father, Todd Barnes, was arrested and tried for child abuse and convicted, despite Glory's tearful defense of him. But even though her mother was ex-onerated, the judge wasn't convinced that Glory would be safe with her. In a surprise move, Glory went into state custody, at the age of thirteen. Her mother didn't appeal the decision.

When Beverly subsequently married Myron Pendleton, at his urging, she tried to get custody of Glory again. But the same judge who'd heard the case against Glory's father denied custody to Beverly. It would keep the child safe, the judge said.

What the court didn't know was that Glory was in more danger at the foster home where she'd been placed, in the cus-tody of a couple who did as little as possible for the six children they were responsible for. They only wanted the money. Two older boys in the same household were always trying to fondle Glory, whose tiny breasts had begun to grow. The harassment went on for several weeks and culminated in an assault that left her bruised and traumatized, and afraid of anything male. Glory had told her foster parents, but they said she was making it up. Furious, Glory dialed the emergency number and when the police came, she ran out past her foster mother and all but jumped into the arms of the policewoman who came to check out her situation.

Glory was taken to the emergency room, where a doctor, sickened by what he saw, gave the police enough evidence to have the foster parents charged with neglect, and the two teenage boys with assault and battery and attempted sodomy.

But the foster parents denied everything and pointed out that Glory had lied about her mother abusing her. So she went back to the same house, where her treatment became nightmarish. The two teenage boys wanted revenge as much as the spiteful foster parents did. But they were temporarily in juvenile detention, pending a bond hearing, fortunately. The foster parents weren't, and they were furious. So Glory stuck close to the two younger girls, both under five years old, whom she had been made responsible for. She was grateful that they required so much looking-after. It spared her retribution, at least for the first few days back at the house.

Jason Pendleton hated his stepmother, Beverly. But he was curious about her young daughter, especially after a friend in law enforcement in Jacobsville contacted him about what had happened to Glory. The same week she was sent back to the foster home, he sent a private investigator to check out her situation. What he discovered made him sick. He and his sister, Gracie, actually went themselves to the foster home after they'd read the investigator's covertly obtained police report on the incident— which was, of course, denied by the custodians. They pointed to Glory's attempt to blame her mother for the abuse that had sent her father to prison, where he was killed by another inmate within six months.

The day the Pendletons arrived, the two teenage boys who had victimized Glory were released to the custody of the foster parents, pending trial. Glory had been running away from the teenagers all day. They'd already torn her blouse and left bruises on her. She'd been afraid to call the police again. So Jason found Glory in the closet in the bedroom she shared with the two little girls, hiding under her pitiful handful of clothes on wire hangers, crying. Her arms were bruised all over, and there was a smear of blood on her mouth. When he reached in, she cowered and shook all over with fear.

Years later, she could still remember how gently he picked her up and carried her out of the room, out of the house. She was placed tenderly in the back seat of his Jaguar, with Gracie, while Jason went back into the foster home. His deeply tanned, lean face was stiff with bridled fury when he returned. He didn't say a word. He started the car and drove Glory away.

Despite her mother's barely contained rage at having Glory in the same house where she lived, Glory was given her own room between Gracie's and Jason's, and her mother was not allowed near her. In one of their more infamous battles, Jason had threatened to have his own legal team reopen the child abuse case. He had no doubt that Glory was telling the truth about who the real abuser was. Beverly had stormed out without a reply to Jason's threats. But she left Glory alone.

It became a magical time for the tragic young girl, belonging to a family who valued her. Even Myron found her delightful company.

After Beverly died unexpectedly of a stroke when her daughter was fifteen, Glory's life settled into something approaching normalcy. But the trauma of her youth had consequences that none of her adoptive family had anticipated.

Her broken hip, despite two surgeries and the insertion of a steel pin, was never the same. She had a pronounced limp that no physical therapy could erase. And there was something else;

her family had a history of hypertension, which Glory inherited. No one actually said that the stress of her young life had added to the genetic predisposition toward it. But Glory thought it did. She was put on medication during her last year in high school. Severely overweight, shy, introverted and uncomfortable around boys, she was also the target of bullies. Other girls made fun of her. They went so far as to put false messages about her on the internet and one girl formed a club devoted to ridiculing Glory.

Jason Pendleton found out about it. The girls were dealt with, one charged with harassment and another's parents threatened with lawsuits. The abuse stopped. Mostly. But it left Glory feeling alone and out of place wherever she went. Her health, never good, caused many absences during the time of turmoil. She lost weight. She was a good student and made excellent grades, despite it. She went on to college and then to law school with the support of her stepsiblings, and graduated magna cum laude. From there, she went to the San Antonio District Attorney's office as a junior public prosecutor. Four years later, she was a highly respected assistant prosecutor with an impressive record of convictions against gang members and, most recently, drug smugglers. Her weight problem was in the past now, thanks to a good dietician.

But in her private life, she was alone. She had no close friends. She couldn't trust people, especially men. Her traumatic youth in foster care had predisposed her to be suspicious of everyone, especially anyone male. She had male friends, but she had never had a lover. She never wanted one. Nobody got close enough to Glory Barnes to hurt her.

Now this stubborn San Antonio detective was trying to force her to leave her job and hide in a small town from the drug lord she'd prosecuted for distributing cocaine.

Fuentes was the newest in a long line of drug lords who'd crossed the border into Texas, enlarging his drug territory with the help of his street gang associates. One of them, with the promise of immunity from Glory, had testified in the trial and despite his millions, the drug czar had been facing up to fifteen years in federal prison for distribution of crack cocaine. A hung jury on that case had let him walk.

After she lost the drug case against him, she'd been sitting in the hall when Fuentes came out of the courtroom. He couldn't resist bragging about his victory. Fuentes sat down beside her and made a threat. He had worldwide connections and he could have anybody killed, even cops. He had, he said, taken out a persistent local deputy sheriff who'd harassed him by hiring a contract killer only two weeks ago. Glory would be next if she didn't lay off investigating him, he'd added with an arrogant smile. Sadly for him, Glory had been wearing a court-sanctioned wire at the time. His arrest had come the very next day.

His fury had been far-reaching. Someone had actually fired a gun at Glory when she walked out of the courthouse two days ago, missing her head by a fraction of an inch. She'd turned to look for her bus when her assailant fired. It had been such a close call that Detective Marquez was determined not to risk her a second time.

"Even if he gets me, you've still got the tape," she argued.

"The defense will swear it's been tampered with," he muttered. "It's why the D.A. didn't put it in evidence."

She swore under her breath. Her color was higher than usual, too.

As if on a signal, the door opened and Haynes walked in with a glass of water and a pill bottle. Sy Haynes was Glory's administrative assistant, a paralegal with a sharp tongue and the authority of a drill sergeant. "You haven't taken your capsule today," she muttered, popping the lid on the medicine bottle and shaking one capsule into Glory's outheld hand. "One close call a month is enough," she added, referring to what Glory's doctor had termed a possible mild heart attack arising from the pressure of the trial. A stress test had detected a problem that might require surgery if Glory didn't take her medicine and keep to her low-fat diet and adopt a low-stress lifestyle.

Marquez wanted her to leave town and she didn't want to go. But what her doctor had said to her was something she wasn't willing to share with Marquez or Sy. He'd told her that if she didn't get out of town, and into some sort of sedentary lifestyle, she was going to have a major heart attack and die at the prosecutor's table in her courtroom.

She swallowed the capsule. "The damned things include a diuretic," she said irritably. "I have to go to the bathroom every few minutes. How am I supposed to prosecute a case when I have to interrupt myself six times an hour?"

"Wear a diaper," Haynes replied imperturbably.

Glory gave her a glare.

"The D.A. doesn't want you to die in the courtroom." Marquez pressed his advantage now that he had backup. "He might not get reelected. Besides, he likes you."

"He likes me because I have no private life," she retorted. "I carry case files home with me every night. I'd miss yelling at people."

"You can yell at the workers on the Pendletons's organic truck farm in Jacobsville," Marquez assured her.

"At least I do know something about farming. My father had a little truck farm…" She closed up like a flower. It still hurt, after all these years, to remember the pain of seeing him taken away in an orange jumpsuit, cringing when she sobbed and begged the judge to let him go.

"Your father would be proud of you," Haynes interjected. "Especially now that you've cleared his name of that child abuse charge."

"It won't bring him back," she said dully. Her eyes narrowed. "But at least they finally found the man who killed him. He'll never get out now. If he ever goes up before the parole board,

I'll be sitting there with pictures of my father at every hearing for the rest of my life."

They didn't doubt it. She was a vengeful woman, in her quiet way.

"Come on," Marquez coaxed. "You need a rest, anyway. It's peaceful in Jacobsville."

"Peaceful." She nodded. "Right. Last year, there was a shoot-out in Jacobsville with drug dealers who moved hundreds of kilos of cocaine into the city limits and kidnapped a child. Two years before that, drug lord Manuel Lopez's men were stormed on his property in Jacobsville in a gun battle where his henchmen had stockpiled bales of marijuana."

"Nobody's been shot at for two months," Marquez assured her.

"What if I'm recognized by any leftover drug smugglers?"

"They won't be looking for you on a farm. San Antonio is a big city, and you're one of dozens of assistant district attorneys," he pointed out. "Your face isn't that well known even here, and certainly not in Jacobsville. You've changed a lot since you went to school there. Even if someone remembers you, it will be for the past, not the present. You'll be a quiet little woman from San Antonio with health problems watching over several fields of vegetables and fruit, thanks to your friends the Pendletons."

He hesitated. "One more thing. You can't admit that you're related to them, or even that you know them well. Nobody in Jacobsville, except the police chief, will know what you really do for a living. We're giving you a cover story that can be checked out by any suspicious people. It's foolproof."

"Didn't they say that about the *Titanic*'s design?"

"If she goes, I have to go with her," Haynes said firmly. "She won't take her medicine if I'm not there pushing it under her nose every day."

Before Glory could open her mouth, Marquez was shaking his head.

"It's going to be hard enough to help Glory fit in," he told

Haynes. "If she takes you with her, a gang member who might not recognize you alone might recognize the assistant who goes to court with her most of the time. Most of the gangs deal in drug trafficking."

Glory grimaced. "He's right," she told her assistant sadly. "I'd love for you to go with me, but it's risky."

Haynes looked miserable. "I could wear a disguise."

"No," Marquez said quietly. "You're more useful here. If any of the other attorneys find out something about Fuentes, you're in the perfect position to pass it on to me."

"I guess you're right," Haynes said. She glanced at Glory with a rueful smile. "I'll have to find a new boss while you're gone."

"Jon Blackhawk over at the FBI office is looking for another assistant," Marquez suggested.

Haynes glared at him. "He'll never get another one in this town, not after what he did to the last one."

Marquez was trying to keep a straight face. "I'm sure it was all a terrible misunderstanding."

Glory let out a chuckle in spite of herself. "Some misunderstanding. His assistant thought he was very attractive and asked him over to her place for dinner. He actually called the police and had her charged with sexual harassment."

Marquez let out the laugh he'd been holding back. "She was a beautiful blonde with a high IQ and his own mother had recommended her for the job. Blackhawk phoned his mother and told her that his latest assistant had tried to seduce him. His mother asked how. Now she's outraged over what he did and she won't speak to him, either. The girl was her best friend's daughter."

"He did drop the sexual harassment charge," Glory pointed out.

"Yes, but she quit just the same and went online to tell every woman in San Antonio what he did to her." He whistled. "I'll bet he'll grow gray hair before he gets a date in this town."

"Serves him right," Haynes muttered.

"Oh, it gets worse," Marquez added with a grin. "Remember Joceline Perry, who works for Garon Grier and one of the other local FBI agents? They gave Jon's work to her."

"Oh, dear," Haynes murmured.

Joceline was something of a local legend among administrative assistants. She was known for her cutting wit and refusal to do work she considered beneath her position. She would drive Jon Blackhawk up the wall on a good day. God only knew what she'd do to him after the other secretary quit.

"Poor guy," Glory murmured. But she grinned.

Haynes glanced at Glory with a worried look. "What are you going to do on the farm? You wouldn't dare go out and hoe in the fields, would you?"

"Of course not," Glory assured her. "I can can."

"You can what?" Haynes frowned.

"You have heard of canning?" Glory replied. "It's how you put up fruits and vegetables so that they don't spoil. I can do jam and jelly and pickles and all sorts of stuff."

Marquez raised an eyebrow. "My mother used to do it, but her hands aren't what they used to be. It's an art."

"A valuable skill," Glory said smugly.

"You'll need to wear jeans and look less elegant," Marquez told her. "No suits on the farm."

"I lived in Jacobsville when I was a child," Glory reminded him with a forced smile, without going into detail. Marquez was old enough to have known about Glory's ordeal. Of course, a lot of people didn't, even there. "I can fit in."

"Then you'll go?" Marquez persisted.

Glory sat back against the desk. She was outnumbered and outgunned. They were probably right. San Antonio was a big city, but she'd been in the same apartment building for two years and everyone who lived there knew her. She'd be easy to find if someone asked the right questions. If she got herself killed,

Fuentes would walk, and more people would be butchered in his insane quest for wealth.

If her doctor was right—and he was a very good doctor—the move right now might save her life, such as it was. She couldn't admit how frightened she was about his prognosis. Not to anyone. Tough girls like Glory didn't whine about their burdens.

"What about Jason and Gracie?" she blurted out suddenly.

"Jason's already hired a small army of bodyguards," Marquez assured her. "He and Gracie will be fine. It's you they're worried about. All of us are worried about you."

She drew in a long breath. "I guess a bulletproof vest and a Glock wouldn't convince you to let me stay here?"

"Fuentes has bullets that penetrate body armor, and nobody outside a psycho ward would give you a gun."

"All right," she said heavily. "I'll go. Do I have to ramrod this farm?"

"No, Jason's put in a manager." He frowned. "Odd guy. He isn't from Texas. I don't know where Jason found him. He's..." He started to say that the manager was one of the most unpleasant, taciturn people he'd ever met, despite the fact that the farm workers liked him. But it might not be the best time to say it. "He's very good at managing people," Marquez said instead.

"As long as he doesn't try to manage me, I guess it's okay," she said.

"He won't know anything about you, except what Jason tells him," he assured her. "Jason won't have told him about why you're there, and you can't, either. Apparently the manager's just had some sort of blow in his life, too, and he's taken the job to get himself over it."

"A truck farm," she murmured.

"I know where there's an animal shelter," Marquez replied whimsically. "They need someone to feed the lions."

She glared at him. "With my luck, they'd try to feed me *to* the lions. No, thanks."

"This is for your own good," Marquez said quietly. "You know that."

She sighed. "Yes, I suppose it is." She moved away from the desk. "My whole life, I've been forced to run away from problems. I'd hoped that this time, at least, I could stand and deliver."

"Neat phrasing," Marquez mused. "Would you like to borrow my sword?"

She gave him a keen glance. "Your mother should never have given you that claymore," she told him. "You're very lucky that the patrol officer could be convinced to drop the charges."

He looked affronted. "The guy picked the lock on my apartment door and let himself in. When I woke up, he was packing my new laptop into a book bag for transport!"

"You have a sidearm," she pointed out.

He glowered at her. "I forgot and left it locked in the pocket of my car that night. But the sword was mounted right over my bed."

"They say the thief actually jumped out the window when he brandished that huge weapon," Glory told Haynes, who grinned.

"My apartment is on the ground floor," Marquez informed them.

"Yes, but you were chasing the thief down the street in your…" She cleared her throat. "Well, you were out of uniform."

"I got arrested for streaking," Marquez muttered. "Can you believe that?"

"Of course I can! You were naked!" Glory replied.

"How I sleep has nothing to do with the fact that the guy was robbing me! At least I got him down and immobilized by the time the squad car spotted me." He shook his head. "I told the arresting officer who I was, and he asked to see my badge."

Glory put her hand over her mouth to stifle a giggle.

"Did you tell him where it was?" Haynes asked.

"I told him where he could put it if he didn't arrest the burglar." He moved restlessly. "Anyway, another squad car pulled up behind him, and it was an officer who knew me."

"A female officer," Glory told Haynes, with glee.

Marquez's high cheekbones actually seemed to flush. "The burglar's tote came in handy," he murmured. "At least I got to ride back to my apartment. But the story got out from the night shift, and by the next afternoon, I was a minor celebrity."

"What a pity you didn't get caught by the squad car's camera." Haynes giggled. "They could have featured you on that TV show *Cops.*"

He glared at her. "I was robbed!"

"Well, he didn't actually get to keep anything he took, did he?" Haynes asked.

"He fell on my new laptop when I tackled him," Marquez scoffed. "Trashed the hard drive. I lost all my files."

"Never heard of backing up with hard copy, I guess?" Glory queried.

"Who expects to have someone break into a cop's apartment and rob him?"

"He does have a point," Haynes had to admit.

"I guess so."

Marquez looked at his watch and grimaced. "I have to be in court this afternoon to testify for a homicide case," he told them. "I can tell my boss that you're going to Jacobsville, right?"

She sighed. "Yes. I'll go tomorrow morning, first thing. Do I need a letter of introduction or anything?"

"No. Jason will let the manager know you're coming. You can stay in the house on the property."

She hesitated. "Where is the manager staying?"

"Also in the house." He held up a hand. "Before you say it, there's a housekeeper who lives in the house and cooks for the manager."

That relaxed her, but only a little. She didn't like strange men, especially at close quarters. She decided that despite the summer heat, she'd pack thick cotton pajamas and a long robe.

Jacobsville seemed much smaller than she remembered it. The main street was almost exactly the same as it had been when she lived nearby. There was the pharmacy where her father had gone for medicine. Over there was the café which Barbara, Marquez's mother, had run for as long as she could remember. There was the hardware store and the feed store and the clothing boutique. It was all the same. Only Glory herself had changed.

As she turned onto the narrow paved road that led to the Pendletons's truck farm, she began to feel sick at her stomach. She'd forgotten. The house was the same one she'd shared with her mother and father, until her mother's explosive temper had shattered Glory's young body and their family. Until now, she hadn't thought about how difficult it might be, trying to live there again.

The old pecan tree in the front yard was still there. She spotted it before she saw the mailbox beside the narrow paved driveway. Years ago, there had been a tire swing on the tree.

The real surprise was the house. The Pendletons must have spent some money remodeling it, because the old clapboard house of Glory's youth was now an elegant white Victorian with gingerbread woodwork. There was a long, wide front porch which contained a swing, a settee and several rocking chairs. Far behind the house was a huge steel warehouse where workers were putting boxes of fresh corn and peas and tomatoes and other produce from the large fields on all sides of the house and warehouse. The fields seemed to stretch for miles into the flat distance.

She pulled up in the graveled parking lot under another pecan tree and cut off the engine. Her small sedan contained most of her worldly goods. Except for her furniture, and she hadn't even considered bringing that along. She was keeping her apartment in San Antonio. The rent was paid up for six months, courtesy of her stepbrother. She wondered when she'd get to go home.

She opened the door and got out, just in time to see a tall, jeans-clad man with jet-black hair and a mustache come down the front steps. He had a strong face and an athletic physique. He walked with such elegance that he seemed to glide along. He looked foreign.

He spotted Glory and his taut expression grew even more reserved. He moved toward her with a quick, elegant step. As he came closer, she could see that his eyes were black, like jet, under a jutting brow and dark eyebrows. She had the odd feeling that he was the sort of man you hope you never meet in a dark alley.

He stopped just in front of her, adding up her inexpensive car, her eyeglasses, her windswept blond hair in its tight bun and her modest clothing. If he was measuring, she thought, she'd fallen short.

"May I help you?" he asked coldly.

She leaned heavily on the car door. "I'm the canner."

He blinked. "Excuse me?"

She swallowed, hard. He was very tall and he looked half out of humor already. "I can can."

"We don't hire exotic dancers," he shot back.

Her green eyes widened. "Excuse me?"

"The can-can is a dance, I believe?"

"Is it, really?" she asked with a mischievous glance. "Would you like to demonstrate it, and I'll give you my opinion of whether it's a dance or not?"

Incredible, she thought. Until now, she hadn't really believed that a man's eyes could explode with bad temper...

CHAPTER TWO

The man's jaw clenched. "I am not in the mood for games," he said in coldly accented English.

"First you talk about dancing, now you're on about games," she said. "Really, I don't care about your private life. I was sent here to help with the canning. Jason Pendleton offered me the position."

His eyes were really smoldering now. "He what?"

"Gave me a job," she replied. She frowned. "Are you hard of hearing?"

He took a step toward her and she moved further toward the hinges. He looked ferocious. "Jason Pendleton offered you a job here?"

"Yes, he did," she replied. Perhaps humor wasn't a very good idea at the time. "He said you needed someone to help put up his organic fruit. I can make preserves and jellies and I know how to can vegetables."

He seemed to be struggling with her presence. It was obvious that he wasn't happy about her coming here. "Jason said nothing about it to me."

"He told me he'd phone you tonight. He's in Montana at a cattle show."

"I know where he is."

Her hip was throbbing. She didn't want to mention it. He was irritated enough already. "Would you like me to sleep in the car?" she asked politely.

He seemed to realize where they were, as if he'd lost his train of thought. "I'll have Consuelo get a room ready for you," he said without enthusiasm. "She's been putting up the jellies and preserves herself. It's a new line. We have a processing plant for the vegetables. If the fruit line catches on, we'll add it into the plant. Consuelo said the kitchen here is plenty large enough to do for a sampling of products."

"I won't get in her way," she promised.

"Come on, then. I'll introduce you before I leave."

Was he going to quit already, then, to keep from having to work with her? she wanted to ask. Pity he had no sense of humor.

She reached back into the car for her red dragon cane. She had an umbrella stand full of the helpful devices, in all sorts of colors and styles. If one had to be handicapped, she reasoned, one should be flamboyant about it.

She closed the door, leaning on the cane.

His expression was inexplicable. He scowled.

She waited for him to comment about her disability.

He didn't. He turned and walked, slowly, back to the house, waiting for her to catch up. She recognized that expression. It was pity. She clenched her teeth. If he offered to help her up the steps, she was going to hit him right in the knee with her cane.

He didn't do that, either. He did open the door for her, grudgingly.

Great, she told herself as she walked into the foyer. We'll communicate in sign language from now on, I guess.

He led the way through a comfortable living room with polished bare wood floors, through what seemed like pantries on both sides of the narrow passage, and into an enormous kitchen with new appliances, a large table and chairs, a worktable, and yellow lace curtains at all the windows. The floor was linoleum with a stone pattern. The cabinets were oak-stained, roomy and easy to reach. There was a counter that went from the dishwasher and sink around to the stove. The refrigerator was standing alone in a corner. It must have offended the cook and been exiled, Glory thought wickedly.

A small dark woman with her hair in a complicated ponytail down her back, tied in four places with pink ribbon, turned at the sound of footsteps. She had a round face and laughing dark eyes.

"Consuelo," the tall man said, indicating Glory, "this is the new canner."

Consuelo's eyebrows arched.

"I told him I can can and he called me an exotic dancer," Glory told the woman.

The other woman seemed to be fighting laughter.

"This is Consuelo Aguila," he introduced. "And this is…" He stopped dead, because he didn't know who the new arrival was.

Glory waited for him to get on with it. She wasn't inclined to help out.

"You didn't ask her name?" Consuelo chided. She went to Glory, with a big smile. "You are welcome here. I can use the help. What is your name?"

"Gloryanne," came the soft reply. "Gloryanne Barnes."

The tall man raised both eyebrows. "Who named you?"

Her eyes grew solemn. "My father. He thought having a child was a glorious occasion."

He was curious about her expression. She seemed reluctant to add anything more.

"Do you know who he is?" Consuelo asked her, indicating the tall man.

Glory pursed her lips. She shook her head.

"You didn't even introduce yourself?" Consuelo asked the man, aghast.

He glowered at her. "She won't be working with me," he said flatly.

"Yes, but she's going to live in the house...?"

"I don't mind sleeping in my car," Glory said at once, very pleasantly.

"Don't be absurd," he growled. "I have to go to the hardware store to pick up some more stakes for the tomato plants," he told the small, dark woman. "Give her a room and tell her how we work here."

Glory opened her mouth to protest his attitude, but he whirled and strode out of the room without another word. The front screen door banged loudly as he went out it.

"Well, he's a charmer, isn't he?" Glory asked the older woman with a grin. "I can hardly wait to settle in and make his life utterly miserable."

Consuelo laughed. "He's not so bad," she said. "We don't know why he took over when Mr. Wilkes resigned. The boss—that's Mr. Pendleton, he lives in San Antonio—told us that Rodrigo had lost his family recently and was in mourning. He came here to pick up his life again."

"Oh, dear," Glory said quietly. "Sorry. I shouldn't have been so sarcastic toward him."

"It rolls off his back," the woman scoffed. "He works like a tiger. He is never cruel or harsh with the men who work in the fields. He is a cultured man, I think, because he loves to listen to DVDs of opera and classical music. But once, we had a worker get into a fight with another man, and Rodrigo intervened. Nobody saw him move, but in the flash of a light, the aggressor was lying on his back in the dirt with many bruises. The men don't give Rodrigo any reason to go after them, since that happened. He is very strong."

"Rodrigo?" Glory sounded out the name. It had a quiet dignity.

"Rodrigo Ramirez," she replied. "He worked on a cattle ranch down in Sonora, he said."

"He came from Mexico?"

"I think he was born there, but he does not speak of his past."

"His accent is very slight," Glory mused. "He speaks Spanish, I guess."

"Spanish, French, Danish, Portuguese, German, Italian and, of all things, Apache."

Glory was confused. "With a talent like that, he's managing a truck farm in Texas?"

Consuelo chuckled. "I also made this observation. He led me to believe he once worked as a translator. Where, he did not say."

Glory smiled. "Well, at least this is going to be an interesting job."

"You know the big boss, Jason Pendleton?"

Glory nodded. "Well, sort of," she amended quickly. "I was more friendly with his sister," she confided.

"Ah. Gracie." Consuelo chuckled again. "She came with him once. There was a cat with a broken leg lying beside the road, a stray that hung around here. Gracie picked it up, blood and dirt and all, and made Jason take her to the nearest vet. She was wearing a silk dress that would cost me two months' wages, and it didn't matter. The cat was what mattered." She smiled. "She should marry. It would be a very lucky man, to have a wife like that."

"She doesn't want to get married," Glory said. "Her real father was a hell-raiser."

"Hers and Jason's, you mean…"

Glory shook her head. "You see, Jason and Gracie aren't related. Her father died when she was in her early teens. Her stepmother married Jason's father. Then her stepmother died and Jason's father married again." She didn't add that Jason's stepfather was also her own stepfather. It was complicated.

Consuelo took off her apron. "I must show you to the guest

room." She turned, and only then noticed the cane, half hidden behind Glory's jeans-clad leg. Her eyebrows met. "You should have told me," she fussed. "I would never have let you stand like that while I gossiped! It must be painful."

"I didn't notice. Really."

"The room is downstairs, at least," Consuelo said, leading the way past the pantry shelves, into the living room, and through a far door that led to another hall, which ended in a bathroom opening into a small, blue-wallpapered room with white trim.

"It's lovely," Glory told her.

"It's small," Consuelo said. "Rodrigo chose it for himself, but I told him he needed more room than this. He has two computers and several pieces of radio equipment. A hobby, he said. There is a small desk in the study that he uses, but he prefers his bedroom when he's doing the books."

"He's antisocial?"

"He has nothing to do with women," Consuelo replied. She frowned. "Although, there was a pretty blonde woman who came here to see him one day. They seemed very close. I asked. But he ignored the question. He does not talk about himself."

"How odd."

"You are not married, or engaged?"

Glory shook her head. "I don't want to marry. Ever."

"You don't want children?"

Glory frowned. "I don't know that I should try to have them," she said. "I have a...medical problem. It would be dangerous." She sighed. "But since I don't trust men very much, it's probably just as well."

Consuelo didn't ask any more questions, but her manner with Glory was gentle.

The truck farm was huge. There were many fields, each with a separate crop, and the plantings were staggered so that something was always ready to harvest. The fruit trees were just being picked. Peaches and apricots, nectarines and kiwi fruit were first to harvest. The apple trees were varieties that produced in the fall. In between were berries, dewberries and raspberries and blackberries and strawberries.

"I'm going to be busy," Glory exclaimed when Consuelo pointed out the various surrounding fields.

"We both are," the older woman replied. "I was thinking about giving up this job. It's too much for one woman. But two of us, we can manage, I think. The jams and jellies and pickles will add a lot to our revenue if they sell. They're popular with tourists. We also stock them at the local florist shop, and they're put in gift baskets. We have a processing plant for the organic vegetables and an online shop that our warehouse operates. They ship orders. But this is early days for our specialty canning. I've only managed to do the usual things, fruit preserves and jellies. I would love to do small batches of organic corn and peas and beans as well, but they mostly do those at the processing center in bulk. Besides, those require the pressure cooker to process and more time than I have had since Rodrigo took charge. He is a dynamo, that man."

"Pressure cookers make me nervous," Glory began.

"We've all heard terrible stories about how they can explode," Consuelo chuckled. "But this is a new age. They all have fail-safe controls nowadays. Anyway, we won't use them here. Let me show you what we're working on. It's an easy job."

Easy. The work was. Glory's hip pained her, and she spent some of her time on a heating pad. But Consuelo found her a stool and she adjusted to the new physical demands of her job.

Rodrigo, however, was not easy. He seemed to have taken an instant dislike to Glory and was determined to say as little to her as possible in the course of a day.

He seemed to think she was a useless person. He was impersonally tolerant of her disability, but he often looked at her as if he suspected that her brain was locked away in a fleshy cabinet and was only taken out occasionally to be polished. She wondered what he'd think if he knew what she did for a living and why she was actually down here. It amused her to consider his reaction.

One day, he brought a new man into the house and told Consuelo that he would be overseeing the men while Rodrigo had to be away over the weekend. Glory didn't like the newcomer at all. He seemed to never look anyone in the eye. He was small and swarthy and he made a point of staring at Glory's body when he spoke to her. Already uneasy around men she didn't know, this one was causing her some real problems.

Consuelo noticed, and she got between the man and Glory when he became too friendly.

"I cannot imagine what was in Señor Ramirez's mind when he hired that Castillo man as an assistant," Consuelo muttered to Glory when they were alone in the kitchen. "I don't like having him around here. He's spent time in jail."

"How did you know that?" Glory asked. She knew the answer, but she wondered if Consuelo was just sensing the man's past or if there was a reason for the remark.

"The muscles in his arms and torso are huge, and he has tattoos everywhere." She mentioned one particular tattoo that marked him as a member of one of the more notorious Los Angeles street gangs.

Glory, who knew about gang members all too well, was surprised and impressed by the woman's knowledge.

"What is he doing here?" Glory asked aloud, pondering.

"I would not dare to ask," came the solemn reply. "Señor Pendleton should be told, but it would be worth my job to mention it outside the house. We will have to trust that Rodrigo knows what he is doing."

"There's a strange bird," Glory remarked. "Rodrigo. He's very cultured and quite intelligent. I'm sure he could write his own ticket in management anywhere he wanted to work. He seems out of place on a truck farm."

Consuelo chuckled. "I would not ask that one anything that was not necessary for the performance of my job," she replied. "From time to time, something upsets him. He is eloquent with bad words, and he does not tolerate sloppy work or tardiness. One man he scolded for drinking on the job was fired the same day. He is a hard taskmaster."

"Yes, I thought he seemed that sort of man. He's not happy."

Consuelo looked at her and nodded. "You are perceptive. No, he is not. And I think that he is not usually a moody person. He must have loved his family very much. I notice how he is with my son, Marco, when he visits me."

"You have children, then?" Glory asked gently.

Consuelo smiled. "Yes, a boy. He has just turned twenty-one. I adore him."

"Does he live nearby?"

Consuelo shook her head. "He lives in Houston. But he comes to see me when he can. Especially when there's a soccer game on cable—he can't afford it, but Rodrigo had it put in here so that he doesn't miss the games."

"Soccer?" Glory's green eyes lit up. "I love soccer!"

"You do?" Consuelo was excited. "Which team do you like best?"

Glory smiled sheepishly. "Mexico. I know I should support our own team in this country, but I love the Mexican team. I have a flag of the team that hangs in my living room during the World Cup and the Copita."

"I probably should not tell you that I am related to a player on that team."

"You are?" Glory exclaimed. "Which one?"

Before she could answer, Rodrigo walked in. He stopped in the doorway, scowling at Glory's radiance when she smiled. "What did I interrupt?" he asked curiously.

"We were talking about soccer," Consuelo began.

He glanced at Glory. "Don't tell me you watch it?"

"Every chance I get," she replied.

He made a sound in his throat, like a subdued chuckle. He turned to Consuelo. "I'm going to be away for the weekend. I'm leaving Castillo in charge. If you have any problems with him, let me know."

"He does not..." Consuelo began, glancing at Glory.

"He doesn't bother us," Glory interrupted with a speaking glance.

"Since you have no contact with him, I can't imagine why he should," he told her. "If you need me, you have my cell phone number."

"Yes," Consuelo said.

He walked out without another word.

"Why didn't you let me tell him?" Consuelo asked worriedly.

"He'd think I was complaining to you," Glory said simply. "If Castillo gives me any trouble, I'll take care of him myself." She smiled gently. "You shouldn't think that my hip slows me down very much," she said softly. "I can take care of myself. But thank you for caring."

Consuelo hesitated, then she smiled. "Okay. I'll let you handle it your way."

Glory nodded, and went back to work.

Castillo didn't bother them. But he did have a long conversation with a man in a white van. Glory watched covertly from the kitchen window, making sure she wasn't visible to him. The van was old and beat-up and the man driving it was as muscular and as tattooed as Castillo. She made a mental note of the van's license plate and wrote it down on a pad, just in case.

She shouldn't have been so suspicious of people, she told herself. But she knew a lot about drug smuggling from the cases she'd prosecuted, and she had something of a second sense about the "mules" who transported cocaine and marijuana and meth-amphetamine from one place to another. Many of the "mules" were in street gangs that also helped distribute the product.

She and Consuelo were kept busy for the next couple of weeks as the fruit started to come in. They had baskets and baskets of it, picked by the workers and spread around the kitchen. If Glory had wondered why there were two stoves, she didn't have to ask any longer. Both were going night and day as the sweet smell of preserves and jams and jellies wafted through the house.

Slowly Glory had become accustomed to seeing Rodrigo in the kitchen at mealtimes. He slept upstairs, so she didn't see him at night. Sometimes she heard him pacing up there. His room was apparently right over hers.

She served Rodrigo bacon and eggs and the homemade bis-cuits she'd made since she was ten, because Consuelo had to go to the store for more canning supplies, including jars and lids. She poured coffee into a cup and put that on the table as well. She'd long since eaten herself, so she went back to peeling a basket of peaches.

Rodrigo watched her covertly. She had her hair in its usual braid. She was wearing old blue jeans and a green T-shirt that showed very little skin. She wasn't a pretty woman. He found her uninteresting. Not that it mattered. Now that Sarina was married, and she and Bernadette were no longer part of his life, not much did matter. He'd hoped that the reappearance of Ber-nadette's father, Colby Lane, would make no difference to the close ties he had with the woman and child. But in scant weeks, Colby and Sarina were inseparable. They had been married years ago and it seemed that the marriage was never annulled. It was like death to Rodrigo, who'd been part of Sarina's family for three years. He couldn't cope. It was why he'd taken on this assignment. It was both covert and dangerous. He was known to the big drug lords, and his cover was paper thin since he'd helped put away Cara Dominguez, successor to famous, and dead, drug lord Manuel Lopez.

Rodrigo was an agent for the Drug Enforcement Administration. He and Sarina, a fellow agent, had worked out of the Tucson division for three years. Then they'd been asked to go undercover in Houston to ferret out a smuggling enterprise. They'd been successful. But Colby Lane, who'd helped set up the smugglers, had walked off with Sarina and Bernadette. Rodrigo had been devastated.

Sarina had promised Colby that she'd give up her DEA job and go to work for Police Chief Cash Grier here in Jacobsville. So Rodrigo had asked for this undercover assignment, to be near her. But Sarina had been persuaded by the DEA to work with Alexander Cobb in the Houston office on another case. Colby hadn't liked it. Rodrigo had liked it less. She was in Houston, and he was here. Colby had remained at Ritter Oil Corporation in Houston as assistant of security for the firm, while Sarina settled back in with the Houston DEA office. Bernadette was back in Houston finishing out the school year in a familiar place.

Sarina had come here to tell him the news. It had been painful, seeing her again. She knew how he felt; she was sorry for him. It didn't help. His life was in pieces. She was concerned that his cover was too flimsy and he stood to be killed if the drug lords found him out. It didn't matter. There was a price on his head in almost every other country in the world from his days as a professional mercenary. This country was the only place left where he wasn't in danger of being assassinated. On the other hand, his line of work was likely to get him killed.

"You don't talk much, do you?" Rodrigo asked the woman peeling peaches beside him.

She smiled. "Not a lot, no," she replied.

"How do you like the job so far?" he asked.

"It's nice," she replied. "And I like Consuelo."

"Everyone does. She has a big heart."

She peeled another peach. He finished his coffee and got up to get a refill for himself. She noticed. "I don't mind doing that," she said. "It's part of my job to work in the kitchen."

He ignored the comment, added cream to his coffee, and sat back down. "How did you hurt your leg?"

Her face closed up. She didn't like remembering. "It was when I was a child," she said, circumventing the question.

He was watching her, very closely. "And you don't talk about it, do you?"

She looked him in the eye. "No. I don't."

He sipped coffee. His eyes narrowed. "Most women your age are married or involved with someone."

"I like my own company," she told him.

"You don't share things," he replied. "You don't trust anyone. You keep to yourself, do your job and go home."

Her eyebrows arched. "Are we doing a psychological profile?"

He laughed coolly. "I like to know something about the people I work with."

"I'm twenty-six years old, I've never been arrested, I hate liver, I pay my bills on time and I've never cheated on my income tax. Oh," she added, "and I wear size nine shoes, in case it ever comes up."

He chuckled then. His dark eyes were amused, alive, intent on her face. "Do I sound like an interrogator?"

"Something like that," she said, smiling.

"Consuelo says you speak Spanish."

"Tengo que hablarlo," she replied. *"Para hacer mi trabajo."*

"¿Y qué es su trabajo, pues, rubia?" he replied.

She smiled gently. "You speak it so beautifully," she said involuntarily. "I was taught Castilian, although I don't lisp my 'c's."

"You make yourself understood," he told her. "Are you literate?"

She nodded. "I love to read in Spanish."

"What do you like to read?"

She bit her lower lip and gave him an odd look. "Well..."

"Come on."

She sighed. "I like to read about Juan Belmonte and Joselito and Manolete."

His eyebrows arched toward his hairline. "Bullfighters? You like to read about Spanish bullfighters?"

She scowled. "Old bullfighters," she corrected. "Belmonte and Joselito fought bulls in the early part of the twentieth century, and Manolete died in the ring in 1947."

"So they did." He studied her over his coffee mug. "You're full of surprises, aren't you? Soccer and bullfighting." He shook his head. "I would have taken you for a woman who liked poetry."

If he'd known her, and her lifestyle, it would have shocked him that she'd even considered doing manual labor, much less read poetry. She was amused at the thought.

"I do like poetry," she replied. And she did.

"So do I," he said surprisingly.

"Which poets?" she fished.

He smiled. "Lorca."

Her lips parted on a shocked breath. "He wrote about the death of his friend Sánchez Mejías in the bull ring."

"Yes, and was killed himself in the Spanish Civil War a few years later."

"How odd," she said, thinking aloud.

"That I read Lorca?"

"Well, considering what he wrote, yes. It's something of a coincidence, isn't it?"

"What poets do you read?" he returned.

"I like Rupert Brooke." In fact, as she looked at Rodrigo she was remembering a special poem, about death finding the poet long before he tired of watching the object of the poem. She thought involuntarily that Rodrigo was good to look at. He was very handsome.

He pursed his lips. "I wonder if we could possibly be thinking of the same poem?" he wondered aloud.

"Which one did you have in mind?" she probed.

"'Death will find me long before I tire of watching you,'" he began in a slow, sensuous, faintly accented tone.

The peach she was peeling fell out of her hands and rolled across the kitchen floor while she stared at the man across the table from her with wide-eyed shock.

CHAPTER THREE

Rodrigo stared at her curiously. She was a contradiction. She seemed simple and sweet, but she was educated. He was certain that she wasn't what she appeared to be, but it was far too soon to start dissecting her personality. She interested him, but he didn't want her to. He was still mourning Sarina. Anyway, it amused him that she liked the same poems he did.

She got up slowly and picked up her peach, tossing it away because Consuelo had waxed the floor that morning and she was wary of getting even a trace of wax in her fruit. She washed her hands again as well.

"I'm glad to see that you appreciate the danger of contamination," Rodrigo said.

She smiled. "Consuelo would have whacked me with a broom if she'd caught me putting anything in the pot that had been on her floor, no matter how clean it is."

"She's a good woman."

"She is," Glory agreed. "She's been very kind to me."

He finished his coffee and got up. But he didn't leave. "One of the workers told me that Castillo made a suggestive remark to you when you went to ask him for replacement baskets for some berries that had molded."

She gave him a wary look. She'd had words with Castillo over his foul language. He'd only laughed. It had made her very angry. But she didn't want to get a reputation for tale-telling. There was more to it than that, of course. Her mother hadn't been the only person who'd been physically abusive to her. The two teenage boys in the foster home had harassed and frightened her for months and then assaulted her. As a result of the violence in her past, she was uneasy and frightened around men. Rodrigo had been away when the new employee had made suggestive remarks, and Glory and Consuelo would have been no match for a man with the muscles Castillo enjoyed displaying, if Glory had antagonized him.

"You're afraid of him," Rodrigo said quietly, watching her reaction to the statement.

She swallowed. Her hand contracted on the knife. She didn't want to admit that, even though it was true. She was afraid of men. It hurt her pride to have to admit it.

"Was it a man, who did that to you?" he asked unexpectedly, indicating her hip.

She was too emotionally torn to choose her words. "My mother did it," she replied.

Whatever reply he'd expected, that wasn't it. "God in heaven, your mother?" he exclaimed.

She couldn't meet his eyes. "Yes."

"Why?"

"She was killing my cat," she said, feeling the pain all over again. "I tried to stop her."

"What did she hit you with?"

The memory was still painful. "A baseball bat. My own baseball bat. I played on my school team just briefly."

His indrawn breath was audible in the silence that followed. "And the cat?"

The memory hurt. "My daddy buried it for me while I was in the hospital," she managed huskily.

"Niña," he whispered huskily. *"Lo siento."*

She'd never had comfort. It had been offered, and refused, several times during traumatic periods of her life. Sympathy was weakening. It was the enemy. She tried valiantly to stem the tears, but she couldn't stop them. The tenderness in Rodrigo's deep voice made her hungry for comfort. Her wet eyes betrayed that need to him.

He took the knife and the peaches from her, set them aside and pulled her up tight into his arms. He held her, rocked her, while years of sorrow and grief poured out of her in a blinding tide.

"What a witch she must have been," he murmured into her soft hair.

"Yes," she said simply, remembering what came after her accident. The arrest of her father and his conviction, the foster homes, the assault…

She should have been afraid of him. The memory of the boys overpowering her in her foster home haunted her. But she wasn't afraid. She clung to him, burying her wet face in his broad chest. His arms were strong and warm, and he held her in a gentle but tight nonsexual way. It was a landmark in her life, that comfort. Jason had held her when she cried, of course, but Jason was like a loving big brother. This man was something entirely different.

He smoothed her hair, thinking how it helped to feel another human body close against his. He grieved for the loss of Sarina and Bernadette, and deep inside he remembered his anguish when the drug lord, Manuel Lopez, had killed his only sister. He knew grief. He began to understand this woman a little. She was strong. She must be, to have survived such an ordeal. He suspected there were more traumatic things in her past, things she'd never told another living soul.

After a minute, she moved away from him. She was embarrassed. She dabbed at her eyes with the hem of her apron and turned to pick up the peaches and the knife.

"We all have tragedies," he said quietly. "We live with them in silence. Sometimes the pain breaks free and becomes visible. It should not embarrass you to realize that you are human."

She looked up at him with red eyes. She nodded.

He smiled and glanced at his watch. "I have to get the men started. Breakfast was very nice. Your biscuits are better than Consuelo's, but don't tell her."

She managed a watery smile. "I won't."

He started out the door.

"Señor Ramirez," she called.

He turned, his eyebrows arched.

"Thank you," she managed.

"You're welcome."

She watched him go, twisting inside with unfamiliar emotions. She couldn't remember any man, except for Jason, holding her like that in her adult life. It had been wonderful. Now she had to put it right out of her mind. She didn't want anyone close to her emotionally. Not even Rodrigo.

The next week, she was surprised to find a police car in the front yard. She went to the front porch and paused as the town's police chief, Cash Grier, bounded up the steps.

She hadn't seen him before, and she was surprised by the long ponytail he wore. She'd heard that he was unconventional, and there were some interesting rumors about his past that were spoken in whispers. Even up in San Antonio, he was something of a legend in law enforcement circles.

"You're Chief Grier," she said as he approached her.

He grinned. "What gave me away?" he asked.

"The badge that says 'Police Chief,'" she replied, tongue-in-cheek. "What can I do for you?"

He chuckled. "I came to see Rodrigo. Is he around?"

"He was," she replied. "But he hasn't come in for lunch, or called." She turned and opened the screen door, leaning heavily on the cane. "Consuelo, do you know where Mr. Ramirez is?"

"He said he was going to the hardware store to pick up the extra buckets he ordered," she called.

Glory turned back to the chief, and found him eyeing her cane. She became defensive. "Something bothering you?" she asked pertly.

"Sorry," he said. "I didn't mean to stare. You're young to be walking with a cane."

She nodded, her green eyes meeting his dark ones. "I've been using it for a long time."

He cocked his head, and he wasn't smiling. "Your mother was Beverly Barnes, wasn't she?" he asked coldly.

She drew in her breath.

"Marquez's mother runs the local eatery," he replied. "I know about you from her. She and Rick don't have any secrets."

"Nobody is supposed to know why I'm here," she began worriedly.

He held up a hand. "I haven't said anything, and I won't. I gather you include Rodrigo in those people who aren't supposed to know why you're here?"

"Yes," she said quickly. "Especially Rodrigo."

He nodded. "I'll watch your back," he told her. "But it would be wise to have Rodrigo in on it."

She couldn't imagine why. The manager of a truck farm wouldn't know what to do against a drug lord. "The fewer people who know, the better," she told him. "Fuentes would love to hang me out to dry before the trial. I know too much."

"Marquez told me. He said he had to fight you to get you to come down here in the first place. The thing is, Fuentes probably has confederates that we don't know about."

"Here?" she asked.

"Very likely. I have a few contacts on the wrong side of the law. Word is that he's hiring teenagers for his more potent areas of vengeance. They go to juvenile hall, you see, not prison. I understand that he's recruiting in a Houston gang—Los Serpientes. If you see any suspicious activity here, or any new young faces hiring on, I want to know about it. Night or day. Especially if you feel threatened at all. I don't care if it's after midnight, either."

"That's generous of you," she said, and she smiled.

"Not really," he sighed. "Tris, our baby girl, keeps us awake all hours just lately. She's teething, so you probably wouldn't even have to wake us up."

"Your wife is very famous," she replied shyly.

He chuckled with pride. "Yes, but you'd never know it to see her pushing baby Tris in a cart in the Sav-A-Lot Grocery Store," he assured her.

Grocery store. The store had a van. Something niggled in the back of her mind. She remembered something. "There was a van," she said suddenly. "This man Castillo that Mr. Ramirez just hired to be his assistant was talking to some man in a battered old white van. Something changed hands—money or drugs, maybe. It was suspicious, so I wrote down the license plate number."

"Smart girl," he said, impressed.

"I put it on a pad in the kitchen. Would you like to come in and have coffee? Consuelo's made a nice peach pie for supper."

"I love coffee and pie," he assured her.

"Come in, then."

He followed her into the kitchen, where Consuelo greeted him, but with obvious suspicion. He got the number from Glory while Consuelo was out of the room.

"Consuelo doesn't like policemen," she confided. "I don't know why. I mentioned something about the extra patrols that were coming past the house, and she was belligerent."

"Could be the immigration investigations," Cash murmured. "They've stepped up in the new political climate."

"What about the extra patrols?" she asked suddenly.

He glanced toward the doorway to make sure Consuelo wasn't around. "One of Ramirez's employees has a rap sheet. We've been keeping a low profile, but we're keeping an eye on him." He grinned. "Nice work, getting that tag number."

She chuckled. "I feel like an undercover narc or something," she murmured as he got up to leave.

He laughed. "I can't tell you why that's amusing, but one day you'll see. Thanks for the coffee and pie."

"You're very welcome." She hesitated. "Can you tell me which employee you've got your eye on?"

He sighed. "You've probably guessed that already."

She nodded. "Castillo has tats and muscles like a wrestler. It doesn't take much guesswork. I've seen his type come through my office for years."

"So have I," he said.

"Do you know Mr. Ramirez well?" she asked suddenly.

"Not really," he said deliberately. "I've seen him around. But I actually came today to check with him about one of your employees who may be in the country illegally."

She wondered which employee. "Should I ask him to phone you when he comes in?" she asked.

"Do that, if you don't mind."

"I'll be glad to." She leaned on her cane, frowning. Another thought provoked her next question. "That illegal," she said slowly. "You don't think it's Angel Martinez, do you?" she added, recalling the sweet little man who was always so courteous to her when he came into the house with Rodrigo. She was fond of him.

His eyebrows arched. "Why do you say that?"

She shifted her weight. Her hip was hurting. "It's just that he and his wife, Carla, have three children. They're so nice, and they're happy here. They come from a village in Central America where there was a paramilitary group. Somebody in the village identified one of the rebels to the government authorities. The next day, Angel took Carla and the children to a healer in another village because one of the children had a sore eye. When they got back, everybody in the village was dead, laid out like firewood on the ground."

He moved closer. "I know what life in those villages is like," he said with surprising sympathy. "And I know what good people the Martinezes are. Sometimes enforcing the law is painful even for professionals."

His sympathy made her bold. "I know an attorney in San Antonio who specializes in immigration cases," she began.

He sighed, noting her expression. "And I know one of the federal attorneys," he replied with resignation. "Okay. I'll go make some phone calls."

She beamed up at him. "I knew you were a nice man the minute I saw you."

"Did you? How?" he asked with real curiosity.

"The ponytail," she told him. "It has to be a sign of personal courage." It was overt flattery.

He laughed. "Well! I'll have to go home and tell Tippy that the secret's out."

She grinned.

His expression became solemn. "Castillo is dangerous. Don't get brave when you're on your own here."

"I realized that early on," she assured him. "He has no respect for women."

"Or men," he added. "Watch your back."

"I will."

He waved on his way down the steps.

Rodrigo was curious about the conversation Glory had with Chief Grier. Too curious.

"Did he say anything about the illegal immigrant he's looking for?" he asked over bowls of soup at the supper table with Consuelo.

Glory hesitated. She didn't quite know Rodrigo enough to trust him with information of a potentially tragic case.

Consuelo grinned at him. "She's afraid you might blow the whistle on Angel," she said in a stage whisper.

Glory flushed and Rodrigo burst out laughing.

"I would never have suspected you of having anarchist leanings," he chided Glory.

She finished a spoonful of soup before she answered him. "I'm not an anarchist. I just think people make snap decisions without all the facts. I know that immigrants put a strain on our economy." She put the spoon down and looked at him. "But aren't we all Americans? I mean, the continent is North America, isn't it? If you're from north, central or south America, you're still an American."

Rodrigo looked at Consuelo. "She's a socialist," he said.

"I am not classifiable," she argued. "I just think that helping people in desperate need is supposed to be what freedom and democracy are all about. It isn't as if they want to come here and sit down and let us all support them. They're some of the hardest working people in the world. You know yourself that you have to force your hired hands to come out of the fields. Hard work is all they know. They're just happy to live someplace where they don't have to worry about being shot or run out of their villages by multinational corporations looking for land."

He hadn't interrupted her. He was watching her with narrow, intent eyes, unaware that his soup spoon was frozen in midair.

She raised her eyebrows. "Is my mustache on crooked?" she asked mischievously.

He laughed and put the spoon down. "No. I'm impressed by your knowledge of third world communities."

She wanted so badly to ask about his own knowledge of them, but she was shy of him. The memory of the fervent embrace she'd shared with him made her tingle all over every time she pictured it. He was very strong, and very attractive.

He finished his coffee, glancing at her. "You're dying to know, aren't you?" he asked with a bland expression.

"Know what?"

"Where I come from."

Her cheeks went pink. "I'm sorry. I shouldn't pry..."

"I was born in Sonora, in northern Mexico," he told her. He

skipped the part about his family and their illustrious connections, including their wealth. He had to remember his concocted history. "My parents worked for a man who ran cattle. I learned the business from the ground up, and eventually managed a ranch."

She felt strongly that he wasn't telling the whole story, but she wasn't going to dig too deeply. It was too soon. "Did you get tired of the ranch?"

He laughed. "The owner did. He sold his holdings to a politician who thought he knew all about cattle ranching from watching reruns of *High Chapparel*, that old television Western."

"Did he really know all about it?" she fished.

"He lost the cattle in the first six months to disease because he didn't believe in preventative medicine, and he lost the land two months after that in a poker game with two supposed friends. No ranch, no job, so I came north looking for work."

She frowned. Jason Pendleton wasn't the sort of man who socialized with day laborers, she thought, even though he wasn't a snob. "How did you meet Jason... I mean, Mr. Pendleton?" she corrected.

He caught the slip, but let it pass. "We were both acquainted with a man who was opening a new restaurant in San Antonio. He introduced us. Jason said that he needed someone to ramrod a truck farm in a little Texas town, and I was looking for work."

Actually he'd approached Jason, with the help of a mutual friend, and explained that he needed the job temporarily to provide his cover while he tried to shut down Fuentes and his operation. Jason had agreed to go along with it.

Their next conversation, the day Glory arrived, had been about Glory going to work on the truck farm. Jason had told him nothing about Glory, least of all that she was his stepsister, but he hadn't liked Rodrigo's remark about Glory being crippled and it was evident. Rodrigo had the feeling that Jason was overly fond of Glory—perhaps they were even lovers. It had been a taut conversation.

Rodrigo was tempted to ask Glory about her relationship with Jason, but he didn't want to rock the boat.

"Well, your English is a hundred times better than my Spanish," she sighed, breaking into his thoughts.

"I work hard at it."

Consuelo was stirring cake batter. She glanced at Rodrigo curiously. "That Castillo man is going to be trouble, you mark my words."

He leaned back in his chair and looked at her. "We've been over this twice already," he said quietly. "You want your son to work here and take his place. But Marco doesn't know how to manage people." He said it in an odd tone, as if he was holding something back.

She glowered at him. "He can so manage people. He's smart, too. Not book smart, but street smart."

Rodrigo looked thoughtful. His eyes narrowed. "All right, then. Have him come and talk to me tomorrow."

Consuelo's dark eyes lit up. "You mean it?"

"I mean it."

"I'll call him right now!" She put down the bowl of unfinished batter and left the room, wiping her hands on her apron as she went.

"Is he as nice as she is? Her son, I mean?" Glory asked.

Rodrigo seemed distracted. "He's a hard worker," he replied. "But he has some friends I don't like."

"I'll bet I have some friends you wouldn't like," she retorted. "It's the boy who'll be working here, not his friends."

He cocked an eyebrow. "Outspoken, aren't you?"

"From time to time," she confessed. "Sorry."

"Don't apologize," he replied, finishing his coffee. "I like to know where I stand with people. Honesty is a rare commodity these days."

She could have written a check on that. She was lied to day by day on the job, by criminals who swore innocence. It was always somebody else's fault, not theirs. They were framed. The witnesses were blind. The arresting officers were brutal. They weren't getting a fair trial. And on and on it went.

"I said," Rodrigo repeated, "will you and Consuelo have enough jars and lids, or should we get more?"

She started. She'd been lost in thought. "Sorry. I really don't know. Consuelo brings them out. I haven't really paid attention to how many we've got."

"I'll ask her on the way out. If Castillo gives you any more lip, tell me," he said, pausing in the doorway. "We don't allow harassment here."

"I will," she promised.

She watched him go into the other room, heard the murmur of his deep voice as he spoke to Consuelo. He really was a handsome man, she thought. If she hadn't been carrying so many emotional scars, she might have looked for a way to worm herself into his life. It was odd that a man like that would still be single at his age, which she judged to be mid-thirties. It was none of her business, she reminded herself. She only worked here.

Two days later, a late model SUV pulled up in the driveway. A slender, pretty blonde woman got out and darted up the steps. She was wearing blue jeans and a pink tank top. She looked young and carefree and happy.

Consuelo was busy washing jars and lids before they started on the next batch of peaches when there came a knock at the door. Glory went to answer it, leaning heavily on the cane. She'd had a bad night.

The young woman grinned at her. "Hi," she said in a friendly tone. "Is Rodrigo around?"

For some inexplicable reason, Glory felt her heart drop. "Yes," she said. "He's at the warehouse overseeing the packing. We're stocking it with fruit preserves and jellies for the internet business."

"Okay," she said. "Thanks."

If it had been anyone else, Glory would have gone back to the kitchen. But the woman fit the description Consuelo had mentioned, and she was curious. She watched as the other woman approached the big warehouse out back. Rodrigo spotted her and his whole face became radiant. He held out his arms and she ran into them, to be swung around and kissed heartily on the cheek.

If Glory had needed reminding that Rodrigo was handsome enough to attract almost any woman he wanted, that proved it. She turned and went back into the house. It hurt her that Rodrigo wanted someone else. She didn't dare question why.

He didn't bring the visitor into the house. They stood together under a big mesquite tree, very close, and spoke for a long time. Glory wasn't spying. But she was looking out the window. She couldn't help it. That those two had shared a close relationship was impossible not to notice.

Finally Rodrigo took the blonde's hand in his and led her back to the SUV, helping her up into her seat. She smiled and waved as she drove away. Rodrigo stood looking after the truck, his smile gone into eclipse. His hands dug into his jean pockets and the misery he felt was evident even at a distance. He looked like a man who'd lost everything he loved.

Glory went back to her canning, pensively. She wondered what had gone wrong for Rodrigo that he and the blonde woman weren't together.

She asked Consuelo, against her better judgment.

"Who is that blonde woman who comes to visit Rodrigo?" she asked, trying to sound casual.

Consuelo gave her a stealthy look. "I don't know," she said. "But it's obvious that she means something to Rodrigo."

"I noticed," Glory replied. "She seems very nice."

"He's fond of her, you can tell." She set the timer on the pressure cooker. "But if you look close," she added gently, "you can tell that it's only fondness on her part. She likes him, but she isn't in love."

"He is," Glory blurted out.

Consuelo glanced at her curiously. "You're perceptive."

Glory smiled. "He seems like a good person."

"He's the best. We all like him."

"I noticed that he seems…"

Before she could finish the sentence, the back door opened and a tall, handsome young man with wavy black hair, dark eyes and an olive complexion came in through the back door without knocking. He was wearing jeans and a pullover shirt, and broadcasting gang colors and tattoos.

Glory didn't dare voice that summary. She wasn't supposed to know about gang symbols. But she did. This young man belonged to the infamous Los Serpientes gang of Houston. She wondered what in the world he was doing in the kitchen.

Before she could ask, he grinned and hugged Consuelo, swinging her around in a circle and laughing the whole time.

"Hi, Mom!" he said in greeting.

Consuelo hugged him back and gave him a big kiss on both cheeks. She turned, her arm around his muscular waist. "Glory, this is my son, Marco!" she announced.

Don't miss Fearless *by Diana Palmer,*
available February 2024 wherever
Canary Press Books and ebooks are sold.

www.Harlequin.com